Crooked Mile

For my wife Judith, without whose patience and understanding this book would never have been possible

Crooked Mile

BEN BEAZLEY

PUBLISHING

First published in the United Kingdom in 2009 by Picnic Publishing
Published in 2011 by Bank House Books.

This paperback edition published in Great Britain in 2014 by DB Publishing,
an imprint of JMD Media Ltd

British Library Cataloguing in Publication Data
A catalogue record for this book is available from the
British Library

ISBN 978-1-78091-414-5

Typesetting and origination by Chandler Book Design

Printed and bound in the UK by Copytech (UK) Ltd Peterborough

Chapter One

The atmosphere in the smoky bar room was charged with tension. Seated behind the deal paymaster's table, Arthur Cufflin felt the first pangs of anxiety. The Irishman was alternately mouthing imprecations at him and bellowing to the men packed behind him in the tiny room.

'It's not enough, you bastard. We want a fair wage! Thirty shillings for six days' work is rubbish – everyone here knows that!'

'And you know that it's the going rate. Five shillings a day,' replied Cufflin, speaking loudly enough to be heard by the men at the front of the crowd while desperately trying not to shout. If he lost control of the situation there would be mayhem, which was the one thing he couldn't afford. The thirty ditch diggers and navvies, who had gathered to collect their weekly pay and had already taken a few pints of George Camm's Burton Ale, were an unpredictable mixture: hard Irish labourers working side by side with local men recruited until harvest-time. A wrong word now and the room would erupt.

As agent for the Shires Canal Company, it was Arthur Cufflin's responsibility to ensure that the new twenty-mile 'canal cut', linking the brick yards at Market Flixton with the wharf on the edge of Kelsford, was built on time and within budget. Friday evening was pay night. During the summer months, when longer days and fine weather permitted the digging to go on into the late evening, he took the heavy pay satchel out to the main cut but now, at the end of December, it was different. Work stopped at dusk and the men were back in town soon after seven o'clock. Few, if any, returned to their dingy lodgings to eat a meal and clean up before visiting the pub. Friday was pay night, and pay night meant drinking night. Since the middle of October, each Friday at nine o'clock sharp Cufflin had sat down behind the wooden table at the far end of the bar in the Prince Albert. The men lined up, and each made his mark or wrote his name in the heavy ledger, receiving his week's money from the depths of the satchel slung on its heavy leather strap across the agent's shoulder.

Some pay nights were fairly relaxed, others not so easy. When the weather was fine and the cutting progressed well, Friday night was good. Arthur Cufflin had been in the business for over thirty years. Starting as a digger for the old Union Canal Company back in the 1850s, he had quickly worked his way up to foreman. Aged twelve he had been working in the blacksmith's shop near to his tiny back-to-back home in Sheffield, pumping the bellows and learning to hammer out the soft molten metal into horseshoes. By the age of fourteen Arthur had gained a rudimentary knowledge of reading and writing from his weekly visits to the Working Men's Evening Institute in nearby Meadows Street. The eldest of five children, and by now a strapping youth, he was determined not to spend his life in the poverty of a city slum. In the hot summer of 1855 a gang of Irish diggers working on the Grand Union Canal became involved in a serious disturbance in the pub two doors from his parents' house, and one of them was locked up in the local Station House on a charge of grievously injuring a constable. Arthur replaced him on the gang, and since that day had been a canal man – first a navvy, then a foreman and later, thanks to his literacy and a facility for reading plans and working with figures, an agent for the company.

At forty-six Arthur Cufflin was still a powerful man, with heavy muscle just beginning to turn to fat where his broad chest and belly pushed against a tightly buttoned waistcoat. He was no stranger to the situation in which he now found himself. Cufflin had learnt years ago to believe in the old adage that when you raise your voice and nothing happens it is time to raise your fist. During his years as a ganger, running a team of navvies, he had been able to convince men such as these to do his bidding. These were hard-working, hard-living labourers, some from the boglands of Ireland, finding work in England to support a family back home. Others, second- and third-generation Irish, were from the slums and docklands of Liverpool and Manchester. It was a spartan and often violent existence – an unmerciful regime of work relieved one night a week by drinking to oblivion and passing out in the bed of some worn-out whore.

What was happening was not in question: the men gathered here to collect their week's earnings were in a state of high agitation, and from experience Cufflin knew he was sitting on a powder keg. But why? This should have been an easy evening. Apart from early frost setting back the digging a little, the contract was running to time. No one had been injured, and the company always paid the going rate. So why were the two fifteen-men gangs looking for trouble?

The big Irishman with curly hair and a beard was the instigator of the trouble. As soon as the queue for pay began to form he had elbowed his way to the front, and had begun to harangue Cufflin about the rates of pay, insisting that, as the cutting was ahead of schedule, a bonus should be paid.

At first Cufflin thought he was drunk, in which case it was his foreman's duty to come forward and remove him, so that the pay parade could continue.

When neither Doherty nor Mullahy, the two gangers, made a move to intervene, Cufflin was puzzled at first and then worried. What the hell was happening? The room became quiet, awaiting the outcome of proceedings at the table, then voices drifted up from the throng as individuals began their own arguments: those who agreed with the big man against others who wanted their money.

At the edge of his vision Cufflin saw a man at the far end of the room reeling backwards into four others, seated at a table laden with ale. The heavy iron-legged table was hurled back against the wall in a shower of beer and broken glass. As if this was a signal, the room erupted into a mass of cursing, fighting bodies.

Arthur Cufflin reacted with surprising speed for a man of his bulk. He had one responsibility in a situation like this – rights and wrongs were a matter for another day – to safeguard the company's money. No stranger to bar room brawls, a lifetime spent on the edge of disorder had taught him the skills he needed to survive. When paying out, he always ensured that he was accompanied by Sam Stone. A one-time fairground prize-fighter, Stone, who had adopted this surname during his days in the booths, was now – at an age approaching Cufflin's own – severely impaired by his many encounters over the years. His slurred speech and lack of coordination gave him the appearance of being permanently drunk. However, standing at six foot four, and weighing in at just over sixteen stone, he was ideal in his role as the agent's protector: the company had required little persuading. Unsuitable for other employment, Sam happily worked during the week as a labourer in the main storage yard at Derby. On Fridays, when Cufflin picked up the pay roll, Sam, with a clean shirt freshly pressed by his landlady, set off with him on the short train journey to Kelsford. In any minor altercation Sam, having received a nod from his master, stepped in and summarily resolved matters – positioning himself between Cufflin and the disturbance, in order to give the agent sufficient time to beat a swift retreat to safety, along with his bag of sovereigns. Experience also prompted the paymaster to position himself near a handy exit.

As the mêlée spread towards him, Cufflin stepped back quickly and slid through an unlocked door into the licensee's living quarters. He moved quickly along the narrow unlit passage, pushed past a dresser laden with crockery, threw open the door at the end of the hallway and slipped silently into the darkened kitchen. Once he was out of the house and across the yard, the alley that ran along the back wall would take him past the houses in Miller's Courtyard and out into the safety of the gas-lit High Street.

His mind focused upon making good his escape, Cufflin failed to register the significance of the open kitchen door in front of him. As he charged through it into the yard, the rope strung across the opening took him just below the knees. He felt the searing pain of snapping teeth and lacerating flesh as he crashed face down onto the rough cobblestones beneath him. Winded and hampered by his heavy bag, Cufflin attempted to roll to one side and protect himself, but an immense weight struck him in the small of his back as an assailant dropped across him with both knees, forcing from his body what little breath was left. Strong fingers twined into his hair, pulling his head back and almost snapping his neck, while a damp cloth was forced against his bleeding nose and mouth. Consciousness fading, he felt the weight of the moneybag slip away from his side, the thick strap severed by the blade of a well-honed clasp knife.

The three assailants worked with the well-rehearsed precision of professionals. While one expertly cut along the stitching of the satchel and transferred its contents into the leather Gladstone bag at his side, a second moved swiftly to the kitchen doorway and recovered the taut rope that had been strung across the opening and wound round the boot scraper near the door jamb. The third, a tall and well-built man, moved quietly to the yard gate to ensure the adjacent alleyway was clear. Nothing appeared out of place in alleyway or yard other than the inert figure of Cufflin sprawled on the cobbles. The noise of the tumult inside the inn percolated from the bar room, along the passage and out through the empty kitchen. Time was precious; any second now and the police would arrive. The chances were high that some would come to the back of the pub to block off one of the rioters' escape routes.

'Come on, move it!' The order was given in the low, authoritative tone of one accustomed to having his orders obeyed.

Moving quickly, the trio picked their way through household rubbish along the hundred yards of narrow alleyway. Concentrating upon avoiding human detection, they were startled by an unexpected eruption of noise from a pigsty at the rear of one of the small dwellings.

'Jesus Christ!' The startled exclamation brought the three to an unnerved halt.

'Shut up, you fool – do you want to tell the world where we are?' The tall man's hissed admonishment brought the others back to their senses. 'It's gone well. When we get to the street Martin and I go left, down to the stables, while you, Eddie, head along Beggars Lane for the canal – just as we arranged. Look normal; don't rush it. At the moment they're not even looking for us. See you in Manchester.'

A thin drizzle was beginning to fill the cold December night air as the first two men emerged from the dark alleyway and strolled casually along the High Street towards Cooper's Court and Harriman's stables. The heart-stopping clatter of heavy boots ringing on the road behind them caused a moment of panic, giving way to a surge of relief as, turning to glance back, they watched the figures of two burly constables disappear down the recently vacated alley.

Another two minutes found the men in a quiet back street, slipping through unlatched double gates into Isaac Harriman's stables. Gasping with relief, the younger of the two pushed the heavy gate closed and leaned his back against it, breathing heavily. His companion took two paces to the left, away from the gate, and went down on one knee, the pistol in his hand pointing steadily into the gloom. Within seconds the sound of a horse easing its stance on the other side of the yard caught their attention. The cocking of the Colt Navy single-action revolver filled the silence.

'Put the gun down.' The voice was nervous. 'It's all right, I've got the horses.'

The tall man straightened, carefully releasing the hammer and tucking the long-barrelled Colt back into his waistband. 'Bring them over.'

The softly spoken words were accentuated by his soft Southern Irish accent. Out of the pitch blackness a short, powerful man with a heavy black beard, wearing an old pair of suit trousers held up by webbing braces, led two saddled horses.

'Any problems?' asked the tall man.

'No. The missus saw me leave for the pub, then went to bed an hour ago. She's sound off – the coast is clear.'

'When the police come nosing round you know nothing, all right?' The gentle Irish voice had not risen in tone, but the emphasis was chilling. 'If this goes wrong we'll be back – you understand?'

Trembling in the darkness, the bearded man nodded. 'Go before they close off the roads.' His voice had an urgency they could not ignore.

Quickly the robbers swung up onto their mounts and clattered into the street, leaving the heavy wooden gates swinging open behind them.

A ten-minute gentle trot brought them onto the road that led from the north side of the town into open countryside. A mile and a half further on they reined in at the Five Ways crossroads. So far the plan had been executed flawlessly. The robbery had gone without a hitch, while Dakin and the others would either escape arrest in the brawl or be locked up overnight and spend a few days in gaol: a cheap price to pay for the Shires Canal Company payroll. Not surprisingly, they had seen no one on the road out of town. By now the drizzle had become a persistent downpour, soaking the riders to the skin and dissuading casual travellers from taking to the road, while the absence of the police was no surprise: they only maintained a check on the access roads to Kelsford during the fair every July. Even then, with the interminable wrangling between borough and county authorities over each other's responsibilities, gypsies and vagrants stood a better than even chance of slipping in without detection.

Resting the horses beneath the sheltering branches of a large tree near the roadside, the two men dismounted and spoke for the first time since leaving the stables.

'You did well, Martin.' The tall man was pleased with the evening's work. 'The laudanum was well thought of. It saved a deal of time. He has a reputation for being a fighting man.'

'I told the chemist it was for the auld woman – to help her sleep and give me some peace. I tell you now, Connor, that agent will be needing some more when the doctor starts in to working on him!'

Connor Devlin became thoughtful. 'Let's hope that Eddie doesn't get into any trouble. He should be on the boat, safe and sound with the money, very soon now. Radbone will set off at first light to be first at the locks by the time the keeper opens up. Now, we split up here as planned. I'll be in Sheffield by six in the morning, and on the eight-forty train for Manchester.'

After brief farewells, and a cursory handshake, the two men parted, riding off in opposite directions.

The towpath, churned into a thick glutinous treacle by the iron hooves of massive horses trudging constantly along the bank throughout the daylight hours, was slippery and dangerous. Eddie Donnelly let out a curse as he stumbled against a heavy metal bollard sunk into the ground at the water's edge, and fell with a resounding thud against the side of the barge that was moored to it. Cursing the rain, the mired path and the night, he pulled himself away from the water's edge. Still tightly gripping the bag in his right hand, he instinctively stumbled away from the boat and into the shelter of the towpath hedge.

After waiting for a full five minutes he was satisfied that his mishap had not attracted any attention. No one had moved on the barge, which meant it was unoccupied. There had been no dogs, or the lantern of a suspicious bargee on an adjacent tub checking for thieves.

Donnelly spent another minute to recover his breath and take stock. On the downside he was soaked to the skin. The flush of adrenalin generated during the robbery and escape had ebbed away during his passage along the towpath, and now he was cold, colder than he ever remembered being in his life. Even during the long childhood evenings in Liverpool, huddled in a shop doorway and waiting for his ale-sodden parents to emerge from the warm, reeking interior of some anonymous pub, he had never felt as cold as this. The icy downpour, while effectively cloaking his passage, had quickly permeated his cheap jacket and open shirt, soaking him in minutes. There would be a change of clothes and a rum and hot water toddy when he got to the barge. December or not, it had been necessary to dress lightly for the job in hand: freedom of movement in a struggle was essential, so an overcoat or cape was out of the question. Connor and Martin had heavy riding capes in their saddle bags and would have escaped the worst depredations of the weather. By the early hours of the morning they would be at the safe houses. After a wash and shave and a change of clothes, Connor would catch the train to Manchester, which Martin Lafferty would join at Derby. No one was going to associate the two smart middle-class travellers with the events of the previous night thirty miles away.

The advantage of Donnelly's situation was that he was almost there. Another ten minutes and he would see the stern light of the *Trojan*. Although the lights were normally extinguished when the vessels were tied up for the night, occasionally a skipper, departing for an evening's business, left one or both on so he could find his way back in the dark. The arrangement was that

Radbone would burn just the red port-side lantern, to distinguish the *Trojan* from any other vessel. Donnelly's right leg was becoming swollen and sore. The initial sickening pain when he had cracked his shin across the heavy iron stanchion had passed, and with his free hand he gently explored the emerging lump. Nothing broken; he had experienced worse. Better keep moving before it stiffened up: there would be plenty of time to rest it during the leisurely boat trip to the Mersey.

Tightening his grip on the moneybag, Eddie checked once more that he was still alone. A slim man in his early twenties, he was young to be entrusted with such responsibility. It was usually an older man, along with an unobtrusive minder, who was given the task of safeguarding the spoils – but it had been decided that he could pass unobtrusively as Amos Radbone's son on the *Trojan*, and help to work the boat without being noticed by those such as police and other representatives of officialdom. Although he would be spotted within hours in the close-knit canal society, one of the elements of such a society is discretion: questions posed by outsiders are not to be answered.

A lifetime of petty thieving around the docklands of Liverpool had provided Donnelly with a sound background for the work in hand. Brought up in the slums near the Mersey, his Irish heritage, combined with a natural ability to avoid detention by the police, had quickly brought him to the notice of those who lived outside the law. By the time he was fourteen he was working as a courier for the gang run by Bryan MacGuire, who in turn was the link man between local criminals and Irish political groups operating on the mainland. Though he had never killed anyone, Eddie was aware that many of those with whom he associated had, and that one day he himself might be called upon to do so. Although not a big or powerful man, the prospect did not particularly bother him: he had been party to sufficient gang operations to know that any killing was done in an organised and professional manner. That way you were safe. It was the fools who lashed out in drunken pub fights, or who in a moment of rage beat an unfaithful lover to death, who were hanged. Thus it was that being chosen for the Kelsford robbery was relatively mundane. At twenty-three, with a taste for smart clothes and good living, he was a cheerful, presentable young man who could pass himself off in any of the lower- or middle-class environments it suited his boss to put him in.

Removing his once stylish bowler hat, Donnelly tipped away the water that had accumulated in its narrow brim and carefully replaced it on his head. A final glance at the overgrown water's edge brought a wry smile to his face. Good job the empty barge was there, otherwise he would have pitched straight into the icy water.

Putting as little weight as possible onto his injured leg, Donnelly moved as fast as he could along the towpath towards the bridge ahead. The *Trojan* was moored about a hundred yards the other side of it, just round the bend. Suddenly, with a surge of relief, he felt the thick mud beneath his boots give way to a paved surface. The Shires had taken the trouble to lay heavy paving slabs along the water's edge at this point, no doubt to facilitate the stacking of cargoes on the bank before they were sent onwards by cart. If he were lucky they would extend to where Radbone was tied up. Despite his painful leg, the Irishman managed to force himself into a slow trot towards his destination.

As he entered the black yawning mouth of Bridge Sixty-Four Donnelly ducked low, trying to extend his view into the gloom and hoping to catch sight of the warm red glow of the welcoming stern lamp. He never knew what killed him. There was no time for pain or fear, simply an immense flash of light as his face and skull caved in – then nothing. The force of the blow sent his body crashing sideways into the wet, curving brickwork of the bridge, his neck already broken by the impact. Sliding sideways down the dull red bricks he came to rest, motionless, in a half-sitting position with his back propped against the wall, the Gladstone bag still clutched loosely in his right hand.

The silent figure in the heavy rain-sodden coat remained immobile for several seconds in the impenetrable darkness as if transfixed, listening to the quiet sound of the rain hissing down upon the still waters outside. Then, slowly and carefully, in order to avoid the warm sticky mess that was beginning to pool around the corpse, the figure bent over, and gently prised open the dead fingers to lift away the heavy bag of sovereigns.

Chapter Two

The taproom of the Prince Albert resembled the 'tween decks of a man o' war in the aftermath of a sea battle. The large teak-cased clock hanging on the wall showed ten minutes past midnight. Two barmen were tidying up and moving broken furniture, picking their way carefully over a floor littered with broken glass and other debris. Behind the bar the licensee, George Camm, was taking stock of the damage.

'At least the big mirror didn't get smashed.'

The constable at the end of the bar, scribbling in his notebook, glanced up to look at the object in question, an ornate wall-length piece of glassware with a legend bearing the name of the house alongside that of the brewery, a credit to the skills of an unknown engraver. 'You're lucky with that one, George. I don't know why they put expensive pieces like that in these places. It's bound to go one day.'

'No, you're wrong there, Harry.' Camm moved down the length of the bar to stand next to the young policeman. 'With the big mirror at the back of the bar I can see what's going on right across the room. A man having a pint and a game of cards doesn't like being watched – so you need to be a bit subtle. Likewise, I can stand pretty well anywhere I want and see what's happening at the tills. It's no secret – any barman worth his salt knows that, so he doesn't fiddle the till.'

'It doesn't stop the old hands, but it certainly slows down the amateurs.' Detective Sergeant Tom Norton leaned his elbows pensively on the polished surface.

Harry North looked across at the tall detective who had joined them. In a small force such as Kelsford Borough everyone quickly knew everyone else, and a young officer such as Harry soon learnt who among the senior men would help him, and who he should avoid. Sergeant Norton was definitely in the first group. A quiet, rather private man, he had a reputation as an experienced detective, and for being fair in his dealings with other police officers and criminals alike. A short time ago Harry had arrested a man for breaking into a pawnbroker's shop. It was the early hours of the morning by the time he had walked his prisoner to the police station and booked him. The only detective left on duty was Sergeant Norton who, although he had finished his shift and was about to go home, had stayed on to help him. Although the man was a vagrant, and to Harry it was an open and shut case, Tom had shown him how to deal properly with the incident.

The young constable thought that Norton looked tired. His slightly angular face was strained and drawn: too much work and not enough sleep – the trademark of detective work, he mused.

Tom shook his head at the small spirits glass that George Camm held up to him speculatively, choosing to light a cigar. The edges of his heavy wheat-coloured moustache lifted as he gave the young officer a friendly smile.

Harry was still young in his trade, thought Tom, but with the right tuition he had potential. It had not escaped his notice that the publican had called the officer by his first name. The Prince Albert was not on North's regular beat: he, along with the rest of the constables, had come running when the call for assistance had gone out. Tom made a mental note and returned to the job in hand.

'Is there a room we can use upstairs, George? We need to have a round table and the Station House is bedlam at the moment – it's stacked out with drunks and Paddies.'

Seated round two of the square tables that they had pushed together in the upstairs function room, the four detective sergeants waited for the arrival of the fifth member of their group. It had been a long night. The disturbance in the pub, while serious in its own right, was not unique. Kelsford was no stranger to public disorder. Forty years ago the town had witnessed the depredations wrought in the name of Chartism, when the factories and homes of wealthy employers had been ransacked.

Situated in the heart of England, Kelsford had, over the last twenty years, progressed from being something of a backwater into an important crossroads for transport and industry. The revolution in transport brought about by the ever-increasing railroad networks that wound back and forth across the country had been particularly important. At first by chance and then by design the rail lines from north to south and east to west all merged and flowed through the town. Lying as it did on the navigation cut earlier in the century through the Midlands by the Erewash Canal, Kelsford emerged as an entrepôt for goods and commerce of all sorts, which led to hitherto-unimagined growth for the locality, and prosperity for those in a position to exploit it. Many outsiders gravitated into the town from other, less fortunate parts of the Midlands as its importance increased. When the ribbon-making trade failed in one place, or a boot and shoe manufacturer went under in another, many of those displaced turned up in the rookeries and lodging houses of Kelsford to augment the growing population.

It was as part of this development that the Shires Canal Company had, eighteen months before, undertaken the ambitious project of cutting a new twenty-mile canal link from the nearby brickworks at Market Flixton to the new warehousing on the north side of Kelsford. The importation of their own Liverpool and Manchester navvies, supplemented by local casual labour, had inevitably led to tensions in the community. High earnings by outsiders, who were living in lodgings alongside the local poor, inevitable caused trouble and, as far as the tired police officers seated in the room were concerned, that trouble had arrived just after nine, this evening, Friday 16 December 1887.

Their musings were cut short by the entry into the room of the imposing figure of Detective Inspector Joseph Langley, accompanied by George Camm. Dropping heavily into the remaining chair, Langley turned to Camm. 'Any chance of a drink, George?' The deep gravelly voice held an undisputed authority.

'I would have thought so, Mr Langley. With what's gone on tonight the brewery won't miss a bit more. What would you like, gentlemen?' 'Five pints sounds good.' It did not occur to the Head of Detectives to ask the others if this was their preference. 'And a drop of brandy to keep us awake.' His heavy moustache lifted upwards in a smile that did not quite reach his dark eyes. 'Then we could do with some privacy, George – all right.' It was a statement not a question.

Taking a pouch from his coat pocket, Detective Inspector Langley proceeded to stuff an old short-stemmed briar with Bondsman tobacco. The room remained quiet while, having packed the heavily carbonated bowl, he applied a match to the pipe. Unobtrusively observing the four men through the billowing blue cloud of tobacco smoke as he carefully worked the flame around the glowing bowl, Langley pondered on how he should best deploy his forces.

On his left was Thomas Norton, definitely the most able of his subordinates. Middle thirties, his wife had died eighteen months ago; a careful and meticulous detective, with just that touch of flair that got results. A combination of intelligence and an ability to resolve difficult cases had, over time, brought him to be regarded as Langley's unofficial deputy. Not for the first time a small warning passed through the old man's mind. A strong character – probably because of the long time he had spent overseas in the army – Tom Norton was perceived by many to be his successor, something that needed watching.

Facing Norton was Sam Braithwaite. A completely different character, he was a large, red-haired, bullish young man. Six feet tall and heavily built, Sam was a slogger – in more ways than one. Renowned rather for the use of his fists than his imagination, the big man fitted nicely into Langley's small team. In a town such as this the inspector needed someone who could command a high degree of respect from the highly disrespectful.

Moving round the table, his gaze settled upon the slim figure of Jesse Squires seated next to Tom Norton. Very bright and very inventive, young

Jesse would go far – probably not in Kelsford, though. He was likely to find his talents better appreciated elsewhere, in a bigger force with more opportunity to develop his abilities. Rather small and slightly built for his chosen profession, Squires was curious about those mysterious things that appeared on the periphery of the police service's vision. While others were aware that obscure scientists could identify people by looking at their fingerprints, Jesse knew how they performed this sorcery. It was he who had devised, with the assistance of Alfred Saunt, a photographer in Ludgate Street, a system for recording the pictures of criminals arrested in the town. Langley dwelt on Squires a moment longer. A clever man was useful; a very clever man could be an encumbrance.

Facing him at the other end of the table, the last member of the department was easier to appraise. Heavy moustache and dark wavy hair, both showing those flecks of grey that women seemed to find attractive and men reassuring, Henry Farmer was the oldest and longest serving of the group. Henry's open visage and friendly manner were in some ways natural and in others carefully cultivated. Of medium height, he was always immaculately turned out, with a silk waistcoat and a heavy silver Albert watch-chain ostentatiously looped across a stomach that was beginning to show the signs of middle age. Stylish black boots buffed to a mirror polish perfectly matched his habitual smart light-grey suit. Despite the lateness of the hour Farmer looked as if he had just walked in from a Sunday morning stroll round the park. The truth was, that having been at work all the previous day, he had just signed the duty register and was about to go for a quiet drink when the taproom of the Prince Albert had erupted.

Inwardly, for the first time since sitting down, Langley warmed to the man opposite him. Henry he understood. They were of an era. No one else in the room could remember Farmer as anything other than a detective. Twenty years ago, as a bright young officer with a knack of talking his way out of fights and into women's bedrooms, Henry had been an ideal candidate for those delicate enquiries that required just a little more than frank answers to blunt questions. Langley paused momentarily to wonder if Henry was still involved with the dark-haired widow who lived on Victoria Road. At least he had enough sense to involve himself with women who were discreet – and over the years had always avoided any breath of scandal. His persuasive personality, combined with a complete lack of morals, put Henry Farmer very high on the inspector's list of allies.

Joe Langley had been a policeman for thirty-seven years, most of which he had spent as a thief-taker. During that time he had seen and dealt with most things in life, from petty theft to murder, from minor assaults to vicious robberies. The events of tonight were going to go on for some time – of that he was certain. It was his job to ensure that they were resolved successfully and did not return to haunt him later. How things were dealt with tonight would make all the difference in the days and weeks to come.

Without removing the smouldering pipe from his mouth, Langley tamped down the contents with a forefinger which after a lifetime of poking at the glowing contents of this and a dozen other such briars was impervious to pain, and cleared his throat.

'It's late and I don't want to prolong this. Let's go through what we've got. Henry, you were first here, what do we know about the trouble in the bar?'

Farmer sat back in his chair. 'The fighting was over by the time I arrived. Ambrose Quinn and half a dozen uniform men had cracked as many heads as they could and managed to quieten things down. It looked like a battlefield, as good as anything I've seen for a long while. They were carting the prisoners off to Long Street when I walked in.'

Langley refrained at this point from asking how many had been arrested. If the number was less than one for every policeman at the scene, including Sergeant Quinn, he would have something to say the next morning. He gave a grunt to signify that Farmer should continue.

'Rodwell and Simmonds found Cufflin when they arrived. Apparently they were running up the High Street to the pub at the same time as Sergeant Quinn. He shouted to them to come in through the back yard. I've spoken to them and they didn't see anyone in the alley. I have to say that the job looks to have been done very quickly. It couldn't have taken more than about two minutes, three at the outside.'

The detective inspector grunted sourly but made no further comment, reserving any discussion for later.

'Ambrose and I went through and had a look at Cufflin. He's had a bad beating but he'll live. We got him off to the infirmary in the Fire Brigade ambulance and I've put a man at his bedside to watch him until he can talk to us.'

'Do we know what happened out there?'

'Not really.' Farmer needed to think carefully. The old man had a mind like a razor and was analysing every move that had been made before his arrival. 'When we found him Cufflin was laying face down on the ground. He had obviously been surprised and knocked down. His face was badly damaged, but I'd say that was most likely done when he hit the cobbles. He was out cold; it took us about five minutes to bring him round. All we could get out of him was that he had gone over some sort of a tripwire.'

'What about the yard? Anything?'

'Nothing. If there had been a tripwire it was removed before they left. Even the yard gate had been closed. A bit later Celia, George's wife, found the week's takings had gone out of the strongbox in the kitchen cupboard.'

'Thomas, tell me about the bar.'

Tom Norton leaned forward and moved his pint pot to one side, in order to sketch with his finger on the table top. 'The pay table is here.' He outlined an oblong on the surface in the damp area left by his glass. 'Cufflin is sitting here, and the door to the living quarters is at the back of him – here. Soon after he began the pay parade a big Paddy came up to the front and started to harangue him about everything and nothing, obviously part of a pre-arranged plan. Then a fight began at the back of the room and Cufflin decided it was time to go. He grabbed his moneybag and dashed through the door and down the corridor into the kitchen.' The index finger of his right hand drew a line over the wet surface to a point a few inches nearer the centre of the table. 'As he went through the kitchen area into the yard, he was attacked and left unconscious, with the money gone. The indications are that a tripwire had been stretched across the doorway. Whoever did it took the time to clean out George Camm's strongbox. So far we don't know how much the agent was carrying, or how much was in the strongbox.'

'Anything left in the yard?' Langley was studying a point somewhere over their heads, between the corner of the room and infinity.

'Clean. The only thing they left was the leather moneybag. Strap cut through, bag emptied, then discarded. If there was a wire they took it away with them. Once the job was done, they were away through the back of Miller's Courtyard.' Guardedly he added, 'I say "they" because I don't think that one man on his own could have guaranteed to put Cufflin down and ensure he stayed down while the money was transferred. And the distraction in the bar took several, so why would you only send one man to do the main job?'

Langley continued to gaze at the unseen point in space. 'Is Cufflin involved?' he asked quietly.

'From the injuries I would say not.' To the others Langley and Norton appeared to be engaged in a private discussion. 'I saw him, and even if he were part of the job and it went wrong, I doubt that he would have allowed himself to be messed up so badly. His nose is all over his face and he's lost several teeth. Possibly his jaw is broken as well.'

'He gave his minder the slip. . . .'

'I don't think so. Stone has been with him for a long while. When I spoke to him earlier I asked why he didn't follow Cufflin out. Just because he's punchy it doesn't mean he's stupid – well, no more than any other man who has earned his living in a boxing booth. I remember Big Sam from when I was a kid. He was good in his day.'

Tom knew better than to allow himself to wander from the matter in hand. As a younger man Sam Stone had been a frequent customer in his father's pub, The Rifleman in Grange Lane. Tom had always looked up to the huge man with the battered face and cauliflower ear as some sort of a local hero, in the way that most adolescents do. At some time during his early life Sam had been a soldier. 'Grenadiers, lad,' he used to say, 'made me the man I am today!' Tom thought momentarily of the mockery that time had made of that statement. Then Tom Norton had gone into the army himself, and when he came back to his home town years later Sam had gone away. It was not until the Shires Canal Company had begun this present venture that he had again encountered the old bruiser. In the intervening years life had taught the policeman not to be surprised at the alteration he found.

'Anyway,' he continued, 'that's history. Sam's job was to allow his man to escape safely with the money. That went according to plan. No one expected an ambush in the yard.'

Langley eyed the younger man speculatively through the trickle of smoke, meandering lazily up towards the ceiling. 'How much was there in George Camm's tin box?'

'He thinks about a hundred pounds.' It was Sam Braithwaite's turn to make a contribution. 'There was the money from the bar for the last week, and ten pounds from a dance that they held in here last night.' Instinctively, each man's eyes, with the exception of Joseph Langley, glanced quickly round the function room as if expecting to see some ghostly signs of the recent event.

'Anything to add? Jesse? Henry?' Both shook their heads. They knew that it was best not to speculate on something that the inspector would most certainly remember in the cold light of morning.

'Have the County closed off the roads leading from the town?'

'I telephoned Sheffield Road. The duty sergeant was going to contact the out stations, sir,' Jesse Squires volunteered.

Sheffield Road was the headquarters of the County Constabulary, situated at its boundary with the borough on the main road running north from Kelsford. Everyone in the room knew it was a pointless exercise. Other than County Headquarters the stations were not equipped with telephones, so it would take hours to contact the local constables – by which time the robbers would be miles away.

Taking his pipe from his mouth, Joseph Langley glowered at the men seated with him. Silently he took a long pull at his pewter tankard. None of the others touched theirs; it was as if no one wanted to draw unnecessary attention to himself. Langley savoured the silence, apparently musing upon the situation. In fact he had no need to muse at all. This was a deliberate ploy to disconcert his officers and to make them aware of his displeasure. For the same reason he had not invited them to smoke; and if he had not badly wanted a drink the ale and brandy would not have been on the table.

Silence sat heavily in the room. A smell of stale beer and sweaty bodies, the legacy of an untold number of dances and cheap wedding receptions, pervaded the atmosphere. The four detectives were tired and wanted to snatch a little sleep before their inevitable return to the Station House in Long Street at some unearthly hour the next morning. Sam Braithwaite was the only one who had actually been on duty when the fracas occurred. Henry Farmer was about to leave for home, while Tom Norton and Jesse Squires had gone off duty a short time before.

Draining the remainder of his beer, Langley set his pint pot carefully back on the table. 'It's a mess.' The words were spoken with a quiet rancour that did not augur well for those involved in the investigation. 'At nine o'clock on a busy Friday night a large-scale disturbance is orchestrated to cover a serious robbery. Those who committed the robbery escaped – presumably, unless they grew wings and flew away, through streets crowded with policemen.'

It did not seem politic for any of the detectives to point out that any policemen in the area were making their way hotfoot to the disturbance, and the cold wet weather had ensured that those folk not in a warm tavern were shut away safely at home. The streets had been virtually deserted.

'We have no descriptions, we don't know how many are involved, and we don't know how much has gone!'

Tom Norton gazed speculatively into his glass. The old man was deliberately being destructive. He had seen him do it many times before. That was his way, and it would be reasonably successful. So long as he kept everyone off-balance he would be able to maintain an iron grip on the situation, ensuring complete obedience. Tom wondered in which local hostelry he had been ensconced when the messenger boy had finally tracked him down. Of one thing he was certain: the detective inspector would not have been home by the fireside of his large suburban house in Wellington Park.

Joseph Langley had a reputation as a prodigious drinker. Each lunchtime he held court at the Pack Horse Hotel, five minutes' walk from the Central Station House. The tavern was a meeting place for businessmen negotiating transactions over an inexpensive lunch and lawyers and barristers, installed behind expensive bottles of claret, playing God with their unfortunate clients. It was a natural haven for Langley, chatting with his cronies, a room brimming with information for the experienced listener who could tune into half-heard conversations. Langley's evenings were spent in the town's lower-class drinking haunts. These inns and beerhouses were a murky world in which small-time villains congregated to surreptitiously exchange their ill-gotten gains over greasy bar counters. The more successful took themselves off to dark corners away from keen ears and prying eyes, while easily seduced women lounged in doorways and against tables, plying their trade or drinking themselves into a belligerent stupor. As if by tacit agreement most touched and parted in the squalid shadowy yards and courts abutting these drinking dens. Dealers haggling hoarsely over prices relieved thieves of their booty. In short and frenetic bursts of energy, their backs against a wall and skirts hitched round their waists, prostitutes in adjacent dark corners relieved those same men of their small gains. Men with an ability to plan swapped warm corners for cold and murky doorways in order to explain to the less bright how to replenish their resources.

Tom, along with the other detectives, was expected to frequent the public houses within his area. It was a game in which both sides knew the rules. Usually with a colleague, and always off duty, they would spend half an hour supping ale and ensuring that their faces were known both to the clientele and the landlord. As soon as the policemen entered the premises any important conversations in their hearing ceased. Uneasy pleasantries were exchanged and business was suspended until they departed.

Tom knew that Joseph Langley understood this routine perfectly: it was one in which he had been a player for the past three decades. Thirty years of consorting with the low life that swam in these murky waters had bestowed upon him a unique knowledge. There were few of those nebulous figures slipping unobtrusively through the shadows to whom he could not put a name, but his real skill was knowing where these miscreants were later to be found. From bitter experience, fathers and sons alike were painfully aware that if Mr Langley visited then trouble would be fast on his heels. He was rarely accompanied on his evening perambulations, and when Big Joe entered a bar room a genuine air of disquiet pervaded the atmosphere. Someone would engage him in a polite conversation while the licensee pulled a pint of ale, for which he would rarely accept the proffered payment. Supping slowly and half-listening, Langley's attention generally lay elsewhere. Who was quietly leaving? Which men, pausing in the doorway before entering, turned to go elsewhere?

This evening the wet and bedraggled potman, dispatched by Tom Norton from the Prince Albert, had tracked him down to a dingy beerhouse in Cooper's Court, comfortably settled in the corner of the room next to the deal plank which served as a counter. The whispered message delivered, Langley sent the lad back to say that he was on his way. Finishing his drink and pulling his heavy Ulster coat around him against the weather, Langley had stepped out onto the wet street and set off towards the Prince Albert, already checking off in his mind what needed to be done.

Langley was speaking again. 'Sam, you and Jesse go back to Long Street, make a start on interviewing the prisoners. I want to know who set this up and how. I'll speak with the night inspector and have every stable yard in the area checked. They either had horses waiting or they're holed up in some Paddy lodging house until it's safe to move. I want to know which it is before morning.'

Braithwaite nodded. 'It's already being done, sir. The uniform men, apart from Harry North, are back on their beats. They've been told to go straight to any stables to make sure the locks haven't been touched.'

The detective inspector nodded his approval. The night beat officers worked a system when checking yards. As each padlock was lifted and pulled to ensure it was securely locked, the beat man turned it over to face in a particular direction. Next time he passed by, an hour later, he would immediately know if the lock had been tampered with.

'Tom, you and Henry go home and get some sleep. I want you back first thing in the morning, say eight o'clock – no later. There's a lot to do tomorrow. First I want that agent interviewed. We need to know exactly what's gone and how much.'

'The pay money was all sovereigns,' Jesse Squires interjected. 'George Camm's was a mixture of sovereigns, change and a couple of five pound notes.'

Langley gave him a sharp glance. 'Who's been changing five pound notes in here?' Squires wished he had not been so specific. Now he had something else to resolve before he could slip home for a couple of hours' sleep.

'I'll find out, sir.'

'I'll arrange with Caleb Newcombe for two of the day men to come in plain clothes. We're going to need more manpower for a while.' Newcombe, the uniformed night inspector, was what Langley described as 'a good hand'. An ex-detective, he could be relied upon to detail two reliable officers.

'We could do with three really.' Tom Norton spoke quietly, almost as if he didn't want to interrupt the other man's train of thought. 'This could be a long job. If we get two men the superintendent will take one back into uniform after a week, leaving us struggling. If we have three in the first place, then we'll have an extra man now when it's busy and still finish up with two.' The grin he shot at Langley evinced a similar reaction from the older man.

'Three it is. Any preferences?'

'Can I suggest young North downstairs? He's quite promising, and having been here all night he knows what's happened first hand.' Tom glanced round the table; there were no dissenters.

'All right. I'll get Caleb to send him home to get some sleep and to come back in the morning.'

As the meeting broke up Langley indicated that Tom should remain behind for a minute.

'You know the minder, don't you?' 'Yes, sir, since I was a kid. He used to tell me his army stories and he even taught me a bit about pugilism.'

'Good.' Langley stood lost in thought for a few seconds. 'Buy him a beer and have a good talk to him – for old times sake. Find out if his man has been doing anything out of the ordinary recently. Any gambling or debts, woman on the side – you know what you're looking for. He could still be involved. Either it went wrong on him, or more likely he's out of his depth with the people who have set this up.'

Tom let himself quietly in at the back door of the small terraced house in Sidwell Place. In the darkened kitchen he struck a match and held it to the gas mantle. A smoky yellow flame slowly dispelled the gloom. At any other time the plate of pork and cheese set out on the kitchen table under a starched tea towel would have been welcome. Whenever Tom was on a late shift it was his sister Ann's habit to leave out something cold for his return. Tonight he was neither hungry nor tired. Taking down a glass from the shelf in the larder, Tom knocked the round glass marble seal from the neck of the beer bottle that stood alongside the plate. Ignoring the food, he went through into the sitting room and dropped heavily into the deep armchair at the side of the black range. Lost in thought, Tom allowed the shadows cast by the fire's glowing embers to steer his mind over the events of the night.

That the robbery of the paymaster and the disturbance in the tavern were all one was not in question. It was a matter of who was behind it and where the perpetrators were now. If, as was likely, they had made off on horseback into the county, they could be anywhere by morning. The probability of a lone constable out on some back road encountering them was almost nil, and from the state in which Cufflin had been left it would be better if that didn't happen: a dead policeman was something to be avoided at all costs. It was typical of the workings of Joe Langley's labyrinthine mind that he should look to the injured man as being part of the team that had set up the robbery. Tom would speak to Sam Stone in his own time to find out if there was anything about the agent that he should know.

Upstairs the low crying of a child disturbed his reverie. Young James, his sister's boy, had been under the weather for a few days with a chill; doubtless his mother had him snuggled up with her in the tiny back bedroom that they had occupied since they moved in with Tom a year ago. Ann's husband John had died eighteen months before in the smallpox epidemic that the hot summer weather had brought to the town.

A combination of the low-lying fields surrounding the borough and the sewage-laden river that overflowed into them created a deadly concoction. During the summer months the town was plagued with a form of dysentery referred to locally as 'summer diarrhoea'. Children under five years of age were particularly susceptible to its ravages, making the town infamous for its high infant death rate and overcrowded fever hospital. It was only recently that piped water, drawn from the newly dug reservoir at Barminster twenty miles away, had provided an alternative to the disease-laden wells and pumps from which every household had drawn its water. A year and a half ago smallpox had added its weight to the scales of destruction. With the impartiality that only death seems capable of exhibiting, it had cut a swathe through rich and poor alike. Among the victims were his brother-in-law and his own wife Kathleen.

The funerals over, and each adjusting to the burdens of their bereavement, it had seemed sensible for Ann and young James to move into Tom's house. Tom needed a housekeeper, and his sister could well do with saving the rent on the cottage that she and John had occupied at the far end of town. During the daytime Ann worked for their father behind the bar of the family pub and James attended Frisby Street Elementary School just round the corner.

With a start, Tom heard the thud of heavy boots coming down the entry between the houses. He must have drifted off for a few minutes: the sky over the houses in the next street was beginning to lighten. Through the net curtains he saw a bulky figure in a tall helmet coming through the back gate. Without trying the door, the figure bent close to the glass and tapped gently on the window.

Already out of the chair, Tom put his hand up in acknowledgement as he went into the kitchen to let the constable in.

'What's happened now, Reuben?' He did not need to be told that the visit was not a social one.

'Body, Thomas.' Reuben Simmonds alternated between attempting to rub some warmth into his cold hands and stroking the heavy dew of early morning from his luxuriant black handlebar moustache. 'Down by the canal, on the towpath.'

'Get yourself warm and tell me.' Tom knew it was no use rushing him. Simmonds had obviously been dispatched either from the Station House or the place where the body was lying. He was one of the officers who had discovered Cufflin in the pub yard, and had been on duty all night.

The feeling returning to his hands, Reuben painstakingly unbuttoned his cape. Leaving the hooks and eyes and the chain with its lion's head clasp at his throat done up, he threw the sodden garment back from his shoulders in order to absorb what little warmth was issuing from the dying coals.

'Boatman, walking his horse just after daylight, come across the body of a man under Bridge Sixty-Four. Got his head well and truly stoved in. Looks like he's been there all night. Sergeant Braithwaite and Sergeant Squires are down there. They said to come and fetch you.'

Tom looked for the first time at the clock on the mantel shelf. He was amazed to see that it was twenty past six. He had drifted off for much longer than he had realised. Glancing through the window at the cold grey fingers of light spreading over the tiny back yard, he calculated that it could not be more than three-quarters of an hour since the boatman's grisly find.

Both men turned at the sound of the sitting room door opening behind them. Ann Turner, her small slim figure made bulky by the heavy robe wrapped around her against the cold, looked enquiringly from one to the other.

'Morning, Reuben.' Her voice was thick with the remains of sleep.

'Morning, Ann.' Although Simmonds was considerably older than Tom's sister, they had known each other for years – first through her brother and later because the constable had been an acquaintance of her late husband.

'I've got to go out, sis. It'll probably be a long day. How's Jamie?'

'He's not had a bad night. Took a while to get off.' She had lived with her brother long enough to understand the hours that his job imposed upon him. Her questioning look was more to ascertain whether Reuben would be remaining behind for a little longer to dry out and have a hot drink.

To the unspoken enquiry her brother replied, 'We're both on our way. I'll see you later.' Tom had already retrieved his heavy grey overcoat and hat from the table where he had draped them when he came in. 'Come on, Reuben. You'll be going to bed soon.' The expression on the constable's face indicated that he would have preferred to be 'going to bed' with a hot cup of tea and some buttered toast inside him.

Approaching from opposite directions, Tom Norton and Joseph Langley reached Bridge Sixty-Four at the same time. Muffled against the cold, and leaning heavily on his silver-headed walking stick, the strain of a night with little sleep and the prospect of a third serious incident within a few hours combined to make Langley look all of his sixty years. Climbing over the small stile that gave access to the towpath from the bridge top, the two men scrambled down the steep embankment.

In the dank winter mist drifting up from the water's still surface, the scene that greeted them was not a pleasant one. During the early hours of the morning the torrential rain had given way to a heavy frost that was biting into those assembled on the canal bank. The corpse in its soaking clothing was frozen solid. Slumped in a half-seated position, his back propped against the inner wall of the bridge, Eddie Donnelly had assumed the aspect of a statue carved in ice and discarded by a disappointed sculptor. His head was slumped forward onto his chest. What remained of his ruined face, transformed by the blow into a bloody mask, had been glazed by the frost.

During his time in the army Thomas Norton had been no stranger to death. After leaving school at thirteen he had spent two years working in his father's inn, serving ale and looking after the travellers who broke their journey overnight in the comfortable rooms over the bar. In common with most of his contemporaries Tom was familiar with horses. From a young age he had helped his father's ostler to feed and groom the mounts of visitors to the Rifleman. By the time he was eight he could ride a nag round the pub yard without falling off, and at ten he was entrusted to take the horses to be shod.

When, in the summer of 1866, a recruiting party of the Royal Horse Artillery stopped over at the Remounts Depot at Sevastopol Barracks to rest their horses, the fifteen-year-old knew that he wanted to be a soldier. His next few days were spent sneaking off to watch the men exercising horses and cleaning weapons, while during the evenings he listening avidly to their tales of far-away places, recounted over foaming tankards of ale in the crowded taproom. With the restlessness of youth he decided, having secured his parents' blessing, to enlist. When the tall, well-proportioned young man told the recruiting sergeant that he was eighteen it did not even provoke a raised eyebrow, and as the battery left Kelsford en route for the next town Gunner Thomas Norton rode with them.

It was purely by chance that the battery to which Tom had been posted was detailed for service in India. Four months later, as winter was settling its cold hand over the English countryside, he was riding the gun carriage of a six-horse team into the cantonments of Peshawar on the North-West Frontier, which at this time was in a perpetual state of conflict. Tom spent the next nine years, when not in barracks, chasing recalcitrant tribesmen up and down the Khyber Pass and across the border into neighbouring Afghanistan.

Despite a deep revulsion for the spectacle before him, Tom steeled himself to look carefully. Provided he did it once, properly, he would not need to repeat the process. His gaze travelled slowly over the macabre spectacle. In the dim half-light of the tunnel, set against the backcloth of smoky grey mist and gently lapping water, the stiff body took on the eerie aspect of a ghostly spectre from another world. An unreasoning dread filled him that at any second the corpse might silently rise up, arms outstretched in supplication, begging the salvation that had earlier been denied by the killer.

With a huge effort Tom forced his heaving stomach to be still and rejoined his companions. Despite the morning cold a thin film of sweat coated his forehead. Turning away, as if intent on surveying the far reaches of the canal, he paused a moment to allow the chill breeze to dry his perspiration.

Jesse Squires and Sam Braithwaite stood at the entrance to the bridge tunnel, quietly awaiting the arrival of their senior officer. Sam was the first to speak. 'One of the boatmen found him just after half past five when he was walking his horse. Looks to have been here most of the night. We've sent for Dr Mallard. We can't search him until his clothing has thawed out.'

With a nod of acknowledgement Langley ducked under the bridge and went down on his haunches to look more closely at the body. Being careful to avoid touching anything in the cramped space between the grotesquely splayed legs and the stone edge of the towpath, he remained motionless for some seconds. 'Any sign of a weapon?' The tiredness was leaving him. This was not a third incident. Everything that had happened during the night was connected, of that he was certain. This could be what he so desperately needed, the first break in the chain. Whoever this man was – unlucky bystander or member of the gang – he was a mistake.

'Not yet, sir. As soon as it's properly light we'll get some uniform men down to make a search.'

Tom's heaving stomach was beginning to settle. With the improving light he was mentally absorbing every detail of the scene, just as Langley was. Later a recollected detail could prove critical. 'Now that it's getting lighter, can I send for Alf Saunt to photograph the body before it's removed?'

Pushing himself up on his stick, Langley nodded. 'Yes – and I don't want a horde of people down here, tell him that!'

'It may be too late,' Tom murmured, staring into the mist at two figures clambering over the stile. As the new arrivals approached the four detectives quickly identified them as Dr Arthur Mallard, the police surgeon, accompanied by Charles Kerrigan Kemp, editor of the *Kelsford Gazette*.

Chapter Three

Perfunctory greetings having been exchanged, the three detective sergeants moved away under the bridge, allowing Langley to steer the newspaperman away down the path. Charles Kerrigan Kemp and Joseph Langley were old acquaintances. Neither friends nor adversaries, both were aware of their ultimate reliance upon the other. Kerrigan Kemp depended to a degree on the early information that Langley supplied him, ensuring that he always stayed a little ahead of his competitors. Langley in turn knew that what he did not tell Kerrigan Kemp he would soon discover from other sources. Most lunchtimes the two exchanged pleasantries across the lounge bar of the Pack Horse, and took careful note of who was speaking to whom.

This morning there would be a verbal fencing match in which both men were well versed: Kerrigan Kemp desperately wanting to see the body and questioning the possibility of an early arrest; Langley cautiously speculating, determined to keep the editor as far from any real evidence as possible.

While this cat and mouse game was being played out, Dr Mallard, his brown leather bag of instruments open beside him on the ground, was hunched over his grisly task. Arthur Mallard was relatively new to the world of the police surgeon; inevitably, within days of being appointed to his new role he was being referred to by the entire force as 'Ducky'. Having qualified in 1881, until two years before he had worked as a junior doctor in his native Yorkshire. The death of a doting maiden aunt had bequeathed upon him a modest inheritance, sufficient to allow him to buy a partnership in the Kelsford practice of Dr Lawton Bradley in Gadsfield Terrace. The practice was a flourishing one and an ideal opportunity for the young Dr Mallard to prove his worth. Lawton Bradley's need for a partner had lain in his own failing health and a desire, aged almost seventy, to look towards retirement. The partnership and the old practitioner's semi-retirement were ended abruptly after eighteen months by the untimely demise of Dr Bradley, following a short illness.

Unable to purchase the remaining share in the practice, Mallard came to an agreement with his late partner's widow, that she should retain her husband's share of the income while he continued *in situ*.

One of Dr Bradley's roles in the town had been that of surgeon to the police force. To the young Mallard, the offer from the watch committee to continue in his partner's place was not one to be passed up. For a retainer of £125 a year, his responsibilities were to attend prisoners taken ill at the police station and to visit police officers who reported sick. For each examination he received a shilling per patient, and the cost of any medication he supplied.

Although Mallard was also required to attend suspicious deaths and perform the subsequent post-mortem, this was the first occasion when the need had arisen and he felt a little nervous. Fortunately the young doctor, who had a naturally amiable disposition, was a popular figure, and it was for this reason that none of the detectives, standing back while he examined the body, asked why he was delving in his medical bag when the corpse was frozen solid. Watching with mild amusement, Tom decided it was time to help out.

'The problem when they're stiff like this is that you can't do anything until the body is thawed out back at the mortuary, can you?'

Gratefully Mallard closed his bag, nodded and withdrew a pace from the unsightly remains. He was well aware of the subtle guidance being proffered. 'No. It'll be much later in the day before I can tell you anything constructive.' With a wry smile he added, 'Obviously he's dead and he's been struck a massive blow to the head, but you don't need a doctor to tell you that.'

'How long do you think he's been dead?' Braithwaite already knew the answer to his question.

Mallard pondered a moment. 'Although he's under the cover of the bridge his clothing is wet through. It rained heavily between about half past eight last night and two this morning. The body is absolutely frozen so I think he was here well before two. I'd guess at somewhere between half past eight and midnight.'

'I was going to have the body photographed by Mr Saunt and then, if you agree, get it removed to the mortuary,' said Tom. It was time that matters here were drawn to a conclusion. They were all beginning to feel the early morning cold gnawing at exposed fingers and creeping through the thin soles of their shoes.

As he spoke, the diminutive shape of Alfred Saunt clad in an ankle-length tweed overcoat and long muffler wound securely around his neck appeared out of the mist. The small boy trudging along behind him was hardly visible under the camera, heavy wooden tripod and box of equipment with which he was weighed down.

Langley took the arrival of the photographer as an opportunity to break off his conversation with Kerrigan Kemp. Shrugging deeper into the warmth of his ulster, the detective inspector walked quickly over to the group of men who had emerged into the morning light and were stamping their feet to restore some circulation in their stiff legs.

'Braithwaite, when Mr Saunt has finished taking his pictures go back to his shop with him and wait while he processes them. I want them on my desk as soon as possible.' With a bleak smile, almost as an afterthought, he added, 'And bring the original plates with you – they need to be locked away for evidence.' Langley had no intention of Alfred Saunt making a few shillings by distributing spare copies to the *Kelsford Gazette*. 'Squires, you stay here and make sure no barges leave. Go up and see Alloway the lock-keeper: he's not to open the lock flight until we say so. I'll send someone down to you and you can start going from boat to boat. Usual enquiries, everybody's name. Any you're not happy with, search the boat.' He stared speculatively into the dank vapour rising from the waters. 'Somewhere here is the weapon that killed him. We're probably looking for a boat hook or a baulk of timber. Not too long, short enough to be swung in a confined space, but heavy enough to kill a man. That's your job, Jesse – it needs finding.'

Jesse Squires nodded briefly. 'What about tracks?' he asked tentatively. For the first time the older man allowed his exasperation to show. 'Tracks! Half the police force, the editorial staff of the *Gazette* and the good doctor, along with a water gipsy and his sodding cart horse, have been walking up and down this path since daylight. It was a mud bath before anyone even arrived: it's hardly likely there are any tracks left!'

While making the appropriate noises, Jesse Squires did not agree with his superior. It was true there had been a deal of inevitable traffic at the scene of the murder, but it had been limited to one area, between Bridge Sixty-Four and the road bridge from Scriven's Walk. From the position of the body it was possible, even likely, that the dead man had come into Bridge Sixty-Four the other way, from Beggars Lane. Later, when left alone, Jesse would examine the towpath on the far side of the bridge.

Langley felt distinctly uneasy. Murders were usually spur of the moment events, carried out with little forethought or planning; a domestic dispute between husband and wife, or a drunken brawl resulting in the death of one of the protagonists. This was different. Although the murder had the appearance of an aberration, it was part of a larger scheme. A scheme that had encompassed a carefully prepared escape plan for those involved. If the killer was not caught at the scene of the crime, or at the outside within twenty-four hours, there was little hope of ever resolving the case: this was one of the basic rules of any murder enquiry. He glared into the mist-laden tunnel at the object of his displeasure. 'At least our leader is away until Monday.' His dislike of the head constable was common knowledge, as was the fact that it was heartily reciprocated by that personage. 'I'm going to get some breakfast. Tom, Sam, go and collect the uniform men from the Station House and start them making enquiries. One of you get down to the infirmary and see Cufflin. The other go and see Ike Harriman: his stables were broken into during the night. That's got to be where they took the horses from. Meet in my office at twelve noon.'

As they watched the back of the overcoated figure stamp off along the muddy path the three men grinned at each other.

'Do you really think he's going to have breakfast?' Jesse, still engrossed with what was behind them under Bridge Sixty-Four, was clearly impressed with the old man's iron constitution.

'Yes. As far as he's concerned that's just a piece of meat in there,' replied Tom. 'He'll go down to the cabmen's hut, have a sixpenny fry-up and at the same time find out if any of the cabbies saw anything unusual on the roads during the night.'

Langley had caught a few hours' sleep in his office instead of going home, reflected the detective. How else would he have first-hand knowledge that one of the night men had reported the break-in at Harriman's stables?

As day broke properly a brilliant early morning sun burst through to whisk away the clammy vapours of the night, its fresh bright rays giving a lie to the recent shadowy events. The air in the stable yard was redolent with the reek of fresh manure and old straw. Strolling into the tack room, Harry North's already overloaded senses were assailed by the heavy odour of sweat-stained leather combined with saddle soap and polish.

Harry was not quite sure what he was looking for. This was not entirely his fault. Exchanging his uniform for his best Sunday suit and bowler hat, he had reported at the Central Station House, as instructed, at eight o'clock prompt. Within a few minutes Walter Swain and Arthur Hudson, the other two uniform officers detailed for plain-clothes work, had joined him in the draughty parade room.

Shortly after a quarter past eight Sergeant Norton, accompanied by Sergeant Farmer, had called the three of them into the inner sanctum of the detective department. For the benefit of the two day men, Tom had related the events of Friday evening, and told them about the unidentified man beneath Bridge Sixty-Four.

North, in a state amounting almost to euphoria at being selected to work with the detectives, listened to every word. In the parade room he had been in the process of regaling his colleagues with the details of the fracas in the Prince Albert – how Sergeant Quinn and Sam Stone had stood back to back in the middle of the main room, cracking heads and laying out any man who came within their reach.

Ambrose Quinn was something of a hero to the young constable. Three years ago Harry had left his father's village shop in Somerton, ten miles outside Kelsford, to join the police force. His parents would have been happier if he had joined the county police and elected for the quieter life of a village policeman, but this was not what he was seeking. He wanted to be in the town, with its convivial public houses and accommodating barmaids. This exciting life had not materialised quite as Harry had imagined. Day shifts were spent patrolling the town centre, and chatting with the occasional pretty servant girl engaged on household errands. The night-shift, of which there were twice as many, was a more attractive proposition. Patrolling a beat in the dead of night, especially if the weather was bad, could be irksome, but it was seldom boring. Harry had learnt early that those whom he encountered out and about at night were seldom steadfast citizens. The more denizens of the night upon whom he shone his lamp, the more he found to be up to no good. Quite soon he had established for himself a reputation of being lucky. Luck, he felt, had very little to do with it. While many of his contemporaries chose to spend the night-shifts slipping away down entries to sleep in a stinking privy at the back of a terraced house, Harry found it preferable to find a deserving suspect to arrest and spend an hour in the warm Station House.

It was in the course of his duties that Harry had come to know Sergeant Ambrose Quinn who, when not out on patrol, was the Station House sergeant. A six foot four giant of a man, with a face that looked as if it had been hewn from a cliff-face, Quinn, who originated in County Wicklow, had arrived in the town twenty years earlier. No one, other than possibly his wife, whom he had met and married soon after his arrival, knew of the Irishman's true origins. There were rumours that before coming to Kelsford he had earned his living as a bare knuckle fighter in the fairground booths around Liverpool, even that he had at one time been an associate of Sam Stone's and that the two had fought each other for a purse. Whether or not this was idle speculation, after Sam had reappeared in the town as Arthur Cufflin's minder, the two men certainly nodded to each other on a Friday evening when their paths crossed. One thing was definite: the conjecture would take on renewed fervour after last night's display.

Cufflin safely out of the way, Sam Stone had moved across the bar in order to engage the curly-haired Irishman who had been the source of the disturbance. Even with his bulk, Sam had not been able to reach his target in time to prevent the man from losing himself in the mêlée. Entering with Harry North and two other constables through the street door, Ambrose Quinn had carved an immediate path into the brawl, and both he and Stone had arrived in the centre of the disturbance simultaneously.

In the unspoken knowledge that they were allies, head and shoulders above any other man in the room, the two had turned back to back and proceeded to take on all comers. Among the roughnecks surrounding them there was an immediate understanding that these were professional fighters. There were no haphazard movements, no lashing out at any moving target. Like a pair of dancers, each judged the other's action by their touching backs and shoulders, the two huge men standing like a two-headed colossus. Stone, parrying a swing from a broken table leg, dispatched his assailant with a blow from a fist the size of a coal shovel. Quinn, his helmet gone, grabbed two-handed at a disorientated navvy careless enough to come within his reach. Pulling him in close, the sergeant buried his right knee deep into the man's groin, before dropping him retching at his feet. In what appeared to be a continuation of the movement, Quinn's right fist came up with the force of a whistling locomotive under the sternum of another contender. Catching the sagging body by the lapels of his greasy waistcoat, Quinn headbutted the man between the eyes before hurling him backwards, the bridge of his nose irreparably smashed, to career unconscious into a table. Within minutes a circle had cleared around the two big men, driving the fight out towards the edges of the room where Harry and the other constables could secure some prisoners.

The part of the story that North had not heard was the discovery of the unidentified body beneath Bridge Sixty-Four. He listened carefully as Henry Farmer outlined the details of the discovery, and explained that the murder was almost certainly connected with the earlier robbery.

Sergeant Norton took up the briefing. Hudson and Swain were to go down to the canal to assist Sergeant Squires in his search for the murder weapon, and were to check over the barges. Sergeant Farmer was going to the hospital in the hope that Arthur Cufflin was able to describe his attackers. They were all to meet back in the office later in the morning.

Once the others had left Tom took out his silver pocket watch and checked the time – it was half past eight. 'Right, young Harry,' he announced brightly, 'we're going down to Harriman's to find out what the story is there. Were the horses stolen, or has someone been helping the villains?'

At the stables in Cooper's Court Tom had instructed the young man to have a look round while he talked to the proprietor. So it was that Harry found himself in the stifling atmosphere of the tack room, doing as instructed. He was intent on succeeding in this latest enterprise: having been on the beat for three years, he was desperate to become a detective. In truth he knew there was little chance of obtaining a permanent posting. Kelsford was behind the times, with a relatively small force; each of the four detectives carried the rank of sergeant, and they were led by the inspector. However, that was bound to change soon, and if Harry could make a success of this temporary employment perhaps he would be among those to be chosen to work in the department as a constable when more men were brought in.

Being a country lad, Harry was familiar with stables and saddlery. Gazing round the low room, he counted the saddles and bridles hanging tidily from sturdy wooden pegs ranged along the side wall. Next he peered into the sacks of horse-feed in a disused stall, stirring the crisp new straw on the cold stone floor as he did so. He poked warily, not sure what he was looking for, at the same time being careful not to get any of the dust billowing up from the sacks on his neatly pressed suit.

He jumped back quickly as a startled rat, disturbed by his attentions at one of the bags, scuttled from its secret corner and ran over his shoe into a bolt hole under the nearby bench. Harry decided that it was time to rejoin the sergeant. He was not frightened of the creatures, but only a fool remained in a confined space where there were rats unless wearing knee-length boots. A frightened rat scurried for the nearest point of safety, which could well be up an unprotected trouser leg.

In the yard, Tom was in deep conversation with the owner of the stables, Isaac Harriman. 'Two of my best riding horses, a gelding with a white blaze and a young mare. Your constable woke us up at about five o'clock. Said the hasp on the padlock had been cut through. Sure enough, both gone.'

'What time did you last check them, Ike?' Tom asked absently, absorbed in an examination of the heavy padlock that he had lifted down from the yard gate.

'About eight o'clock, just before I went off to the pub.'

'Still going to Matty's place – the Black Lion?'

'Yes, dropped in for a couple, then home to bed.'

'What time?'

The hackmaster pushed his cap to the back of his head, scratched at his sparsely covered pate with a dirty finger nail and pulled the cap back into place. 'Bit late actually, Sergeant. I got into company with a few friends. It was after midnight, I suppose.'

'And you didn't see anything?' Tom was twisting the lock in his hand, examining first the face side then the back plate.

'I didn't come in through the yard. Through the front door and off upstairs.'

Tom turned his attention from the padlock to the damaged hasp – a substantial steel fitting, showing the signs of age, its outer shell dark with the ionisation of rust. The sawn-off cross section gleamed in the sunlight like a piece of newly polished silver. 'Any strangers hanging around during the last few days?'

'Nothing, Sergeant, not even any new customers.' The attempt at humour fell flat, and Harriman shuffled his muddy boots uncomfortably.

Handing the now redundant padlock back to its owner, Tom returned his attention to the yard. 'Let's take a look round, shall we? See if anything else has gone.'

The three men moved purposefully, peering through half-open stable doors and picking their way through the dung-strewn aisle of the main barn past the six heavy cart horses haltered in open bays.

Out in the crisp morning air once more, Tom paused, looking pensively across the cobbled yard at the two empty stables that, until a few hours ago, had housed the mounts upon which the thieves had made their escape. Shrugging his shoulders deeper into the warmth of his overcoat, he buried his hands in his pockets. Tilting his head slightly, he gazed intently at the shorter man. 'Nothing else to tell us, Ike?'

Just for a second, looking into those cold pale blue eyes, Harriman felt as if his very soul was being scrutinised. Sinking his face into his heavy black beard, he swallowed hard, dragging saliva into his tinder dry mouth. 'No, Mr Norton. I just want to get my horses back.'

When Harriman looked up again the detective had a humourless smile on his face. Staring into those eyes, he felt an icy chill of apprehension. If this went wrong it was not only the Irishmen he needed to fear.

'Oh, I think your horses will turn up, Ike. I'll be interested to see where.' The voice, like the eyes, was cold and full of steel.

Tom looked carefully round the yard again. Always stand still and have one last look: you might just see the thing you missed. He could hear Joe Langley's gravelly voice in his ear. 'I'll see you again, Ike,' he murmured, and, nodding to North, he turned and walked slowly out into the street.

Watching the backs of the two policemen as they turned left out of the gate towards the High Street, Isaac Harriman realised that, despite the chill morning, he was sweating profusely.

Tom Norton and Jesse Squires sat in a secluded corner of Phipps' Coffee House. Having sent his new assistant back to the Station House to check for information concerning the stolen mounts, Tom had slipped off for a quiet rendezvous with the other detective. Apart from two middle-aged ladies seated at the opposite end of the room, deep in conversation, they were the only customers.

Squires sipped appreciatively at his steaming brew, allowing the caffeine to percolate luxuriously through his system. In a back room a hungry grinding machine could be heard chomping at the raw beans being poured into its funnel.

'So you think Harriman is involved?' An eagerly straining ear at the next table would have been hard pressed to have tuned into the quietly spoken words.

Tom peered into the depths of his cup. 'Definitely. There's no rush. We'll let him run for a while, but he's involved all right. They must have arranged for him to have the horses ready in the yard. He tried to make it look like a break-in by sawing through the hasp on the gate. He hadn't got the sense to do it with the padlock in place, so there are no saw marks on the lock. He says he must have left the tack room undone, which is rubbish. No reputable hackmaster is going to leave a room full of expensive saddles and harness open all night. And when young Harry went in there it had been cleaned out and fresh straw put down. Not the sort of thing you do if you've just had the burglars.'

Jesse nodded quietly. Glancing casually round the room to confirm they could not be overheard, he said, 'We know who he is, and what killed him.'

Tom replaced his coffee cup and saucer on the crisp white tablecloth. From an inside pocket he produced a slim cigar case. Kate had bought it for him the Christmas before she died. Two stiff brown leather halves, one slotting inside the other, made a secure flat sheath. 'Better than one of those hinged cases,' she had said. 'This will take all different sizes.' Not a drinking man, Tom's only real indulgence was a good cigar. His favourite, a slow-burning mellow smoke, was produced locally by Goodman's at their small factory on the corner of Lampton Street and Willow Lane. At threepence each, five nicely filled Kate's case. Every time he handled the warm leather, absently rubbing a thumb over its shiny surface, he saw her finely chiselled face and thick chestnut hair in his mind's eye: 'better than one of those hinged cases . . .'

Having carefully made his selection, Tom placed the cigar between his teeth and applied a match. A swirling cloud of thick blue smoke drifted lazily between the two men, mingling in the atmosphere with the aroma of freshly ground coffee to produce an almost soporific effect. Leaning forward to rest his elbows on the tablecloth, Tom indicated to his companion that he had his full attention.

'First, there was nothing on the body at all.' Squires was savouring the moment. 'We had to cut the clothes off, then thaw them out. No money, no identification, nothing. Anyone who was on legitimate business would have had something in their pockets. Not this one. He had no intention of being identified if he was stopped or arrested. But do you know what? They brought his bowler hat in with him, and the silly sod had printed his name inside the sweat band! Edwin Donnelly. Thank God for education. Even criminals learn to read and write these days.' Abandoning his moment of theatre, Squires became serious once more. 'I'd bet anything he was involved in the job at the Albert. As soon as we leave here I'll speak to Langley: we need to get telegrams off to London, Birmingham, Liverpool and Manchester. I'll be surprised if we don't get something back fairly quickly.'

Tom grunted his acquiescence. 'What about the murder weapon, Jess?'

'Barge hook. We found it in the rushes going back towards Scriven's Walk. Timber haft about two feet long with a heavy iron claw hook on the end. Sort of thing bargees use for pulling the boat into the side when they're close to the bank. It would be lethal in an enclosed space. Looks as if the killer threw it into the cut but it caught in the reeds.'

'Which means', reasoned the other man, 'that the murderer must have come in from Scriven's Walk and waited for – what was his name?'

'Donnelly.'

'Waited for Donnelly under the bridge, killed him and then left by the same route.'

Sitting back in his chair, Jesse put his hands together and rested his chin on steepled fingers. 'Supposing that Donnelly was involved in last night's affair, the next question is what was he doing under Bridge Sixty-Four.'

His companion removed the cigar from his mouth, and regarded the thin trail of smoke drifting up from its smouldering tip thoughtfully. 'That's what I've been asking myself, Jesse. I think he may have been the banker. Do we know yet how much money has gone?'

Squires gave a nod. 'Cufflin is up and about now. Langley has been to see him at the infirmary, which should cheer him up.' He gave a quick grin. 'He's confirmed that he was carrying the crew's payroll, which was a little over £200.

That on its own is not a huge amount, but in his bag he also had the monthly settlements for suppliers. That was another £350.'

Tom bent his head slightly, tucking in his chin and scowling. As if addressing the tablecloth, he murmured, 'And the rest.' Squires gave a questioning look. 'I think we can add another £250 onto that. The agent doesn't just pay the bills. He's the trusted servant who squares everybody off. Friday night he pays the diggers. Saturday morning he has quiet little meetings with the people who matter. Suppliers' managers who make sure that the merchandise is available, carters who see that things get delivered on time, someone at the council who makes sure that no one is objecting to anything. So I would think that, irrespective of what the Shires Canal Company says, the total haul would stand at £800 minimum, perhaps nearer to nine.' Jesse Squires sucked the air in through his teeth, whistling as he turned the proposition over. 'We need the answers to a couple of questions. Why was he there and why was he murdered. Let's look at it first from the planning standpoint. Once the robbery had been carried out the gang needed to get away safely and dispose of the stolen money. Logically they're going to split up, go their separate ways and meet again later. One of them has got to be responsible for the money. I think that was Donnelly's job. Harriman is reporting two horses as stolen, which means two on horseback riding out of town. They would draw off any pursuit. Donnelly meanwhile slipped off on foot to a pre-arranged rendezvous with someone along the canal, probably on one of the barges. That would make sense – he'd just change his clothes and become a crew member.' Tom drew deeply on his cigar while he marshalled his thoughts. 'Whoever killed him knew who he was and where he was going. That narrows it down either to the person he was meeting or one of his companions. Either way, all the evidence points to a double-cross. The biggest question is who are we actually dealing with? Who set this thing up, and why?'

'I found something interesting down at the mortuary, Tom.' Jesse's dark brown eyes had taken on the aspect of a clever gun dog patiently watching his master. Tom knew the look of old; he had come up with something worthwhile. From his waistcoat pocket Squires drew a small cylindrical object the size of a man's little finger. Under the cover of replacing his empty cup he slid it across the table. Tom drew the object to him, at the same time taking a sip of his coffee. To any observer, one of the men was putting down an empty cup, the other picking up a half-full one. Inconspicuously he examined the heavy brass-jacketed bullet. Its weight seemed disproportionate to its size, the coldness ebbing from the metal as it absorbed warmth from his hand. He raised his eyebrows in an unspoken question.

'In his jacket there was a small change pocket, you know the sort of thing, a pocket within a pocket. It was in there. I would imagine that when he emptied his things out before going on the job he missed it.' Tom remained silent, waiting for his friend to continue. 'It's the calibre that's interesting: .44. Most of the heavy pistols we encounter aren't that calibre. German weapons such as Mausers or Mannlichers have a metric calibre – 7.62 or similar. A Webley would usually be a .38 service model. I know that some years ago they produced a double-action .45 for the Royal Irish Constabulary – but that fired an Adams cartridge, which this is not.' Jesse paused.

'So what's special about this, Jesse?' Tom could sense his colleague's excitement – his slim body leaning forward, the softly spoken words barely audible across the table. Out of the corner of his eye he caught sight of Elsie Phipps, tidying chairs and casting covert glances in their direction. Better drink up and go soon, before curiosity got the better of her and she moved within earshot. Elsie knew well enough who her mid-morning clients were. News of the murder was all round the town, and she was a naturally inquisitive woman.

'This ammunition is American,' Jesse continued. 'Look at the back end. Stamped on the rim are the letters HC – HARTFORD, CONNECTICUT. That's the Colt Works in America. Although the Colt revolver is probably the most popular handgun in North America, it isn't seen very much here. The killer must have taken Donnelly's gun off his body. If Donnelly was carrying a Colt it's more than likely that the others were as well. Which means . . .'

'. . . that we're either looking for a gang of Americans, which is highly unlikely – or people who have access to smuggled American weapons and ammunition.' Things were now beginning to make more sense to Tom. Jesse was in full flow. 'We're looking for an organised group of people who have access to firearms, are able to create large-scale distractions while they commit crime, and are prepared to kill. Add an American connection and we appear to be dealing with some form of political or dissident group. The question is which?'

Tom pondered a moment before replying. 'The only groups we know of that would fit are the Russian and East European anarchists, or the Irish Fenians. With a name like Donnelly and an American connection, I think we can discount the Russian option.'

Chapter Four

A damp December mist shrouded the centre of Manchester and wrapped itself around Connor Devlin as he trudged purposefully along Market Street on his way to Swinburne Court. Hands thrust deep into his worn jacket pockets, he looked just like any other tired workman making his way home from a hard day's work. A grey muffler wound loosely round his neck and a peaked cap pulled down over his brow completed the effect. In truth it had taken Devlin more than an hour, carefully following a pre-arranged route, to complete the short journey from his lodgings in Aylmes Street to the house where the meeting was to take place. Having avoided his landlady, he slipped quietly out of the back door and made his way through the maze of alleyways that led behind the Eagle Foundry and out into South Street. Turning left and away from his destination, his route took him to the Exchange railway station, where he spent some time mingling among the prospective travellers before slipping out into the street and heading for the river. A circuitous route round the back of the cathedral brought him to his present position, east of the river.

As he made his way along the busy thoroughfare, Connor Devlin turned over for the thousandth time the vexed question of how he and his companions in the Brotherhood would eventually bring the English government to heel and secure a lasting independence for his homeland. Every Irish schoolchild knew the story behind the history of their country. Since that fateful day in 1172 when Henry II of England had pronounced himself to be King of Ireland there had been no respite for the Irish people. Over the next 700 years a succession of English monarchs and politicians had attempted, with varying degrees of success, to impose their will upon the island. Henry VIII had forced a Protestant regime, while his daughter Elizabeth had dispatched Essex with an armed force to silence dissenting voices. Oliver Cromwell's Parliamentary Army had ruthlessly established Protestant ascendancy in the province. The 'Rising of United Irishmen' less than a hundred years ago had sealed Ireland's fate, with the resulting Act of Union and direct rule from Westminster.

When the great famine came in the winter of 1845–6 no assistance was sent by the English government to the starving thousands, despite the urgent pleas of the people. Devlin's own grandfather, penniless and unable to find food for himself or his family, was among the hundreds of unfortunates who had died tramping the frozen winter roads seeking sustenance.

Peter Devlin, having paid his last two pounds to the captain of a mail boat, already loaded to the gunwales with Irish emigrants, arrived in England with his dead brother's grieving wife and three sons in the spring of 1846. Moving from lodging house to lodging house, he found that life in the stews of Liverpool was little better than back in Ireland: too many men with too many families vying for too few jobs. Detested by the English working class in the town, who were themselves living at only just above subsistence level, the immigrants soon drifted into their own communities, first of streets and then, as time went by, whole areas.

More from expediency than love, Peter and his late brother's wife Corah, Connor's grandmother, had married after a few months of living in England. Although there were no more children life was still a daily struggle. Peter Devlin queued each morning with all the other hopefuls at the dockyard, puffing at an evil-smelling clay pipe and waiting to see who the yard foreman was going to be. The 'coddy' was, without doubt, the single most important person on the docks as far as the men seeking casual labour were concerned. Each day, depending on which vessels were to be unloaded, he had a quota to fill. If he were a fair man the strongest and fittest got a day's work. If, as so often happened, the selections were based upon who had bought him the most ale in the local tavern the night before, then men such as Devlin went hungry for another day.

Thus it was that in the spring of 1848 Peter Devlin became a member of a newly founded cell of the Fenian Brotherhood in Liverpool. Dedicated to driving the hated English out of their homeland, the nascent organisation was funded by ex-patriot Irish who had emigrated to America – the land of milk and honey – in earlier years. Now, with access to apparently unlimited funds, they were more than willing to provide backing for those at home with the will to fight a common enemy.

Under the tutelage of the Fenians, Peter Devlin set his mind to fusing the hitherto disparate talents in the local Irish neighbourhood. The majority of the men, Devlin included, were big strong countrymen, accustomed to earning their living with the sweat of their brow and the muscles of their arms. Strong physiques, combined with the notorious Irish temper, made them ideal for the purposes envisaged by the Fenians.

Discreetly supplied with the necessary funds, Devlin quietly began to assist the needy and the useful: a pair of shoes for a child here and a pint for a thirsty man there. Before long the line that formed at the dockside in the early morning gloom was totally Irish. Working in crews of twenty men, they presented the coddies with a more appealing prospect than free ale of a night. A coddy hired twenty men as a gang for the price of fifteen. At the end of the day he put five men's wages in his pocket, and nodded when told whose team would be arriving tomorrow.

It was a system in which, on the face of things, everyone involved profited. The foremen quickly became wealthy men; the unloved Irish found regular work where previously there had been none; and the employers benefited from the increased efficiency generated by teams of men who habitually worked together. In reality Devlin and the organisation soon had both employers and foremen in a stranglehold, and could bring the docks to a halt by withdrawing their labour at a moment's notice. The increased hostility shown to them by the local English in the district also suited their purposes well. It was time that these arrogant 'Scouses' learned what it felt like to be out of work and hungry.

After ten years of reorganising labour, and political scheming, the Devlin family had become a force to be reckoned with in Liverpool. With his three burly stepsons – Michael, the eldest, now aged twentyone, Sean, twenty, and Martin, eighteen – Peter had set the iron hand of Fenianism over a large section of the town. When James Stephens established the Irish Republican Brotherhood in 1858, it was Peter Devlin whom he selected to be his mainland commander in the north-west of England.

Always mindful of the need to remain within his own social class, Devlin continued to live buried deep within the Irish settlement, in a little two-up, two-down house within sight of the dockside warehouses. The one indulgence that the Brotherhood leader allowed himself was that he no longer broke his back loading and unloading ships' cargos, but instead spent his time as an organiser and proponent of labour and political doctrine, his office whichever local hostelry was convenient. So it was that in the summer of 1864 the first Liverpool commander of the Irish Brotherhood met his end, not in a running battle with the police or the military but in the back room of the Cap and Cushion public house in Lime Street. At the age of forty-four, while planning a two-day labour stoppage in the unloading of a recalcitrant importer's cargo, over a pint of bitter and whiskey chaser, Peter Devlin suffered a massive stroke. By the time the Fire Brigade ambulance arrived he had been dead for ten minutes.

Following his stepfather's death, and leaving his two younger brothers in Liverpool with their mother, Michael returned to Ireland with his wife Maureen and their children, five-year-old Connor and his younger sister Mary. It was in Dublin that Connor was to spend his early years, forming and developing an almost pathological hatred for the British and what they stood for in Ireland. At the Rourke Street Board School he listened, totally absorbed, as Mr Ormrod, the school's only teacher, taught his pupils how Irish history had been shaped and distorted by an occupying power that controlled their land from a distant country over the water. During the evenings, an ear to the parlour door and shivering on the cold linoleum, Connor and Mary overheard the political discussions of their father and his associates. Connor soon began to understand that his father was an active patriot, involved in illegal activities against the detested British – waylaying rent collectors and relieving them of their takings, and ambushing small parties of English soldiers on isolated country lanes.

Leaving school at thirteen, Connor was put to work in a grain warehouse owned by a local businessman named Edward Summerville, who was a friend of his father. Summerville was an important man in the Irish Brotherhood. With an office in Manchester, his business, which shipped grain from the mainland into Ireland, placed him in a unique position to assist the affairs of the Brotherhood. Michael Devlin and Summerville had long ago agreed that, once versed in the ways of commerce, young Connor could become a valuable asset to the organisation. If he displayed sufficient aptitude, at the right age he would be sent to Summerville's Manchester branch to work for the Brotherhood in England. In the meantime Connor's understanding of politics and his dislike of everything English were sharpened and whetted by his father with the care of a craftsman honing a scalpel. Ten days after his nineteenth birthday, in March 1878, he set sail on the steamer SS *Lombardy* for Liverpool.

In the nine years that had elapsed since his arrival in England, Connor Devlin had been employed by the Brotherhood, initially as a courier and later as a member of the special teams responsible for the commission of organised crime. Always with a political agenda, the matter in hand could be a robbery or a raid on a military arms depot. Split into three or four main cells, each in the charge of a lieutenant who was in turn responsible to an area commander, the teams rarely knew the identity of any Brothers outside their own group. If anyone was arrested, which often happened, he could only betray a limited number of accomplices.

Connor quickly established himself as a reliable and resourceful operative. On one occasion, while relieving a dozing militia man of a highly prized service rifle, his group had been disturbed by a regular soldier on piquet duty. Almost without having to think about what he was doing, Connor stepped in close to the startled sentry and pushed his long, thin-bladed fish-gutting knife into the man's ribs and up through his heart. The soldier died without making a sound, and thereafter Connor Devlin was regarded as a man always to be relied on and never to be trifled with.

Devlin's mind returned to the task in hand. He needed to concentrate. He had a meeting to attend – one at which difficult questions would be asked, and where wrong answers would not be tolerated.

Stopping near the end of New Brown Street, he moved back into the shadows cast by the gas lamp outside a deserted pawnbroker's shop, and leaned against the entry door between two houses. Pulling an old briar pipe from his coat pocket, and half-turning, he knocked the dottle from its bowl against the wall. Taking his time, he mechanically filled the pipe from a leather pouch, tamping down the tobacco and turning away from the wind to apply a match to the mixture. The ritual took over a minute. To the casual observer he was putting together a smoke before resuming his onward trek to some lodging house; in fact it was his final check to ensure he was not being followed before taking the next turning on the left into Swinburne Court. Had there been any hint of danger he knew that the entry door was off the latch, and two stout, well-greased bolts would secure the door in place long enough for him to make his escape down the entry and over the back gardens.

Cold in his thin clothes, Connor clamped the pipe between his teeth and turned quickly into Swinburne Court. The grandiose title was immediately revealed for what it was on entry: on the right-hand side half a dozen terraced houses came to an abrupt end where a brick wall, reaching up to the first-floor bedroom windows and running from one side of the street to the other, sealed off any further access. Opposite the houses was the featureless façade of Israel Silverman's garment factory.

The women who had just finished their shift were streaming out of Silverman's gates in a river of chattering humanity. A few men, foremen and timekeepers mingled with the throng. It was not difficult for Connor to lose himself momentarily in the crowd and slip unnoticed into the gloomy entry between number 9 and number 11. Like everything else that afternoon, the timing of his arrival had been carefully planned. With the entry gate firmly bolted behind him, he pushed his way through the lines of washing hanging limply from slack ropes on either side of the passage wall and made his way through a second gate into the tiny yard at the back of the house. The kitchen door was on the latch, and the Brotherhood lieutenant slipped silently through into the parlour and the warmth of a blazing range.

Number 11 Swinburne Court was one of the Brotherhood's many safe houses. Always located in districts that were sympathetic to the cause, they were used for hiding away fugitives from the law, storing arms and contraband and, as on this occasion, for holding high-level meetings. Access was strictly regulated; routes to and from were carefully monitored. The occupants, Mr and Mrs Kiernan, although caretakers for the Brotherhood, had been sent out to the tiny beerhouse in the next street with instructions not to return until after eight o'clock. Michael Loughlin and Peter Tumelty, the Kiernans' lodgers, were both at their posts, Loughlin seated in the shed at the bottom of the garden with a double-barrelled shotgun, to prevent any surprise entry from the rear, and Tumelty kneeling upstairs in the blackness behind the front bedroom window, a Martini-Henry rifle trained on the street. The flickering gas lamp outside Silverman's factory, bathing the cobbled approach in soft eerie light, created a killing ground through which anyone approaching number 11 had to pass.

Inside, on the dingy landing, a short wooden ladder gave access through an open trapdoor to the loft above. At the first warning of danger the senior officers present at the meeting, or the fugitive who was being hidden, could make good their escape into the loft space. Once there it was easy for the escapees to pick their way carefully along the rafters and over the ceiling joists of the intervening houses to the end of the block. Here a hole large enough for a man to pass through had been cut into the roof space of 22 Meerbrook Place, on the other side of the wall built across the road outside. The arrangement provided a swift and secure escape route into the neighbouring street, while any police were being held off in Swinburne Court.

In the parlour Connor Devlin took a seat at the table opposite a thin dark-haired man who held a tall bottle across the table between them. As the amber liquid splashed into the glass set out for him, Connor took in, as if for the first time, the legend on the label declaring that Bushmills Irish Whiskey had been slaking thirsts since 1690.

Liam O'Dowd placed the bottle between them with studious care, sat back and regarded Devlin with a long appraising stare. Connor, his glass untouched, leaned forward, elbows on the table and chin resting on his interlocked fingers. This was going to be a difficult interview. The man opposite was an old hand, and was deliberately not saying anything: he was waiting for Connor to break the silence and lose the advantage. Senior officer on the mainland, Liam O'Dowd was a powerful and dangerous man; Connor knew him to be totally ruthless and dedicated to the cause.

Almost a minute elapsed before O'Dowd's harsh Belfast accent broke the silence. 'So what the fuck went wrong, Connor?' No apparent malice – just a flat question demanding an answer.

'I don't know, Liam. The job went exactly as planned. We turned the agent over and were away with the money before the first copper came through the front door. We split up as arranged: me and Martin on horseback to lead away any chase, Eddie with the money down to Radbone's boat.'

Connor began to perspire: a wrong answer now and he was dead. It was after the gang had parted that things had gone wrong. He and Martin, having said their farewells at the crossroads, had gone their separate ways. Early the next afternoon the train from Sheffield had deposited him in Manchester. As arranged he went directly to the Pelican just round the corner from the station, and passed an hour chatting in the bar with the licensee and a few cronies. 'Show your face as soon as you get back; the more people who say you were at home the better. By the time anyone asks they'll have forgotten what the time was, and will be telling the law you were in the pub an hour before the train got in from Sheffield.' Martin Lafferty had similar instructions – the problem being that Martin had never arrived back in Manchester.

The next day the local papers carried the full story of the Kelsford robbery, along with the news that the body of one of the suspects had been discovered on a nearby canal towpath. Connor was stunned. Just before lunchtime a small boy called at his lodgings and passed him a terse message to be at Swinburne Court the following evening, at exactly twenty-five to seven.

O'Dowd's face remained expressionless, eyes cold. 'What's your assessment?'

'As far as I can see there are three possibilities.' Connor's voice was hoarse. 'First, someone realised what was cracking off and followed Eddie down to the cut, brained him and took the money. Second, and far more likely, Martin doubled back after we separated, got to Eddie before he made the rendezvous and killed him. The third possibility is that Eddie and Martin had their own plan, met to divide the cash and Martin double-crossed him.'

On the face of it the suggestions were reasonable; in reality Connor knew they were not. Whatever had come to pass that evening, he as the unit leader was now on trial. The job had gone badly wrong and the responsibility was his. That alone could cost him his life, as an example to other leaders.

The other man sat in silence, musing. Head down, his unshaven jaw resting on his chest, his cold eyes never left Devlin's face. Even now Connor found time to admire Liam's ability to blend into almost any background. Although not of an age, they had worked together on and off for many years, at home in Ireland and on the mainland. Aged fifty, O'Dowd had the ability and the education to stand, suited and booted, in front of a political gathering and expound the rights of a free Ireland, or, as now, sit unshaven and in cheap clothes, every inch a factory hand home from a day's work.

'There's another possibility.' The harsh voice took on an edge of authority. 'How about you and Martin following Eddie down to the cut? You come in from opposite ends and ambush him. No way about it, he's got to die. You take the money and go for the horses. Martin disappears for the time being while you come back here and brass it out.'

Connor felt perspiration trickling down his back, his mouth full of ashes, as he attempted to clear his throat. Despite the rule that firearms could only be carried when on a job, he wished he had brought a pistol. Not, he thought grimly, that it would have availed him much. It had not escaped his notice that the commander was already seated behind the table when he entered the room, nor that O'Dowd poured the whiskey left-handed, his right remaining casually out of sight in his lap, a loaded gun across his knees.

'You're bound to wonder, Liam. In your place so would I. Think about it, though. If that's what happened I'd have been a bit shrewder. I'd have made it look as if the job had gone totally wrong, that Martin had tried to do for both of us and escaped. And you know Martin as well as I do. He's no genius. If I was going to pull something I'd never choose him as a partner.'

The words hung in the air between them, the atmosphere stifling in the closed room. Connor suddenly became aware of a clock ticking somewhere to his left on the mantel shelf. Raising his head slightly, the Brotherhood commander stared at him balefully. 'Check the yard; I heard something move.' The voice, still devoid of expression, cut through the silence, and Connor felt his bowels turn to water. Both men knew there was nothing in the yard except a lookout with a loaded twelve-bore shotgun. As soon as he opened the kitchen door, framed in the light from the gas mantle, he would be executed. That was the decision of the judge and jury facing him across the table.

Fighting a losing battle to control his heaving stomach, Connor pushed back his chair and stood up slowly. Ponderously he walked towards the door, and the inevitable blinding flash that would be the last thing he would see in this world. His hand resting on the cold brass door knob, Connor's mind raced to find some way to avert what was about to happen. Behind him there was the heavy click of a revolver being cocked. It was a simple choice. Open the door and accept the judge's decision, or plead for mercy and be shot in the back.

Cold night air rushing in through the open door turned the perspiration bathing Connor's body into ice. The silent blackness enveloped him, robbing him of his vision. He stood motionless for a full thirty seconds before turning back into the parlour. The .45 Webley revolver was pointing unwaveringly past him through the empty doorway into the murky void of the yard.

Slowly, with infinite care, Liam O'Dowd allowed the hammer of the pistol to settle back safely over the chamber before he placed the gun on the green velvet tablecloth. The warm, friendly smile that had persuaded so many people over the years to do his bidding creased his sallow features. 'You've not drunk your whiskey,' he chuckled. Not for the first time Connor remarked to himself that O'Dowd's smile never quite reached his eyes.

For the next hour their discussion revolved around what had gone wrong and what was to be done next. After examining all the possibilities they decided that until Martin Lafferty had been found no definite conclusions could be drawn. The word was to be spread that Lafferty was wanted urgently by the Brotherhood – preferably alive.

O'Dowd's attention then turned to other matters. The Shires robbery had been planned to pay for a consignment of firearms that had recently arrived in Liverpool from America. Connor had been aware for some time that American Brotherhood supporters were sending shipments of pistols and rifles direct to Ireland; that some were arriving at mainland ports was news to him. 'You've kept this close, Liam,' he murmured, the warmth of the whiskey from the almost empty bottle spreading luxuriously through his body. He decided not to drink any more: it was early and he had to make his way home.

'The fewer that know the better. Our friends in the States have taken care of everything. They have a man who's an importer and exporter on the Eastern Seaboard. Until now the cargoes have been delivered to Scottish ports and then taken to the "Auld Country" by fishing smacks. Now it's time for something different. This consignment is safe in a warehouse not far from here. Three hundred brand new Colt .45 revolvers and two hundred Winchester repeating rifles, and ammunition.'

Connor digested the information. A regular supply of weapons to the mainland changed things. There would be no more need for risky hit and run raids on military armouries, and the potential for terrorist activities was unlimited. On the other hand, large quantities of firearms were not easy to conceal. 'How are we handling them?'

A knowing, almost crafty look passed across his companion's swarthy face. 'I want you to go back to Kelsford. Rent a house – you know the precautions. When you've set it up let me know, and I'll send the whole lot down to you by barge.'

Connor nodded slowly. They had moved contraband through the canal system many times before. For some reason the English police rarely stopped and checked canal boats. 'Fine. But who will you use?'

'The Radbone family, I think. We'll need someone like Amos and his sons, who run along that stretch of the Erewash regularly. The guns can be hidden under their legitimate cargo.'

'How many consignments are you thinking of?' Connor knew that storage and distribution would be his responsibility.

'A lot. What we don't use ourselves we'll sell on to these European gangs – anarchists and dissidents.'

Connor looked up sharply. 'That's a bad idea, Liam, if you're talking about Russians and Latvians. They're a menace. They're hotheads. No proper organisation and no security. They'll be a danger to us.'

The senior officer's response was dismissive. 'Leave that to those who know what they're doing. Look after your own job.'

Connor shrugged. The prospect of dealing with these groups appalled him – but time would tell, and at the moment time was on his side. 'I'll need to organise a safe warehouse to store the stuff when it arrives.'

Again a crafty look crossed Liam O'Dowd's countenance. 'That's already taken care of. We have a contact in the town . . .'

Chapter Five

S tanding to one side of the tall, heavily netted window, Ruth Samuels moved the edge of the brocaded curtain and gazed out onto the busy street below. The wide expanse of Victoria Road was almost deserted at this time in the afternoon. A solitary horse-drawn tramcar advertising Nestlé's milk products was stationary in the centre of the street, the horses stamping and pawing their hooves on the light covering of early snow. Across the road the windows of Bradshaw's newspaper shop were brightly decorated with festive streamers and coloured baubles in readiness for the Christmas festivities. The rest of the shops in the block and the houses just visible in the adjacent side street were also decked out with the small tinsel-covered trees made popular by the late Prince Consort. From the arm of one of the tall ornate lamp standards that were a feature of the broad thoroughfare someone had hung a small paper lantern. Two warmly clad middle-aged ladies freshly returned from an afternoon's shopping in the town centre disembarked, and the tramcar resumed its course, the sound of the horses' hooves muffled by the freshly falling snow.

Henry Farmer studied the woman in the half-light of the bedroom as she stood naked at the window with her back to him. His eyes focused on her long legs and heavy buttocks. Most women in their early thirties were starting to lose their attractions. For those in the lower and middle classes child-bearing and hard work took their toll: thick, heavy bodies, worried eyes peering from careworn faces. Paradoxically, for the upper classes good living tended to have a similar result: a comfortable existence, combined with producing a large family, endowed most of the wives with a matronly figure before they were thirty-five. Ruth, at thirty-two, had escaped many of the vagaries of life. She was tall for a woman, almost five foot six. Her heavy breasts and narrow waist were those of someone much younger, the result, Henry mused, of never having borne children. It was the shoulders that prevented her figure from being classically statuesque. Instead of sloping gracefully away from her neck, they were broad and strong – the shoulders of a peasant woman whose homeland was the Dniester river and the Russian hills.

She turned to speak, long ebony hair flowing loosely down over her shoulders and framing her high cheekbones. Dark brown eyes set above a long straight nose and wide sensuous lips told of her Semitic heritage. The thick pelt of dark hair curling up her belly began to arouse him again. Ruth caught his appraising gaze. 'Satisfied?' she asked. Her mischievous grin didn't tell Henry whether she was referring to what he was seeing or to their recent lovemaking.

Reaching into a humidor on a small table near the window, Ruth took a cigar, lit it and, having inhaled deeply, passed it over to Henry. Acutely aware of his new stirrings, he lifted the covers and indicated for her to return to the bed.

Despite her Russian birthright and Jewish upbringing, Ruth Samuels had been born and bred in Kelsford. Her parents, Aaron and Rachel Kosminski, had fled their home village near Lvov before she was born. After trekking across Europe they had arrived on a packet boat at Dover in the early summer of 1854. From there, through the influences of the local synagogue, Aaron had been steered towards Kelsford's burgeoning Jewish community. Living in one room, in a tiny back-to-back house in the Downe Street district, the young Russian had made a living repairing watches. Later, using carefully hoarded money, he had rented a small shop on Oxford Road near the army barracks and had begun to ply his trade as a jeweller. It was during these difficult years, in 1855, that Ruth had been born. As the Jewish community in Kelsford grew and prospered, so Aaron Kosminski became both a respected member of the synagogue and a wealthy man. By the time Ruth was seventeen her father owned not only large premises in Kelsford High Street but also two other shops, in nearby Derby and Sheffield.

An influential figure in Aaron's success had been Isaac Samsonov, an older man. The Kosminski and Samsonov families both came from the village of Brovinska, near the Dniester river in the western province of Ukraine, so it was a matter of honour for Samsonov to assist Kosminski in his business venture; and when his wife died in 1872 that the seventeen-year-old Ruth should be considered a suitable prospect to replace her.

Isaac Samsonov had come to England forty years earlier – like his friend Kosminski to escape from the oppression and intolerance of the Tsarist regime. In 1830 the twenty-four-year-old goldsmith and moneylender had left his wife and baby son in their village while he journeyed north to Kiev on business. When he returned a month later the only trace of his shop and home was a heap of charred rubble and timbers. On instructions from St Petersburg the local Cossack garrison commander had conducted a pogrom against all Jews living in the Lvov district. The subsequent depredations of the mounted soldiery reduced every Jewish business and synagogue in the area to ruins, while all Jews who failed to escape into the forests were rounded up and summarily executed.

Neither finding nor expecting any consideration from the remaining Christian and Greek Orthodox members of the community, Samsonov decided to leave. After paying a visit to the recently dug mass grave that was the final resting place for his family and so many friends he left the province, never to return, taking only the clothes he was wearing. During the ensuing months he made his way north into Latvia, at Riga managing to obtain a place as a deckhand on an English vessel loaded with timber. Leaving the Gulf of Riga, the sailing ship headed first for Gotland and then, having called at Karlskrona, made its way up through the Kattegat and into the North Sea, arriving at Grimsby after nearly six weeks.

Tired of travelling, Isaac Samsonov made his way to the nearby synagogue, where he spent his first night in England on a palliasse in a tiny storeroom. Abandoning his original idea of making his way to America, the young man accepted the advice of the rabbi and decided to seek his fortune in England. The consensus of opinion was that his best opportunities lay either in Manchester or in a Midlands town where there was a growing Jewish population.

Electing for the latter, the following morning Samsonov set off on the final stage of his travels, armed with a letter of introduction to the Jewish leaders in Kelsford and a gold sovereign from the synagogue contingency fund.

Like so many of his contemporaries, once established in his new land he changed his name to one that was more acceptable to the English ear. Jacobus Steinburg became Jacob Stein, Szac Marcovitch Samuel Marks, Josif Rizckovski Joseph Richards ... and Isaac Samsonov became Isaac Samuels. Working in the closely knit confines of orthodox Jewry in the town for five years, by living almost at subsistence level he scraped together sufficient cash to open a small pawnbroker's shop at 4 Grey's Court – ideally situated in the heart of the Downe Street district. The Christian poor deposited and redeemed household goods on a weekly basis, while the Jewish poor were given interest-free loans. While these didn't earn any money, they were more than offset by Isaac's increasing status among his fellow citizens.

In the spring of 1842, along with two of his closest friends, Solomon Meyer and Jakob Peters, Samuels went into the business of banking. Selling the pawnshop in Grey's Court, which by now he owned outright, he and his colleagues opened the Kelsford Bank of Commerce in Cumberland Place. The gamble was a huge one. Capital for the venture was raised through business and banking contacts in Manchester, where the Jewish community was firmly established. Failure, which was too dire to be contemplated, never materialised, and after ten years the three partners were well on the way to becoming very wealthy men.

That Isaac Samuels had been lastingly affected by the loss of his first wife and small son was beyond any doubt. Although it was a matter he discussed with no one – not even his second wife Hannah, whom he married in 1845 – the influence upon his life was deep. Nurturing an abiding hatred for the

Russian political and class system, and the anti- Semitism that it engendered, he became deeply involved as a covert Jewish activist. As the years passed, and more European Jews fled from persecution in their native lands, so an influential support network known as the 'Pipeline' had evolved – in which Samuels played his part. Jewish communities in France, Belgium and the Netherlands, along with those of the free Scandinavian countries, had created a series of sophisticated escape routes out of the Russian Empire, based on couriers and escorts who met escaping refugees at the borders of the Russian satellite states. Fugitives were provided with new papers and identities before being taken to safety through Austria or the newly federated German states, and once in a safe country with access to a western seaport they were provided with financial and other support so they could begin a new life in either England or America. Because of the dangers it was usual to take individuals rather than families through the Pipeline.

With Hannah's death, a third marriage to the young Ruth Kosminski suited Samuels very well. He had known the girl since childhood and was aware that, unlike many of her friends, she was a mature and welleducated young lady. Aaron Kosminski had ensured that his only daughter came to womanhood well equipped for the trials and tribulations of life. A private education at a young ladies' school in the south of England had ensured she had all the attributes required to procure a successful marriage, while Aaron had spent many hours versing her in the intricacies of book keeping and business practice. Ruth was set above her fellows by an unusual aptitude for languages. Brought up in a closed Jewish community among first-generation adults from all over Europe, many of whom had only a basic understanding of English, the young girl's skill flourished. By the time she was ten Ruth could speak English, Dutch, German, Russian, French and Yiddish flawlessly. On her return home from Miss Saunderson's Boarding Academy for Young Ladies, aged fifteen, Ruth set to work as an interpreter in her father's flourishing business. Foreign clients who wished to conduct business with Mr Kosminski usually took no notice of the smart young lady taking notes of their meetings, little thinking that asides made to their companions in *plat Deutsch* or in French laden with Marseille patois were faithfully transmitted to their host at each coffee break. During crucial meetings Kosminski often called a short halt to proceedings on receipt of a pre-arranged signal from his daughter, only to return to the table a wiser man.

One of the reasons that a marriage to Ruth suited Samuels well was that he wished to use her in his dealings with the Pipeline. As his wife she could travel round Europe with unrestricted freedom, ostensibly on bank business, meeting various important contacts and on occasion bringing back important refugees. Also, thanks to her sound business knowledge, she could genuinely close overseas business contracts on his behalf.

The marriage, solemnised in the Kelsford synagogue in 1872, lasted for eight years until, at the age of seventy-four, following a short respiratory illness that the doctor attributed to overwork, Isaac Samuels died peacefully in his sleep.

In the seven years since she had become a young – and very wealthy – widow, Ruth had taken stock of her life. Domestically the eight years with Samuels had been pleasant if unexciting. In his late sixties when they married, her husband had been relatively undemanding as a bed partner, and certainly there had been no prospect of a family. While her husband's lack of interest in such matters did not displease Ruth – she had never found him attractive – the young woman had needs of her own. When her expectations of a full married life were not fulfilled she decided to discreetly remedy matters. Travelling abroad regularly presented opportunities that might otherwise have been denied her: the clandestine nature of her activities for the Pipeline brought her into contact with a number of active and exciting men, most of whom were interested in a short-term relationship with an attractive woman.

Her ally in these liaisons was Mirka Sloboda. Two years older than Ruth, Mirka had come to Kelsford from the Ukraine with her parents when Ruth was sixteen. Settling in the town, Mirka's father had found employment in one of the local factories, and his daughter went to work as a parlourmaid for the Kosminski family. While maintaining the required social distance, the two girls had become firm friends, and when Ruth married Isaac, Mirka had moved with her to Victoria Road as her personal maid.

Lighting a fresh cigar to replace the one that had burnt out in the bedside ashtray during their second bout of lovemaking, Ruth turned on her side and looked pensively at her partner. Her affair with Henry Farmer was the first occasion when she had allowed herself to become involved with a Kelsford man. Over the years she had been careful to have only one lover in England – a business contact of her husband's in Liverpool, a town she visited for the bank two or three times a year. The affair ended when he was moved to his firm's head office in Copenhagen.

Ruth had initially met Henry Farmer through the bank. Small amounts of cash had been disappearing from the main banking hall tills and he was the officer who investigated the matter. The thefts were quickly traced to an elderly cashier, setting out to improve his financial position before retiring, and the matter was discreetly closed – but because of the delicate nature of the enquiry Henry had arranged to deal with one partner only – Ruth – and to make his reports away from the bank, at her home. She found the urbane and elegantly dressed detective very attractive, although he was several years older than her. As he was a widower of many years, living alone, she decided it would be safe to embark upon an affair with him. Her instincts were correct. Farmer was a discreet lover who expected no more from the relationship than being compatible partners in bed.

'I've got to go away for a while,' she said. Her voice – which was what had first attracted Henry – was deep for a woman's, beginning somewhere in the back of her throat. He looked at her quizzically. 'After Christmas I'm going to conclude a loan settlement in Amsterdam.'

'How long will you be gone?' It was not the query of an insecure young amour but the straightforward enquiry of a good friend.

'Probably about a month, I think. While I'm there I may catch a train to Paris for a few days. The capital's supposed to be in a turmoil over this international exhibition that's being planned – they're supposed to be building a huge metal tower – and I wouldn't mind having a look.'

That she was lying did not particularly bother her. Ruth was going to meet an important political émigré and conduct him safely to England, but Henry did not need to know this: it was part of her life that was of no concern to him. She wondered what her policeman lover would do if he discovered that his attractive Jewish widow was involved in such highly dubious political activities. Ruth could have called a halt to her part in the Pipeline when her husband died, as unlike him she did not have a deep hatred of all things Russian and she did not share his extreme political views; but she enjoyed the exciting and occasionally dangerous nature of the work.

'If it were not for "your Christmas", I'd be going this week,' she laughed.

Farmer grinned back. As well as he knew her, he could never get used to Ruth's way of life and her dismissal of such important events as Christmas. 'If I get myself circumcised tomorrow can I come with you?' he asked.

'If you get yourself circumcised tomorrow you'll be no good to me until I get back.'

Chuckling, they tucked themselves under the sheets in companionable silence, passing the cigar back and forth.

After Henry had gone, let out through the tradesmen's entrance and down the passageway round the corner from Victoria Road by a vigilant Mirka, Ruth began to dress in readiness for her meeting with Joshua Howkins. The fact that she did not like Howkins irritated Ruth, because she was acutely aware that her feelings were reciprocated – and this animosity tended to influence her business judgements. An influential businessman in the town, and chairman of the watch committee, Howkins did not like to conduct business with a woman, but it had been made clear to him from the outset that if he wished to negotiate a cash loan for the new canal basin on the north side of town he would have to deal with Mrs Samuels. The meeting, in the bank's luxurious boardroom, was a routine matter. At the outset of the Shires Canal project, Howkins and a group of his associates had been quick to realise the potential for a swift profit. Forming a group headed by Howkins, they had unobtrusively acquired several tracts of land on the north edge of Kelsford, where the canal swung east. This they intended, subject to the demolition of some terraced housing, to convert into a large warehouse complex centred on a canal basin. Having unloaded in the basin, barges would follow a new extension of the canal out of the complex and swing back to rejoin the main channel. The cash outlay to complete the dig and erect the warehouses was considerable – in excess of £100,000 – and expenses had to be defrayed by borrowing from various sources, including a proposed £20,000 from the Kelsford Bank of Commerce.

Ruth looked up from the papers spread in front of her. 'To obtain a cash loan, Mr Howkins, even if it is well secured, your consortium will be paying a considerable amount of interest. The plan that you have put to us, which envisages repayment within the first five years, would result in excess of £30,000.' Howkins, sitting on the opposite side of the wide conference table, waited. Still looking directly at him, trying to persuade him to make eye contact, Ruth continued. 'I've discussed the matter with my co-directors and we feel that an option you may find more advantageous would be for the bank to purchase from your group an agreed percentage of the share stock in . . .' she made a pretence of checking the document in front of her '. . . Kelsford Warehousing. The advantage would be mutual. For your part the capital amount borrowed would be substantially reduced, thus decreasing repayments and interest. We would take a gamble upon the shares flourishing and thus receiving a limited interim dividend. At the expiry of the five-year period we would sell you the shares at, say, five per cent below market value. Our opinion is that the projections are healthy and should prove financially rewarding for both parties.'

It was now her turn to wait. The bank could, by being involved in the early stages, realise more than its original investment, withdrawing before there was a downturn in canal transport. Her two partners, Solomon Meyer and Jakob Peters, were in agreement that the new warehousing and canal basin was a sound business proposition. Initially, after Isaac Samuels' death, they were unhappy that his widow had been foisted upon them as a partner under the terms of his will. However, time had shown that she was an able businesswoman and, they were forced to admit, an asset to the company.

Joshua Howkins turned to gaze down the huge polished rosewood table towards the large bay windows that looked out onto the quiet of Cumberland Place. The possibility of such a proposition had been anticipated and discussed well before the meeting – not whether it should be accepted, but how best to deflect it. 'Thank you, Mrs Samuels, but that will not be necessary. The group I represent does not anticipate a share flotation. The undertaking will be based upon an equally divided partnership – although I agree that in the early stages it's more expensive for us to negotiate a direct loan.'

Ruth nodded slowly. His refusal surprised her slightly. The bank's proposal was a sound one, and would have eased the consortium's cash flow considerably. She returned her attention to the file of papers on the table. There were, apart from Howkins, three other partners involved in Kelsford Warehousing: Lucas Sangster, an American machinery manufacturer currently living on the outskirts of the town in Great Olston, Oswald Langran, who owned a string of shops selling boots and shoes, and Brewitt Gotheridge, an engineer who with the advent of the new craze for cycling had made a fortune producing 'safety bicycles' at his factory in Coventry. All four of the men were, in the eyes of the bank, a sound investment, and the loan had already been agreed by the other two partners. She was, however, enjoying Joshua Howkins' moment of uncertainty.

The dapper little man across the table had over the years created a highly successful chain of grocery shops in Kelsford and the surrounding district. To this he had quietly added various plots of land in and around the town, and was not above using his influence as a member of the corporation to develop or dispose of them, at a considerable profit. A fact to which few were privy was that Howkins owned large areas of property near Downe Street – and Ruth thought grimly to herself that he would not be at all happy to discover she was aware of this; or, for that matter, that the Kelsford Bank of Commerce was actively buying adjacent plots and premises in order to prevent his establishing a monopoly. When the time came to demolish Downe Street there would be an immense profit to be made, a profit that she and her partners were determined their bank would share in.

Giving Howkins a pleasant smile, Ruth stood up. 'I think we can accommodate you in this matter, Mr Howkins. If you call upon us later this week with your solicitor, I'll have the necessary papers drawn up.'

Joshua Howkins pushed back his chair carefully and rose to his feet, tugging at the edges of his waistcoat to straighten it. Ruth rang a small polished brass bell on the table next to the file of papers. The heavy double doors of the conference room swung open and a uniformed attendant appeared. Shaking Ruth's proffered hand and expressing his satisfaction with the afternoon's business, Howkins allowed himself to be escorted down the stairs into the banking hall, without realising that he had been dismissed.

It was less than ten minutes after he had left that Ruth followed Howkins out of the bank and into her waiting carriage. 'Mr Issitt's house, please, David,' she said to the coachman as she climbed into the plush but cramped interior.

As the brougham rattled at a brisk trot on its short journey through the busy streets of the town, Ruth's mind jumped to her forthcoming meeting. Manfred Issitt was the Midlands regional organiser for the Pipeline. Like Ruth he was a second-generation immigrant, whose political conscience drove him to help his fellow Jews escape from the oppressive domination of the Tsars. Presumably, she thought, the arrangements for her current trip had now been made, and this meeting was her briefing.

Passing the imposing grey stone walls of Sevastopol Barracks on his left, the coachman swung sharply into a wide suburban street a hundred yards further on. Halting the carriage outside 6 Leaminster Gardens he dropped nimbly to the ground, and touched his silk hat as he opened the carriage door.

'I expect to be at least an hour,' Ruth informed him. 'Please return at six o'clock.' Bobbing his head, David Capewell gave the highly polished bell-pull a tug, and stood to one side while a maid invited his mistress into the house.

In the library the lamps had been lit and their warm glow was reflected in the heavy mellow woodwork and dark leather-bound books of Mannie Issitt's extensive collection. The walls were lined from floor to ceiling with tomes on Judaism and classical literature from all over the civilised world. The difference between Mannie and so many other men in his position, thought Ruth, was that he had read most of them.

Issitt smiled with genuine pleasure as the attractive woman entered the room. 'Shalom, Ruth.' The soft well-modulated tones accorded completely with the man, who was tall and immaculately dressed, his crisply pressed white shirt and dove grey cravat perfectly matching his dark trousers and long coat.

'Shalom, Mannie,' Ruth replied. 'How are things with Rachel and the children?'

'Rachel is away with Edward and Jonathon at her mother's – she'll be back for the new year.' The fact that he had given his children anglicised names did not escape Ruth. After exchanging pleasantries and waiting for the housemaid to bring them tea and biscuits on a large silver tray, Issitt addressed the matter in hand. 'We now have details of your trip,' he said quietly, dropping almost without thinking into Yiddish just in case an inquisitive servant should be hovering by the library door. 'This one is important.' His voice was low and unusually tense. 'The émigré is of extreme interest to us. He's employed by the government as an inspector of taxes and for the last ten years has been our man in the Lvov district. He acts as the initial contact point for potential escapees. About a month ago he sent word that he thinks he is under suspicion, and wants to leave Russia before the Ochrana have sufficient evidence to arrest him. Since this recent attempt to assassinate the Tsar all hell's been let loose. The police are rounding up suspects every day.' Issitt paused for a moment, but Ruth nodded for him to continue. 'His escape won't be well received. It'll confirm the Ochrana in their suspicions, and it's not beyond the bounds of possibility that they'll try to recover him.'

'Where am I to meet him?' Ruth turned over the possibilities. If she was contacting the man somewhere like Switzerland it should be fairly straightforward; if it was in Austrian territory it would be more difficult.

'Near to Unghvar, this side of the border.'

Ruth glanced sharply at Manfred. Unghvar was in Galicia at the foot of the Carpathian Mountains, as far east across Austro-Hungarian territory as a traveller could go. The mountains that separated the eastern boundary of Franz Josef's empire from Tsarist Russia were wild and desolate, not a good place for a stranger to be alone. 'They still have vampires there,' she remarked, a feeling of misgiving gnawing at her stomach.

'And your parents' village was a hundred miles further east,' said Issitt. 'You can speak the dialect like a true native. If things become difficult you can blend into the countryside without the slightest problem. No one would be able to tell you from the local Cossacks.'

'Except,' pointed out Ruth, 'that I am Jewish, and a woman travelling alone.'

'Rushka, this is a most important trip. You won't be alone. The man will be escorted to your meeting point, and from there you'll be with friends all the way home. You've done this a dozen times before.' Manfred's voice was urgent. If the Ukrainian tax collector were to be arrested and tortured by the Tsarist secret police – the Ochrana – then their whole network in the Lvov region would collapse. Dozens of their people would be taken up and imprisoned. A pogrom would be ordered by St Petersburg and whole communities would be wiped out. He did not need to explain this to his visitor; she already understood the implications.

Ruth sat quietly for a while. Irrespective of which route had been arranged for her to travel, it was well over a thousand miles from Kelsford to Unghvar; she would have to cross Europe in the middle of winter. Her promise to Henry Farmer that she would be back in a month appeared to be a fairly accurate estimate, but if there were any problems it could be nearer five or six weeks. Taking a deep breath, she said, 'I'll have to make the necessary arrangements at the bank.' In fact her business was not a great problem. Both of her partners belonged to the Pipeline organisation, their role to provide finance, along with many other wealthy supporters.

Issitt relaxed, touching his hand to his immaculate cravat, and smiled his appreciation. 'Thank you, Ruth, you'll be doing us a great service.' His voice had recovered its usual confident tone.

There was a time when Manfred Issitt had entertained certain aspirations concerning Ruth. Growing up together as part of a wealthy, if narrow, community, a marriage match had been discussed by their respective parents. Manfred found Ruth a very attractive woman, and her marriage to the elderly Samuels had disappointed him. Always a practical man, Mannie contented himself with a comfortable marriage to Rachel Jacobs, another local girl, and was soon the father of two healthy and active boys. A couple of years after Ruth was widowed Issitt had made a perfunctory approach to her that she could have interpreted as brotherly affection or otherwise. The worldly Ruth declined to pursue the implied offer, and the two remained simply friends.

For the next hour, the door to the outer hallway securely closed, they discussed arrangements for the journey.

Chapter Six

Frederick Judd, his pen poised over the column of figures that he was busy tallying, looked up as the bulky figure of Joseph Langley passed his office door. Of the five inspectors on the force Langley and Judd were the most senior, holding equal rank, not that the detective would ever acknowledge this fact. To Joseph Langley, uniformed officers were there for the convenience of his detectives, and as such should know their place. Langley, as head of detectives, was the longest serving and Judd, as chief clerk, was responsible directly to the head constable for the administration of the force. Joseph Langley held the often-expressed opinion that the chief clerk's role was that of 'a useless pen-pusher, who would be better employed counting sacks at Sibson's Wharf'. This morning, as on every other morning, he strode down the corridor, pipe clasped firmly between his teeth, making no acknowledgement of the other inspector's presence.

Judd glanced at the polished brass ship's clock mounted on the wall to his left. Eight minutes past eight: the old man was late. The chief clerk had noticed recently that Langley's timekeeping was not as strict as it used to be – the result, he presumed, of heavy nights spent in a local tavern.

His concentration broken, Judd laid his pen down carefully in the grooved tongue of the heavy wooden inkstand on his desk. Sitting back in the comfortable leather round-backed chair, he stretched his arms above his head and decided that the names and figures could wait a while. Tomorrow – Wednesday – was the force's weekly pay day, when every man presented himself between the hours of two and four in the afternoon for his wages envelope.

Langley's disdain for the chief clerk was fully reciprocated. As far as Judd was concerned, the detective inspector was a bigoted fool. An experienced and ambitious police officer, far from being a 'pen-pusher', Judd had served his time both as a constable and a sergeant in the streets and back alleys of Sheffield. Langley was good at his job, but limited by his perceptions of others.

It was, and always would be, a basic truth that thief-taking was a fundamental of police work, but Judd had realised many years before that without an able administrator no organisation, least of all a police force, could function.

Two years earlier Fred Judd had made a careful study of the backgrounds of recent successful candidates for the office of head constable. It was no surprise to him that, in over half of them, the appointment had gone to an officer serving as a chief clerk. But he was also aware that the Joe Langleys of this world wanted head constables to be appointed from the ranks of the army officers, civil servants, school teachers and coastguards whose names filled the application sheets. The less a chief constable knew about police work, the safer Langley and his peers remained. It would not be long, Judd decided, before he himself made a move; it was a matter of waiting for a suitable opportunity in a suitable town. Meanwhile he would continue to give good value for the forty-eight shillings a week that he earned in Kelsford.

A small grin touched the corners of Judd's mouth as he thought back to his days in Sheffield. Not everything, he thought, worked out as planned. While he was a sergeant in the charge room, the clerk of a small borough force in the next county had emptied the force's bank account and disappeared without trace. Absentmindedly scratching his heavy beard, he searched the recesses of his memory for the man's name. Allen, that was it – Horace Allen. A thin weedy man who didn't look as if he had it in him. Judd had met him once or twice in the course of his duties. Inspector Allen, he recollected, had gone off to the bank to collect the week's wages one Wednesday morning, having first emptied the petty cash tin, pocketed the warrants money and cleaned out the coffee fund. Adding the wages to his haul, the chief clerk was last seen at the railway station, purchasing a ticket for London.

Judd's reverie was interrupted by Joseph Langley's deep growl further down the corridor as he interrogated the duty constable in the public enquiry office about an entry in the occurrence book. Each morning the detective inspector followed a fixed routine. Coming in through the side door in Grey Street, his first stop was the main enquiry desk in the public waiting area to examine the overnight occurrence book. From there, he went into the charge room to look at the detained persons book, to find out who was in the cell block. Heaven help the unfortunate charge sergeant who had inadvertently released someone overnight whom Inspector Langley had an interest in. With any luck, thought Judd, when the old man eventually goes – as some day he must – someone like Tom Norton will replace him.

His deliberations were interrupted by a small person darting past his open door. 'Arthur!' Judd bellowed. 'Where do you think you're going?'

The slim figure slid to a halt and returned to the office doorway. 'Sorry, sir, I was going down to Mortimer's to get Mr Langley an ounce of Bondsman. Sorry, sir!'

Arthur Hollowday was a small, thin lad of thirteen, whose spiky ginger hair looked as if it had been cut at the weekend by his mother. The boy was terrified of Detective Inspector Langley, and did his best to avoid him. On the other hand, he regarded the bulky figure of Inspector Judd with a respect bordering upon reverence. One of six children, Arthur lived with his mother and five siblings in a tiny terraced house in Wordsworth Lane. His father had been killed in an accident at Sibson's Wharf three years earlier, when Arthur was only ten, and since that time his mother had been making ends meet by taking domestic cleaning jobs during the day and bar work in the evenings.

When a local beat officer had spotted Arthur in the street, poorly clad and barefoot, he had put in an application for the family to receive assistance from the Kelsford Police Poor Children's Association. It was pure chance that it had been Fred Judd who made the visit to the Holloday household to assess their situation. From that time onwards, warmly clad in a second-hand pea jacket and a pair of sturdy boots from the police stores, Arthur had viewed the chief clerk as his personal saviour – and twelve months ago, when he took his leave of Slate Street Elementary School, a job had been found for him at the police station, running messages.

'What about my coffee, then?' Judd immediately regretted the brusqueness of his tone.

The boy's expression was one of confused despair. 'Sorry, sir. I'll get it for you now, before I go to Mortimer's, sir.'

'No, lad.' Fred was well aware of the cause of young Arthur's dilemma. 'Fetch Inspector Langley's tobacco first.'

'Thank you, sir.' Arthur's relief was visible as he scurried off along the passage.

He would have to do something with the boy, thought Judd, before the likes of Langley destroyed whatever potential he might have. Settling himself deeper into the warmth of his comfortable chair, the chief clerk returned to tallying up his figures.

When Tom Norton arrived at Long Street the clock on nearby St George's Church was just striking nine o'clock. After exchanging greetings with the elderly constable on desk duty he went through the door at the rear of the public office and along the passage to the detective's office.

Sam Braithwaite was already squeezed into the chair behind his desk in the far corner of the room. Obviously awaiting Tom's arrival, he put a cautionary finger to his lips, then with a conspiratorial grin tapped his nose with his forefinger. Tom glanced quickly at the closed connecting door between the detective's office and Langley's room; by listening carefully the sound of muted voices could just be distinguished. Joseph Langley's deep baritone was punctuated at intervals by another, less grating tone. Tom recognised this second voice as that of Superintendent Robert Archer Robson, the head constable.

'The old man's explaining why he hasn't caught the Shires robbers yet,' whispered Sam, gleefully.

Archer Robson had come down to take command of the Kelsford Force five years previously from the Scottish border country north of Berwick. That he and Langley had taken an instant dislike to each other was common knowledge. To most members of the force it was a constant delight that two of the most senior officers at Long Street were in a state of permanent disagreement.

Less than a minute later the stocky figure of the head constable, a stack of court files under his arm, emerged from the next office. Without pausing to close the door behind him, he strode off purposefully in the direction of the magistrates' court.

'Come through, Thomas.' The detective inspector, unlit pipe clenched between his teeth, appeared unruffled by his recent encounter and waved Tom into the chair opposite to his desk. 'Our leader's not happy.' With the door closed behind them, Langley's gravelly voice was pitched so that no eavesdropper could overhear. 'For once it's a sentiment I share.' Tom knew Langley well enough to know that in this mood he was at his most devious – and dangerous. 'He wants to know why there have been no developments after four days. No prisoners. Why we're no further forward.' Langley struck a match and busied himself with his pipe, watching the sergeant through the emerging smoke.

'I'm not so sure about that, sir,' Tom ventured cautiously. 'We know who the dead man was. The Manchester police know him, and are working at tracing his associates. It's just a matter of time before something turns up.'

'You're talking about good luck, and the only sort of good luck that policemen find is what they make for themselves.' The older man's face creased into a macabre grimace that Tom recognised as the inspector's interpretation of a smile. 'We need a confession.'

Tom felt his stomach lurch. So that was what this was all about. He had to think quickly, stay ahead of the old man before he was committed to something he would regret.

'I think we should have Ike Harriman in and talk to him – just the two of us.' Langley removed the briar from his mouth, blew a thin stream of blue smoke across the room, then gazed reflectively at the stem held perfectly still in his right hand. A whisper of smoke drifted up from the burning embers in its bowl. Langley seemed to be lost in contemplation of his proposal. Almost fifteen seconds elapsed before he spoke again. He was playing a game at which he was an expert: allow the words to sink in, then continue; don't allow the other party time to reply. 'You and I will interview him, Thomas. Things need to move on and we both know that he's involved.' The voice was soft, avuncular, with no trace of its unsettling growl.

The atmosphere in the room had suddenly become stifling. There was no way in which Tom could go along with the proposition. Langley was testing him. If he agreed he would be Langley's creature for the rest of his career. If he refused the inspector would ensure that he was quietly removed from the department, with a comment on his record that was guaranteed to end his prospects forever. Gathering his senses, he leaned forward slightly. In a voice that was little more than a whisper he said, 'That might be a little premature. The Manchester police say Donnelly was involved with an Irish Fenian group. They're sending me details, which should be here in a day or two. If we're in a position to talk to him about this Irish thing he might just tell us something. If not, we can still come away winning.'

Now it was Tom's turn to play the game. With any luck the information from Manchester would be sufficient to unsettle Harriman. If not, at least it would buy him a little time to deflect Langley from this particular scheme.

Joseph sat quietly for a few moments, considering what Tom had said. He had great respect for his sergeant's abilities, which was why he had decided to move their relationship on by involving him in his plan. 'All right.' The conspirator was gone; he was once more the brusque, authoritative inspector. 'Let's see what comes down from Manchester before we do anything else.' Tom was about to leave when Langley spoke again. 'Meanwhile we'll rattle a few cages.' This time the grin was genuine. 'Meet me in the Pack Horse at half past one: we'll take a little walk round the town.'

Tom's head throbbed like a traction engine as he weaved his way unsteadily down the narrow entry towards his back gate. He desperately wanted to sleep but knew that the moment he closed his eyes he would start to throw up. Joseph Langley's 'little walk round the town' had consisted of an afternoon and evening drinking in every pub, beerhouse and brothel in Kelsford.

Having met Langley in the Pack Horse as arranged, Tom was introduced to several of the inspector's associates, some of whom he already knew. Among the company at the bar was the editor of the *Gazette*, Charles Kerrigan Kemp, who, having bought a round of drinks, attempted to wheedle information about the Shires robbery and murder enquiry out of him. After half an hour of dissembling the two detectives left for less salubrious climes.

The first of Langley's haunts they visited was a beerhouse in Lothair Street, owned by one Edith Knapp and known to one and all as 'Crooked Edie's'. It was an old cobbler's shop which, on the death of her husband some years before, Edie had converted into a drinking den, after paying eight shillings for a beerhouse licence. The original shop counter had long ago given way to a sturdy deal plank mounted on six heavy beer barrels, two at each end and two supporting the centre. Behind the counter, on substantial brick plinths, stood a further four barrels. Three were filled with Starr's Ale, the fourth with a strong Irish stout, all drawn direct from the wood. Half a dozen drinkers, all workmen taking a pint or two after finishing the early shift at one of the nearby factories, stood in the tiny room between the door and the bar.

Crooked Edie, so named because of her pronounced limp, the result of a broken hip when she was kicked by a wagon horse as a child, kept her thin pale face impassive as she spied the two detectives entering through the narrow doorway. The meaningful glance she shot at the serving girl busy clearing away empty glasses dispatched her into the back room to warn the other customers.

'Two pints of Starr's, please, Edie.' Langley's glance was already taking in the drinkers. Tom's eyes followed the broad back of the young girl as she disappeared into the adjacent room. The beer in the pint glass that the woman placed on the timber counter was flat and uninviting. Brought up in his father's pub in Grange Lane, Tom was well aware of the properties of different ales, and beer drawn from the wood was not his favourite. Tiny beerhouses such as this, with no cellar or storage space, could only sell their wares direct from the barrel, and the result was a flat drink that demanded an acquired taste – one that Tom did not have.

Having enquired of Mrs Knapp's health and that of her children, each of whom Langley appeared to know personally, the detectives made their way into the dingy back parlour. Tom blinked as his eyes adjusted to the gloom of his grimy surroundings. The dozen or so men and women in the room filled it to overflowing. The air was thick with tobacco smoke and the rancid smell of stale beer and unwashed bodies. In the empty space where a kitchen range would have stood was a rickety table cluttered with glasses of ale, and a single gas mantle fought a losing battle against the deteriorating afternoon light. A large unshaven man of indeterminate age, with a sallow-faced woman draped across his lap, removed his hand from inside her skirts and acknowledged the inspector.

'Will you have a drink, Mr Langley?' His heavy Glaswegian accent made it difficult to judge whether he was drunk or sober.

'Thank you, Brindley, that seems a good idea.' As the serving girl disappeared to bring the inspector a fresh glass, Tom could not fail to wonder at his companion's capacity for drink. As he sipped cautiously at his own flat beer a fresh one was pushed into his free hand.

While he had never previously visited Edie Knapp's beerhouse, Tom had been in a hundred others like it. He registered that his companion had with deceptive casualness leaned his back against the wall in the corner of the room, where he could watch the door to the front bar and no one could get behind him. As if listening to the conversation between the old man and Brindley, Tom slipped closer to Langley at an angle that allowed him to cover the only other door leading into the back kitchen, where two girls aged about twelve were washing glasses in a stone sink. He noticed that their feet on the greasy stone floor were bare and dirty. Looking further, through the open kitchen door, Tom watched a grey-bearded man in a navvy's cap buttoning his trousers as he left the nauseating privy next to the coalhouse.

After a few minutes occupying himself by half-listening to the desultory conversation between Langley and the Scotsman over the pros and cons of a promising racehorse called Cromford Glory, and trying to decide which of the house's unsavoury denizens was Edie Knapp's minder, Tom turned his attentions to the rest of the room. Apart from the doxy with Brindley, there were two others among Edie's customers. One was a stout blowsy female with a raddled face, wearing a large black hat with a crushed crown that had seen better days and more than one owner, who was engaged in quiet conversation with an individual in a reefer jacket whose back was to the detectives. The third, he realised, mildly annoyed with himself, had slipped away unnoticed while his attention was elsewhere.

Tom's interest returned to the conversation taking place beside him, which had turned to a different subject. 'I don't get down here much these days. How are things at the yard?' Langley took a long pull at his beer, almost draining the glass.

'Fine, thank you, Mr Langley. Are you busy yourself?'

Before Langley could reply, the woman on Brindley's knee, who was obviously deeply drunk, pushed herself upright and glared owlishly at her companion. 'I'm a busy woman.' Now he could see her face, Tom saw she was older than he had originally judged – probably about forty. Her narrow coarsely veined cheeks made her particularly unattractive. 'Do you want business or not?'

'Hello, Queenie. I've not seen you for a while.' Langley's deep growl had been replaced by a soft razor-edged murmur.

Victoria Bartholemew registered a mixture of confusion and fear as, in her befuddled state, she understood her error. 'Jesus, Mr Langley, I didn't know it was you. Sorry, sir!' Somewhere in the background Tom could discern the remnant of an Irish accent, almost lost after years spent in English stews and brothels. With some difficulty the woman pulled together her disarranged skirts and, sliding from the Scotsman's knee, made her way unsteadily towards the back door, mumbling to no one in particular that she needed to get off home.

Unbidden, a twinge of sympathy for the woman flashed through Tom's mind. Not for the first time, he wondered what might have been his sister's fate had she and Jamie not been able to come and live with him.

Ignoring the interruption, the inspector continued his line of conversation. 'This new wharf that the Shires are building. Will it affect you much?'

Half-listening to the reply, Tom's gaze wandered back round the room. For a fleeting second his eyes locked with those of a pale-faced man whom he had not noticed previously. He was a short, thin man, whose lopsided mouth and drooping bloodshot eye clearly bespoke a stroke at some time in the past. His unhealthy pallor told even more clearly of a recent release from prison. The features quickly filed away, Tom released the man's gaze and continued his sweep of the room.

Understanding where Langley was steering the conversation, the thickset Glaswegian rubbed a horny hand across his stubbled jaw. 'I dinna think so, Mr Langley. These Irishmen,' he stole a quick glance at the other customers, 'these Irishmen are no' interested in the goods yard. We use our own labour.

They dinna bother us.' Some of the tension visibly left the room; the detectives' unwelcome visit was simply a fishing expedition.

Tom drained his glass and made his way through the kitchen into the squalid back yard. An area thirty feet long by twelve wide, it was littered with boxes and empty bottles, overspill from the dismal scene inside. Avoiding the fetid privy, Tom took his place next to a tall dark man in working clothes at the kitchen drain. Unbuttoning his fly, he urinated against the wall and into the drain hole, which was only marginally less noxious than the adjacent lavatory. Neither man spoke, and by the time the policeman had finished his tall companion had disappeared into the parlour again.

When Tom returned, Langley, his discussion with Brindley concluded, signalled to him that they were leaving. Tom noticed with approval that Langley had not removed his high black silk hat, despite the room's low ceiling, and that he maintained a firm grip on his heavy, silver-headed cane. In places such as this only a fool failed to be cautious.

The remainder of the afternoon and evening was for Tom a blurred kaleidoscope of beerhouses and drinking dens, each one a replica of, and less memorable than, the last. Langley spent the time engaged in discourse with an endless succession of men whose faces, as the afternoon wore on into evening, became less clear to his companion. Tom was forced to admit that Joe Langley was quite good company when he was on a spree. As time passed, and the weight of ale that he was sinking began to take hold, the old man brought forth a host of tales from his eventful past, so that Tom had an interesting – almost enjoyable – time. A dark door was pushed very slightly open, revealing intriguing insights into Langley as a younger man. Listening to the anecdotes, interspersed with information concerning those they were meeting, Tom's respect for the inspector's knowledge strengthened.

It was Langley's capacity for drink that was causing Tom some difficulty by early evening. Although not a heavy drinker himself, he had, as a stock in trade, developed the ability to hold his liquor. A few pints consumed while touring his area or the inevitable sessions with other policemen on promotions and retirements were one thing, but a night out with Langley was another. Despite his formidable reputation, by nine o'clock even the detective inspector was becoming unsteady and decided to call a halt. At a quarter past nine a decidedly worse-for-wear Detective Sergeant Norton, his grey bowler hat perched precariously on the back of his head, jacket and waistcoat unbuttoned, bade farewell to the old man outside the Lamb and Pheasant to make his way unsteadily home.

While Tom snored away the effects of his day, the tall, dark-haired man with whom he had shared Edie Knapp's kitchen wall was busy. When the two detectives had walked through the parlour door of Edie's back room Connor Devlin had been momentarily disturbed. He had only been back in Kelsford a matter of hours, and his hand luggage lay on the single bed of the tiny upstairs room that Edie was renting him until he found a permanent lodging. In the first few seconds after the men had appeared in the doorway Connor raced through the possible reasons for their presence.

Only Liam O'Dowd and the man with whom Connor was conversing softly knew of his return to the town. That Crooked Edie assumed he was involved in some criminal venture was reflected in the inflated price that he was paying for the squalid attic r oom, but his return and identity were, he reasoned, unlikely to be known to the police – although he could have been seen on the night of the robbery and by some misfortune traced to the beerhouse. Swiftly examining the possibility, the Irishman dismissed it: if it were so, these two would be accompanied by uniformed officers. As he watched the pint pots being handed to the men he visibly relaxed. This was an unofficial visit. Half-watching the policemen unbuttoning their heavy overcoats in the warmth of the room, Connor almost imperceptibly shook his head at his companion.

Shifting his position slightly, Connor turned his face away from the policemen and resumed his conversation. His companion, Clancy Taft, a builder and carter by trade, was reliable, a member of the Brotherhood; they had worked together in Manchester. He was employed as a contractor by the Shires Canal Company on the Flixton canal cut, and his job, running one of the gangs that built the deep locks and laid stone edges on the towpath, made an ideal cover for Brotherhood activities. Among the labour force there were fifteen hard-core members of the organisation, a sufficient number, it had been decided, to be operationally useful while not attracting attention. Without declaring themselves, they quietly identified and cultivated those in their gangs who might at a future time be worth approaching. Clancy was the only one who would ever know of Connor's identity, thus reducing the inevitable risks if anyone came to the attention of the police.

In answer to the question in Taft's eyes, Connor took a sip of his ale and murmured softly, 'We stay. They're interested in who's leaving.'

Taft nodded in agreement. 'I'll fix you a room at Susan Burke's,' he muttered. 'It's on the edge of the rookeries. The fewer people who know you're here the better, and you can slip in and out easily.'

Connor pondered for a moment. It was a sensible idea. The Downe Street area, with its square mile of common lodging houses, known as the rookeries, was a tightly knit immigrant community. For the last two generations poor Irish families and itinerant workers along with a smattering of east European refugees had crowded into the district. Two or three families shared a tiny four-room terraced house, sleeping in shifts and often simply renting bed space. The houses, eight or ten crammed into tiny courts, were difficult to approach without being noticed, while being relatively easy to escape from if necessary. On the other hand it was a notoriously unhealthy part of the town. Filthy privies, usually one between three houses, leaked sewage into the soft earthen yards and thence into the communal wells. Typhoid epidemics were an annual occurrence, and cholera was not unknown.

Although corporation wagons, driven by the 'dilly men', were supposed to cart away night soil, Downe Street seldom saw them: the sheer density of inhabitants prevented any such system working; and the occasional dilly cart during the hours of darkness was more likely to be bringing in the proceeds of some nefarious activity than taking out human waste. Yes, a lodging in Downe Street would suit him nicely.

Connor allowed his attention to wander back to the two policemen while he considered Taft's suggestion. If they knew their business one of them, probably the younger, would be going out to check the yard soon. Finishing his beer, Connor placed his glass among the others on the crowded chimney breast. 'Fix it. I'll stay here tonight,' he murmured, then turned to slip out into the yard.

As he expected the detective came out into the area a few moments later. Having taken a cursory glance round, he joined Connor to relieve himself against the wall. Finishing first, the Irishman turned away to leave before the policeman got a proper look at him, but not before he had ensured that he would know the detective again. A quick glance was sufficient: tall, light brown moustache brushed up at the ends, carefully trimmed side whiskers, pale blue eyes. Connor Devlin would recognise him, even without the smart grey bowler hat and slim cigar clenched between his teeth.

Watching other people inconspicuously was a skill that Saul Meakin had acquired as a young child. Brought up in the back streets of Sheffield, with little schooling, he had learned in his formative years to steal and to observe. That he had developed the latter skill to a higher level than the former was proved by the amount of time he had spent in prison over the years; his natural bent as a watcher, and consequently as an informer, was second to none. Meakin's slightness of build and furtive demeanour had resulted in his being dubbed the Weasel at an early age; so long ago was it that few people knew him by any other name.

Weasel Meakin had been carefully following the conversation between two Irishmen when the arrival of the detectives had interrupted his concentration. That something was being planned by Clancy Taft, whom he knew by sight, and the dark-featured stranger was apparent. Good information was a commodity that needed to be handled carefully if it were to realise its full potential. Whom to impart it to, and how, was critical.

Before his recent release from gaol Weasel had made the fatal error of informing a trusted warder about the activities of a group of prisoners involved in a tobacco smuggling venture. Unfortunately, when those concerned had been disciplined by the prison governor, Meakin's name had leaked out. Kept thereafter in a secure area of the prison until his release, the little man was lucky to have escaped with his life. Suffering a minor stroke during this period, he had been given an early release on the governor's recommendation. It was in fact a mutual benefit: for Meakin it meant that his return to society came slightly earlier than he had hoped, while the prison service no longer had to go to extraordinary lengths to protect him while in custody. On regaining his freedom, the one thing that Meakin dared not do was return to his old haunts in Sheffield. News of his activities in prison had been swiftly leaked to associates of those who were now suffering the consequences of his treachery, and promises had been made that the matter would be dealt with.

At half past six on a rainy morning, just over a month ago, a side gate of Leicester Prison had been opened and Meakin had slipped unobtrusively out into the dimly lit street. Twenty minutes later, having asked the uniformed booking clerk at the nearby Midland railway station about the destination of the next train, he was on his way north – to a new beginning in Kelsford.

That the two men were police was patently obvious to him, and after a fleeting glance in their direction Meakin turned his attention back to the conversation he had been listening to. Finding that the Irishmen were no longer discussing their plans, he carefully scrutinised Langley and Norton again. The older man was obviously senior, and of a breed that Weasel had long ago learned to distrust. The younger was more interesting. He did not appear to be relishing the poor-quality ale, and was giving his attention to the occupants of the room. Meakin took a pull at his beer and, waiting for the detective's gaze to settle upon him, allowed their eyes to meet for a second – just long enough for the contact to register – before averting his gaze.

At another time, in another place, the detective would remember him.

Chapter Seven

Tom Norton awoke the following morning to a world bathed in winter sunshine and the worst headache that he could remember. He cursed Langley and every tavern keeper in Kelsford as he swilled cool water over his face from the jug on the night stand. Ann was less than sympathetic when her collarless and bleary-eyed brother presented himself in her kitchen. Without speaking she indicated the kettle bubbling on the parlour hob, the water ready for him to shave with; her stiff back and silence as she continued to prepare Jamie's breakfast indicated her annoyance. About to speak, Tom changed his mind, overcome by a wave of nausea as he caught a whiff of the bacon frying on the stove. Forcing his mind to concentrate, he took his open razor from its case on the shelf and began to lather his stubbled jaw. Relenting slightly, Ann placed a mug of tea beside him and asked him how he felt. Tom made a face.

The time spent together since their bereavements had brought them much closer than either had expected. Ann had grown to understand much about the peculiar lifestyle that her brother's work imposed upon him: the irregular hours, meals prepared and uneaten; occasionally she did not see him for days at a time. She was irked this morning because, having been at work all day, she had first prepared a meal for herself and Jamie, when he returned home from school, and then cooked again for her brother. That he had stumbled through the door much later, mumbling drunken apologies, and gone straight to bed, where his befuddled snoring kept her awake until the early hours, had not improved her mood.

Tom deeply appreciated his sister's presence in the house since Kate's death. They had much in common. Growing up together in their parents' pub, they had been close companions: Tom, the older brother, hefting barrels and crates into the cellars of the Rifleman and working as an ostler; Ann, slightly built and wiry, standing at the kitchen table helping her mother prepare food for the customers.

When Tom left to join the army his sister was a child of nine. On his return she was an eighteen-year-old woman, already courting her future husband John. After Jamie was born Kate had become very close to Ann, the two women often being mistaken for sisters out shopping together, taking turns to push the baby in its perambulator. Thus it was that, having both lost their partners, it seemed only natural for the brother and sister to come together, sharing their loss and rebuilding their lives.

Sipping gratefully at the sweet tea, Tom paused in his ablutions to peer through the door into the parlour. Little Jamie was becoming very much like his father to look at. Not overly tall, he had John's rounded features and hazel eyes. The boy was going to need a father sooner or later – of this Tom was acutely aware. He wondered if Ann had come to the same conclusion. Reuben Simmonds had been dropping in to see Ann when his duties permitted, although, as far as Tom was aware, they had not walked out as a couple yet. Significantly, the tall, moustachioed constable had been avoiding Tom at work. He resolved that, when an opportunity presented itself, he would speak to Reuben and clear up any misunderstanding.

'How are things at school, son?' Tom needed to break the atmosphere.

'All right, thank you, Uncle Tom. Will we be going to the baths on Saturday?' The boy's voice was eager. On a Saturday, if Tom was free, he took the boy to the newly opened public swimming baths in Vicary Lane.

'I don't know, Jamie, probably not this weekend. I think I'll be working.' There was no point lying. Tom knew beyond any doubt that he would be fully occupied until the Donnelly killing had been resolved.

'Was last night part of this enquiry?' Ann Turner was not a malicious woman. Annoyed as she was with her brother, she knew that drunkenness was not part of his character and there would be a good reason for his condition.

'I'm sorry, sis, truly I am. Things are at a standstill and Langley decided that he and I should go out and visit some drinking dens. I couldn't refuse, and you know what he's like.'

Yes, thought Ann, she and everyone in Kelsford knew what Joseph Langley was like. A drunken brute of a man who should have been removed from office years ago. The fact that her brother respected the man's professional abilities did not change her opinion. Tom did not seem to have considered the matter, but when Langley eventually retired her brother was the most likely person to succeed him.

'It's probably best if I work from day to day for the time being.' Ann started to think ahead. If Tom was going to be working unpredictable hours, she would leave cold food out so he could eat as and when he managed to get home for a change of clothes and a shave. If her brother ever remarried, she thought ruefully, it would have to be to a very understanding woman.

'Thanks, love.' Tom was beginning to feel a little better. Putting his hands on his sister's shoulders, he kissed her gently on the cheek. 'Thanks. When this is finished we'll do something. Perhaps if I can get a couple of days' leave we'll take Jamie somewhere nice for Christmas.'

'Yes, that would be nice.' Ann's ill humour had dispersed. Looking at the heavy clock on the mantel shelf, she turned her attention to more pressing matters. 'Come along, James. Uncle Thomas has got to go to work and you'll be late for school.' Grinning impishly at her brother, she said, 'Kiss Mr Langley for me.'

At half past eight in the morning the Station House was a hive of activity. In common with Langley, Tom's first stop was usually the charge room. The duty sergeant, Bartlett Horspool, was busy supervising the morning's prisoners and escorts, who were getting ready to go across to the police court in the nearby Town Hall.

Bartie Horspool, the longest-serving uniformed officer on the force, was, at sixty-two years of age, overdue for retirement. A short, thickset man with a grizzled white beard that failed to conceal the absence of any front teeth, Horspool worked permanently as the day duty office sergeant. More years ago than he cared to remember, in a fracas in the Downe Street area between a crowd of Irish immigrants and some out-of-work local men, he had lost his teeth to a blow in the face from a baulk of timber, which for good measure had also badly broken his nose. Five years ago, while leading a posse of constables against a mob of ungrateful paupers at the workhouse, he had suffered a hernia after being severely kicked. As a result of Sergeant Horspool's injuries, Dr Mallard's predecessor had recommended that he be excused nights and given a job in the Station House. The result was that he was now working at a reduced salary, and desperately attempting to avoid being 'superannuated' at twenty shillings a week. Never an amiable man, Sergeant Horspool was in a particularly sour humour. There were five prisoners to go across to the court, but he only had two escorts – and the file of evidence for one of the prisoners had not yet been delivered to him.

Tom's presence was greeted with a sour glare, as Horspool lifted his balding pate from the charge book that he was studying and turned to survey the group of prisoners lined up before his desk. Three men and two women were being handcuffed together by a young constable in readiness for court. One of the men gave a sharp curse as the young officer shackling him caught his wrist in the lock of the handcuff as he snapped it shut. The expletive drew Tom's eye to the line. One of the women, stout and in her fifties, was familiar to him – Elspeth Richards, a petty thief who specialised in preying upon young servant girls. She would approach an unsuspecting parlourmaid out shopping and, pretending to be a destitute widow, sell the girl her wedding ring for a few shillings. The ring, which was made of brass and worthless, would be replaced around the corner by another secreted in her bodice.

'Still working the widow's lurk, Elspeth?'

The woman raised her head and glared out at him from beneath her crumpled black bonnet, tied under the folds of her voluminous chin with a dirty old ribbon of the same colour. Whatever was in her mind she knew better than to antagonise the detective.

'A woman's got to earn a living, Mr Norton.' The voice was tired and conciliatory – the tone in which she would tell her story to the magistrates, thought Tom. From the papers on the charge desk, he saw that it was her file of evidence that was missing, and that Sam Braithwaite was the officer dealing with her.

'I'll get Sergeant Braithwaite to take the file across to court for you, Bart,' Tom said. The charge sergeant grunted in acknowledgement, engrossed in checking a prisoner's meagre possessions which he was handing to one of the escorts.

As he turned to leave, Tom's attention was caught by a woman being led from the cell corridor to join the end of the line. Looking back at the charge ledger, he saw she was booked in as Mary McCarthy, 22 Elder Street, unlawfully drunk in Mercer Lane, and the arresting officer was PC 114 Chote. Little wonder that he was careless with the handcuffs, Tom thought, looking at the number on the collar of the young policeman who was staring out of the door at the waiting prison wagon. Young Chote had been on duty all night and, having arrested a drunken woman causing a nuisance, he was now going to spend his morning at the police court, waiting to give his evidence.

Tom touched Chote on the arm and, checking that they were out of earshot of the charge sergeant, moved with him to the end of the line. The woman, still half-drunk, appeared to be unaware of his presence until he spoke to her. 'Hello, Queenie. I've not seen you for a while' – the words that Langley had used the previous afternoon. Dark, shifty eyes turned slowly towards him, glowering malevolently. About to say something, Queenie Bartholemew bit back the words and turned her gaze towards the floor. Tom doubted if she cared that her ruse had failed. Now, rather than a fine of two and sixpence, she would probably get seven days' hard labour – an occupational hazard as far as she was concerned.

Daniel Chote was dismayed. This was his first session of night duty on his own since he joined the force a month ago: a big, strong lad of twenty, he had decided that there were better ways to earn a living than as a railway porter at the Midland station. He had found the woman with a client in an alleyway off Mercer Lane just after two o'clock. It had been his intention, having got rid of the man, to send the prostitute packing, but she had proved troublesome, and when she had kicked his shin the constable decided to arrest her. The consequences of allowing her to be charged in a false name were, he surmised, dire. Stealing a glance at the surly Sergeant Horspool, he turned back to the detective.

Silently, Tom took the charge sheet from Chote's hand and with a stub of pencil from his pocket, drew a line through the woman's name. Carefully, his back to Bart Horspool, he wrote, VICTORIA BARTHOLEMEW (ALSO KNOWN AS QUEENIE) – NO FIXED ADDRESS – PROSTITUTE.

KNOWN TO DETECTIVE SERGEANT 8. NORTON. 'Give this to the court officer, have her name amended, and say nothing to Sergeant Horspool,' he said quietly.

Constable Chote nodded, and glared angrily at the woman who had fallen again into her semi-drunken stupor. Looking round to thank the detective, he was just in time to see the tall figure disappearing through the outer door into the passageway.

Sorting through the litter of papers on his desk, Tom decided that nothing required his attention so urgently as a walk in the fresh air to clear his aching head. He had been in the office about ten minutes when Jesse Squires arrived, accompanied by Harry North. As Tom had correctly surmised, once the immediate flurry of activity had subsided the head constable had withdrawn two of his uniformed officers from the Shires investigation, leaving only Harry to assist the detectives. The young man was still setting out to impress, Tom noted. To his dark trousers and stylishly cut jacket had been added a sea green silk cravat, held in place by an ornate silver stickpin. Tom grinned to himself. Henry Farmer had better watch out: his reputation for sartorial elegance was soon to be in for a challenge.

'I'm going down to have another word with Ike Harriman,' Tom said to Jesse. 'Do you want to come with me?'

Squires looked tired. He had been in the office until late the previous night, examining Saunt's photographs of the scene at Bridge Sixty-Four. Once alone at the murder scene with the photographer and his young assistant, Jesse had set to work to record as much as possible. As far as Langley was concerned, the photographer's job was to take pictures of the corpse for identification purposes. Jesse viewed the matter differently. Over the next hour, under the detective's supervision, Saunt had recorded the entire scene in detail. Squires knew that when Langley saw how many pictures had been taken – and the bill for them – there would be trouble, but he would worry about that later.

Pausing in the act of unbuttoning his overcoat Jesse looked across at Tom. 'Do we have something new?' he asked.

'No, but Ike doesn't know that. He has a good idea that we don't believe his story and I want to keep some pressure on him. An early visit will keep him off-balance.'

Jesse buttoned his coat back up. 'All right. Harry, you come with us. If we go now we'll beat "himself" – he's late this morning and I can do without seeing him. Fred has Saunt's bill on his desk.'

The fresh air and bright sunshine began to revive Tom's spirits. Wednesday was market day in Kelsford and the streets were already busy with an influx of people from the surrounding countryside. Dogcarts pulled by freshly groomed ponies clattered along the streets, making crossing the road perilous. Despite a recent by-law prohibiting the driving of cattle through the town centre, the trio deemed it prudent to stand aside in the doorway of Fielders and Curtis' grocery store while an obstinate farmer led a young bull, tethered through its nose ring to a three foot long staff, past them.

Arriving in Cooper's Court, Tom was still not sure what his approach with Harriman was going to be. Identified by Harriman's mark on its saddle, one of the 'stolen' horses had been recovered on Sunday morning, tethered in the yard of a hotel in Sheffield. That would do for a start.

The entrance to the stable yard was unlocked, as the hackmaster had not yet replaced the sawn-off hasp. Closing the gate behind them, the detectives stood in the middle of the yard taking stock of their surroundings. Away from the bustle and clatter of the town streets, in the quiet atmosphere redolent with the tang of horses and saddlery, Tom felt his head beginning to clear. That they were alone was apparent. Other than the stamping of a horse's hoof somewhere in the stable block, the yard was silent.

Harry North was the first to speak. 'It looks as if our man is away to market, Sergeant.' His voice was pitched low, as if, should his assumption be wrong, he would not be overheard. Tom did not answer immediately. This was an opportunity not to be missed. Harriman's wife, he recollected, kept a food stall in the market place on a Wednesday. She and the servant girl would have been out since early morning selling pies and pastries to hungry farmers. If Ike was also out then a search of the premises might prove most profitable. Jesse had already moved quietly across the yard and was trying the back door of the house. Turning to the others he shook his head, indicating that it was securely locked.

Tom spoke quietly to Harry. 'Stay here. If anyone comes in keep them talking.' North nodded and took up a position near the gate where he could spot anyone approaching without being seen himself.

By the time Tom joined him, Jesse had found an insecure kitchen window and was working on the catch with a heavy lock knife. In less than a minute the sash was unfastened and the window raised. Climbing through head first, Tom scrambled over the sink and dropped awkwardly onto the flagstoned floor. Opening the door with the key that was in the lock, he admitted Jesse into the kitchen. Both stood perfectly still for a moment, listening for any sounds of movement. Satisfied that they were alone, Tom secured the window and the two men moved into the main sitting room.

The house was large and laid out in the style of a farmhouse. The kitchen was spacious: a deep fireplace accommodated a heavy black cooking range, which was freshly cleaned and blacked. Doubtless the servant girl had been up since dawn, cleaning and polishing before her day out at the market with her mistress. Two large airy rooms led off from a passageway to the front door. The first was a living room, with a comfortable armchair either side of the oak-beamed fireplace. A heavy dining table covered with a dark green velour cloth occupied the rear of the parlour. The distinct chill in the house confirmed that the occupants were out for the day; no early morning fire had been laid against the morning cold.

Jesse moved into the front room to begin his search while Tom ascended the wide staircase. A quick look round the bedrooms on the first floor revealed little of any interest, and he moved quickly to the top floor of the building. At the head of the stairs a narrow landing led to the left to the parlourmaid's room, which he ignored, turning his attention to the rooms at the other end of the landing. Two were filled with junk: old papers and ancient horse tack that the parsimonious hackmaster refused to throw away. The third was what Tom was looking for: Harriman's office.

To his surprise, the lid of the roll-top desk under the window was unlocked. The slatted lid made a slight clicking sound as it slid back, and a heap of invoices and bills spilled untidily onto the floor, revealing a worn green leather writing surface let into the desktop. Scooping the papers from the floor, Tom placed them on the swivel chair in front of the desk, and began a careful examination of the four small recessed drawers running along the top above the writing pad. They contained nothing of any interest: a gold watch-chain, three gold sovereigns, two sets of collar studs, a rosette for second prize at a horse show and a bottle of blue ink. Five minutes spent sifting through the papers on the chair proved no more profitable. It was apparent that whatever his skills as a horseman, Ike Harriman was not an enthusiastic bookkeeper. From the look of things, his accounting method consisted of piling all his bills and receipts in a heap in the drawer and sorting them out when necessary. Among the stack of bills for horse-feed, wagon hire and veterinary fees was a recent cutting from the *Kelsford Gazette*, referring to last Friday's robbery. Not unexpectedly, underlined in pencil was the section that referred to the perpetrators having escaped on stolen horses from Harriman's stables.

Tom stood back and surveyed the rest of the room. A tall cupboard let into the back wall held a sleeveless leather jerkin hanging on a peg and a large bundle of documents tied with brown string. A paper label declared them to date from 1880. Propped against the back wall of the cupboard was a heavy gauge shotgun. To his surprise, when Tom broke the weapon open he found it to be loaded. He frowned. Harriman might be a dilatory businessman, but he was a countryman, and countrymen did not leave loaded shotguns lying around. Out of habit he threw the weapon up to the light and peered along the barrels: sunlight glinted along the brightly oiled metal. He closed the gun, and replaced it exactly as he had found it before stepping back onto the landing. There was nothing in the office to incriminate Harriman. The loaded shotgun could be a precaution against burglars, but Tom doubted it. Isaac Harriman appeared to be worried about something more than being investigated by the police.

Once more in the parlour, Tom and Jesse stood in the middle of the room taking a final look round. Jesse had found nothing in the downstairs rooms, and it was time to leave before their presence was discovered. A picture over the oak mantelpiece caught Tom's attention, an old watercolour in a plain walnut frame. The scene was a tiny cottage kitchen. In the centre was a plain table, and an upturned jug of milk was overflowing across the kitchen floor. Four tiny piglets lapping the milk filled the foreground, while in the background an old lady in white apron and bonnet was entering through the cottage door. Tom smiled. How many children, he wondered, had gazed at the scene and speculated on what the old lady would do to the miscreants when she found what had happened in her kitchen?

An urgent tug on his sleeve interrupted his reverie, and glancing round quickly he saw what it was that had caught his colleague's eye. Harry North, his face pressed against the kitchen window, was gesturing to them. Jesse had the door into the yard open by the time Tom joined them.

Harry's face was pale in the cool air. 'You'd better come and have a look at this.' His breathing was heavy and his voice husky.

The two sergeants followed him across the yard. Entering the fodder store at the top of the exercise yard, they stood for a moment to allow their eyes to adjust to the gloomy surroundings. The store was a small barn about twenty feet deep and fifteen wide, its dim interior containing several wagonloads of hay, neatly baled and stacked round the walls as feed for the winter months. The centre of the floor was kept clear so that a hay wagon could be drawn up and unloaded with the heavy hoist that was fixed to a beam running the width of the barn. Hanging from the hoist, his boots about three feet from the earthen floor, was the body of Isaac Harriman.

Badly shaken by his discovery, Harry explained that while guarding the gate he had noticed the insecure barn door. Having previously visited the stables, Harry knew that, in the absence of the owner, the fodder store should be locked. His curiosity aroused, he had left his post to make a quick search. Tom could well imagine the young man's fright when he walked into the gently swinging corpse in the poorly lit store.

Questions raced through Tom's mind as he took in the situation. It was not possible for this to be an accident. Harriman knew that the police were deeply suspicious of him: had the pressure of his situation been sufficient to cause him to take his own life? The alternative was that someone had wanted him dead, for some reason. The detective's mind slipped back to the loaded shotgun in the cupboard.

Harry, who by now had recovered his equilibrium, was sent off to Long Street to inform Langley of the latest development. Meanwhile, Jesse went into the adjacent street, grabbed a passing errand boy, relieved him of his basket of groceries and, on the promise of a sixpence, sent him to find Dr Mallard at his surgery.

Alone for a short while, Jesse and Tom began a methodical search of the fodder store. Tom was annoyed that they had not discovered the body on their arrival. The three of them had trampled back and forth round the yard and house, destroying any traces that might have been left by a possible intruder. After twenty minutes of futile poking about they conceded that there was nothing of any relevance immediately apparent. Brushing dust and straw from their clothing, they returned to the yard to await the arrival of the doctor.

Tom checked the time on his silver pocket watch: three minutes to ten. Taking out his slim cigar case, he offered a Goodman's panatella to Jesse. As he carefully replaced his light-coloured bowler, from which he had been picking wisps of straw, Jesse gratefully accepted the smoke. They were in the process of sharing a match when Harry returned, accompanied by Arthur Hollowday.

'I couldn't find Mr Langley.' North was flushed with his exertions. 'Inspector Judd says that he'll find him and get him to join us. Meanwhile he's sent the lad to run errands and take messages.'

Not for the first time Tom silently gave thanks for the efficiency of Fred Judd. He had no doubt that Fred would find Langley, and sending the boy meant that Tom could use North for other things.

At ten minutes past ten Dr Mallard arrived, closely followed by two uniformed constables who had also been dispatched by Inspector Judd. Tom was vaguely puzzled that Langley had not arrived, but put the thought to the back of his mind while he dealt with more pressing matters. He instructed the two constables to remain inside the yard, close to the gate. Anyone arriving and wanting to gain entry was to have his name taken, and be held until one of the detectives had spoken to him.

Inside the barn, Harry explained to Dr Mallard the circumstances of his discovery. Mallard, taking a stepladder from where it was propped against the wall, climbed up to examine the body. He was still engaged in this when Alfred Saunt and his apprentice bustled into the yard. Tom shot an enquiring glance at Jesse. 'It's all right,' he responded. 'I sent the boy for him – we'll need some photographs.' He did not add 'before Langley arrives and stops him'.

Tom nodded in agreement. It was not Saunt's presence that bothered him but the manner of his arrival. People would have seen the police activity in Cooper's Court, and he didn't want to have a crowd of spectators outside.

With meticulous detachment, the photographer spent a quarter of an hour photographing the body and the interior of the fodder store. Far from displaying the irritation with the delay that many of his peers would have exhibited, Arthur Mallard was totally absorbed in the processes taking place around him. He – correctly – considered himself to be a good doctor, and was also aware that his expertise could only be broadened by experience. Many of his contemporaries considered the role of police surgeon to be a lucrative sinecure, but in Mallard's opinion he could learn as much from spending time at a crime scene as he could from watching a surgeon perform a complicated piece of surgery. If he was to give evidence at an inquest or trial then it was crucial that he be fully conversant with the events taking place before him.

Alfred Saunt, his work finally done, began to pack away his equipment and loaded up his young assistant with tripod, camera and cloth covers, before leaving to process the photographic plates clutched tightly under his arm. Tom turned towards the open barn door and caught sight of Arthur Hollowday's spiky head peering in. 'Get out of here, boy – this is no place for you!'

Taken aback by the sharpness of the detective's voice, a startled Arthur jumped away from the doorway. Peering cautiously round the door jamb he squeaked apologetically, 'Sorry, sir, sorry, I was just having a look, sir.'

'Go down to Mr Poleworth's funeral parlour and ask him to come up here. Tell him to bring his handcart and speak to me or Sergeant Squires.' The body had to be taken to the police mortuary for examination as soon as possible. 'After that go to Mr Saunt's and wait for the photographs to be developed. Take them to Long Street and hand them to Inspector Judd.' The boy scuttled off, and disappeared through the yard gates towards the town.

The officers carefully released the pulley rope from the retaining cleat on the wall around which it was fastened, and lowered the body to the ground to await the arrival of the undertaker. On Dr Mallard's instructions the hoist rope was cut through some twelve inches above the knot, leaving the rope to be removed from Harriman's neck at the post-mortem.

Tom had just dispatched one of the uniform men to find Mrs Harriman and bring her back to the house when the burly figure of Superintendent Archer Robson appeared in the gateway. Over the next few minutes Tom outlined to the head constable the events of the morning, studiously avoiding any reference to the unauthorised search of the house earlier. 'Unfortunately, Inspector Langley has not arrived yet, sir.'

'Inspector Langley is not at work today. He is indisposed.' Tom noted the flat and dispassionate tone in which the information was delivered, and ventured no query about the nature of Langley's indisposition.

The head constable could guess all too easily what was wrong with Langley: he did not doubt that, after a night's carousing, the detective inspector was suffering from a monumental hangover. If it were not for Langley's connections with members of the corporation, and consequently the watch committee, Archer Robson would have got rid of him long ago – with a quick vote of thanks and a gold watch. Unfortunately Langley's cronies in high office made him virtually unassailable, and until a compulsory retiring age was brought in Archer Robson was stuck with him.

Having been informed by Inspector Judd of the death in Cooper's Court, Archer Robson decided that the incident presented him with a valid reason to escape from his morning duties as prosecuting officer in the police court. Handing the stack of court files to Judd, he set off for Cooper's Court. An added incentive to take the air was the beginning of a nagging toothache. A back molar on the left side of his lower jaw had for the last week been exhibiting signs of tenderness, and this morning he was plagued with a dull ache. A brisk walk might postpone the inevitable visit to the dentist.

Having listened carefully to what the sergeant told him, Archer Robson appeared satisfied. Pensively stroking his heavy black walrus moustache, he asked, 'Do you think it's suicide, Sergeant?' His soft Edinburgh accent was inaudible to anyone standing more than a yard away.

'I think it would be wrong to make that assumption, sir. For him to have killed himself he would have needed something to stand on, and there's nothing. I think it far more likely that he's been murdered.'

Archer Robson was about to take his leave when the sound of raised voices at the yard gate caught their attention. Charles Kerrigan Kemp was arguing with the policeman blocking his path. Kerrigan Kemp, accustomed to being given early access to scenes such as this, was not about to be turned away by a uniformed constable.

'I do not wish to speak to Sergeant Norton, nor will I wait outside like a common sightseer. I am the editor of the *Kelsford Gazette*. Find Inspector Langley and tell him that I am here!' The voice carried harshly across the quiet yard.

A slow, almost self-satisfied smile spread across Archer Robson's round face. His heavy eyebrows lifted quizzically as his eyes met Tom's. 'You carry on, Mr Norton. You have enough to do. I shall speak with the editor of the *Kelsford Gazette*. He is, I feel, in for a disappointing morning.'

Watching the superintendent as he stumped off across the yard, Tom realised that he was seeing a side of the man of which he had not been previously aware. He warmed considerably towards the Scotsman as he watched him, apparently effortlessly, turn Kerrigan Kemp around and walk with him out into the street, while the constable secured the heavy gate behind them.

'It's definitely not suicide.' Arthur Mallard's quiet tones hung pregnantly in the heavy atmosphere of the detective office. The day's sunshine had been replaced by a late afternoon chill. With Langley absent, Tom had convened a meeting of his colleagues to hear the doctor's report first hand.

For Mallard it had been a busy day. The morning spent at Cooper's Court had delayed his rounds, which in turn had meant that he could not perform the autopsy until after lunch. It was after two o'clock when he had handed the reins of his pony and trap to the small boy with spiky red hair in the police station yard and made his way into the mortuary. He had made a mental note to speak to someone concerning the mortuary facilities: the tiny, airless room, with a transom window set high in the wall that let little light and no air in, barely had space for him to move round the table. This was the first time he had needed to use the room, and he was appalled at the total absence of cleaning or washing facilities. A pitcher of cold water, which had been left for his use by some unknown station cleaner, stood by a stone sink that drained into the soakaway in the station yard. What bothered him most was the lack of any post-mortem instruments. To perform the autopsy he had to use the surgical instruments from his medical bag, which would now have to be boiled clean before being used on any of his patients. He had no doubt that the police force was going to have to dig deep into its pocket very soon if he was to perform further post-mortems.

Returning to the matter in hand, Mallard continued to address the small group of policemen. 'The rope from which the body was suspended didn't kill him. Once the rope was removed there were marks underneath of a much finer ligature that was used to strangle the victim. From the marks I would say he was attacked from behind, then put onto the hoist in an attempt to make it look like suicide.'

'How long would you say that he had been dead?' asked Henry Farmer.

'Not long. I would think no more than an hour, as rigor mortis hadn't started to set in. He wasn't put onto the hoist straight away. I think he'd been dead about half an hour before that happened.'

Sam Braithwaite broke the silence. 'What makes you think that?'

'The body had lain on its left side for some time. After death, once the heart stops beating, blood drains to the lowest point. In this case it had drained down and coagulated on the left side of the body – the area becomes dark and suffused; it's quite unmistakable. Had he been hung up immediately I'd have expected the blood to gather in the legs. I suggest your man was strangled, then allowed to lie on the ground for up to half an hour before being moved.'

While the five policemen assimilated this information, Mallard took the opportunity to glance round. This was the first time he had been in the detective department's main office. Until now his visits had been confined to visiting drunken or injured prisoners, and to taking the morning sick parade in the muster room at eleven o'clock as part of his rounds, when he examined any officer who wished to report sick. This, he mused, was something else that needed to change: there was absolutely no reason why those men could not visit his surgery in Gadsfield Terrace.

The doctor was not sure what he had expected to find in the office. The room was quite large, each detective having his own desk, all piled with varying amounts of paperwork and sundry items of criminal paraphernalia. On Sam Braithwaite's a screwdriver and small case opener, taken from a prisoner charged with shop-breaking, lay among the stack of case files. On Henry Farmer's there was a short-handled bludgeon, the result of an officer 'shining his lamp' on a suspicious character the previous night. Beside Tom Norton's desk stood a set of three lamps, which for some days had been an annoyance to everyone who had to walk around, and into, them. They had been recovered from a yard in Cutler's Row, and Tom was loath to part with them until he knew who the owner was. The shelves three deep along each wall were stacked with old files and bundles of papers. This, Mallard rightly assumed, was the office filing system.

Discussion of the manner of Harriman's killing continued a little longer until the doctor, an evening surgery to attend, excused himself from the meeting.

Walking him to his trap in the yard, Tom said companionably, 'I saw you looking round. It could be improved, but it'll take money.'

'Not before I get a new mortuary,' grinned the doctor, untying his horse.

As the pony and trap clopped out of the gates into Butler Lane at the rear of the police station, Tom pushed his hands deep into his trouser pockets and pondered the implications of the doctor's findings. Whoever killed Harriman had probably slipped into the yard at daybreak and waited in the feed shed for him to come out to tend to the horses. From Farmer's conversation with Harriman's widow earlier in the day, they knew that she had left with Elizabeth, the servant girl, at half past seven for market. Harriman was in the habit of feeding the horses at about half past eight, which was when the killer would have surprised him from behind, probably as he bent over a feed bin, with no chance to defend himself. Although obviously premeditated, the killing had been rushed; the attempt to make it look like suicide had been clumsy. If the murderer had had more time, Tom thought, he would have lured his victim to somewhere more secluded and faked an accident. That the house had been searched was obvious from the insecure kitchen window. So why was it necessary to kill Harriman quickly, and what did the murderer want?

Chapter Eight

J oseph Langley awoke as usual just before six o'clock, the dull winter's light filtering through his half-open bedroom curtains. For a few moments he lay perfectly still, not wanting to disturb the pain in his skull by moving. The brandy fumes swirling through his head were like a poisonous all-consuming fog, the source of an incredible pain that lanced through his temples and made it difficult for his rheumy eyes to focus. A thick glutinous mucus coated the inside of his mouth, refusing to allow his tongue to move or saliva glands to function.

From the apple tree just below the bedroom window a sparrow's twittering began to filter through. Seconds later this was followed by the rhythmic clopping of iron hooves as an early morning dray, fresh from Halyard's Brewery in Castle Lane, passed down one of the streets behind the house. The screech of its metal wheels on the cobbled surface sent shafts of blinding light lacerating through Langley's senses, making him want to vomit. He lay perfectly still for several minutes, acutely aware that sooner or later he would have to get up. Irrespective of his aching head and nauseous stomach, there was a pressing need to attend to the demands of a bursting bladder.

With the infinite caution that only acute pain, or a monumental hangover, can dictate, he swung his legs out of bed and rested bare feet on the cold linoleum. The shock of the chilly floor blissfully enveloped him for a few fleeting seconds before the waves of nausea returned. Sitting perfectly still, he waited until he had recovered sufficiently to grope around with his hand under the bed for the handle of the ornate chamber-pot. Dragging the receptacle into a position between his feet, still seated on the edge of the bed, Langley urinated noisily – grateful for the marginal relief.

Standing up cautiously, the old man began, painfully, to function. Waking with a hangover was commonplace nowadays. He knew that by mid-morning the headache would be gone and his heaving stomach would be ready to receive solid food. Pulling on his trousers and yesterday's shirt, which he had thrown over the chair under the window before falling into bed, he silently cursed the unsteady hands that refused to allow him to do up the buttons. Pulling up his braces and tucking the shirt into his undone trousers, Langley recovered the silk waistcoat from the floor where he had dropped it the previous night. Now he was fully awake he was conscious of the crisp morning air blowing in through the half-open sash window. Slipping the waistcoat on, he searched for the white silk muffler that he habitually wore when he went out of an evening. Finding it where it had fallen, he knotted it loosely round his neck and, leaving the bedroom, crossed the landing.

Pausing outside Clarice's bedroom, he listened for a moment to the sound of soft snoring coming from her room. It would be another hour before she was up and about. Unsteadily, Langley negotiated the steep flight of stairs, automatically avoiding placing any weight on the middle of the third tread from the top, which squeaked. Down on the ground floor he paused to regain his breath and allow the pounding in his temples to ease. The cold, which had initially served to counter the effects of the hangover, was now becoming insidious. He began to shiver uncontrollably in the cold hallway. This was one of the few occasions when he regretted the parsimony that refused to allow him the luxury of employing a maid, who by now would have lit some fires.

The warmth from the glowing coals left overnight in the kitchen range went a little way to raise the temperature in the room. Stooping over the sink, Langley sluiced cold water over his face, gulping some down in the process. The icy deluge hit his heaving stomach with the force of an avalanche. Within seconds he was vomiting uncontrollably in a bout of nausea that lasted for several minutes. When it passed, he released the grip that he had taken of the stone sink to give him some measure of support. Using cupped hands he washed out his mouth, being careful not to swallow any more of the water. Wryly the thought came to him that at least there was running water in the house now – not as in the old days, when you had to go out to the pump.

Seating himself in the armchair at the side of the range, Langley began to feel the benefit of the meagre heat that gradually warmed him and returned him to some semblance of normality. In a few minutes he would make a pot of hot sweet tea; there was enough heat in the range to boil a kettle. Before that, though, there was something he needed to do. He studied his shaking hands: hands that would not button a shirt or trousers, and certainly could not cope with a boiling kettle. Pushing on the arms of the chair, he levered himself upright and, with the resignation of one who recognises his own condition, lumbered over to the kitchen cupboard and took down a bottle of Wood's Navy Rum and a half-pint glass.

The old man did not return to the armchair, but instead sat down at the kitchen table with the glass and bottle in front of him. With shaking hands he placed the bottle between his knees and, after several frustrating attempts, managed to remove the cork from its neck. Still using both hands, he poured a generous measure into the large glass before setting the bottle back on the scrubbed surface.

By now the shakes had worsened and he could hardly keep a limb still. It was always the same; the physical and mental effort of preparing the antidote seemed to exacerbate his condition. Tugging at the silk muffler, Langley removed it from his neck. After a deal of exertion he succeeded in wrapping one end round his right wrist, and using his teeth he tied it into a secure knot. The old man paused briefly to get his breath back and to allow the pounding in his head to subside.

Taking hold of the loose end of the scarf, he passed it behind his neck and over hunched shoulders into his left hand. Gripping the tumbler with difficulty in a trembling right hand and bending over almost to touch the glass, he pulled steadily downwards on the scarf with his left hand. The resulting action raised the glass to his mouth, and held it steady long enough for him to take down its contents in one swallow.

Joseph sat quietly for a few moments, head in hands, elbows resting on the table, giving the alcohol time to take effect. Slowly and deliberately he reached out and poured another measure of the rum, then without any hint of a tremor carefully replaced the cork in the bottle. In a minute he would make a pot of tea and take some upstairs to Clarice, before making up the fire and boiling a kettle on the range for a shave.

Langley's disposition was not improved by what he found in the police station yard on his arrival. Instead of entering the station through the main office as usual, thanks to a gang of men digging up the pavement in Long Street he had to go in through the stable yard in Butler Lane.

The cobbled yard was a hive of untidy bustle. A middle-aged constable with his tunic unbuttoned was attempting to back a restive horse into the traces of the prison van. Standing at the stable door, holding it tight closed, was the portly figure of Sergeant Alfred Vendyback. Through the open upper portion of the door Langley could see two other men, in shirts and braces and with their backs to him, poking about with pitchforks in the hay.

'What's going on, boy?' he demanded of young Arthur Hollowday.

'Rats, sir! PC Morton nearly got bit by one when he went in to get the 'orse, sir – big bugger, it was. It jumped at 'im and run over 'is shoulder!' In his excitement the lad dropped back into a broad local accent. Fred Judd would have despaired: for months now he had been attempting to improve the boy's speech.

In Joseph Langley's experience everyone had an Achilles heel, a weak point that provided the key to controlling them. His most deeply buried secret was that he was terrified of rats. At the age of twelve he had gone to sea for a short period as a ship's boy. Early on, to his horror, he had discovered that a prime sport of the men with whom he shared his living space in the fo'c'sle was rat-baiting. The mess deck cleared, a man was posted at the foot of the companion ladder against the arrival of any inquisitive officer, and the sport began. Bets were laid and a pig-tailed sailor, his hands tied behind his back, entered a circle formed by his mates, proceeding to do battle with the other occupant of the circle – a large recently caught bilge rat. The sport was to see how many of the rodents the man could kill with his teeth before he was too exhausted or too badly bitten to continue.

From the outset young Joseph had more sense than to reveal his feelings to his shipmates. Instead he always ensured for himself a place well to the back of the group of onlookers, or took post at the foot of the ladder.

A sudden unearthly squeal came from the back of the stables. Arthur's attention swung back to what was happening. For several seconds the agonised squealing continued in a nerve-wracking crescendo. It ended abruptly as a third man, who appeared from the shadows inside the stable, swung a heavy shovel at something on the ground. There was a dull thud, and then silence. Sergeant Vendyback opened the stable door sufficiently wide to allow one of the officers, his trouser legs secured with baling twine, to slip out into the yard. Impaled on the long tines of his pitchfork was the body of a large black sewer rat.

In the middle of the yard the mare shied away and reared at the sight and smell of the rodent. Seth Morton, trying desperately to quiet the animal while avoiding being trampled, bellowed obscenities at the man with the pitchfork.

Arthur Hollowday, turning to speak to Inspector Langley, found that he was alone.

'I may need to go to Manchester, sir.' Tom paused to judge the inspector's reaction. It was common knowledge that to approach Joseph Langley before mid-morning was courting disaster. The detective inspector glared up at him from the papers he was reading on his desk. More from habit than the need for a smoke he picked up his pipe and began poking about in the bowl with a match. For some reason, which he had not bothered to analyse, Langley felt resentment towards Tom for Harriman's death. Not, he acknowledged, that Tom could necessarily have prevented it. More importantly, had he agreed to bring the man in earlier, his demise could have been turned to their advantage. A fictitious interview and a concocted statement that could never be disputed would have enabled them at least to close the book on the Donnelly murder. This was, Langley did not doubt, a case of thieves falling out. Harriman was one of those thieves, and therefore could have been conveniently held responsible for the killing at Bridge Sixty-Four. As it was, there were now two unsolved murders and no suspects.

'Why?' The monosyllabic response was not encouraging.

'I've spoken on the telephone with the police at Central Manchester.' Tom took a deep breath; the old man was going to be difficult. 'A Detective Sergeant Millward. They have a special department that's looking into the activities of these Irish political activists. He feels he may be able to help us, but obviously it can't be done by telephone or telegraph. He's asked that I go to see him.'

'What's his information?' By now Langley had succeeded, with the aid of a pen nib, in scraping some of the coke that had accumulated in the pipe bowl onto his blotting paper.

'He may be able to identify one of the ringleaders, sir.' Tom needed to be careful because he was not being strictly truthful. The Manchester officer had said that if he wished to discuss the subject it could only be done face to face. Tom agreed with him: the newly installed telephone in Fred Judd's office was most definitely insecure. All the calls were connected through the post office switchboard, and he was certainly not prepared to have some nosey operator listening in.

The inspector's head ached intolerably. He wanted to conclude the conversation and take a walk in the fresh air down to the Pack Horse for a livener.

'Go tomorrow morning,' he grunted, 'and be back the day after – no later!'

Tom closed the door behind him and sat back down at his desk. He had taken a gamble that Langley would not telephone Manchester to speak to Sergeant Millward himself. It was well known that the detective inspector hated the new telephone, claiming that before long someone would be electrocuted. The trip to Manchester was an opportunity to see how a big detective department was organised, and with any luck he would discover something that would help with the events in Kelsford.

'I think this is a two-man job.' Sam Braithwaite's deep fruity voice boomed across the office, and he gave a knowing wink to Henry Farmer who was busily writing at his desk.

'Shout a bit louder and the old man can come out and discuss it with you,' retorted Tom, grinning across at him.

Henry raised his head and smiled back absently. He was depressed that after today it would be some considerable time before he saw Ruth Samuels again.

In view of the nature of the journey and the distances involved, to Mirka Sloboda's delight Ruth had decided to take her maid with her. The plan outlined by Manfred Issitt was that Ruth should travel on legitimate business as far as Vienna, where she would stay at the home of a wealthy Austrian banker who was a member of the Pipeline. From there she would travel as the wife of a Russian government official to Lubch, a small town a few miles east of Unghvar in the Carpathians, where she would be met by a local contact.

The house in Victoria Road was a flurry of preparations for the mistress's imminent departure. Ruth and Mirka were to catch the half past seven train the following morning for Liverpool Street station, whence they would travel to Harwich. The following day, Tuesday 3 January, they were to take the Great Eastern Railway's ferry to Antwerp.

New Year's Day had been busy for Ruth. At the bank she had spent the morning going through papers and handing over business responsibilities to Jakob Peters' son Maxwell. Ruth Samuels' relationship with Max was an uneasy one. On Isaac Samuels' death, Max had expected to be appointed a partner; that the position had gone to Ruth was something he deeply resented. While on the surface he maintained an affable and obliging façade, Ruth was aware that there were occasions when he actively worked to undermine her. It was not something she could specifically point to – just the odd vote against her on critical issues, or a client changing his mind following a quiet lunch with Peters. She hoped he would not compromise the Kelsford Warehousing Project during her absence. For the time being Ruth decided that she had more urgent affairs to consider.

The afternoon was occupied by a visit from Mannie Issitt to finalise last-minute arrangements. Unfortunately this meant she had not been able to say goodbye to Henry. He would, she knew, try to be at the railway station when she left.

By six o'clock in the evening everything was ready. While the cook prepared dinner in the spacious kitchen downstairs, Ruth and Mirka, closeted away in Ruth's bedroom, packed the single heavy trunk that Ruth always took on trips abroad. Measuring three feet long by two feet wide, and two foot six high, it was not as large as the popular steamer trunks taken by the gentry on cruises, but was slightly larger than the average rail passenger's baggage. It was in fact a carefully tried and tested piece of equipment. Its size meant that both Ruth and Mirka could pack sufficient clothes and toiletries for most journeys – but a sturdy leather carrying handle at either end ensured that, in the absence of a porter, the women could carry it easily between them. In the base of the trunk was a shallow false bottom, cleverly added by the Pipeline cabinetmaker who had built it. The concealed compartment was large enough to stow documents or other small items, and almost impossible for even the most zealous of customs officers to detect. It was in this recess that the forged papers for the Russian tax inspector would later be concealed. For the time being its only secret was the well-oiled and carefully wrapped .30 Mauser revolver and a box of cartridges, which nestled snugly at one end.

Neatly packed away underneath their clothes were two of Ruth's dresses, which had been altered to fit Mirka. Once they departed from Vienna, as they neared their destination, Mirka and Ruth were to swap identities – a simple procedure that had served them well on previous occasions. Although of different builds, they were of an age and their travel documents only gave basic descriptions of them. The plan was that they would book into a hotel in Lubch and Mirka, posing as Ruth, would remain there while Ruth slipped away to the rendezvous. That this might take a few days did not pose a problem, provided that Mirka remained in her room and did not accept any social visits. Posing as the wife of a government official would be particularly helpful in discouraging any such approaches.

Ruth eyed her travelling companion speculatively. Although Mirka was slightly shorter and heavier than her across the hips, she had not inherited the heavy Slav features of the Russian peasant. Her small nose and black eyes, the tiny epicanthic folds at the edges of which lent her broad face a slightly oriental perspective, bespoke her Tartar ancestors. At a push, they could both wear almost any of the clothes in the trunk.

She wondered if Mirka would at some time marry. Like herself, the woman was over thirty now, and not unattractive. That she had taken lovers over the years Ruth was in no doubt. Inwardly she smiled to herself. What was the old saying about the women of the Don? 'The only virgins are the ones who can run faster than their brothers . . .' Ruth was fairly sure, from one or two things that she had picked up – a glance, a quick touch in passing – that her maid and David the coachman were romantically involved. It would be interesting to see what happened tonight. It had been agreed that, once the trunk was packed, Mirka would sleep on a single bed in Ruth's room. If she slipped away in the early hours, Ruth's suspicions would be confirmed.

At seven o'clock the following morning Kelsford railway station was bleak and inhospitable. An icy east wind blowing across the open platform cut through the women's heavy travelling coats. Clutching their narrow-brimmed travelling hats to their heads they huddled together in the shelter of the closed station buffet doorway.

Even without the bad weather, Mirka Sloboda was in a foul mood. A disturbed night and a quarrel with David Capewell before they left the house had soured her day. Once she was satisfied that her mistress was asleep, Mirka had slipped from her bed to spend the night with David in his third-floor room. Usually this was an easy matter. The servants shared the top floor of the house, so for the two of them to visit each other in their rooms merely required the rest of the household to be asleep and caution to be exercised. Last night, having said their farewells between the sheets of David's narrow bed, she had been tiptoeing along the landing just before three o'clock when she encountered Mary, the housemaid, coming out of her bedroom en route to the privy. Having recovered from the shock of bumping into someone in the dead of night, Mary enquired with a knowing grin if Mirka had 'forgotten her way'. The response that if she did not keep her mouth shut and her eyes closed she would be extremely sorry sent the young girl scurrying back into her room. This morning, while loading the trunk onto the four-wheeler carriage, Mirka had spotted David in deep conversation with Clarice Jenkins, the new – and young – housekeeper next door. Mirka's presumption that the conversation was not an innocent one provoked a heated row between the couple, which ceased abruptly when Ruth Samuels called her in to get ready to leave.

The sound of the bolts on the buffet doors being drawn back signalled that the staff were opening up.

'Would you like a coffee while you wait, Highness?' Mirka asked.

'Stop calling me Highness. The term is Madam,' Ruth retorted testily. Ever since she had been told she was to accompany her mistress on this trip, Mirka had reverted, more as a joke than anything else, to Russian serf mannerisms and the vocabulary of her native land. Ruth was annoyed. That her maid was excited at the prospect of visiting her homeland was understandable, and they were good enough friends not to stand on ceremony when they were alone. The fact that Mirka had slipped away during the night for a lover's tryst did not bother her; her ill humour did.

Because of the early start they had eaten breakfast at half past five. That there was an atmosphere among the servants was obvious. Mary, the little housemaid, scuttled about trying to avoid the murderous glances being shot at her by Mirka, while later Ruth had been forced to intervene in a row between the two lovers. Well aware of Mirka's hot temper, and her propensity for long periods of sulking, Ruth lost no time in pointedly telling her maid that she had no intention of spending the forthcoming trip 'with a truculent Cossack mare who was about to lose her source of oats for the foreseeable future'. Despite the mood that had overtaken her, Mirka was well aware that to cross her mistress was not to be done lightly: although of different social classes, she and Ruth shared the same heritage and temperament. Ruth was quite capable, even at this late hour, of leaving her in Kelsford and going on the trip alone. Nodding submissively, Mirka had gone off to complete the arrangements for their departure.

'Da, Madam,' she replied sulkily. It was still not too late for this arrogant Kulak to send her home – in which case she would ensure that everyone at Victoria Road, and David Capewell in particular, had an extremely miserable new year.

'And stop speaking in Russian. You're not even on the boat yet.' Frustrated, Ruth pushed past Mirka into the welcoming warmth of the buffet, and made for a seat near the window from where she could watch the train arrivals.

It was while they were drinking the strong hot coffees that the waitress brought them that the well-groomed figure of Henry Farmer walked in. Taking a seat at a nearby table, he ordered a pot of tea and looked casually around the room. The tables in the buffet had begun to fill with people anxious to escape the cold, while businessmen wearing top hats and dark frock coats, on their way to meetings in London, were assembling on the platform. One or two couples, off to visit relatives, congregated under the large station clock, watching a uniformed porter who was towing a large water bowser behind him, hosing down the platform.

Allowing his gaze to come to rest on the two women, Henry, well-feigned surprise lighting his face, smiled at them and nodded politely. Folding his newspaper, he got up and strolled across to their table. Raising his bowler hat politely, he said, 'Mrs Samuels. How nice to see you. How are things at the bank?'

'Very well thank you, Mr Farmer,' Ruth replied. 'Would you care to join us? Our train's not due just yet.'

As Henry settled himself on the hard upright chair, the young fair-haired waitress brought his tea. Ruth turned to her maid. 'Mirka, please can you check that the porter has secured our luggage safely.' To any onlooker the casual meeting and exit of the maidservant would appear to be totally natural.

Dropping her voice almost to a whisper, Ruth said, 'I'm sorry I couldn't see you yesterday. I had meetings all day.'

'That's all right. I understand there's a lot to do. Will you be able to write?' Henry's voice was almost inaudible.

'I'll try. It depends upon the post – you know what it's like abroad. I'll probably be home before the letters get to you.' Ruth had already decided to write a couple of post-dated letters, and leave them in Vienna for her contact to put in the mail on pre-arranged dates. He was well aware that the trip would be a long one, as she had told him she had to go to Austria as well as the Netherlands.

Henry was just about to tell her to be careful while she was away, when to his annoyance he spotted Tom Norton, muffled up against the weather in a long Inverness overcoat, its cape buttoned to his throat, strolling in through the buffet doors. 'Damnation,' he muttered. He had completely forgotten that Tom was going to Manchester. Ruth shot him a look of enquiry, then began to discuss the inclement weather in a normal conversational tone.

Tom, his back to them, walked over to the tobacco counter, made some purchases and, turning to leave, spotted his colleague. Walking across, he first raised his hat to Ruth, then said to Farmer, 'Good morning, Henry. I didn't expect to see you here.'

'Waiting to catch you, old chap,' lied Henry. 'There's a man coming in today to see me about some lamps that he's had stolen. May I show him the ones next to your desk?'

Tom nodded agreeably. 'Please do. I'll be interested if he has a claim on them.'

Politely refusing Ruth's offer to join them, as his train was due at any moment, Tom excused himself and made to leave. Henry, unable now to legitimately linger in the buffet, also excused himself. As he moved to get up from his chair a firm pressure under the table, as Ruth placed her foot on his, held him a moment longer.

'It's nice to see you, Mr Farmer. I hope we'll meet again soon.'

Henry, not looking into her dark brown eyes, knew that he was going to miss her deeply for the next weeks. 'And you, Mrs Samuels,' he replied politely. The pressure on his foot was withdrawn. Pushing his chair back, he followed Tom onto the busy platform.

Seated opposite a middle-aged couple in the cramped compartment of the Manchester train, waiting for the guard to blow his whistle, Tom looked speculatively out of the window. Just what game was Henry playing? The reason for his presence at the station was certainly not the one he had given.

First of all, he hadn't known which train Tom was going to catch. Secondly, Tom had the distinct feeling that, had he not gone over, Henry would have allowed him to leave unnoticed.

Out on the platform, walking to the Manchester train, Farmer had told him that the lady was Mrs Samuels, a partner in the Kelsford Bank of Commerce, that he had happened to see her with her maid and had been invited to join them for coffee. Tom remembered his friend's investigation into the missing money at the bank some time ago. It was unusual, thought Tom, for a lady who chanced to meet a casual male acquaintance in a station buffet to send her servant away on an errand, and out of earshot. Tom smiled broadly at the elderly lady opposite and lit a cigar. No, Henry, he thought, your secret is safe with me, and I definitely admire your taste.

Exhaling a plume of fragrant blue smoke, he caught sight of a tall dark-haired man wearing a three-quarter length double-breasted coat of the sort favoured by seamen, who was about to climb aboard. For some reason the man appeared to change his mind and, pulling his long woollen muffler tighter round his neck and chin, moved off down the train. The face was vaguely familiar, but try as he might the detective could not place it. Giving up after a few moments, Tom relaxed in his seat as the train pulled noisily out of the station.

Chapter Nine

The small town of Lubch, nestling at the foot of the mighty Carpathian Mountains, was, Ruth thought, as pretty as it was isolated. Half a dozen narrow streets, flanked by tiny two-storey houses with red tiled roofs, radiated from a small market square with a tall stone church at one end. Here in the Zakarpatska region of the Carpathians, at the south-western edge of the Ukraine, looking up towards the snow-covered mountains, Ruth and Mirka were at the farthest corner of the Habsburg empire. When the train from Miskolcz deposited them at the station in the centre of Unghvar it went no further: the heavy locomotive turned round and, having taken on fresh supplies of coal and water, retraced its route back to Vienna. Wrapped in warm furs against the cold, the two women completed the last thirty-five miles of their journey by coach. As planned, they had swapped identities on departing from Vienna, much to Mirka's delight and Ruth's amusement. Its summer wheels removed, their coach was fitted with sledge runners during the winter months; it was a bone-shaking ride but the only form of transport available. After four hours of jolting and jarring along the mountainous roads that, fortunately, were kept open by regular traffic between Lubch and Unghvar, the driver deposited them in the market square.

Although it was only half past four the light was beginning to fade, throwing long shadows across the cobbles. Just visible was the distant outline of an ancient castle, almost hidden by the tall trees of a pine forest and grimly glowering down upon the town.

Mirka patted the rump of one of the steaming horses before making a sign against evil towards the castle. In Kelsford, thought Ruth, anyone spotting the gesture would have considered it bizarre. Here, where peasants still believed in vampires and werewolves, it was completely natural.

Burying her hands deeper in the fur muff attached to a thin cord round her neck, Mirka nodded curtly to the two young boys who were grasping the handles of the trunk. Hitching up her long skirts, she set off towards the Hotel Kaiserhof, which was visible further along the main street at the opposite end of the square.

Pulling off her heavy winter coat and throwing her hat onto a chair, Ruth dropped gratefully across the huge double bed in her first-floor room. The journey from Vienna had been a long one, and she was looking forward in eager anticipation to undressing and taking a hot bath before slipping between the clean sheets under the heavy wolfskin cover. Although she would not admit it to her companion, Ruth was enjoying herself. The short stay that they had made in Vienna, and now the spectacular mountain scenery and snowscapes, excited her as much as the mission upon which she was engaged. Vienna was probably her favourite European city. She loved the atmosphere of the brightly lit coffee houses, with their orchestras playing Strauss waltzes softly in the background, and comfortable leather chairs in snug alcoves, where businessmen met for morning coffee and private discussions and ladies gathered in the afternoon to sample the *Gugelhupf*, or the whipped cream pastries, while exchanging the latest gossip. She enjoyed wrapping up warmly against the January cold and strolling through the Vienna Woods, the pathways cleared of snow as fast as it fell by an army of busy workmen. An evening at the opera followed by supper at Frau Sacher's was perfection. Ruth also realised that to visit Vienna was better than to live there. The upper classes were ossified into a rigid and snobbish society, with the ageing Emperor at its head, and the strutting, gold-braided officers of the Imperial Army would not have been out of place on the stage of a comic operetta. Ruth knew that after a while she would have lost patience with this – but to be an observer was a wonderful experience.

On their arrival in Vienna, Ruth and Mirka had been met by Joachim Schallmeier, a long-time associate of the Kelsford Bank of Commerce and a dedicated member of the Pipeline. Ruth and the elderly banker were old friends: when she had been married to Isaac, Ruth had made several visits to Vienna, always staying with Schallmeier and his wife Esther in their luxurious mansion on the Rennweg. She had grown very fond of Joachim, with his long white beard and air of quiet authority, speaking Yiddish with a soft and lilting Viennese accent. To her he was what the Austrians called *gemütlich* – gentlemanly, polite and lovable.

Stretching luxuriously on the soft bed, Ruth allowed herself a moment of reflection. Although Joachim was an old friend of her husband, he had from the outset, with an almost uncanny perception, known that the equation of a young woman and an older man would, if the marriage were to succeed, require a certain degree of latitude. So, even in the early days when Ruth had set off of an afternoon, at a time when most reputable Viennese were taking a nap, he had always made his two-horse carriage available for her. Prudently, Schallmeier had also ensured his personal driver fully briefed him concerning the afternoon's activities. Ruth reflected not upon the fact that she had been able to spend her afternoons with a certain young Uhlan cavalry officer, or an influential politician, but that neither she nor Joachim ever mentioned the fact. At moments such as this, Ruth often wondered where the old man had gained his understanding of human nature.

During the week she spent in Vienna with the Schallmeiers, Ruth negotiated a contract with Joachim to purchase an interest in a coalmining enterprise in Bohemia. Irrespective of her main mission, this deal alone made her trip to Vienna worthwhile for the bank. With the papers signed, Ruth and Mirka were at liberty to relax and pass some time shopping in the various stores off the Kärntnerstrasse. It was with a tinge of regret that they had finally boarded the eastbound sleeper train for Miskolcz and the borders with the Ukraine.

Reaching to one side, Ruth tore open the sealed white envelope that had been handed to her by the desk clerk on their arrival, while Mirka was signing the visitors' book in the name of Nadia Koroschenka. (No one had troubled to ask her maid's name.) The envelope contained a single, unsigned sheet of folded paper asking her to be in the town square at nine o'clock that evening.

Five minutes before nine, after an excellent meal of rassolnik soup served with sour cream, followed by a filling dish of Chakhokhbili chicken, cooked in true Georgian style with a delicious walnut sauce, Ruth made her way to the foyer of the hotel. By the reception desk an Austrian guards officer, his light cloak thrown back over his shoulders and held at the throat by an ornate silver chain, was in conversation with a Russian officer of the Imperial Army. Ruth frowned slightly: it looked as if some sort of military exercise was taking place in the district. She hoped it would not interfere with any of her plans.

Out in the street it was pitch dark and snow had begun to fall gently, adding its cover to that which already blanketed the unmade road. At least, thought Ruth, with the temperature somewhere near ten degrees below zero the roadway beneath was frozen solid. Once the spring thaw came it would be a quagmire for two months until the hot summer sun dried everything out. In England snow was something that caused total disruption, but here, where the amenities at best were primitive, snow was an annual event – arriving in November, staying until March and disrupting nothing.

It was neither the snow nor the brittle cold that bothered Ruth as she walked down the middle of the darkened street. There was something about this rendezvous that bothered her. There was something in the way it had been set up that made her uneasy, something important that she couldn't put her finger on.

As she approached the square, Ruth became aware that she was not alone. Emerging from somewhere deep in the shadows a large figure, wrapped in a heavy sheepskin, dropped in a few paces behind her. Risking a fleeting glance over her shoulder, Ruth confirmed what she already knew:

that the man was definitely following her, and they were alone in the street. She examined the possibilities, her mind racing. It was unlikely that he was a casual pedestrian – not at this time of night – and in a small town such as this it wasn't likely that she was about to be robbed. Ruth was engaged in a potentially dangerous undertaking: assisting a fugitive to escape from Tsarist Russia was a serious offence. Had she been followed from Vienna by the Austrian or Russian secret police? This she quickly discounted. If it were the case, they would not disclose their presence now; they would wait until she had made her rendezvous.

Ruth tensed as the figure came alongside her, ready to run – not that she would get far in a long skirt and voluminous overcoat. A heavy hand closed momentarily over her forearm. The pressure was released almost as soon as it was applied. Hardly pausing in his lumbering stride, the man whispered in a deep baritone, 'Please follow me, Highness.'

After ten minutes of following her guide along narrow streets and back alleys, Ruth found herself on the outskirts of the town. The broad silhouette twenty paces ahead of her, striding deceptively quickly through the snow, was difficult to keep up with, and she was quite out of breath. Suddenly, and without warning, she realised the man had disappeared from her view. Ruth cursed silently: how could she be so careless? The snow was falling quite heavily now, bringing visibility down to a few yards; a momentary lapse of concentration, and she was alone on a deserted road at the edge of town. The possibility that she had walked into a trap crossed her mind.

Looking around, Ruth saw that the small cottages on either side of the road were neat and well cared-for. Light from the windows reflected off the snow to reveal a tiny garden in front of the nearest, and a path leading from the road to the front door. Standing perfectly still she attempted to get her bearings, listening for any sounds.

'It is well, Highness, we have not been followed.'

Ruth almost passed out with fright as the deep voice spoke from the darkness. How he had done it she did not know, but somehow her guide had moved unseen to position himself behind her, the snow deadening his footfall.

Before she could recover herself sufficiently to answer, the bear-like figure led her to the rear of the house, where a dark-haired young woman in her late twenties, a paraffin lamp in her hand, was waiting in the kitchen doorway. Once they were inside she closed the door behind them and locked it. Placing the lamp on the wooden table in the middle of the room, she turned to Ruth and said politely, 'Good evening, Madam, welcome to my house.'

Ruth was about to reply when the door into the passageway opened and a young man came into the room. Even without his dark jacket and celluloid collar, Ruth immediately recognised the reception clerk from the Kaiserhof Hotel. Like the woman he was in his late twenties, small and slim. His black curly hair was prematurely shot with silver grey streaks, and the small pebble glasses perched in an almost scholarly attitude on his broad nose served to accentuate his Semitic features. His business suit had been replaced by baggy peasant trousers and a collarless open-necked shirt.

Holding out his hand to Ruth, he repeated the greeting. 'Shalom, Madam, welcome to my house.' Indicating one of the heavy upright chairs arranged round the table he continued, 'Please – sit down. We will remain in here if you don't mind: it's less overlooked than the front room.' To the big man who was busy shrugging off his sheepskin he said, 'Any problems, Akim Timofeivich?'

For the first time since he had approached her, Ruth was able to get a proper look at the man. He was even bigger than she had realised. About six foot five inches tall, he must, she thought, weigh around twenty stone, none of which was fat. His weather-beaten face, dominated by a huge sweeping white Cossack moustache, was that of a man in his mid-sixties. The resemblance to a great bear was even more pronounced in the confines of the small kitchen.

Akim shook his head and grinned, revealing surprisingly good teeth beneath the huge moustache. 'No. On a night like this only fools and bandits are out. We didn't see a soul.'

Ruth suddenly realised what had been bothering her. She was, she thought, becoming careless and should have spotted it straight away. When they booked in at the hotel the clerk had ignored Mirka and given the envelope containing the rendezvous instructions to Ruth. He had known from the outset that she, not Mirka, was the person he was looking for.

'I am Grigoriy Yavlinskiy and this is my wife Lukeria,' the young man continued. Yavlinskiy's wife, Ruth noticed, was extremely attractive, with long dark hair and expressive brown eyes. 'And this is my very good friend Akim,' he said, waving towards the old Cossack.

Akim Timofeivich glanced up from the glass of vodka to which he was helping himself. 'Highness,' he growled, making a half-bow to Ruth, his face once more splitting into a huge grin.

'And I,' she said, 'am Ruth.'

Introductions completed, they sat round the kitchen table for a while discussing Ruth's journey from England while picking at a plate of sweetmeats. The vodka that accompanied the food was, Ruth noted appreciatively, a top quality Zubrowka, not the usual home-made spirit distilled and drunk by peasants the length and breadth of Ukraine and Russia.

Yavlinskiy refilled Ruth's glass, and gazed appreciatively at the tall bottle with the strand of bison grass anchored in its base. 'One of the advantages of being in the hotel trade,' he murmured. 'We are still in Austrian territory this side of the mountains, and good vodka is easy to obtain here.' Dropping his head for a moment, his chin resting on his chest, he gnawed on his lower lip as if in some doubt about the best way in which to broach the subject they were to discuss. Pushing back in his chair, he addressed himself directly to Ruth. 'You have, I believe, escorted people out of Russia before.' It was a statement rather than a question.

Ruth nodded.

'On this occasion the man is of particular importance to us. For the last ten years he's been a crucial link in our activities, and now it's imperative that he himself is taken to safety. His name is Alexander Simonov and he's a government tax official in the Lvov district. He contacted us some time ago to let us know that he's under suspicion and the Ochrana are closing in on him. An arrangement was made that he should make a trip to complete some business in Stry, just south of Lemberg, from where he would be brought by one of our men over the mountains.' Pausing for a moment, Yavlinskiy looked over his spectacles at the others. 'We know from our friends on the other side that he arrived safely in Stry. He was to leave there today. The journey through the mountains should take two to three days.' He looked across at Akim for confirmation.

The big man cleared his throat and pushed aside his vodka glass. 'It depends upon the snows and how fit he is. If the passes are reasonably clear I could do it in two. With a passenger three, possibly four. I'd begin to worry if he was not here by Wednesday.'

'How old is he?' Ruth asked.

Yavlinskiy gave a small shrug. 'A good question. Unfortunately we don't know. Until recently we didn't know his true identity. We only have it now because it's necessary in order to arrange his escape.'

'What about family?' Any members of his family would, she knew, be arrested as soon as his disappearance was discovered.

'He has none,' the clerk replied. 'Our information is that he is a bachelor.'

'I'd prefer to be at the rendezvous when he arrives,' Ruth continued. 'I'll be able to have a good look at him before we begin my stage of the journey.'

Akim Timofeivich pulled a long face, the ends of his huge moustache dipping towards his chin. 'It is not seemly, Highness. The mountains are dangerous for a woman. I'm quite capable of bringing him down myself.'

'I'm sure you are, Uncle,' she replied calmly, 'but I've been in the mountains before and I will doubtless be in the mountains again. I'll be going with you.'

Akim took a deep breath and held it a moment before nodding his acceptance. The next hour was spent in quiet discussion. Akim, Ruth discovered, lived with his wife in a small farmhouse about a mile further along the rutted track that led out of town. A professional hunter, he spent the summer months in the mountains, trapping and selling furs in the towns on both sides of the border. In the winter, accompanied by his pack of dogs, he earned a living taking any visitors who were sufficiently intrepid – usually army officers on leave – up into the mountains to hunt wolves.

It was agreed that Ruth should spend the following night at the Yavlinskiys'. In the meantime Lukeria would go into Lubch and purchase men's clothing for Ruth to wear. At daybreak on Tuesday, after Akim had picked her up, the two of them would set off for the rendezvous. To any observer Akim would merely be taking another traveller through the mountains.

The snow had stopped by the time Ruth arrived back at the hotel. This time her companion was Grigoriy Yavlinskiy. It had been necessary for him to return with her as the main doors of the hotel were securely locked by now, and he needed to let her in through a side door using his duplicate key. Having accompanied her through the unlit kitchens to the foot of the main stairs, he took his leave and slipped away, securing the door behind him.

Back in her room, Ruth found an anxious Mirka awaiting her return. The maid had ordered a cold meat pie and a bottle of Crimean white wine to be sent up before the kitchen closed, and was now pacing up and down nervously. Although she had eaten earlier, Ruth realised that after the evening's activities she was hungry again. While Mirka recovered the bottle of wine from the window-ledge, where she had put it to keep cool, Ruth cut the pie into halves for them to share, and in a whisper told her of the arrangements for the next day.

White hoar-frost clung to the ends of Akim Timofeivich's whiskers and shimmered wetly in the wool of his heavy sheepskin as the sleigh passed smoothly over the deep snow. Ruth sat, exhilarated, under a fur travelling rug on the back of the horse-drawn sleigh, the icy wind whipping across her face, bringing tears stinging to her eyes and taking all feeling from her features.

It was soon after five o'clock in the morning when the sleigh, driven by Akim's wife, had collected her from the Yavlinskiys' house. It was impossible for Ruth even to guess at the woman's features, wrapped up as she was in heavy clothing on the exposed driving seat. Akim, filling the back seat and looking in his furs even more like a great brown bear, moved over to make room for her.

About six miles out of the town the sleigh slowed down and came to a halt near a small stone bridge. Dropping nimbly to the ground, Akim put out a hand to help Ruth down. Slinging a large hunter's bag across his back, he fished about under the seat for a heavy hunting rifle on a sling that he threw across his shoulder. His mouth split into its familiar grin. 'Ready, Highness?' The deep voice seemed to echo in the stillness of the morning.

Ruth grinned back. 'Ready, Uncle.'

With a curt wave to her husband, the woman on the sleigh turned the horse expertly in the narrow roadway, and with a slap of the reins across the horse's back disappeared into the night. For a short while neither spoke, enjoying the beauty of the setting and the profound silence. The first traces of dawn were beginning to show in the eastern sky, giving the great peaks in front of them a majestically menacing definition. Traces of pale pink light reflecting from the snow-covered stonework of the tiny bridge lent a fairy tale atmosphere to the scene. Hoisting his rifle into a more comfortable position, the Cossack nodded his head towards a path that was just becoming visible on the far side of the bridge, and set off.

As the morning wore on the sun began to shine warmly through the clear mountain air. Following the steeply climbing track for several hours, sweating from their exertions, they eventually arrived at the base of a small waterfall that gave out into a clear, bubbling stream. At some long-forgotten time in the past shiny stepping stones, now polished with age, had been laid at careful intervals across the water to allow travellers to pass. Ruth saw that the pathway on the other side dropped away sharply into a rocky valley before resuming its winding route into the mountains.

Pausing for a short break, Akim produced some fish patties and a bottle of cold tea from the depths of his bag. Realising how hungry she was, Ruth consumed her share with relish as she sat in the shelter of some rocks. Dressed in a man's sheepskin coat and fur boots, Ruth found that in spite of the low temperature – although the sun was shining it was still well below freezing at this altitude – she was snug and warm.

When they had finished eating, Akim started to climb among the shale and small boulders of the watercourse to their left, instead of crossing the stream and following the path. Scrambling up the waterfall after him, Ruth soon realised they were heading for a crease in the rocks some distance above. The climb took nearly an hour before, out of breath and perspiring heavily, she found herself standing on a narrow ledge a hundred feet above the spot where they had stopped. The ledge, she saw, was what she had taken to be a crease in the rocks.

Giving her a few minutes to rest, Akim moved ahead and round a corner to check that the way ahead was clear. When he returned he seemed very pleased with himself. 'Everything's all right,' he growled. 'No one's been up here since I last used the track. Don't worry: it's easy going from now on.'

As she edged along the precipitous rock face, Ruth was not sure that she agreed. The track below had disappeared from view and a sheer drop of several hundred feet into an icy landscape yawned giddily only inches from her feet. The tiny ribbon of silver water below them was, she could see, the beginning of a larger outpouring. She wondered if it was the beginnings of the river Lytha, which ran back down through Lubch and into Unghvar.

Taking a sudden sharp turn to the left, the ledge widened into a track that ran down towards an area of dense snow-clad fir trees. At the point where they came into the trees the track opened out, and Akim struck off across a stretch of sloping ground before disappearing into the firs. After a walk of about ten minutes, penetrating deeper into the woods, they arrived in a clearing with a large log cabin set to one side. Built of cut timbers with a sloping roof that swept down almost to touch the ground, it was the sort of place that was used during the season by hunting parties. In winter, concealed by the woodland and covered in snow, it was almost undetectable.

Motioning Ruth to stay hidden among the trees, Akim disappeared into the woods again, coming into view shortly afterwards at the rear of the building. Moving out into the clearing, he waved to Ruth to join him.

The single room inside the cabin was simply but comfortably furnished. Hunting trophies adorned the walls, while at one end was an old-fashioned cooking range with a pile of cut kindling stacked neatly beside it. Along the back wall in two tiers were six bunk beds, confirming that this was indeed a hunting lodge. In the middle of the room stood a long wooden table, with chairs set along two sides.

Akim lit the twigs and sticks laid in the fireplace. The fire starting to draw to his satisfaction, he piled some logs on top of the kindling and turned to Ruth. 'It is mine,' he said, in answer to her unasked question. 'During the season I bring parties into this area. The bear and wolf hunting is good. Usually we stay for a week or ten days, until they get fed up. The money is useful, and along with a bit of fur trapping it sees me through.'

'It's a good way to live,' said Ruth wistfully. The peaceful solitude of the place appealed to her.

'We're about ten miles into the mountains now,' Akim explained. 'The next inhabited place from here is Torka, thirty miles across the mountains to the north. Unless you know the passes there's no road from that side of the mountains to here. That's where our man will come from, with a guide who knows the paths.'

Before nightfall the old hunter took his gun and set off into the snow to check that they had not been followed, and to see if he could win some meat for an evening meal. Ruth went outside to look for the food store. As she had expected, in a small pit sealed with a large stone at the back of the lodge were several joints of what she presumed to be bear meat and a quantity of cabbages, all carefully stored away and frozen solid.

While she was placing one of the joints in the fireplace to thaw out in readiness for the next day, the flat crack of a single rifle-shot told her that their meal was safe. By the time Akim returned, with a large hare hanging from his belt, she had lit the oil lamps and was busy at the range preparing a pan of cabbage soup. Despite the old man's protests that this 136 was not work for her Highness, Ruth, thoroughly enjoying herself, took his hunting knife from him and in the remaining light went out onto the step, to skin and gut the hare.

After the meal of soup followed by spicy stewed hare, they sat back and looked at each other – tired and content. In the short time they had been together an affinity had grown between them which, Ruth reflected, could only exist here in the mountains.

The old Cossack wiped his moustaches with the back of his hand in an extravagant gesture. Ruth smiled at him: she knew that he dearly wanted to let out a mighty belch but dared not. Misinterpreting the smile, Akim said politely, 'A truly delicious meal, Highness, I thank you.'

Continuing to smile broadly, Ruth said, 'It's a pity there's no vodka to finish it off.'

Understanding the permission, Akim's great grin reappeared, his white teeth flashing. He got to his feet, lumbered to the door and stepped out into the snow. Seconds later he returned with the bottle of home-made spirit that had been buried under the step for safe-keeping. Filling two tumblers, he set one before Ruth and one in front of himself. Picking up the glasses, they both took an initial sip, licked their lips and threw the liquor back in one swallow. Banging her glass on the wooden table, Ruth reached for the bottle and refilled their glasses.

Chapter Ten

The next day the weather was dull and lowering. A heavy mist hung in the surrounding forest glades and snow-filled clouds clung to the mountain peaks, reducing visibility to a few yards. As dusk was beginning to fall at about four o'clock in the afternoon, Akim Timofeivich slung his rifle over his shoulder and disappeared along the track leading away from the log cabin, acting upon some sixth sense.

About an hour later, as Ruth was setting the soup bowls and wooden spoons on the table, he returned accompanied by two men. Closing the timber door behind them, Akim dropped the heavy bar to secure it. Moving to one side, he laid his gun across two pegs set in the wall while his companions began to remove their furs.

The smaller of the two Akim appeared to know, and addressed over his shoulder as Demkov. He was a small wiry man, with long black hair and several days' growth of beard. His dark eyes were red rimmed and tired, and he looked as if he had not slept for some time. The second man was of average height, and younger than she had expected: he was, she surmised, about thirty-five years old. His thick dark hair was wavy, cut short and pushed back in an oddly careless wave, with a parting just off centre. His features were pale, the skin slightly pockmarked from some childhood illness. He would, she thought, have been quite handsome had it not been for the cold hazel eyes gazing arrogantly at her from beneath finely drawn eyebrows.

Ignoring Ruth, the man with Demkov addressed himself to Akim, speaking in a harsh and commanding voice. 'How long do we stay here?'

Akim glanced at Ruth, who put her head down and busied herself with putting the crumbly buckwheat bread on the table. 'Probably tomorrow, Excellency,' he replied. 'Get a good night's rest. The trip across the mountains is a tiring one, and we all have further to travel yet.'

The guide from the Russian side nodded in agreement. They had been on the trail for two days and nights, during which time he had not slept.

'I'll get some rest, then I'll return tonight. It's going to snow again and I want to get back to the top of Klinsterpass before it's too late.' He chuckled. 'I don't want to be stranded on this side of the mountains in daylight.'

Walking over to warm himself by the blazing log fire, the Russian looked round the cabin for the first time, taking in his surroundings. 'Time is important,' he said, rubbing a hand over his stubbled jaw. 'I have urgent information for our people in Unghvar. If there's any sign of us having been followed, Demkov, you must come back and tell us.'

Demkov nodded and seated himself at the table, smiling gratefully at the woman as she placed a steaming bowl of soup in front of him. Akim and the tax collector joined him, and together the men hungrily devoured the meat pie and koulebyaki that Ruth served them. Once the meal had been consumed it was obvious that the two men were worn out by their journey over the mountains. Demkov threw himself onto one of the lower bunk beds and was soon sprawled out in a dead sleep, while his companion sat talking quietly with Akim Timofeivich. Their conversation was desultory and uninformative, confining itself mainly to the treacherous conditions in the passes. The Russian said little about his journey from Lemberg, or the reasons for his hasty flight. Ruth, meanwhile, busied herself in the background, stacking dishes and bringing in firewood for the night. While the guide slept peacefully on the bunk bed she put the remains of the cold pie and some German sausage into a cloth for him to eat on his journey home.

After a while she stole quietly out and made her way up the snow-covered track to ensure that the Russian and his guide had not been followed. Ruth was uneasy. She had made a number of these trips over the years, and there was, she knew, something wrong this time. Alexander Simonov should be at least middle aged, while the man in the cabin was no more than thirty-five; but what really bothered her was that while his Russian was very good it was not perfect. She thought he might be Polish or from one of the Baltic States, Latvia or Estonia possibly, but he was definitely not a Russian. Having checked the track for about a mile she turned back, satisfied that there were no other footprints along the barely visible path, or in the trees bordering their route.

By the time Ruth returned to the cabin it was dark. The guide was pulling on his fur hat and heavy boots ready for the trek back. Bidding him farewell, Akim and the Russian returned to their places at the table. While Ruth lit the old oil lamp, Akim produced a new bottle of vodka from the snow near the door, along with three glasses. The Russian took the thick glass that Akim offered him and sipped its contents. He nodded in approval and threw back the remainder of the glass in one gulp. As he leaned forward to place the tumbler on the wooden table for it to be recharged, his eyes opened and the satisfied smile froze on his face.

The cold barrel of the heavy Mauser pushed deep into the flesh at the back of his neck. In the sudden silence that had fallen in the cabin, the dull click of the pistol being cocked behind him sounded like the slamming of a cell door.

'Now, *Pan Polski*, who are you really?' Ruth's voice was quiet and menacing.

'What's going on? Are you bandits? I have no money . . .' The man's harsh voice was loud, protesting.

'I'll give you ten seconds to tell us the truth.' The pistol bored deeper into his neck, over his spinal column, forcing his head forward.

'What the hell is this crazy bitch doing? I tell you I have no money to give you . . .' His voice was filled with panic now. Beads of perspiration were trickling down his face, his eyes wide with fear, appealing to the Cossack.

'Are there others with him, Highness?' Akim's face remained impassive, his eyes not leaving the man's face as he asked the question.

'No. I've checked the track; he wasn't followed. They may be waiting further up in the forest for the guide to show them the way back down here.'

'I've known Demkov for many years.' Akim's voice showed his concern. 'I don't think he's a traitor, but money has a loud voice. Shall I go after him, Highness?'

'There isn't time. We have to decide what to do with this one and then leave.'

The realisation dawning upon him that it was the woman who was in charge, the prisoner attempted to turn his head to speak to her. The gun barrel jabbed viciously into his vertebrae, forcing his head further down onto his chest. Almost as if it were inside his head, he heard a single quiet click as the woman behind him, her thumb holding back the hammer of the pistol, pulled the trigger and held it back with her finger. Mother of God . . . the slightest movement on his part now . . . if her thumb were accidentally dislodged from the hammer, nothing in the world could stop the gun going off.

'You now have five seconds, *Pan Polski*.' The same flat menacing tone.

For some reason he could not explain, an unbidden thought flashed through the man's mind that the woman had an almost mesmeric voice. He had no doubt that here, in this isolated place, he could be easily killed and his body disposed of. 'Wait.' Holding his hands up in resignation and taking a deep breath, the man made a decision. 'My name is Eugene Leschenko. I am Latvian, not Polish. My father is Russian, my mother is Latvian, I was born in Daugavpils near to the Daugava river.' He was talking quickly, desperate for the woman to remove the gun from his head. When neither of the others spoke he continued, his voice cracked with fear. 'I was involved in a plot to kill the Tsar. Some of the others – they were Poles – were arrested. I escaped, and went to the house where Alexander Simonov was staying in Stry. I knew that he was also suspected. He allowed me to hide in his house and said that he would help me to escape with him. The evening before we were due to leave the secret police came to the house. He was an old man, and would not have been able to escape them. He took some poison that he had laid by in readiness. I knew you would not help me on my own, so I escaped through the back of the house and pretended to be him.'

The pistol did not move. 'And Demkov?'

'When I reached the rendezvous Demkov knew immediately that I was not the old man – but he did know who I was. He agreed to bring me here and leave me with you.'

'I will see to it that the treacherous bastard is killed, Highness.' Akim was angry. This breach of security could result in all of their deaths.

Ruth ignored him. 'And how do you prove all this?' she asked coldly.

The man sighed with resignation. 'I have some papers. I was previously in contact with Simonov and he trusted me. He uncovered the names of some Ochrana agents who are working in the Unghvar district and gave them to me for safe-keeping when he knew he wasn't going to be able to escape.'

'And you were going to use the list to buy yourself a passage out of Russia.'

Not daring to nod, the man made a gesture with his hands. The barrel of the gun in his neck was extremely painful. 'Please – take the gun away. I've been involved with the Lettish Resistance since I was a youth. I had to leave Latvia because the group I was working with was infiltrated. A Russian dragoon detachment was attacked in Riga by some hotheads. Some of our group who were involved on the sidelines were arrested and sent to Riga Central Prison. The authorities are still rounding up suspects. I escaped and joined a Terbatan group in Estonia. From there I went into Russia to help with the scheme to kill the Tsar. That was the most stupid move I could have made: these Poles are mad. Bronisław Piłsudski has been arrested, and they're looking for his brother Józef. Lenin's brother is in prison . . .'

Akim Timofeivich was retrieving the hunting rifle from its peg on the wall. 'I'll take him out and kill him, Highness, then we should leave. It's not safe here now.'

Ruth needed a few moments to think. Taking a step back from the table, she allowed the hammer of the Mauser to drop gently back into its closed position, and released the pressure on the trigger. Keeping out of the man's vision, she moved across to the cabin window and looked out. If Leschenko – even if that were his true name – was telling the truth, then to kill him would be an unnecessary mistake. With a feeling of shock, Ruth realised that she was seriously considering disposing of the man in cold blood. The truth was that if he were a spy their original mission was dead and buried, along with the man whom they had been sent to find. Should that be the case, Leschenko was directly responsible, and was also putting her life and that of other Pipeline members in the region in jeopardy.

On the other hand, his story could be checked quite quickly. Their contacts in Lemberg would know the truth. Was the tax inspector dead? Was Leschenko's story genuine? As for their immediate course of action, the decision had been made for her. Outside it had started to snow. Not the gently swirling flakes that gradually covered the busy streets of Kelsford, but a white and impenetrable curtain that blanketed the ground outside the cabin in minutes, wiping out the track into the forest and reducing visibility to a few feet. If there were soldiers further up the mountain it would be impossible for them to find their way down to the hut in the snowstorm.

'We stay here tonight, Uncle,' she said, moving round the room to a position behind Akim, where she could look at the Latvian's face. 'No one can get through this storm. Even the wolves will be staying at home tonight. Tie him to the chair, and we'll take two-hour watches. At dawn we'll make our way down to the road.'

Leaving Akim to take the first watch, Ruth, the pistol held loosely in her hand, curled up on a bunk bed and dozed fitfully.

Shortly after half past six the next morning the Cossack woke Ruth with a steaming glass of tea from the samovar, which he had put on to boil before rousing her. Contrary to her instructions, he had allowed her to sleep through while he watched their prisoner. Leschenko appeared to have been considering his position during the night, and some of the previous evening's arrogance had returned to his manner. In order to allow him to complete his ablutions, Akim had untied him, and he was now sitting with his hands spread open, flat on the table. His cold eyes fixed Ruth with a long stare. 'You're making a great mistake,' he said in a flat but authoritative voice. 'I'm an important member of the Latvian underground. I'm carrying papers which are of crucial urgency. You will, I can assure you, be in serious trouble when this matter is resolved.'

'I can't comment on your first claim.' The steel in the woman's voice removed some of the arrogance from Leschenko's manner. 'What your standing is in your own organisation I neither know nor care.' Moving away, she walked to the window, checking the weather and deliberately turning her back on him. 'Your other two assumptions are wrong. You did have some papers, which may or may not be of interest to us.' Reaching her arm out, she casually waved a sheet of closely written notepaper. 'For a leader of the Lettish underground, you're little better at concealing documents than you are at pretending to be someone who you are not.'

Leschenko's face was pale with rage. 'Return those papers immediately!' he spluttered. 'They're confidential . . .' But not well hidden, thought Ruth. It had taken Akim a matter of minutes during the night to cut them out of the lining of the man's fur while he dozed in the chair. 'Thirdly.' Ruth spun to face him, her eyes blazing.

'Thirdly, the only person who is likely to be in trouble is you! Until we have verified who you are you will be treated with the utmost caution. At the very best, if you are who you say you are, you have placed us all in a position of jeopardy. If you are not what you claim to be, or we are followed out of these mountains, then either Akim Timofeivich or I will kill you and drop your body into a pass. In these snows your corpse won't be found before the thaw, and I doubt anyone will bother too much even then.'

The big Cossack, waiting silently in the background, quietly approved of the manner in which the woman was dealing with the situation. He wondered if she would actually kill the Latvian should it prove necessary. It was, he decided, of little consequence. If the necessity arose and she did not, then he would. The matter of the Russian guide bothered him considerably. Knowing that the man was an imposter, he had still brought him. Very soon there would be a reckoning between himself and Demkov.

'We could move if you wished, Highness,' he rumbled. 'The trail will be closed for at least two days. We can be in Lubch before anyone gets through.' Akim was worried about the possibility of any pursuit while he had a woman and an unknown man on his hands.

Without taking her eyes off Leschenko, Ruth replied, 'Yes, Uncle, I agree. Let's get back to the village and make a few enquiries about *Pan Polski*.' The flash of annoyance that crossed Leschenko's face at being addressed as a Pole made the jibe worthwhile.

The trek back up the mountain slope and along the precipitous shale ledge to the waterfall took them until mid-morning. They were slowed down considerably by Leschenko, who, already tired from his earlier journey, was not in good condition and found difficulty maintaining the pace that Akim set. Following at the rear, Ruth also struggled to keep up – and was grateful for the delays caused by the Latvian.

By the time they reached the waterfall the weather had once more deteriorated, and heavy snow had again begun to fall. Looking down the dangerous descent to the stream, Ruth began to have serious misgivings. The hundred-foot escarpment was made up of loose stones and heavy boulders without any discernible path. Negotiating the slope in this deteriorating weather was going to be a perilous venture.

Akim also appeared to be concerned. 'We must take it very slowly and carefully, Highness. Follow me closely.' Cautiously, with Akim in the lead, followed by the Latvian and Ruth bringing up the rear, the trio began to descend.

They were twenty feet from the bottom when Ruth slipped. Shifting precariously from one foothold to another, her Cossack boot slipped on the glass-smooth rock beneath her feet as she put her weight down. Legs splayed, her hands clawing to find a fresh grip on the wet surfaces, she began to slide on her back towards the two men below her.

Hearing her cry, both looked round in time to see Ruth, her body gathering momentum, crashing towards them. Gripping onto a tree root with one hand, Leschenko swung round and grabbed at her arm as she hurtled past him. For a split second he was able to hold onto her – long enough to break the momentum of the fall and slow her down – before Ruth dragged him down after her. Throwing himself backwards out of their path, the Cossack allowed the two figures to roll past him and come to a halt ten feet further down. Sprawled in an untidy heap, a few feet from each other at the bottom of the drop, Leschenko and Ruth lay winded for several seconds. By the time Akim had picked his way carefully down to them, both were sitting up and recovering.

'Are you all right, Highness?' The anxiety in his voice was clear.

'Yes, thank you, Akim Timofeivich, my boot slipped,' Ruth gasped.

Looking across at Leschenko, she said, 'Thank you for grabbing me. Are you all right?' Her concern was genuine.

Leschenko's face was twisted in pain as he examined his left ankle. 'I don't know. I can't move my foot. I felt something crack when you pulled me off-balance.'

'Let me look,' grunted the Cossack. Although less than enthusiastic about their companion, Akim was careful and thorough in his examination of the ankle. 'I think it's badly sprained,' he said, more in annoyance than commiseration. This would slow them down. He had an arrangement with Magda, his wife, that this afternoon she would go to the bridge with the sleigh. If he were delayed she would return after dark. That they would not make the afternoon rendezvous he was certain, but he did not want to miss the later one and have to spend a night in the open.

Finding a stout tree branch at the edge of the water for Leschenko to use as a stick, they set off again. While Akim led the way the Latvian, supported by Ruth, hobbled along, making the best time he could.

By the middle of the afternoon, as the day began to lose its light, Akim judged they were still about a mile away from the road leading into Lubch. Leschenko was in poor condition. His ankle and leg were badly swollen and he was having great difficulty walking. Resting in the shelter of an outcrop of rocks at the side of the road, they agreed that Akim should go on ahead to meet his wife, and then return with the sleigh pony to carry the injured man. Watching the old Cossack's broad back striding off down the snow-covered track, Ruth felt vulnerable for the first time. She still had mixed feelings about Leschenko. It was quite possible that he had been in contact with the Russian whom she was supposed to have met, and that Simonov, fearing capture, had entrusted to him the list of Ochrana agents. If he were telling the truth, which she was inclined to believe, then he presented a problem. From what she knew of the Latvian and Estonian nationalist groups – or Anarchists, as they preferred to be called – they were badly organised and prone to acting first and thinking later; and their security was nil. Anyway, she reflected, this was not her problem now. Once back in Lubch he would become Grigoriy's worry. Slipping a hand inside her heavy sheepskin, Ruth closed her fingers reassuringly around the butt of the Mauser. If, on the other hand, he was a Russian spy . . .

Her reflections were interrupted by the man speaking. His harsh voice, tired and dulled by pain, had lost its arrogant edge. 'He calls you "Highness", yet I would wager money that you're not from this part of the world. Who are you?'

'If you're telling the truth then you may find out later. If you're an imposter it's irrelevant.'

'At least give me a name to call you by,' he insisted. After a minute's consideration she nodded. 'Ruth.'

'That's a Jewish name.' Leschenko sounded surprised.

'And who,' Ruth replied coldly, 'did you think that Uncle Sasha Simonov was coming to meet? The Hungarian cell of the Black Hand Anarchists?'

The Latvian looked thoughtful. 'I'd not known him for long. When the plot to kill the Tsar went wrong I made my escape. Being involved with the Terbatans was a huge mistake. They had been infiltrated for a long time, and it was just a matter of waiting for the police to round them up. I knew that Simonov had some sort of escape plan in place, so I asked him to take me with him. He agreed to get me through the mountains; after that I was to be on my own. It was only hours before we were due to leave the house that the police came. He knew it was hopeless. I escaped with his list, and he went into the study and took some strychnine.' When the woman did not reply he continued, desperate to convince her. 'It's the truth, I promise. I only thought of him as a political activist. It never occurred to me that he was working for a Jewish group.'

Ruth sat in silence, watching the track and fingering the pistol inside her coat. 'We'll see when we get to Lubch,' she said quietly. 'Until then, try to get some sleep while I keep watch.'

Nearly two hours passed, and the light was becoming poor when Ruth eventually spotted Akim Timofeivich returning along the path leading the sleigh horse. She stood up and stretched her aching limbs. The cold had got into her bones, and she was so stiff that any form of movement was a supreme effort. Waking Leschenko from the uneasy doze that he had fallen into, she helped him to his feet.

After perfunctory greetings had been exchanged, Akim glared at Leschenko and said to Ruth, 'There are problems, Highness. He is indeed wanted by the cursed Ochrana. Word has arrived ahead of us that Demkov has been arrested and police have been sent into the mountains. They'll have been held up at Klinsterpass, but as soon as it's open again they'll be here.'

Ruth was thoughtful. There was no telegraph through the mountains, which meant that for word to have travelled ahead of them Grigoriy and his associates must be using carrier pigeons. Provided that the bird did not succumb to the weather, it could cover the distance between Lubch and Stry in a matter of hours.

'What does Grigoriy want us to do?' she asked.

Jabbing a thumb towards Leschenko, and speaking low enough for only Ruth to hear, the Cossack whispered, 'We put him on the horse and take him to my barn. You, Highness, are asked to meet Grigorovich Yavlinskiy to discuss matters.'

Nodding her agreement, Ruth helped Akim to haul the injured man onto the horse's back, and they began to trudge back through the snow to where Magda was waiting by the roadside with the unharnessed sleigh.

In the kitchen of Yavlinskiy's cottage, Grigoriy paced nervously, the oil lamp on the table throwing his shadow back and forth. 'This is a total mess,' he said in an exasperated tone. 'We have to move him on within the next twenty-four hours, before the pursuit can clear the Klinsterpass and they arrive here in force.'

'May we just go over what we have got once more?' Ruth asked patiently. It had been a long day. She was very tired and wanted to sleep: she, Grigoriy and Lukeria had been talking for nearly an hour.

On their arrival at Akim Timofeivich's farmhouse, Grigoriy had been waiting to help them get Leschenko down from the horse and into the Timofeis' spare bedroom. Now that the Latvian was injured, it was no longer necessary to secure him in the barn. Akim and his wife remained at the house with their unwelcome guest while Ruth and Yavlinskiy returned to the Yavlinskiys' cottage to discuss the situation.

'First,' she extended the forefinger of her left hand, 'Simonov is dead, which is infinitely better for us than if he had been arrested.' Grigoriy nodded unhappily. 'Second,' her thumb shot out, 'the papers that he was going to bring with him are valuable and are now safely in your possession – which makes the mission worthwhile.' Ruth waited for a response. During the last hour she had realised it was going to be up to her to resolve their difficulties.

It was Lukeria who answered. 'Yes, without a doubt. The list gives the names of fifteen men and twelve women living in the Miskolcz area who are in the pay of the Russian secret police. Now that we have that information we can deal with them accordingly. Some can be quietly removed; others we will feed false information to. One of the most important is a man called Andrei Passalbessi, the stationmaster at Unghvar. He's obviously been monitoring strangers travelling through the district, which, unfortunately, also means that your presence here may have been reported.'

Ruth made a face. That could complicate the plan that had been forming in her mind. 'Third,' her middle finger joined the other two digits, 'it's now fairly safe to assume that Leschenko is genuine.' The others nodded slowly in agreement. 'So we now need to remove him and me from the region as quickly as possible.'

'Do you have a plan, Ruth?' Grigoriy Yavlinskiy sat down at the table with the women, a worried expression on his face. There were probably two, no more than three, local police officers and a couple of customs men in the small township. They all knew that in this isolated corner of the Habsburg empire a detachment of armed Russian police arriving out of the mountains would be able to do anything it wished.

Ruth's idea was simple. The following morning she and Mirka would pay their bill at the Kaiserhof and catch the mid-morning coach to Unghvar, where they would purchase rail tickets on the overnight train to Vienna. Meanwhile, Akim Timofeivich would take Lukeria and Leschenko in his sleigh to the railway station at Varanisz, a small town five miles up the line from Unghvar. There they would also board the Vienna train when it stopped to replenish its boilers and to pick up the mail and any rural passengers.

At some convenient point on the overnight journey Ruth and Lukeria would swap places, Lukeria arriving in Vienna with Mirka, and Ruth with the Latvian. Lukeria could spend a few days with relatives in the city before returning home, while Mirka would return to England by way of Cologne. Ruth and Leschenko would then continue by train across Austria into Switzerland. From there it was a day's journey to the great railway intersection at Basel, and on through France to one of the Channel ports.

One weakness in the scheme was that Leschenko would have to use the forged travel documents that had been obtained for the Russian tax collector. While the papers did not carry any description of the holder, Simonov was considerably older than Leschenko, which created a problem. Grigoriy studied the travel document closely. Giving a slow nod of his head, a satisfied smile replaced the worried expression on his face. 'The date of birth is shown as 3 May 1821. The ink is washable, so the figure two can be made into a five, to make him born in 1851,' he said, almost to himself. Catching the questioning glance that Ruth shot at Lukeria, the clerk continued, 'I served my apprenticeship as a printer. I worked for my father in Lemberg until he died and the authorities seized his business in lieu of what they described as "back taxes". The truth was that the regional administrator had been given an amount of cash by another printer, who was not Jewish, to ensure that the competition was removed.' The bitterness in his voice explained much to Ruth. 'This will take some careful work, but I can make the alteration undetectable,' he murmured.

Ruth wondered if Grigoriy was the forger who had originally prepared Simonov's papers. It would explain how he was so sure he could match the inks. It was, she decided, not her business, and she returned to the matter in hand. Once the date of birth had been altered there should, she mused, be few problems. The papers were made out in the name of Marek Birak, a representative of the Baczewski Liquor and Liqueur Distillery in Lvov. This choice of occupation meant that his travelling on the Austrian side of the Carpathians was normal – while an over-inquisitive official could be readily deflected with a bottle of Zubrowka or Wyborowa produced from his travelling case.

The general outline of the plan seemed to ease Grigoriy's anxiety to a certain extent. That he wanted Leschenko to be as far away as possible was obvious. 'It'll work,' he said. 'I'll have your hotel bill prepared and everything ready for you after breakfast tomorrow. The snow coach leaves from the square at ten o'clock and arrives in Unghvar in time for the six o'clock overnight train to Vienna.'

Ruth yawned and stretched her arms above her head. 'Good. And now, if you don't mind, I'll change into a dress and return to the Kaiserhof to get a night's sleep next door to my mistress.' The couple, noting the lateness of the hour, realised for the first time how tired Ruth must be.

Walking back through the silent streets to the hotel, Ruth and Grigoriy went over the details of their plan. She had not, he told her, been missed from her room by any of the Kaiserhof staff. The forthcoming military manoeuvres in the district had made the hotel busier than usual, so the fact that Madam Koroschenka and her maid had elected to eat in their rooms had passed unnoticed. Several times during the day he had removed the key to the room that Ruth was occupying in her guise of maidservant, replacing it later to make it look as if she had been coming and going on errands.

Entering the kitchens again with Yavlinskiy's duplicate keys, Ruth stole silently through the deserted corridors and up to her first-floor room. Within seconds a light tap on the door indicated that Mirka had been waiting for her return. Her maid stepped quickly into the room, and Ruth, sitting on the comfortable bed, quietly explained what had happened.

Like Akim Timofeivich, Mirka was sceptical about Leschenko. 'Even if he's genuine we can't take him with us,' she protested.

'Unfortunately we have to. If we leave him here it'll endanger the whole local operation. He'll be arrested, and so will anyone else in Lubch who can be connected to him. If he's not here when the Russians arrive they'll simply continue looking elsewhere.'

'You should have left him in the snow, down a crevasse,' Mirka snorted. 'As it is, we're going to have problems with his injury.'

Ruth had to agree. For all her abrasiveness, Mirka was not only a good friend but she was eminently practical. The Latvian's injury was something that needed to be addressed. 'This is what we're going to do. You'll go on to Vienna as arranged. Take the train and return home with your own papers as Mirka Sloboda. I'll take this man south and then west. I'm sure there'll be a train direct from Vienna central station through Linz to Salzburg and then to Innsbruck. It'll probably take two days, but by that time we'll be far enough away from here to have effectively disappeared. At Innsbruck, if necessary, he can rest for a few days in safety.'

Mirka scowled; she did not like the idea at all. 'It would be better if we all three travelled together,' she whispered urgently. 'What happens if you get into trouble with this babushka? It would be much safer if I were with you.'

Ruth turned it over in her mind. Mirka had a point – but three people would attract too much attention. No one remembered a couple.

'No.' She shook her head. 'We'll do it my way. He'll travel as my cousin, who's on business. After we leave Innsbruck it's only a day's travel to Basel. From there we can revert to our true identities. He'll be one of hundreds of émigrés fleeing to England.'

Although Mirka continued to protest, Ruth's mind was made up. Declaring the matter closed, she pulled off her long grey dress, the hem of which was soaking after dragging through the snowy streets, and within minutes she was sound asleep between the crisp clean sheets of the large double bed.

Letting herself out soundlessly, Mirka locked the door behind her and returned to her own room.

Chapter Eleven

Over a breakfast of coffee and rolls the following morning the two women confined their conversation to mundane matters, such as the deteriorating weather and their journey back to Vienna. As she was sipping the strong dark coffee Ruth noticed that they were the subject of a surreptitious scrutiny by an army officer at the next table. Lifting her eyes to look directly at the man, she saw that he was dressed in the day uniform of a Prussian Uhlan officer. He wore what was becoming known as a 'Kaiser moustache', the ends waxed to stiff points in the manner of the German Kaiser Wilhelm. The fact that he had a round, soft and flabby face with small eyes, and wore on his pudgy nose wire-rimmed pince-nez attached to a length of black ribbon, resulted in the slightly comic effect of a pig wearing spectacles.

Following Ruth's gaze, Mirka fixed the officer with a cold stare. Undeterred, he smiled politely at the women and returned his attention to his breakfast. The clatter of hooves in the street abruptly drew their attention to what was happening outside. Through the dining room window they saw a troop of soldiers in tall fur hats reining in their mounts. The long black Cherkeska tunics with crossed ammunition bandoliers, and rifles slung across their backs, were those of Cossack cavalry from the other side of the mountains. Without further ado Ruth and Mirka finished their coffee and left the dining room. The soldiers could only have come into the town through the mountains from Stry, which meant that the Klinsterpass had been re-opened much more quickly than Akim had anticipated.

Back in Mirka's room they swiftly checked that everything was packed and their trunk was securely fastened. A few minutes later a light tap at the door announced the presence of Grigoriy with their bill, accompanied by a porter who removed the trunk to the lobby ready for loading onto the coach. Ensuring that the porter was out of earshot, Grigoriy said, 'A company of Cossack troops has arrived. Some have gone to the square to check anyone arriving or leaving on the snow coach. The rest are in the kitchens at the back of the hotel being fed.'

'What about the others?' asked Ruth, worried by the new development.

Yavlinskiy grinned. 'Akim Timofeivich is a crafty old fox. He collected Lushka at first light in the sleigh. They'll be halfway to Varanisz by now.'

Ruth gave a sigh of relief. The untimely arrival of the Russian soldiers had unsettled her.

'The military manoeuvres are almost ended,' Grigoriy continued, 'which means there's a considerable amount of traffic in and around the town. It may help you to blend into the background. The coach has arrived, and the horses are being changed so it can make the return trip before it starts to snow again. You need to leave now.' Embracing the two women and wishing them a safe journey, he took his leave and returned to the hotel reception desk. Ruth was sorry that she would not see Akim Timofeivich before she left. She had grown very fond of the old Cossack, and would miss his reassuring presence in the days to come.

When they descended to the lobby Ruth and Mirka found it to be a hive of activity. Grigoriy was busy booking in some new arrivals, while several Austrian and Hungarian army officers wandered aimlessly round the reception area. The lieutenant in command of the Russian detachment, Ruth noted, was at the desk, examining the hotel visitors' book. As they were about to walk through the hotel's tall glass doors to board the coach, a figure hovering to one side approached them. Ruth gave a small grimace of annoyance as the stout Prussian officer who had occupied the next table at breakfast planted himself firmly in their path. He was, she saw, aged about fifty and quite short. His eyes, the pince-nez now removed, were a watery blue and bulbous.

Looking straight past Ruth, clicking his heels and giving a little bow, he addressed himself directly to Mirka. 'Madam Koroschenka, may I present myself. Colonel Franz von Rasche of the Imperial German Army.' The voice was unexpectedly guttural, lending a coarseness to the words. 'We are, I think, to be fellow travellers on the coach to Unghvar. May I be allowed to escort you?'

Ruth bowed her head slightly, interested to see how 'Madam Koroschenka' would deal with this unwanted companion. 'Thank you, Herr Oberst, but that will not be necessary.' Mirka made to continue towards the doors.

The colonel persisted. 'I am informed, Madam, that there is an armed and dangerous criminal at large in the vicinity. The good lieutenant over there has pursued him from over the mountains. While he's still at large I really feel that you would benefit from my protection.'

Ruth gently nudged Mirka. There could be an advantage in having the man with them until they arrived in Unghvar. No one would suspect two women in the company of a genuine army officer of being anything other than what they purported to be.

Mirka appeared to consider the matter for a brief moment before replying, ungraciously. 'Very well. My maid and I will be pleased to accept your company as far as Unghvar.'

The Russian at the desk is not the only one who has been checking the names on the hotel guest list, thought Ruth, as von Rasche bowed them out into the street.

In the square two of the Russian soldiers were checking the papers of the few passengers waiting to board the coach. Ruth handed her travel document to the one nearest to her. He was a thin, tired-looking man of about forty with badly snaggled teeth and in need of a shave. From the way in which he peered first at the paper in his hand and then at her, Ruth realised he could neither read nor write. Handing the paper back, the soldier gave a curt nod, and she climbed onto the coach step.

Doubtless because of his German uniform von Rasche was not challenged, and went to the back of the coach where a porter was stacking the passengers' travelling trunks.

'It looks as if you have an admirer,' Ruth chuckled to Mirka as the stout Prussian fussed about, checking that their luggage had been safely stowed.

'Pretentious little shit,' grunted Mirka, hauling herself onto the step and into the interior of the coach.

During the journey from Lubch to Unghvar the Prussian colonel proved to be every bit as boring as the women had anticipated. He was, it transpired, on the staff of General Alfred Graf von Schlieffen, and had been sent to the Carpathians as an independent observer of the war manoeuvres and exercises that had taken place during the recent weeks. By the time the coach drew up outside Unghvar railway station, the pompous little officer had spent over three hours alternately expounding his knowledge of Clausewitz's theories on strategy and lauding the military genius of his master, the Kaiser.

'Ah, Unghvar,' he proclaimed unnecessarily as the runners of the snow coach slithered to a halt. 'May I escort you to lunch, madam?' The glare that Mirka fixed upon him would have deterred a more sensitive man. Blithely the Prussian continued his approach. Smiling in a ludicrously conspiratorial manner, he leaned forward and continued. 'Although this is the most desolate of places, Madam Koroschenka, as a regular visitor to the region I'm well acquainted with one or two quiet little hostelries on the outskirts of town. Our train for Vienna doesn't depart for several hours.'

Ruth almost burst out laughing. The man had an unbelievable arrogance. He was a minor Prussian noble, brought up in luxury somewhere on the eastern borders of what was now the German empire, no doubt married to some fat countess who was living on the family estate with a string of children. This obnoxious buffoon was seriously propositioning a woman whom he had met only a few hours before.

To Ruth's delight, Mirka smiled broadly at the fat colonel and, looking deep into his piggy little eyes, said in a confidential whisper, 'Thank you, Herr Oberst, but I already have an appointment that will detain me for most of the remainder of the day.'

Von Rasche's obsequious expression was momentarily replaced by one of annoyance. With a polite nod of understanding he hauled himself from his seat and climbed out of the carriage, in readiness to hand the women down.

Mirka and Ruth grinned openly at each other. 'Oily little shit,' said Ruth.

A short distance from the railway station the women found a small tavern – der Adler – hidden from the main road in a narrow cobbled thoroughfare, along which the upper storeys of the ancient buildings leaned, almost touching. Safe from the attentions of Colonel von Rasche, they ordered a light lunch of Schnitzel, washed down with a chilled bottle of Moselle wine. Rather than draw attention to themselves by wandering aimlessly round the town until the train arrived, Ruth, feigning a migraine on her mistress's part, rented a room for the afternoon. Having finished their meal, Ruth left strict instructions with the innkeeper that her mistress's sleep was not to be disturbed, and they adjourned upstairs to discuss their plans for the rest of the journey.

The main problem that Ruth faced was what to do about Eugene Leschenko. Had it not been for his injury, she would have had no compunction about travelling to Vienna with him and then parting company. As it was, his papers in the name of Marek Birak had been hastily prepared and, while adequate to pass the scrutiny of any officials checking the passengers on a train, would not withstand careful examination, while his cover story was ill-prepared and very thin.

Ruth was uncomfortably aware that had it not been for Leschenko breaking her fall on the mountainside he would not now be injured. This unfortunate circumstance created a responsibility that she could not avoid. Although she disliked the idea, it was becoming apparent that she might have to take the Latvian onwards through France, and possibly even as far as England. In either of those countries his political status would not create a problem, and he could revert to his true identity.

Mirka was genuinely worried about leaving Ruth to travel across Europe with a man about whom they knew very little. 'When we get back to England, how are you going to explain why we've brought back an unauthorised escapee through the Pipeline? He isn't even Jewish!'

Ruth shrugged her shoulders in resignation. 'It's been bothering me, but I don't see any way round it. They'll have to accept that Simonov is dead and that he entrusted his papers to this man. The value of the list means we have an obligation to help him further.' She was oversimplifying matters, she knew. However, as a trusted agent of the Pipeline she had to be allowed the right to make decisions when an operation went wrong.

Soon after four o'clock they locked the room up and returned the key to the innkeeper. In response to his enquiry as to the state of Madam's health, Mirka smiled wanly and touched a hand to her forehead in a gesture of suffering.

As they were not due at the railway station until half past five, Ruth indulged Mirka by following her round the shops. From the time they had left Kelsford, Mirka had declared her intention of returning home with a genuine Russian samovar. In the confusion of the last few days it had completely slipped Ruth's mind, but now Mirka was intent on tracking one down.

The fourth shop they tried stocked varying sizes and shapes. Bearing in mind she would have to carry it, along with the heavy trunk, all the way back to England, Mirka took her time examining and peering into, under and around every item in the shop. It was almost a quarter past five before Ruth, accompanied by a highly satisfied Mirka, emerged from the shop clutching a polished, double-handled copper samovar.

To their dismay, at the entrance to the station, waiting for them in the covered area where horse cabs and coaches deposited their fares, stood the portly figure of Franz von Rasche, pince-nez dangling. Clicking his heels, he made a curt bow and dropped in beside them. Descending the steps to the platform, it was obvious that the train was going to be half-empty. A handful of heavily muffled passengers were waiting to board the train which, having turned round further up the line, was just pulling into the station, hissing steam and belching smoke.

More importantly, standing at the foot of the stairway with the stationmaster were two grey-clad Austrian police officers. The stationmaster must be the man whom Grigoriy had mentioned as being on Simonov's list, thought Ruth. What was his name? Andrei Passalbessi: that was it. A tall, cadaverous figure, he looked less like a spy or a police informer than anyone Ruth had ever seen. The question was, how much information did he and the police have? It could not be a coincidental routine check: they were looking for Leschenko and anyone who might be helping him to escape.

Gambling on the Prussian's pomposity, Ruth turned to von Rasche and said, 'Herr Oberst, could you wait a moment with Madam at the checkpoint? I have stupidly put our papers at the bottom of my handbag, and it may take me a minute or two to find them.'

'We'll not be waiting anywhere,' he asserted and, drawing himself up to his full height, strutted down the remaining stairs to confront the officials. 'I am Colonel Franz von Rasche, adjutant to General Alfred Graf von Schlieffen of the Imperial German Army. This lady is Madam Koroschenka. She and her maid are travelling in my company.'

'Do you have your papers, please, Herr Colonel?' the older of the two policemen asked respectfully.

A deep puce colour spread up the back of von Rasche's neck as it began to expand against the tight constraints of his high tunic collar. His voice rose to a hysterical bellow. 'I am a senior officer of the German Army. How dare you insult the uniform of the Kaiser! If you wish to question my authority, then you do so at your peril.'

As Ruth had hoped, the Austrian policemen immediately stepped back with profuse apologies, and, with much clicking of heels and saluting, allowed the party to sweep past unchallenged.

The night train to Vienna left Unghvar station on time at precisely six o'clock. Twenty minutes later, with a whooshing of steam and a squealing of metal tyres grabbing at the rails, the locomotive shuddered to a halt alongside the wooden platform at the rural station of Varanisz. Ruth watched intently as the engineer swung a long canvas hose from an overhead water tower to feed water into the engine's great boiler. A uniformed porter manhandled a large four-wheeled trolley laden with sacks of mail towards the guard's van at the rear of the train. With a surge of relief she spotted the slim fur-clad figure of Lukeria walking slowly across the platform arm in arm with the limping figure of Eugene Leschenko, who was leaning heavily on a sturdy walking stick. She lost sight of them as they moved out of her view along the platform, but a moment or two later they passed along the corridor as they sought an empty compartment. Ruth realised they had been watching out as the train pulled in, and had made sure they had boarded her carriage.

Loaded with mail, its boilers full, the train began its long journey north and west to Vienna.

Eugene Leschenko relaxed in the comfortable window seat and closed his eyes in an attempt to sleep. Seated opposite him in the other window seat, Lukeria looked tired and worried. As they were the compartment's only occupants they were both able to stretch out comfortably. Neither had slept much the night before and the early start had left them worn out. Within minutes Lukeria had slipped into a deep sleep, her head gently bumping against the window as the train gathered speed.

Sleep eluded Leschenko, however. Eyes closed and head back, his mind was busy. Up to now things had gone relatively well. Escaping from the Russian police had been his major problem. He still could not believe that he had been so fortunate as to have found his way into the Pipeline. When he approached Alexander Simonov for help he knew that the tax officer was involved in political matters, but had no idea he was a Jewish activist. It was, Leschenko thought, regrettable that it was his carelessness that led the Ochrana to the Russian. They had picked up his trail at Lemberg and followed him to Stry. It was, he mused, doubtful that they even knew Simonov was in the house when they arrived. As soon as he realised the police were at the door the old man's nerve had completely gone and he had panicked, certain it was him they had come for. However, Leschenko realised that the tax collector's suicide had provided adequate diversion to allow him to make his escape – and it was by no means certain that Simonov would have made the journey over the mountains.

After leaving Simonov's house, just minutes ahead of the police pursuit, Leschenko had hidden in a derelict barn for the night before making his way to meet the guide. Once he had shown Demkov the list of names that he was carrying, the Latvian had found little difficulty in persuading the Russian to take him to the rendezvous point on the western side of the Klinsterpass. Taking stock of his present situation, it was, Leschenko decided, Ruth who was the key to furthering his escape.

Once clear of the Zakarpatska region of the Carpathians, it was essential to his long-term plan that he pass unchallenged across the Habsburg empire into France, and thence to England. Leschenko allowed himself a small self-satisfied smile. England, the home of democracy and freedom, was fast becoming a Mecca for every displaced revolutionary in Europe. There he would be able to make contact with others in the Anarchist movement, and lie low for a year or two while formulating his plans for a free Latvia. Although he had no specific idea of where to go, Leschenko had been advised to make for an area of London known as Whitechapel. There, he had been told, men such as himself could live among fellow spirits in safety from the spies of the Ochrana, or the English police. One thing was certain, he thought: he would never again involve himself with maniac Poles such as the Piłsudski brothers, or incompetent bunglers like the Terbatan Group. In England he would establish his own Anarchist cell, and when the time was right he would return to Latvia as a political force to reckoned with.

As he eventually began to fall into a light doze, Leschenko's thoughts drifted towards the woman who seemed to be in charge of this venture. Who was she, this woman whom he only knew as Ruth? She was obviously well placed in this organisation. That she was now returning to England, a fact that Lukeria Yavlinskiy had let slip on the sleigh ride to Varanisz, exactly fitted his plans. He just needed to convince her to take him with her. Leschenko thought vaguely that somewhere along the way there might even be an opportunity to seduce her. He found her husky voice and full figure, which neither the man's clothing that she was wearing when they first met nor the travelling clothes she now wore could disguise, deeply exciting. Throughout his adult life Eugene Leschenko had found little problem in convincing women to succumb to his charms, and he saw no reason why this one should be any different.

Waking to a light tap on the compartment door, Leschenko realised he must have gone off into a deep sleep. An attendant had been along the train to light the small oil lamps hanging from brackets along the corridor. Through the glass panel of the door, thrown into dark shadow by the lamp directly outside the compartment, he saw Ruth. She tapped again, this time more urgently. Lukeria, also now awake, pulled back the door catch and admitted her. After an exchange of greetings, Ruth said, 'I must be quick. I've just slipped out to stretch my legs. There's a slight problem: we have an unwanted companion . . .'

Ruth explained about the Prussian officer. 'He was useful at the checkpoint, but if we're to change compartments we have to lose him somehow. It may be that we'll have to make the swap at the Vienna Bahnhof.'

Leschenko thought briefly. 'Wait and see how things develop. It's not urgent until morning when we reach Vienna. In the meantime I might be able to resolve the problem.'

'What have you in mind, Eugene?' Ruth asked. It was the first time she had addressed him by his Christian name.

'Leave it with me,' he said, still pondering the matter. 'I'll work something out.'

Ruth dozed fitfully as the train rattled through the darkened countryside. The constantly changing motion, as it clattered down one side of a gradient in readiness for the slow pull up the other, alternately lulled her into a light sleep before jolting her back into consciousness. Changing position to ease her aching back, she took out a small engraved fob watch from the change pocket let into the skirt of her travelling jacket. It was a quarter past two. Another four hours until dawn, and about eight before the train pulled into Vienna's Zentral Bahnhof. The constant motion, combined with the stuffy atmosphere in the compartment, was making her head ache.

As she settled back again into her seat she saw that the fat Prussian was watching her. He was wide awake, his porcine eyes moving from her bust-line to a point just above her knees. In response to her annoyed glare, von Rasche raised his eyebrows quizzically and gave a lascivious smile. On the point of saying something to him, Ruth thought better of it. In her role of maidservant, the German would consider her to be fair game for his attentions, and it would not be appropriate for her to speak out. Seeing that Mirka was sound asleep in the corner seat, Ruth decided to go out into the corridor to get some air.

Gathering her skirts together and pulling at the lapels of her jacket to straighten them, she stood up. Giving the smirking little man a cold stare, she slid open the compartment door and stepped into the dimly lit passage.

The train had slowed down again to negotiate another of the interminable gradients. Ruth pulled at the leather strap that released the window in the carriage door. As it dropped down, the blast of cold air took her breath away. The sudden gust caught the gently swaying paraffin lamp behind her, extinguishing the guttering flame and plunging her part of the carriage into darkness. Pulling on the strap, Ruth raised the window to its halfway position, reducing the flow of night air to a refreshing breeze on her face.

The blatant effrontery of the German officer irritated her. It was the fact that he displayed every courtesy to Mirka, but she, presumed to be a servant, warranted no civility whatsoever. Still seething over her inability to remedy the situation, and easing her aching head in the refreshing air, Ruth became aware that she was no longer alone: the portly figure of von Rasche had appeared next to her. As if wishing to share the breeze from the open window, he moved close, and calmly slid his arm round her waist. Smouldering with fury, she turned abruptly to face him. Instead of releasing her, von Rasche used the movement to bring them into a close embrace.

'Take your hands off me right now!' Ruth's outrage, bursting through in her angry tones, was pitched low and menacing.

'Or you will do what, Liebchen? Your mistress is fast asleep, and I am a senior officer of the Imperial Army. I mean you no harm, and I can assure you I will reward you well for any . . . favours . . . that we might share.'

The pudgy fingers of von Rasche's free hand caressed Ruth's cheek, running the backs of his nails gently down her cheek and along her jawline. At this proximity Ruth noticed the faint aroma of an expensive perfume that the little man was wearing. Inclining his head slightly to one side, he moved his face close to Ruth's in order to kiss her on the lips.

Turning her head violently to the side, Ruth spotted a movement further down the corridor. Leaning heavily on his stick against the swaying motion of the train, Eugene Leschenko was making his way along the carriage towards them.

Also aware of Leschenko's presence, von Rasche glanced down the corridor. The limping figure was now only a few paces from them. With a polite smile Leschenko murmured, 'Bitte sehr,' and made as if to pass them in the confined space.

Presuming that the passenger was making his way to the toilet compartment at the end of the carriage, von Rasche squeezed in closer to Ruth so Leschenko might pass. His left arm, still round her waist, dropped down slightly, and with his hand he took firm hold of her buttock, drawing her onto him.

At the same time that Ruth felt the stiffness of von Rasche's erection pushing against her, she saw over his shoulder that instead of moving past them Leschenko had taken a step back, and was steadying his balance with his left hand against the side of the carriage.

In horrified fascination, Ruth saw him reverse his heavy stick, take a two-handed grip and bring it down in a crashing arc on the back of the German's head. The sharp crack as von Rasche's skull fractured was audible. For a split second his eyes opened wide in shock and incomprehension, before the blankness of death filled them. The hand gripping Ruth's flank tightened in a momentary spasm, then fell loosely away.

Dropping the stick, and putting all his weight on his good leg, Leschenko threw an arm round the sagging body and, leaning against the partition wall, held the dead man upright. 'Open the carriage door,' he ordered. Frozen into immobility by what she had just witnessed, Ruth did not seem to hear him. 'Open the carriage door, woman – quickly, before someone comes!'

The urgency in his voice, and the likelihood that at any moment another passenger, inquisitive about what was happening, might appear from one of the compartments, galvanised Ruth into action. The heavy carriage door could only be opened from the outside. Leaning out into the night, she stretched her arm down the outer panel of the door and searched blindly for the latch. Within seconds her fingers were freezing in the icy slipstream. If she did not get the door undone very quickly, Ruth knew she would have to withdraw her arm and massage some feeling back into her hand, losing vital time.

Suddenly, feeling a recess in the panel, her extended fingers wrapped round the door latch and she pushed it sharply downwards. The catch released and the door swung dangerously outwards, throwing Ruth off balance. Grabbing at the inside frame to steady herself, she pulled herself back into the corridor. Taking hold of the lapels of the officer's tunic, she eased the weight of the body from Leschenko's grip.

'When I say "ready",' gasped the Latvian. Ruth nodded grimly.

On the word, in one concerted effort, they heaved the body out through the unfastened door. They were unable to believe their luck: any noise they were making was drowned by a long piercing whistle blast, signalling the approach to a tunnel. Snatching at the door, Ruth slammed it closed. Leaning her shoulders against the side of the carriage, with the increasing speed of the train vibrating through her shoulders and feet as it picked up acceleration in the tunnel, she began to feel sick.

Leschenko quickly checked up and down the corridor. They were alone: no lights under any of the compartment doors and no sound of movement, other than the rattle of the train wheels and the whooshing sound peculiar to trains passing at speed through tunnels. Relaxing, he gave Ruth a long slow smile. 'I said I'd deal with the problem,' he said, matter-of-factly.

Gazing at Leschenko in disbelief, Ruth pushed herself upright and grasped the doorframe for support as the train began to rock from side to side as its speed increased. 'Not like this, for God's sake. We'll have the entire Austrian police force on our trail when they find he's missing!' The moment of panic had passed and Ruth was now thinking clearly and quickly. The abhorrence of being involved in a murder and an awful fear of its consequences gripped at her stomach.

'Think it through.' Leschenko's usually harsh voice was soft and surprisingly gentle, considering that he had just killed a man in cold blood. His cold eyes, Ruth noticed, were burning with a deep fire, almost akin to sexual arousement. As if a great truth were being revealed, she knew that this was not the first time that Eugene Leschenko had killed. 'He was travelling alone. When he fails to arrive at the other end there'll be enquiries made and his luggage will be found. Some time in the next few hours or days – it doesn't matter – the body will be found. The injuries will be consistent with his having fallen from the train. An unfortunate accident. Even if foul play is suspected we'll have passed through Austria and be halfway to England before any enquiry begins.'

Leschenko paused. This was the first time he had spoken openly of going to England, and he wondered if Ruth had picked it up.

Ruth smoothed the front of her skirts with her hands, as if to brush away the memory of the Prussian's erect member pushing against the inside of her thigh. So, in the midst of everything else this strange, and obviously dangerous, revolutionary hoped to travel with her to England. That was something she would have to consider properly later on. At the moment it was a matter of some urgency that they leave the corridor before they were discovered.

Recovering his walking stick from where it had fallen, Ruth helped Leschenko into the compartment which until recently she had shared with Von Rasche and Mirka. Waking the gently snoring Mirka, Ruth sent her to fetch Lukeria so they could discuss the latest development.

Seeing them standing on the main platform at Vienna's Zentral Bahnhof the following morning, no one would have guessed that the three smartly dressed women and their male companion were anything other than fellow travellers bidding each other farewell at the end of a journey.

Once Lukeria and Mirka knew what had happened, they gathered up von Rasche's hand luggage and moved it into an unoccupied compartment in a carriage further down the train. When no trace of the officer's presence was left in the compartment that they had shared, Mirka moved into Lukeria's compartment and Eugene Leschenko settled in with Ruth, as arranged. From that moment Ruth and Mirka reverted to their true identities, their false Russian papers being torn up into tiny pieces and scattered from the moving train window.

As they said their goodbyes, Ruth was filled with a sadness that she would not see Lukeria Yavlinskiy again. In a matter of a few days they had become drawn together by a series of common bonds, not least of which being the murder of Franz von Rasche. Ruth could not believe that she had known the young woman for less than a week. 'Look after yourself, Lushka,' she said as they embraced.

Lukeria nodded, at a loss for words. From here she was to catch a tramcar to the home of a cousin who lived on the outskirts of the city. After spending a few days with her relatives, and laden with the shopping that would add substance to her visit, she would return home to Lubch.

Mirka, burdened with the heavy travelling trunk, was to spend a few days with the Schallmeiers while Joachim made travel arrangements for her return journey to England. It had been decided that Leschenko, travelling with Ruth as her cousin from the Ukraine, should keep his identity as Marek Birak until they were safely on a train from Basel to the French coast.

Returning to the station concourse, Ruth took one final look at her two friends. Mirka, putting down her newly acquired samovar, raised a hand and waved. All that was left was for Ruth and her charge to make the two-day rail journey to Basel.

Chapter Twelve

S itting in the driving seat of the two-wheeled gig, a light early summer breeze in his face and a Goodman's cigar firmly clamped between his teeth, Tom Norton was at peace with the world. The previous morning a note had arrived for him from Arthur Cufflin, the Shires Canal Company agent, requesting that they meet at the site of the Flixton canal cutting. Although it was short notice, Cufflin had suggested that it would be opportune. Tom had to admit that he was intrigued to know why Cufflin wanted to speak to him. It was over four months since the robbery had occurred and neither the police nor the canal company had made any noticeable progress in tracking down the culprits. As was usual in any such cases, the Kelsford police had confined their enquiries to the borough while the canal company had employed their own investigators to take the search further afield.

Fortunately Joseph Langley was away from work with a heavy cold and, as senior sergeant, Tom had not needed to seek permission from anyone else to meet Cufflin. Borrowing the gig and pony from his father, and exchanging his formal bowler hat for a smart new straw boater – the very sight of which would have given Joe Langley apoplexy, Tom reflected cheerily – he set off in the warm May sunshine for a morning in the country.

At first sight the canal workings at Flixton looked to Tom very much like one of the pictures he had seen of an American gold rush town. Pulling the gig off the road into an adjacent field, he tied the pony to the bough of an overhanging oak tree and strolled across to the gap that had been cut in the hedge to give access for the contractors' wagons.

Once through the hedge Tom climbed up to the middle of a newly constructed brick bridge that spanned the dry canal bed. From this viewpoint he spent several minutes taking in the scene laid out before him. The cutting ran away in an arrow-straight line, twenty yards wide and six feet deep, to a point about half a mile away where it veered in a gentle right-hand sweep out of view towards Kelsford. Spread out on the left-hand side of the newly laid towpath and extending into one of the nearby fields were several long wooden huts. These, he assumed, were primarily for the storage of tools and materials, while navvies who were not lodging in the town presumably slept in them. The smoke curling up from the tin chimney at the rear of the furthest hut indicated it was a cookhouse. Criss-crossing the trench at intervals were a series of plank bridges, over which an army of men trudged back and forth pushing heavily laden wheelbarrows. These they were tipping into the hopper of a steam hoist on the far bank, which was laboriously lifting the spoil onto waiting carriers' wagons.

A single line of narrow gauge railway track had been laid down the middle of the cutting to facilitate the removal of waste from the furthest ends of the workings. As Tom watched, a hand-operated trolley pumped by two navvies started its journey back along the track, laden with an assortment of tools and ballast.

'There are over a hundred men working on this stretch now, Mr Norton.' Tom turned to see the burly figure of Arthur Cufflin approaching. Joining him on the bridge, Cufflin leaned on the parapet to get his breath. Taking an old briar pipe and tobacco pouch from his pocket, he stuffed the bowl with a dark black twist. 'Water table's going to be a problem if we don't get it finished before the end of the summer,' he continued. Tom noticed for the first time that water was lying in the bottom of the wide trench beneath the plank walkways, almost reaching the cross-members of the railway track.

Tom nodded. 'And is the job going to come in on time, Mr Cufflin?' he asked politely. He had not seen the agent since the days immediately after the robbery, when he had interviewed him. The man appeared to have made a full recovery from his injuries, although Tom noted that the front teeth in his lower jaw were missing.

'That's what I wanted to talk to you about.' Cufflin gazed speculatively at the hopper, instinctively checking its rate of work. 'I've been in this business for longer than I care to remember, and there's something wrong with the way this dig is running.' Taking the pipe from the corner of his mouth, he glared at it in disgust. 'Bloody thing! I can't keep it in since I lost my teeth.' He thrust the dead pipe back into his pocket.

Tom offered Cufflin a cigar, taking one for himself. Inhaling the smooth tobacco smoke, his interest aroused, he said, 'Tell me about it.'

Cufflin looked directly at the detective. He was not sure that it was right to discuss this, but if he were to resolve his problems he was in need of an ally outside the company. 'First there was the robbery. That was never done for the value of the money. Had it been a quick snatch and grab in the street I might have believed it, but this was an organised thing. With the cash gone the men weren't paid until the following week, which in itself spelt trouble. Since then there have been several other things, like gangers demanding increased rates for certain jobs. And on both sites equipment keeps breaking down. The spoil contractor, Clancy Taft, is suddenly asking that his contract be reviewed because of what he calls unexpected haulage problems. It all adds up to outside interference. What I don't know is by whom.'

The hand-pumped trolley had reached the bend in the diggings and swung away out of sight. Tom considered what the agent was saying. 'Your men aren't local. Do they travel the country for the company, or do you recruit them for each individual job?'

Cufflin was watching the hopper again. The belt was temporarily halted while the carter levelled off his load before moving away to make room for the next wagon. 'It varies. Almost without exception they're from Ireland. Some come over here for a year to work for us on a particular job and then go back home with their money. They're usually family men. Others have been in this country for years and follow the jobs all over the place. I usually keep them as the core of each gang and supplement them with the casuals.'

'There are really only two likely causes of your problems,' Tom said, glancing round to ensure they could not be overheard. 'Either someone's trying to disrupt the project, or another company's attempting to sabotage the job with a view to taking it over. Do you have any political activists among the gangs?'

Cufflin relaxed a little; the detective was no fool. 'They all come here with a vision of an oppressed Ireland. They either want to escape for ever and live in this country, or earn some money and go back home to make it a better place. Every single one of them is political. The problem lies with the ideas that are fed to them by people with a vested interest in such matters.'

Tom's eye followed the two-horse wagon as it pulled away from the hopper. With a whoosh of steam the belt re-started, feeding muck and debris into the next cart. His mind went back to the visit he had made to Manchester central police station earlier in the year. He had spent the day with Detective Sergeant Vincent Millward, a man of about his own age with an impressive knowledge of the Irish situation and activists in the Manchester area. From what Millward had told him, it was obvious there was a problem on the mainland that was neither understood nor acknowledged, except by a very few police officers.

Controlled by powerful elements based in Ireland, a network of active political cells, dedicated to procuring a free Ireland, was being established in places such as Manchester and London. Organised on a military basis, each unit was under the command of an activist who lived permanently in England. Trained in the hotbed of violence that surrounded any such activities in their homeland, these groups financed their existence by crimes such as the Shires robbery. Tom had been startled and not a little disturbed. He remembered the incident in Dublin about five years ago – shortly after he joined the detective department – when the Chief Secretary for Ireland, Lord Cavendish, and one of his assistants had been murdered by a terrorist group in Phoenix Park on the outskirts of Dublin. At the time he had dismissed this as an internal affair, confined to the province. Millward made him realise he was wrong. The assassinations had been carried out by a group of Fenians known as the Invincibles, whose actions had caused a furore within the Irish fraternity and had lent strength to the movement for Home Rule, championed at Westminster by a Member of Parliament named Charles Parnell. It was in part this movement, agitating for the establishment of an Irish parliament, that was at the centre of the present difficulties.

Ranged against Parnell was the Irish Republican Brotherhood, which had been formed nearly thirty years before. This group, dedicated to achieving its aims by violence, was part of the Fenian movement, so called after an Irish armed force whose origins could be traced back to the times of myth and legend. The armed military wing of the Fenians was, Millward told him, known as the Irish Republican Army, and had been active in mainland England for many years. The sole objective of the Brotherhood was to organise a major uprising in Ireland, funded by criminal activities on the mainland. The information that the police had gathered concerning the Brotherhood's organisation was sparse. Obtained through rumour, and observations of known members, it amounted to remarkably little. Any gang members who were arrested proved singularly difficult to interview and almost impossible to turn into informants. On the odd occasion that a member of the Brotherhood was persuaded to speak about the group's activities, he had always disappeared without trace when released from police custody, presumably killed by his associates for passing information. The only other known fact was the enormous amount of support for the Fenians among the ex-patriot Irish community in America.

Vincent Millward was interested to learn the details of the Kelsford robbery, and not at all surprised at the possibility that arms and ammunition for the commission of the crime had originated in the United States. The dead man, Eddie O'Donnell, was well known to the Manchester police as a petty criminal, and had long been suspected of having an involvement with the Brotherhood.

The fact that a cartridge manufactured by Colt had been found on his body was, Millward felt, of enormous importance. 'It's inevitable,' he had said, 'that shipments of arms will begin to flood into this country from the States. Now that their own civil war is ended there's a huge armaments industry looking for a market. The manufacturers aren't bothered where the guns go, provided they're paid in cash. Once a system is set up here to receive and distribute the weapons it'll become big business.'

As part of the fight against the Fenians mounted by the small group of officers in Manchester, details of all passenger ships entering the port of Liverpool from anywhere in Ireland were supplied by the steamship companies, via the Liverpool police, to their office. It was a painstaking process. Anyone who travelled back and forth with any degree of regularity was scrutinised. Names of known suspects or the aliases that they used were searched for and noted. Most importantly, a small library of photographs of arrested suspects was being compiled.

The Irish Republican Brotherhood, according to the little that Vincent Millward's team knew of the group, was extremely active, and had a history of violence in the north of England and in London, and was thought to have been behind several recent robberies in the Liverpool and Manchester region and at least two murders. It was thought that the group was commanded in the northern part of England by a man known as William, or Liam, O'Dowd. Nothing except the man's name was known, and the Manchester police were desperate for more substantial details. Millward's information, put together from eavesdropping in public houses and overhearing conversations between prisoners in cellblock passages, indicated that O'Dowd was probably one of the most powerful men in the Brotherhood.

Tom had left Manchester with much to think about. It was, he thought, logical that in the course of furthering their interests the Brotherhood should expand into the Midlands. Kelsford, with its railway links and canal network creating a centre for transport and communications, was an ideal base.

Waiting on the platform for his train back to Kelsford, Tom was given one final piece of advice by Millward before they took their leave of each other. 'Tread carefully. These people are dangerous. One of your biggest problems will be in convincing your people that the organisation exists in your town. If they say a problem doesn't exist then it isn't a problem, but if they acknowledge its existence it becomes a problem.'

Returning his thoughts to the present, and exhaling a thin plume of blue smoke, Tom regarded Cufflin closely. 'Have you ever heard of an organisation called the Irish Republican Brotherhood?'

To his surprise the older man nodded. 'Yes. Everyone has: every Paddy who can swing a shovel. On a pay night the collectors go round each table for a subscription – a shilling a man.' Cufflin was amazed that the policeman had asked the question.

'No, everyone doesn't know about the Brotherhood,' Tom replied ruefully. 'You know because you work with Irishmen. I, on the other hand, have a lot to learn.'

Cufflin studied the glowing end of his cigar. So this was what it was all about. The Brotherhood. If they were operating in the Midlands it would explain a lot about his difficulties – but not everything. Still contemplating the cigar, he said, 'There's something else. Something I'm not sure about.'

Tom controlled his instinct to look at the agent directly again. Something in the man's tone told him this was important, and that Cufflin was unsure whether to speak or not. Continuing to stare ahead, Tom deliberately continued his scrutiny of the workings. The hopper had resumed the clattering delivery of its endless load. In the distance the trolley was returning down the rail, just one man on it this time. Throwing his cigar butt over the bridge, he said quietly, 'Go on.'

'We also have the contract to dig out the system for the canal basin and the warehousing project at the north end of the town. It makes sense, because we're responsible for taking this cutting through to the town and do all the linking up at that end. The construction work there is a very big job – digging out, putting in underground water tunnels to feed water from the back of the canal loop into the basin and building the wharves. As the Shires has got all the necessary manpower and equipment in place we were the obvious choice to take the warehousing contract. And, although we won't do it ourselves, we've agreed to be responsible for subcontracting the erection of the offices and warehouses.' Tom remained silent, waiting for Cufflin to continue. 'One of the reasons I asked you to meet me here this morning is because a group of the backers and some bank officials are coming over – any time now – to have a look at the way this end of the job is progressing. It's not unusual for a group of money men to put up the capital for this type of a project, as an investment. But what I don't like is that they're saying we must use a particular quarry over in the Hope Valley, Batsford Stone, for all the hardcore on the dig, the foundations and the stone for top-dressing the buildings. I know Batsford Stone. They're a sound enough company, Mr Norton, but they're much too small to supply the amount of material we'll need. I've explained this to my directors, but they say the backers are paying and that if it goes wrong it's up to them.'

'I don't know much about the construction business,' Tom replied warily. 'I'm afraid you're going to have to spell it out for me.'

'I've seen this done before,' Cufflin explained. 'The company in question is working beyond its means, so it doesn't have the resources to supply the materials that are needed. The client is asked for a cash advance to purchase the shortfall in materials. Once a supply from other companies has been sub-contracted they declare the original company bankrupt and pocket the cash advance. This means that in order to secure the materials – which they can't manage without – the client has to pay for them a second time; and if that's not possible, that company in turn is declared bankrupt.'

Tom rubbed a hand across his jaw and fished in his pocket for the flat leather cigar case. 'And you think that's happening here?'

Cufflin took the proffered cigar and touched a match to it. 'Yes. This move to control where the contracts lie is suspicious. It's usually a fraud worked by the supplier, but what I find worrying is that it appears to be the backers themselves who are setting this up.'

A group of people had begun to merge from the gap in the hedgerow: five men and a woman. The men, led by Joshua Howkins, were attired in top hats and morning coats, while the woman – who Tom recognised as Ruth Samuels as she drew nearer – wore a straight grey skirt and matching jacket with puffed sleeves over a high-collared white blouse.

'It looks as if your guests have arrived,' Tom said quietly, although they were still well out of earshot. 'What do you want me to do about this?'

'Nothing at the moment,' replied the agent. 'I need to know you're aware of what might be going on. If anything definite comes to light I'll contact you.'

'Fine. In the meantime it might be helpful if I stay for a while and become acquainted with your backers.'

Declining Max Peters' arm, Ruth Samuels hitched the skirts of her long dress up a few inches and strode purposefully ahead of him towards the entrance through the hedge. That this was neither ladylike nor polite did not for the moment bother her. She was furious with Peters, and had this not been a business meeting with a group of wealthy clients she would have had no compunction about starting a row there and then.

Since her return from Russia Ruth's relationship with her co-directors, and Max Peters in particular, had been uneasy. The journey back from Vienna with Eugene Leschenko had been surprisingly uneventful. As she had planned, Ruth made a stopover at Innsbruck for three days in order to allow the Latvian to rest his ankle, which with constant use had become extremely painful. Although the injury was still far from mended, the short recuperation allowed Leschenko to complete the journey to Dover, where Ruth gave him a small amount of money for living expenses and put him onto a train for London.

An assiduous search of the newspapers had, on the third day after they left Vienna, resulted in Ruth finding a small piece in a local Swiss paper concerning the death of von Rasche. The report merely stated that the body of a German officer had been found by a shepherd at the foot of an embankment in a remote mountain area of the Zakarpatska to Vienna railway line. With typical military paranoia, the report gave neither the officer's name nor the exact location. The report concluded that it was a freak accident; he had somehow fallen from the night train travelling to Vienna.

As far as Eugene Leschenko was concerned, Ruth sincerely hoped she would never see him again. During the time she had spent alone with him, Ruth had come to thoroughly dislike the man. His cold, arrogant manner, and the fact she had seen him kill von Rasche for no other reason than his presence being an inconvenience, made her wary of him. His conversation consisted of long rambling monologues concerning the future of his country and its political leadership, interspersed with vociferous diatribes against the Russian state and the Tsarist regime. At one point, during their stay at Innsbruck, he had made a half-hearted advance that she had quickly rebuffed. Ruth had deliberately taken single rooms at the Franzkaner Hotel, which was near the railway station and large enough for them to pass unnoticed. On the second night, while she was dressing to go down for dinner, Leschenko let himself into her room on the pretext of discussing how he should best seek out contacts in London. Seated in front of her dressing table, pinning up her hair, she had watched him in the mirror as he moved up behind her as if to continue the conversation, then bent over to kiss the back of her neck. Curtly she had brushed him off, telling him that if he wished to see England he was never to do it again. As she had expected, far from being embarrassed at the rebuff the Latvian had merely appeared to be mildly annoyed, and had returned to his own room. As with von Rasche, it was more the casual presumption that annoyed Ruth rather than the action itself.

Back in Kelsford, the fact that the mission had not gone as planned was accepted philosophically by her Pipeline co-conspirators. It was readily conceded that on an operation such as this things could go badly wrong, and Ruth's action in bringing Leschenko back to England in order to ensure the security of the Carpathian network was not questioned. It was, however, developments at the bank that had caused problems. The warehousing project had, during her absence, progressed at a faster pace than she might have wished. The original loan and a further £10,000 had been authorised, bringing the bank's commitment to £30,000. It was not this that had led to a deterioration in relations between Ruth and her partners, but that between them Max Peters and Joshua Howkins had managed to persuade the board of directors, Solomon Meyer and Jakob Peters, to hand over management of the bank's involvement to Max.

'Ruth, it isn't relevant who represents the bank; it's the fact that the business is transacted successfully that matters.' Solomon had tried to placate her when she was told of the change at the first board meeting she attended after her return. The reason was, he explained, that this all-male group of financiers preferred to do business with another man, especially as one of them was an American who was not used to concluding business deals with a woman. Ruth was in no mood to be mollified and the meeting was concluded – as was inevitable – with her acceptance of a *fait accompli*, while secretly vowing to settle her grievances with Max Peters at a later date.

The reason for her current ill temper was that on the way out to the dig Max had calmly informed her he had been offered a place on the board at the end of the current financial year, in view of his recent success in brokering the warehousing project. Ruth was speechless. As a board member she could not believe she had not been consulted in such an important matter. It was another example of Meyer and the older Peters making decisions behind her back and telling her afterwards – except that on this occasion the beneficiary of their collaboration could not keep the secret. When, she wondered, would they have told her? Probably in a few months' time – at the opening of the Kelsford Warehousing Company's newly completed premises, as a celebration of the bank's success.

Stepping purposefully through the hedge onto the towpath she was met at the foot of the bridge by a stocky middle-aged man who introduced himself as the agent for the Shires Canal Company. The agent was accompanied by a tall smartly dressed man of her own age wearing a straw boater, whom she recognised as Sergeant Norton of Kelsford Police.

That Mrs Samuels had walked on ahead of her companions, combined with the expression on her face, was not lost on Tom. He doubted she was naturally of a sour disposition, which left the obvious conclusion that something had happened, probably on the short journey from Kelsford, to spoil her humour.

By the time Cufflin had introduced himself, and Tom and Ruth had exchanged polite greetings, they were joined by Howkins and his group, who were being ushered along by Max Peters. They were a mixed bunch, Tom thought. Howkins was a tiny, doll-like man, standing not much over five foot three inches tall. His narrow unsmiling face, white hair and neatly trimmed snowy beard gave him the appearance of a bad-tempered goblin. In contrast, the man introduced to the gathering as Brewitt Gotheridge looked more like a prosperous bookmaker. A heavy paunch bulged against his tight waistcoat, pushing the wings of his morning coat back so that the expensive garment was impossible to button up. The red face and fleshy nose told of good living and a predilection for strong spirits. Oswald Langran, the third member of the group, was less easy to assess. Of medium height, clean-shaven and immaculately dressed in his light grey morning suit, he was of indeterminate age and could have been anything from a shop manager to a banker. What Tom did not know was that this was not an inaccurate assessment. Langran had begun his career forty years previously as an assistant in a Northampton shoe shop. By dint of thrift and a sound business ability he had, at the age of fifty-three, become the owner of a chain of boot and shoe shops throughout the Midlands, and a very rich man into the bargain.

Peters was introducing the fourth and last of the backers to Cufflin. 'May I present Mr Sangster, he represents our overseas interests . . .' From the expression on her face Ruth Samuels was about to explode, Tom thought. Apparently the term 'our overseas interests' did not sit well with her.

Sangster, a large man, almost as broad across the shoulders as Cufflin himself, removed the half-smoked cigar from the corner of his mouth with his left hand while pumping Cufflin's with his right. 'Pleased to make your acquaintance, Mr Cufflin,' he boomed in a deep baritone, which must have carried to the other side of the workings. Replacing the chewed cigar, Sangster gazed appreciatively at the activity taking place around him. 'You've hit the water table from the looks of it. Will you be able to get out of here before the rain stops you?'

Cufflin looked at the man with a degree of interest. 'Oh I think so, sir. Are you an engineer yourself?'

Sangster made a gesture. 'I've done a bit of mining back home. The goldfields of California when I was younger.' He laughed amiably. 'You've got to get your hands a bit dirty before you get your hands on dirty money.'

The group, with the exception of Ruth, laughed politely at the American's little joke. Mrs Samuels, Tom observed, busied herself with straightening her already immaculate skirts. Excusing himself as Cufflin prepared to show the group round the site, he made his way over to the opposite bank where a gang was fixing stone edges into place alongside the towpath. The long stone blocks were too heavy for one man to move on his own, and while a workman busied himself cementing one into place, the ganger supervised the careful lowering of the next block by three labourers, who were using ropes to support it. Tom stood behind the foreman to watch as, with practised skill, the four foot long square-cut block was dropped precisely into position in readiness for mortaring. As soon as the stone was in place the men roped up a fresh one from the pile further along the path. The foreman straightened up, turning to face Tom. In his early fifties, his weather-tanned face, broken nose and twinkling blue eyes were framed by a huge grey beard shot with white. The whole was surmounted by a battered black bowler hat, while his torn suit jacket, originally of the same colour as the hat, was grimed beyond repair with mud and dust.

'Morning,' said Tom pleasantly. 'Do these go all the way along the dig?'

George Taft, known to one and all as 'Clancy', smiled amiably back at him. 'No. They'll go as far as the lock over there.' He indicated the great pit being dug some thirty feet further along. 'Other than at the locks, we only put them in where barges are going to tie up. We'll be putting iron bollards in next for the boat ropes to lash onto. You'll be with the party from the bank, will you, sir?'

Tom nodded. The foreman had a pleasant southern Irish accent which perfectly matched his tough and battered appearance. 'Yes, just having a look round. This is the first time I've been out to the dig.'

Clancy Taft smiled again. And you're a lying bastard, he thought. He had first noticed Norton on the bridge in deep conversation with Cufflin, and had immediately recognised him as one of the two policemen whom he had seen in Edie Knapp's just before Christmas. That he was 'just having a look round' Clancy had no doubt. The question was, why was he snooping? What was he talking to the agent about?

For the next five minutes Tom and the Irishman discussed what was happening at the workings, and how the deep lock construction, for which Taft was also responsible, was undertaken. With the return of the labourers, a new stone block slung on a pole between them, Tom took his leave and allowed the foreman to return to his work.

Making his way back to the other side of the canal, he joined the main party at a trestle table that had been set up outside the canteen hut with refreshments. A small, shifty-looking man with a twisted face was busily handing round a tray of drinks. Taking a glass of chilled white wine from the proffered tray, Tom moved to one side and stood alone, watching the men working on the dig. There was, he thought, something vaguely familiar about the little man; he had seen him before but could not place where.

As he was idly turning the matter over, Ruth, seeing that he was alone, strolled over. She was, he thought, an extremely attractive woman – not pretty by any means, but definitely attractive. 'You're a long way from home, Mr Norton,' she said pleasantly.

'In what respect, Mrs Samuels?' asked Tom, not sure whether she was making an idle comment or referring to his being out of place in the present company.

Ruth flushed slightly. 'I was under the impression that the jurisdiction of Kelsford Police didn't extend beyond the town. I was merely curious that you were so far from home.'

Aware that he had embarrassed her, Tom regretted being unnecessarily abrupt. 'You're right. I'm sorry, my mind was on other matters.' He gave his most charming smile. 'It was a beautiful morning and I had time on my hands, so I decided to take a drive out to see how the canal was progressing. I had no idea there was to be a party of visitors here.'

'We're not exactly visitors. My partner and I have come out on behalf of the bank to meet some of the businessmen involved in the project.' The tall and rather good-looking policeman interested Ruth. She knew from conversations with Henry that Thomas Norton was a pleasant and well-respected man among his colleagues. That she had got off on the wrong foot with him was unfortunate; Ruth did not like offending people unnecessarily.

'Can I get you a drink, Mrs Samuels?' Tom made a small gesture with his hand to the waiter, who was hovering nearby.

Ruth shook her head. 'Thank you, but no. I have work to do. You're fortunate to have a free morning to enjoy the sunshine.'

Tom did not have a free morning. Langley was away, and now he had spoken to Cufflin there was no point in staying. 'Unfortunately I don't have that much time. I slipped away for an hour's peace and quiet, but I think I should get back.'

On the spur of the moment, Ruth said, 'If you're returning to Kelsford perhaps I could beg a lift with you. My own business is concluded, and I don't particularly want to be delayed by the social gathering. It would be a great help if you could oblige.'

Tom readily agreed, and after a short and what appeared to be terse conversation with Max Peters, Ruth rejoined him to be escorted to the waiting gig. On the short journey back into town Tom found himself warming to the woman. They discussed the progress being made with the canal, and how it was likely to influence the town's future. He was particularly impressed by her detailed knowledge of the project, and which businesses and properties would be affected by the canal's opening. It was a long while since he had chatted so amiably with a woman, especially one as well informed and personable as Ruth Samuels.

All too soon the pony was clattering along Victoria Road towards the large house at the corner of Holmwood Road. Jumping down at the gate to help Ruth from the tiny carriage, Tom looked up at the rounded slate roof on the corner. 'This is a beautiful house,' he said admiringly.

'Yes it is. My late husband had it built before we were married. The wing with the rounded roof that you're looking at was added a few years later, I would think about sixteen years ago.' As Tom climbed back into the gig she added, 'You and your wife must come and visit some time, Mr Norton. Please come for dinner one evening.'

Tom smiled down as he picked up the reins. 'Thank you, Mrs Samuels, that would be nice, but unfortunately I'm a widower.' Raising his boater politely, Tom clicked to the horse and gently slapped the reins across its back.

Damnation, thought Ruth as the pony cart clopped away, how could I be so stupid? As soon as she made the invitation she remembered that Henry had told her that Tom Norton's wife had died a couple of years ago.

Ruth had enjoyed Tom's company. Heaven knows, she thought as she went into the house, there are few enough men about whom you can say that!

Pulling the gig into the yard of the Rifleman, Tom was still thinking about the dark-haired woman. He had little difficulty admitting to himself that the ride back from Flixton, pressed close to Ruth Samuels on the narrow seat, had been particularly pleasant. It was, he mused, the first time he had been in such close proximity to a woman since Kate died. He had never bothered to seek the company of women for casual interludes, and on this occasion he had not intentionally sought out Mrs Samuels. Probably, he decided, it was the chance nature of their meeting that had made it so pleasant.

As for accepting a dinner invitation, that would most definitely not be sensible, knowing what he did about her and Henry Farmer. The last thing he wanted was for Henry to think he had a rival. Idly, Tom wondered if anyone else had worked out that the two were having an affair. He thought not. Henry, always a discreet man, never discussed such things with anyone, and Tom doubted she would want the fact known. A sudden thought intruded: did Langley know? Tom decided he might – not for any reason other than that Langley knew everything about everyone, especially if it concerned those who worked for him.

Unharnessing the pony, Tom took him into the stable to brush and feed him.

Chapter Thirteen

J oseph Langley was not sure what it was that awoke him. Lying in bed, sleep clouding his brain, he was aware that it was still dark in the room, and that a pleasant night breeze was blowing through the partially open window. A soft scratching noise in the far corner of the room brought him fully awake. At first he wondered if it was a trick of his imagination. Lying perfectly still, he waited to hear the sound again. It seemed as if several minutes had passed before his now alert senses detected a small movement in the corner near the dressing table.

Moving his head just sufficiently to allow his eyes to focus on the source of the movement, Langley found his gaze returned by two tiny pinpoints of amber light glaring balefully at him from out of the darkness. Its attention attracted by the man's slight movement, the rat froze and watched him patiently, as if daring him to make the first move.

Beads of perspiration broke out on the old man's forehead. He could not believe that a rat had found its way into his bedroom. Moving only his eyes, he glanced at the bedroom window. The breeze had died down and the curtains hung limply in the humid atmosphere. The window was raised no more than a couple of inches but that was, he knew, sufficient. Out scavenging, the inquisitive rodent had found little difficulty in squeezing through the aperture. Desperately, Langley tried to overcome his terror and gather his thoughts. If he lay perfectly still it was just possible that the rat would lose interest in him and exit by the same route. He immediately dismissed the hope: he knew it was not going to happen.

Looking again at the corner of the room, he choked back an involuntary cry. The eyes had been joined by another malevolent pair. Dear God Almighty, there were two of them! The first rat, sensing the fear emanating from him, had become sufficiently emboldened to move very slowly in his direction. Reaching up on its hind legs, it gripped the counterpane with its tiny forefeet and, like a sailor swarming up a rope, pulled itself nimbly onto the foot of the bed.

Almost passing out with terror, the old man lay perfectly still, hypnotised by the bright little eyes, six feet away from his face, gazing unwaveringly at him. The rat was, he saw in the dim light, large and grey, not much smaller than a domestic cat. Its long pink tail twitched obscenely back and forth across the bed, tiny sharp teeth framed by long grey whiskers pushing out from under the top lip of its tightly clenched jaw.

The rodent remained motionless, deciding what its next move should be. There was a slight scuffling noise and it was joined on the counterpane by its companion. This, Langley saw to his horror, was an even larger and heavier specimen – obviously the male. While the female, nose twitching, unblinkingly held Langley's gaze, her mate began inching purposefully along the bedclothes towards his face. Bathed in icy perspiration, his eyes bulging with an uncontrolled terror, Langley was only vaguely aware of the hot wetness on his legs as his bladder emptied. With a breathtaking swiftness, the rodent leapt the last two feet and landed full on his face, clawing for a grip at his beard and nose. It was joined a fraction of a second later by its fellow, this time tangling in his hair in its efforts to sustain a grip.

Langley's thin and piercing screams instantly awoke his wife in the next room. They carried through the open window to the street beyond, bringing a sleeping vagrant in the doorway of Foster's grocer's shop lurching to his feet, and freezing into the stillness of their bed the young couple making love in a bedroom nearby.

'Mr Langley is ill. He's not coming in today. In fact he won't be coming back to work again.' Tom listened to the head constable's words, without fully comprehending what he was saying. Langley ill? Not coming back? He had been all right the previous day when Tom had spoken to him.

When Tom had arrived ten minutes earlier for his day's duty he found Fred Judd waiting in the detective office, with an instruction that Mr Archer Robson wished to see him immediately. Judd, an expression on his face that hovered somewhere between concern and satisfaction, refused to answer any questions, merely reiterating that the head constable was waiting. Ushering Tom through the door, Judd said cryptically, 'Come to my office on your way back down. Then we can talk.'

Standing in front of the head constable's heavy polished mahogany desk, Tom waited in silence for the explanation that he knew was about to follow. Carefully weighing his words, Archer Robson sat back in his chair and folded his hands in his lap. 'During the night – about a quarter past two to be precise – Inspector Langley suffered a severe attack of *delirium tremens*. His own doctor attended, along with Dr Mallard, and they have had him committed to the asylum. I was summoned by Dr Mallard, and we've decided the inspector will not be returning to work again. I have an appointment with the chairman of the watch committee at ten o'clock this morning when I shall arrange for his retirement to be confirmed. The reason given publicly will be that he has had a breakdown.' Whatever the truth of the matter, Archer Robson had no intention of announcing to the world at large that one of his most senior officers was a hopeless alcoholic. Tom, inclining his head slightly, remained silent; there was obviously more to come. 'In view of what has happened, Mr Norton, I am promoting you to the rank of inspector. You will now take over as head of the detective department.'

Tom was stunned. Although he had turned the idea over in the past, and others seemed to have taken it for granted that he would one day succeed Langley, he had never seriously considered the prospect. Archer Robson stood up abruptly and held out his hand. 'You will have a lot of things to attend to, Mr Norton,' he said, in polite dismissal.

After the door had closed the superintendent sat for some time, beaming contentedly at the picture of the old Queen hanging on his wall. She in turn glared disdainfully back at him. It was, he reflected, worth being turfed out of his bed at four o'clock in the morning to be told that Joseph Langley was being taken away slobbering to the lunatic asylum. Now, relieved of the old man's malign influence, perhaps he could bring about some of the changes he had previously been unable to achieve. With Thomas Norton and Frederick Judd as his deputies, Archer Robson intended to restructure Kelsford's police force. No longer would his every action be blocked by Langley and his political cronies on the watch committee.

Opening his desk drawer, Archer Robson took out a single sheet of paper, a handwritten note dated 15 April 1888. The elegant copperplate script, addressed to 'My Dear Joseph', briefly thanked the recipient for his assistance in presenting such evidence to the magistrates as was needed to secure the termination of the licence, and subsequent closure, of the Black Dog in Chandler's Lane. The note ended with a short paragraph informing Langley that if he cared to call in at the offices of the Kelsford Bank of Commerce a package of one hundred shares in the Kelsford Warehousing Project was awaiting his collection. The signature at the bottom of the letter was that of Joshua Howkins.

The head constable's smile became one of deep satisfaction. While the attendants were bundling a babbling Langley into the waiting hansom cab, he had quietly taken his leave of the doctors and Langley's distraught wife and made his way through the deserted town to Long Street police station. Slipping in through the back yard, unseen by the night staff and using the office keys on the ring that he had slipped into his pocket from Langley's bedside table, he let himself into the detective inspector's office. During the next hour Archer Robson made a thorough and careful search of Joseph Langley's desk and filing cupboard. By half past six, the early morning sunlight streaming through the window, Robert Archer Robson was seated at his own desk, carefully sorting through a thick pile of the old man's personal papers and stacking on one side those he had read. The Scotsman placed the one he was now rereading securely in his desk drawer.

The Black Dog was, he knew, a run-down and disreputable hovel situated at the end of a stinking alley on the north side of the town. As police court officer, Archer Robson had recently presented to the licensing justices a file of evidence, prepared and signed by Langley, to the effect that it was a long-established brothel and, as such, should be closed down as a disorderly house. Despite the licensee's protests, the magistrates had accepted the evidence without question and terminated the licence. It interested the head constable that the Black Dog stood on land that the Kelsford Warehousing Project needed to acquire before the canal basin could be completed.

Archer Robson looked across at the ticking clock on the wall over the fireplace. From the opposite side of the room Queen Victoria, a glazed expression on her face, was also staring at the timepiece. It was five minutes before ten. Any moment now the chairman of the watch committee would be arriving. That he would already have been informed by other sources of the recent turn of events Archer Robson had no doubt, but it was his duty as head constable to report the matter officially to the watch committee. More importantly, he wished to tell the chairman personally of his decision about Langley's successor, and on this occasion, he mused grimly, there would be no argument.

A soft knock was followed by Frederick Judd's bearded figure in the doorway. 'Mr Howkins is here to see you, sir,' he announced.

By the middle of the morning Tom had cleared his desk and removed his possessions to his new domain. Everyone at Long Street was now aware that Joseph Langley was not returning and that Thomas Norton was the new detective inspector. Among his immediate colleagues, Sam Braithwaite, Jesse Squires and Henry Farmer, there was an atmosphere approaching euphoria. While Sam was gleefully planning a party to celebrate the promotion, which Tom knew he could not avoid, Henry and Jesse individually and privately came to see him in the inspector's office to pledge their allegiance. Both were pleased he had been given Langley's job, while at the same time acknowledging that, with Tom's altered situation, their relationship must change.

For his own part, after a brief and cordial meeting with Fred Judd, Tom spent the larger part of the morning stowing away his papers and personal effects in the desk drawers and cupboards, wondering how on earth he was going to fill up his newly acquired space. He was mildly puzzled by the complete lack of personal documents, which, in view of Langley's sudden departure, he would have expected to find. It was, he thought, almost as if someone had been in before him and cleaned up.

Soon after midday Tom decided to have a lunch break and take a walk in the sunshine down to the Rifleman to share his good fortune with his sister and his parents. Lifting his grey bowler from its hook on the coat stand just inside the door, he caught sight of Langley's heavy walking stick propped next to a filing cupboard. Picking it up, he hefted it in his hand to feel the weight and fine balance of the dark Malacca wood. For the first time he had the opportunity to examine the stick closely. It was, he surmised, very old, probably something that Joe had acquired by dubious means many years before. The solid silver head was shaped to fit snugly into the palm of the hand; twisting it, Tom half-expected to find that he was holding a sword stick, but nothing happened: it was simply a very nice walking stick. About to replace the cane in its resting place, Tom changed his mind. Langley's reign in the town had ended, and the fact needed to be signalled to those who mattered. Carried with him wherever he went, the silverheaded cane had over the years almost become his badge of office. In which case, Tom decided, it could continue to be exactly that – a badge of office.

Fixing his hat firmly on his head, he tucked the cane under his arm and strolled happily through the front door of the station into Long Street, and off towards the Rifleman.

While Tom was celebrating his promotion over a pint of porter with his father and sister, ten miles away in a deserted barn a meeting of a different sort was taking place. The three men, seated on packing cases that had been drawn up to form a circle on the cleanly swept floor, were intent upon their discussions, safe in the knowledge that the only approach to their hideaway, a narrow track, was protected by two armed men, while two more were covering the blind side towards the canal.

Liam O'Dowd leaned forward. In the dim interior of the barn his dark saturnine features and unshaven jaw made him look more like a swarthy Spaniard than a native of Erin's Green Isle. Picking up the half-empty bottle of Bushmills, he held it out. Connor Devlin and Lucas Sangster both tendered their glasses for refills.

O'Dowd replaced the bottle beside him and indicated, with a small movement of his hand, the contents of the barn behind him. 'There are fifty-four cases of Winchester .45 calibre repeating rifles stacked up by that back wall, along with ten cases of ammunition. Every one of the cases contains fifty boxes of one hundred rounds each, making a grand total of fifty thousand rounds.' He regarded the other two men questioningly; neither interrupted him. 'It's taken us two weeks to bring them down here from the Pool in two separate barges, travelling a day apart.' Catching the questioning glance that Sangster shot at Devlin, he added quickly, '"The Pool" is Liverpool.'

Sangster grunted; he would never understand this god-damned Limey lingo. He glared down at the chewed cigar butt in his hand. Although he was longing for a smoke to go with the excellent Irish whiskey, there was no way he dared light it with the boxes of ammunition stashed round him.

'For the moment they remain here under guard.' O'Dowd resumed, speaking now to Devlin. 'Later we move them into one of this gentleman's nice new warehouses in the Kelsford Basin under a thousand bags of corn, or some such, until the time is right.'

Devlin now understood the comment made by Liam at their earlier meeting in Manchester. This American must be the man he referred to as the contact who was already in place in Kelsford. 'What are you thinking of when you say "the time is right"?' he ventured.

'Thanks to the potential supplies from the States, I propose to stockpile enough weapons to arm a force here on the mainland. A similar arsenal will be put together in the Old Country. At the right political moment a rebellion will be started at home – probably in Dublin – and we'll do the same here.' O'Dowd's eyes burned with patriotic fervour. 'Meantime, there'll be sufficient guns – rifles and pistols – for us to sell on to some of the East European anarchists who are based here, for them to use in Russia and the Balkans.'

Connor was worried. 'You know my feelings on that, Liam. They have no security and some of them are absolutely mad. A couple were chased through the streets of London only a few weeks ago. They'd bungled a pay roll robbery at a factory in broad daylight, for Christ's sake! They killed two policemen and a passer-by before they stole a tramcar – and the police shot both of them.'

Liam took a pull at his whiskey. Patiently, as if explaining to a child, he said, 'It doesn't matter, don't you see? As long as nothing is traceable to us it doesn't matter what they do. Let them rear up at the police and get themselves killed: all we want is their money.'

Easing his aching back, Lucas Sangster pulled himself to his feet and stretched his arms. 'There's a lot of money in this, Connor,' he murmured, picking up the thread from O'Dowd. The brashness that he had exhibited at his meeting with the bank officials was gone, the booming voice replaced by a deep Texas drawl. A lifetime spent on the California goldfields and in American frontier towns had honed the man's instincts to a fine edge. Sangster was an excellent judge of situations – he had to be; on occasions his life had depended upon it – and he realised it was important to convince Devlin that the plan was sound.

Walking over to the far side of the barn, he reached into an already opened crate and pulled out from the straw packing a repeating rifle encased in oiled paper. Carefully removing the paper, he wiped the excess oil from the gun's mechanism and brought it to where the others were sitting. 'My associates in the States can provide you with almost any commodity you need. An army rifle sells here for about two guineas – but the problem is you can't buy them. We're supplying you with a better and faster firing weapon for the same money. You can sell them on to these piss-kitty amateurs for as much as you can get with no loss to the cause.' With a single practised movement Sangster dropped open the breech, checked that the action was clear and handed the weapon, butt first, to Connor. 'It's the latest model. Winchester 1886,' he continued, now the practised salesman. 'For the past ten years your British Army has been using the Mark II Martini-Henry. It's a good solid weapon that will throw a .45 shell eighteen hundred yards – and at less than that will drop a bull in its tracks with one hit. The problem is that it's a single-shot weapon, which means it's got a relatively slow rate of fire. This new Winchester has been on the market for just under two years. It's the same calibre as the Martini – fires a .45–70 slug – but it has distinct advantages.' Sangster was in full flow, and had his audience's undivided attention. 'This little beauty is thirty-eight inches long and weighs nine pounds, which is a bit heavier than the Martini-Henry, but the real advantage is that it has a nine shot magazine. You just put it to your shoulder, pull the trigger and pump the next one into the breech without taking your eyes off the target. Because it's eleven and a half inches shorter than the Martini it can be hidden away or carried much easier.'

'What's its accuracy like?' Liam O'Dowd interrupted.

Sangster's meaty jowls lifted in a huge grin. 'I can put all nine into an inch group at fifty yards in eight seconds flat. I tell you, three good marksmen armed with this son of a bitch would take out an entire company of Brits before their first man could get a shot off!'

Connor rubbed a hand over his stubbled jaw. 'Word is that the Brits are going to be issued with a new rifle soon.'

The Texan nodded. 'That's true. They know the limitations of the Martini-Henry and have been looking at a recently developed Lee-Enfield, but believe me, it'll still not come up to these Winchesters. For a start it'll have a bolt action, which can't compare to this under-the-butt lever attached to the trigger guard. This is the weapon for you: fast and easy to conceal. Do the sums, Connor. As Liam says, provided everybody is careful it doesn't matter what happens to the foreigners.' Watching Connor, Sangster knew they had won. Whether he liked it or not, Devlin was unable to put forward an argument against the proposition.

Their meeting concluded, the three men stepped out of the barn into the warm afternoon sunshine. Privately, Sangster was turning over in his mind what Devlin had said about the instability of the Anarchist groups. Lack of security, he had come to understand, was one accusation that could not be levelled at the Irish Republican Brotherhood. Before this meeting he had been given a specific time at which to board a barge named the *Trojan* as it passed through Bridge Sixty-Four in Kelsford. Once aboard the slow-moving craft, Sangster had wondered if he had dropped into another world. The vessel, towed along by a plodding carthorse, was steered from her bench in the stern by a silent old crone dressed in a tattered man's cap and filthy apron. The stump of a broken clay pipe clamped securely between her toothless gums and one eye glazed over by a cataract gave her the appearance of an old witch. The barge's other two occupants were Connor Devlin, whom he had not met previously, and an old man referred to only as Amos, who appeared to be the crone's husband. Sangster had soon realised that transporting him like this to his rendezvous with the head of the Brotherhood in mainland England was actually a carefully prepared exercise. Two younger men – the couple's sons he presumed – flanked the towpath on foot, both armed with shotguns, and from time to time they disappeared into the adjacent fields. Because of the slowness of their progress it was, Sangster had realised, difficult for anyone to follow them without detection, while it was relatively easy to mount a guard. Liam O'Dowd, he presumed, had made the journey down from Manchester on one of the two barges that had delivered the cases of rifles, securely hidden under a cargo of several tons of loose coal.

Shaking hands before taking leave of each other, O'Dowd gave Sangster a knowing look. 'Speaking of payroll robberies that didn't work out exactly as planned, perhaps you should tell Connor here about our latest developments.'

Sangster looked sharply at the Brotherhood commander, sensing that the Irishman was playing a game to which he was not privy. 'I had a cable from a friend the other day, saying he might soon have some information for us about what went wrong with your Shires job,' he said to Devlin.

Chapter Fourteen

The May heat in New York was stifling. Picking his way down the rubbish-cluttered stairs from his tiny second-floor apartment, Martin Lafferty examined the thermometer hanging in the hallway. Eighty-five degrees. It was nine o'clock on Sunday morning and his cotton shirt was already dark across the back and under the arms with unsightly patches of sweat. He decided that he would carry his linen jacket until he arrived at his destination. Turning sideways, he examined his reflection in the cheap boxwood-framed mirror hanging on the wall of the lobby.

Lafferty's appearance was at odds with his surroundings. The polished shoes and freshly pressed trousers, held up by a pair of red braces, or suspenders as they were known by the Americans, were set off by a clean white shirt and an emerald green bow tie. The smart straw boater with its red and green striped band, which he carefully adjusted to a jaunty angle on his pomaded auburn hair, was carefully chosen to match his tie and braces.

Down on the Manhattan quayside, where he was heading, he had the air and polish of an accredited shipping agent, ready to receive and direct new arrivals from the old country towards their new lives in America. Here, in the streets and bars surrounding his apartment house, three blocks back from the docks, in one of New York's poorest districts, he was recognised for exactly what he was – a cheap crook.

It seemed an age since he had stood at the stern of the SS *Corinthian*, watching the bleak Liverpool skyline fading away in the wintery November mist. Studying his reflection in the glass, Martin checked his carefully knotted silk tie as he pondered his good fortune.

While Connor Devlin and Eddie Donnelly had been busy securing the yard gate and fixing the trip rope across the kitchen door of the Prince Albert, it had been Martin's job to check out the kitchen. Once in the darkened room, the first thing Lafferty had come across was George Camm's cash box standing on the Welsh dresser. Scooping the pile of loose money up, he had distributed it quickly between his trouser and jacket pockets, deciding there was no need for the other two to know of his find.

The robbery had gone to plan. Leaving the agent sprawled unconscious in the yard, the three had made their escape exactly as planned. He and Connor had split up at the crossroads, while Eddie had taken the money down to Amos Radbone's barge. It was only when he had ridden almost into Derby, where he was to catch the train from Sheffield to Manchester the following morning, that Martin stopped to count his windfall.

Squatting on his haunches in the broken-down cowshed just off the road, Lafferty could not believe the amount of money that was laid out on the ground in front of him. Taking his time, he re-counted it, fingering every coin lovingly. Sixty gold sovereigns, forty halfsovereigns, two five pound notes and fifteen in loose change: £105. The young Irishman had never seen so much money in his entire life; this must represent the entire takings of the pub for the whole of the previous week.

Like most of his contemporaries, Martin Lafferty had grown up in difficult circumstances: a hard childhood among hard people. His participation in the activities of the Irish Republican Brotherhood were more from self-preservation than any deep political motivation. Membership of the Brotherhood meant he could indulge in criminal activities under the protection of the organisation. Although he was totally uneducated, those activities had developed in him a quick and agile mind. That the theft of the money would be discovered Lafferty had no doubt, and that he would not be allowed to keep his ill-gotten gains was equally certain. Once back in Manchester he would have to give the money to Connor, who might allow him to pocket a couple of sovereigns as beer money – if he was lucky. Slowly a plan formed in his mind: he was not going to allow that to happen.

Tomorrow morning he would wait until the Sheffield train had passed through Derby station on its way to the north-west, and take the first available train he could find in the opposite direction. When he failed to join Connor on the train his accomplice would merely think there had been a delay. That Lafferty had absconded would, if he were lucky, possibly not be discovered for a few days.

At first light, having turned his horse loose in an orchard on the outskirts of Derby, Martin decided to walk the last mile into the town. Worn out by the night's activities, just after six o'clock he boarded a passing tramcar, which deposited him under the ornate railway bridge in Deansgate near to the town centre. By this time he had formulated a scheme that, while ambitious, was in his judgement sound. His aim was to get to America. No longer would he have to skulk about the dismal back alleys of the industrial north, taking orders from men who were little better off than himself. In America, the land of plenty, his new-found wealth would allow him to set himself up in some sort of business and become rich quickly. Lafferty was acutely aware of the risk he was taking. Defection from the Brotherhood was not tolerated, and disloyalty was punished with a brutality intended to deter any other would-be dissenter. If his scheme went wrong he knew that no mercy would be shown by his masters.

Martin's plan depended upon his entering Liverpool and boarding a ship unseen by any of his associates, who would undoubtedly be looking for him. In order to achieve this he would, he decided, first need to catch a train to Hull. Coming as he did from Liverpool, Lafferty was familiar with the ways of European emigrants who passed through England on their way to the United States. His idea was to join a group coming into the country from Scandinavia, travel with them by rail to Liverpool and board the boat undetected.

Once in Hull it had taken him three evenings of trawling the dockside pubs and drinking dens to find what he wanted. After a few quiet conversations with some of the anonymous faces who were always in the background if you knew where to find them, Martin was steered towards the Sultan Vaults in East Street. There, sitting at a table in the corner of the taproom, reading a newspaper, was the man with whom he needed to speak.

Sven Olafson, if such was his name – which Martin doubted – had obviously been forewarned of the Irishman's enquiries. A thin, sparsely built man in his late middle age, he did not look typically Swedish other than for his thinning, once blond, hair. He was not, Martin noted approvingly, overly well dressed: his collarless shirt was seedy, and a grubby white muffler was tucked into his greasy waistcoat front. There was nothing out of the ordinary that would give a casual observer cause to remember him. A workman's flat cap lay on the beer-stained table in front of him.

'You're looking for something?' The Swede came straight to the point.

'I need to become Swedish for a short while,' the Irishman said softly, taking the chair next to him.

'Go and live in Sweden then,' replied the other man, staring coldly over his paper.

Lafferty gazed across the almost empty bar. Why do these places always have red and gold flock wallpaper? he wondered.

'Don't let's piss about with each other,' he said, laying on a thick Irish accent for effect. 'I'm not from the police and I'm not from the immigration commissioners. I want to go with the next boatload of Swedes who come in here en route to Liverpool. It's as simple as that. I'm told that you can arrange such things.'

Olafson carefully folded his newspaper and picked up the pint pot at his elbow, draining it in one long swallow. Wiping his mouth on the back of his hand, he gave Lafferty a long appraising look. 'As you say, let's not piss about, Irish. That you're not from the local commissioners I already know. The police I'm not bothered about, and anyway I'm assured you're not from them.' The point he was making was not lost on Martin. Olafson was paying off contacts in the local police force and immigration commission. 'The arrangements and a suit of clothes will cost ten pounds. You'll meet me here tomorrow night at seven o'clock.'

Standing up to leave, Olafson picked up his cap and pushed it onto his balding head. Almost as an afterthought, he bent confidentially over the Irishman and said, 'If you're playing games, Irish, remember that you're a long way from home, and the water in the docks is very cold.'

The following evening at the appointed time Lafferty walked into the bar of the Sultan and, without having time to buy himself a drink, was given a signal by the waiting Olafson to follow him out into the back yard. It was cold and dark. If he was being set up, this was where it would happen, thought Lafferty, his mind flashing back to another night and another pub yard when he had been part of the team waiting for a man. That he had not been given time to buy a drink or signal to anyone watching out for him in the room was something that he understood – a precaution that he himself would have taken.

Pausing to take a breath and to allow his eyes to become accustomed to the gloom, Martin stood perfectly still, listening. He need not have worried; the elderly Swede, apparently alone, was waiting for him with a parcel of clothes and identity papers in the name of Gustav Jenson. Lafferty had no qualms about the authenticity of the documents. In every port where poor emigrants washed up there were men such as Olafson. A prospective emigrant with an infectious disease or some other problem, turned away at the quayside by the shipping company's doctor, had nowhere left to go and rarely any money. The only way to fund his passage home was to sell the one item of value that he possessed – identity papers.

'Listen carefully to what I'm telling you.' The Swede's heavy voice cut through the darkness. 'You're in luck. The *Christiana* docked this afternoon with a cargo of travellers from Copenhagen to New York. At half past six tomorrow morning be at the hostel in Alders Lane. There will be seventy-five people there, all Swedes and Danes, waiting for the wagons to take them and their baggage to the railway station. Supervising them will be the White Star Line agent. Show him your papers: he'll be looking out for you. He'll give you a boarding permit for the train. Speak to no one. If anyone questions you, pretend you don't understand a word of English. After that you're on your own.'

The rest had been relatively easy. For an extra ten pounds Olafson had agreed to telegraph the White Star offices in Liverpool and purchase a second-class ticket for Martin in the name of Michael Laughton. Once safely aboard the SS *Corinthian*, Lafferty had slipped away from the party of emigrants as they made their way to the steerage accommodation in the forecastle and taken up his cabin on the passenger deck.

Twelve days later, when the ship docked in the Hudson, Lafferty strolled casually down the gangplank, clutching the cheap suitcase of clothes that he had purchased in the small ship's chandler's shop. Armed with a new set of papers in the name of Samuel Kendrick Spencer, which he had stolen the previous evening from a cabin while its occupant was enjoying his last dinner on board, Martin Lafferty climbed onto the barge for Castle Garden and registration by the American Immigration Centre.

In all his carefully executed planning, Lafferty had, through no fault of his own, missed one important item. Because he had spent the days immediately after the Kelsford robbery either travelling or involved in setting up his disappearance, he had not had time to read a newspaper – and therefore was blissfully unaware that Eddie Donnelly was dead and the entire proceeds of the robbery were missing.

Martin grinned back at the reflection gazing out at him from the mirror. The identity papers that he had used during the registration process were deposited in the first rubbish bin he saw after leaving the dock gates. Once the real Spencer reported the theft, to use his name would be to court disaster.

Lafferty was now Niall Kierney. Renting the cheap apartment near the docks, Lafferty had spent a couple of weeks quietly examining his surroundings and becoming accustomed to the American way of life. Two things quickly became apparent to him. First, in this multinational melting pot, like gravitated towards like. The Italians, the Germans and the Irish all set up their own communities, creating what were known as neighbourhoods. The tenement block in which he lived was in the centre of a strictly Irish enclave. Any Wops or Spiks venturing into the Paddy neighbourhood did so at their peril. Second, it was a society in which crime and the criminal flourished. Provided the small man paid his dues to whoever ruled the streets in his area, he could engage in almost any schemes that the human brain could devise. Martin was intrigued and pleased with this. Free enterprise was actively encouraged – a contrast with the strict regulation of members of the Brotherhood. He intended to remain here just long enough to put together a comfortable bank balance before moving on to pastures new; in fact, the venture he had settled on meant he could not remain in the area indefinitely.

Having established himself with Lorchan Kelly, the Irish gang boss for the area of Manhattan in which he was living, Lafferty, his fertile brain working overtime, set to work to carve out a niche for himself. His ploy, if totally immoral, was quite simple. When an immigrant boat docked in either the Hudson or East river, the passengers were first taken by barge to the old opera house at the tip of Manhattan, which was now the Castle Garden Immigration Centre. Any who had become ill on the voyage were separated and placed in quarantine on Staten Island. Once the immigrants' arrival in the United States had been officially registered, they passed through into America proper. While legitimate porters and carriers arranged with the new arrivals to transport their meagre possessions to various parts of the city – forty cents a piece to 59th Street, fifty cents to Brooklyn – Lafferty mingled among them selling offers of employment and prosperity. Each day that he knew a boat from Ireland was due in he went down to Central station and purchased twenty or twenty-five single tickets to places such as Chicago, or some other Midwest city. Once the area outside the registration centre was full of travellers, and the legitimate agents were busy dealing with newly arrived families, he set to work. Spying out suitable targets, usually a man and wife with a family, surrounded by their worldly possession in suitcases and paper parcels, he approached the couple, posing as a business agent, and offered to sell them rail tickets, along with a contract of employment with a fictitious company. It always worked. A fellow Irishman offering everything that they had expected was too good to ignore. Of course, to secure the employment contract the man first had to pay Lafferty a sum of money, varying between twenty-five and fifty dollars depending on Martin's quick assessment of the family's financial state. Sold at face value, the rail tickets ensured that the victims were several hundred miles away before they realised they had been duped, and return was almost impossible. With the crowds of steerage passengers numbering as many as two thousand per boat, there was little chance of Lafferty being identified by one of the genuine company agents – but he reckoned that controls would have been tightened up by the end of the summer, and he would have to move on to something else. There was also a rumour that more dock police were going to be employed, and that a new immigration centre was to be established on Ellis Island.

This morning, according to the shipping lists published in the *New York Times*, two vessels were due in: Cunard's SS *Aurora* from Liverpool and the *Altmeister* from Bremen. This was an opportunity not to be missed. There would be at least three thousand people coming off those two boats, and while he targeted his fellow countrymen the hordes of Germans would serve nicely to confuse the overworked officials on duty.

Satisfied with his appearance, Martin stepped out into the blistering heat of the morning and strolled off down the street. Already people were 'up and doing', as his mother used to say. That was the one thing to which he had not grown accustomed here: the pace at which things moved. Even though it was Sunday morning horse-drawn wagons clattered along the wide streets, and barkeepers were setting out tables on the sidewalk – reminding Lafferty of something he found fascinating: the differences in vocabulary. The man whom he had just passed, clearing refuse from some bins in an alley, was a garbage collector, the pavement was called a sidewalk, and the horse-drawn tram that he mounted at the corner of East 23rd Street to take him the mile and a half into the docklands was a streetcar.

Idly watching the world pass by, Lafferty did not notice the thickset man in a heavy, unseasonable tweed suit who got onto the tramcar at the same stop as himself and took a seat in front of him. Nor was he aware of a second man, also waiting at the car stop, who took up a place behind him.

Descending from the streetcar on West 14th, Lafferty ambled slowly along in the sunshine towards the dock area. Still marvelling, after nearly six months, at the wonders surrounding him, he stopped outside the City Limits bar to light a smoke. Since his arrival he had put away the briar pipe and shag tobacco that he had been puffing since he was fourteen, and embraced the new

American habit of cigarette smoking. Flicking the dead match into the gutter, he looked to his left and let his eyes move skywards to take in the massive statue looming above the building line from Bedloe's Island. A man in a bar had told him over a pot of the pale insipid beer that seemed so favoured by the New Yorkers that it was three hundred feet high and had been brought on a boat from France eighteen months ago. Had he been back home, the Irishman would have pulled the man over the table for such a blatant lie. As it was, he contented himself with picking up his beer and, having asked the man what sort of an ignorant Irish Mick he thought he was, moving away to another table.

Debating whether to take an extra half-hour and have a beer before addressing the business of the day, Lafferty became aware of the two men who had joined him. Gazing speculatively over the buildings at the huge figure of the woman with the torch held high above her head, the older of the two, a florid looking man of about fifty, smiled amiably at Martin. 'The Lady of Liberty Enlightening the World. The first thing that they see when they come in up the river.' His voice was a throaty growl, the accent originating somewhere in Brooklyn. Removing the curly brimmed Derby that matched his brown suit, he mopped the sweat running down his forehead.

Martin drew deeply on his cigarette and nodded. 'Aye. A wonderful sight on a wonderful morning.'

The florid man pushed a thick finger down behind his stiff collar and eased it away from his neck. Martin wondered how he could bear to be wearing the thick tweed suit, which was clinging to him like a damp rag. 'It's a warm morning,' he remarked idly.

'It'll be cooler in the cab,' the man replied.

Martin looked at him in puzzlement. 'You're off somewhere then?'

'We all are,' said his companion, still smiling amiably.

For the first time the second man spoke. Moving in very close behind Lafferty, in a low, clear voice he said, 'Police officers. We've been watching you for some time now, Kierney. You're under arrest for defrauding immigrants of money and other goods in the Hudson and East river docks. Keep your hands in front of you where we can see them.'

Lafferty was too stunned to think about making an escape. Besides, the gun that the officer was pressing into his spine decided the issue. One of the other things that Martin still had to come to terms with was the fascination that firearms held for Americans. Almost everyone in the criminal classes habitually carried a gun. Every day the newspapers carried reports of fatal shootings and murders in the Bronx and Manhattan. That this law enforcement officer would not hesitate to use the pistol Martin did not doubt.

'As my colleague says, keep your hands in front of you and in sight all the time.' A badge had magically appeared in the florid man's left hand. With a fist the size of a small ham, he took a firm hold of Lafferty's shirtsleeve.

To the elderly road sweeper, leaning on his brush and watching from the other side of the road, it was a common enough event. The man in the straw hat, carrying his jacket slung over his arm and being led to the awaiting cab by two police officers, was just another petty crook whose turn it was to spend a weekend in the pokey. Clearing his throat noisily, he hawked and spat into the dry dust at his feet before taking his weight off the broom handle and resuming his work.

The ride in the closed cab was conducted in silence. Martin, sitting bolt upright on the squat seat, was crushed up against the side of the vehicle by the bulk of the man next to him. He was now able to get a proper look at the second detective sitting opposite. He was younger, slim and marginally taller than his partner. The expression on his hatchet face was not reassuring. Like Martin, he was wearing a straw boater in deference to the heat, and his lightweight jacket still retained a degree of style in spite of the stifling atmosphere in the vehicle. The heavy revolver in his right hand was now directed unwaveringly at a point somewhere between the Irishman's crotch and his navel. The older man with the Brooklyn accent needed a shave and smelled heavily of stale sweat and tobacco. The reek was so overpowering that Lafferty soon began to feel as if he would vomit.

The journey was a long one, and he began to wonder how far the precinct station was from the docks. After about fifteen minutes curiosity turned to unease. 'Which station house are we going to?' he asked. When neither man replied he repeated the question, aggression and worry showing in his voice. 'I want to know right now where we're going.'

'Shut the fuck up, Limey.' The younger detective's tone was cold and dispassionate.

Lafferty was becoming desperate. 'I want to see your badge. I don't believe you're police.' He was beginning to realise that if these men were not what they claimed then they must be gangsters. Although he worked alone, and paid his dues in the approved manner, it was common knowledge that rival factions from time to time attempted to take control of each other's territory. If he was caught in the middle of some dispute, Martin knew his situation could be perilous.

The older man chuckled loudly, 'Oh, we're definitely cops, Paddy. Now shut up before my friend blows your bollocks off.'

By now the cab was passing through an area that Martin did not know. The streets were narrow, and a stink of fish pervaded the air. Warehouses were the only buildings that he could see through the tiny side window against which he was jammed. Apart from the odd sign he caught sight of, proclaiming Minsky's Processing Plant and Gorchen & Company – Ice Packers, they were grey anonymous sheds.

After another ten minutes the cab came to a halt at the mouth of a narrow alley that led down between two of the warehouses. The only significant thing about the latter part of the journey that registered with the Irishman was that he had passed Minsky's premises twice, the obvious implication being that the cab driver had been taking a circuitous route in order to confuse him.

Climbing out of the cab first, the younger man covered Lafferty as he stepped down into the deserted roadway. The heat was bouncing up from the cobbles in miniature hammer blows, and Martin's head was beginning to ache from the heat and smells. 'Look,' he said desperately, 'whatever's going on I'm not involved. I don't work for anyone. If it's money you want I can fix that. . .'

It was pointless. The big man was now standing next to him, his brown Derby hat screwed tightly down onto his head, a short-barrelled pistol almost lost in his heavy fist. 'Walk!' he ordered, his amiable smile replaced by a grim look of menace.

At the end of the alley the thin man tapped lightly on a heavy side door, its securing padlock and bar swinging loosely in the shadows. As it was being opened from the inside the screech of machinery rent through the Sunday morning quiet as a steam-driven crane somewhere nearby began its labours. Martin, his mind working overtime, realised that wherever they were the smell of fish and the crane meant that they were once again near a quayside, probably much further up the East river.

A gun barrel in his back forced him through the open door into the darkened warehouse. After the brilliant light outside, Lafferty was completely blind for several seconds. As his eyes grew accustomed to the gloom he saw a man in front of him with what looked like a short-barrelled shotgun pointed at his midriff. There was no sign of his escorts from the cab, and he assumed they had gone, their task completed.

Suddenly, without warning, a thin rope was thrown round his neck from behind, and his head jerked backwards from the force with which it was pulled tight. Lafferty gasped for breath, and his hands flew to his throat to try to release the pressure. His head felt as if it were bursting, and bright lights flashed and scattered across his brain as he lost consciousness.

Chapter Fifteen

When Lafferty came to he was seated, his hands and ankles securely bound, on an upright chair in what appeared to be some sort of an office. The room was quite large, and was dimly lit by a paraffin lamp that swung on a piece of chain hanging from the ceiling. Turning his pounding head to look round, he saw that he was in the weighing room of a disused fish store. Empty boxes and rickety shelves littered the floor and walls. Over to his left, facing an open door into the main building, was the long counter on which the fish would be thrown in readiness to be weighed by the tally man. That the place was now derelict was obvious from the general air of decay and the thick layer of dust that coated all the surfaces.

Facing him about six feet away, also seated on a hard-backed chair, was a man. The chair upon which he was sitting had been turned round, his folded arms leaning on its back.

'What's going on?' Lafferty croaked. The effort of speaking was excruciating, the result of his being almost garrotted by the rope.

'Now that's exactly what we want to ask you, Martin.' The voice was soft, a pleasant drawl, unlike the harsh New York tones to which Lafferty's ear had become accustomed. Somewhere buried in the background were the echoes of an almost forgotten Irish brogue.

In the ensuing silence it took Lafferty almost a minute to comprehend that the dim figure had called him Martin. Not Niall, as he was known to his acquaintances in the apartment block, or Kierney, as he had been referred to by the men who picked him up.

The figure opposite remained silent as he watched the realisation of his true situation dawn upon the Irishman. He had spent the last thirty years interviewing men and knew the value of silence. For some reason that he did not fully understand, people could not cope with the vacuum that it created. No matter how precarious the situation, leave a man in an empty silence and he will have to fill it with words.

As he expected, Lafferty eventually spoke, his voice cracked with fear and the pain in his throat. 'What is it you want?'

The man relaxed. Up to this point he had not been absolutely certain that this small-time operator who worked the immigrant boats was in fact the person for whom he had been looking. He allowed himself a self-satisfied smile. Tracing Martin Lafferty was, he felt, something to be pleased about. His quarry had, the man felt, done well to make it this far and to stay at liberty for so long. Fortunately for the Brotherhood, in planning his escape Lafferty had made one basic error: he had followed the procedures ingrained in him during his training.

Members of the Brotherhood were taught that should it be necessary to go to ground and effect a false identity they were to assume a name that kept their own initials, and to quote their true date of birth. The reasoning behind this was simple. A man who has personal items that carry his initials, such as a signet ring or an engraved watch, is much more credible if his assumed name accords with these items. It was also a standard police tactic, after a prisoner had been in custody for several hours, to see if he could remember what details he had given when arrested. A false name was easy to remember; not so a fictitious date of birth.

Once Liam O'Dowd realised that Lafferty was on the run he lost no time in putting out a general alert. A price of one hundred guineas was offered for his detention alive, and fifty for him dead. A clerk in the White Star offices in Liverpool, who was paid a regular retainer against just such an eventuality, quickly came up with the name of a Michael Laughton, whose date of birth tallied with Lafferty's and who had sailed for New York on the SS *Corinthian*. The ticket had been purchased over the telegraph against a bank account in Hull by one Sven Olafson, a well-known local fixer. Once apprised of the nature of their enquiries, Olafson, who had no wish to have any trouble with the Brotherhood, was most cooperative – and his description of the Irishman for whom he had obtained false papers and a passage to the States was that of Martin Lafferty.

By the time the enquiry reached the Brotherhood in Brooklyn, the *Corinthian* was safely back in the Mersey and the trail was apparently cold. However, a contact at New York's Castle Garden Immigration Centre had, for a few dollars, spent a quiet hour during the night-shift scanning through the passenger lists for the day when the *Corinthian* docked in New York. The search revealed that, though he had travelled as a second-class passenger, Laughton had not left the ship when it tied up; but it appeared that a second-class passenger by the name of Spencer had reported his cabin broken into and his travel documents stolen at the time the ship berthed. No one was surprised to discover that a man posing as Spencer had registered at immigration before disappearing through the dock gates into obscurity.

This information, along with a verbal report that the fugitive appeared to have made good his escape, was passed to the man who now sat facing

Lafferty. Unlike those who were out on the ground searching for Lafferty, Miles Ellingworth was not convinced that the matter was closed. After a lifetime among the world's most proficient wheelers and dealers, Ellingworth knew a lot about finding people. Forty years ago, as a twenty-year-old deck-hand from Cork, he had jumped ship while it was loading in the East river, and had never looked back. He had begun his career in America as a clerk in the Long Island offices of Josiah Clarkson, before seducing and marrying Clarkson's daughter Harriet. The fact that Ellingworth had a young wife and daughter living in County Cork did not enter too deeply into his calculations: as he was never going back to Ireland, the young man felt that to disclose such a detail would be somewhat counterproductive. When Clarkson died three years later, Harriet had inherited his not insubstantial business, and her young husband had ensured that it was he who replaced his father-in-law as company president.

From that moment on, his talent for making money and closing deals ahead of his competitors ensured that by the time he was thirty-five Miles Ellingworth was a dollar millionaire. Always true to his instincts, he rarely passed up the opportunity to turn a deal. If a venture required that certain people were paid for services rendered, then he freely accepted that this was the way of life. On the other hand, if someone did not accept this process there were people who could, as the Americans said, lean on them. With this philosophy and an ever-increasing bank balance, it was not long before Miles Ellingworth's business empire became intertwined with what was rapidly becoming known as organised crime.

In a society that was tailor-made for corruption to flourish, Ellingworth became pre-eminent among those who could arrange almost anything for anyone, provided the price was right. Politicians needed to be bought, police officers suborned and the up-and-coming trade union leaders shown the path from rags to riches. The end result was that at sixty years of age Miles Ellingworth was an immensely rich, powerful and ruthless man, and along the way had acquired an insight into the make-up of men that was second to none.

During his early years in New York Ellingworth had briefly fallen in with a fellow ex-patriot, John O'Mahoney, and had helped him to form the Emmet Monument Association, a predecessor to the American Fenian movement. Although they had gone in different directions, the two men had maintained a loose contact until O'Mahoney's death eleven years before. One of the results of this was that for many years Ellingworth had been a covert supporter of the Irish Republican Brotherhood, not through any deep political motivation but because to do so was in the long term a distinctly sound financial strategy. For a thousand dollars a month paid into a discreet bank account in Chicago, which was then transferred to a similar account in London, he could, when circumstances dictated, call upon the services in New York of a whole army of ex-patriot Irishmen, who all believed in an independent Ireland at any cost.

Of late this association had led him into a very lucrative, if highly illegal, business undertaking. The Brotherhood on the other side of the Atlantic was in dire need of armaments such as handguns and rifles. Such weapons were freely available in the States. Since the Civil War gunsmiths such as Samuel Colt had made American firearms the finest in the world. The transfer of the weapons from America to England was a simple matter for a man with Miles Ellingworth's connections. He soon established a number of small firearms dealerships in the Midwest, all of which conducted legitimate business with the American public. Supplying them through a central company based in New York, he was able to divert large quantities of guns and ammunition into his warehouses along the East river. From there, packaged as machine parts, they were simply transported to their destinations in Britain and Ireland.

'What is it you want?' Hoarsely, Lafferty repeated his question. The pain caused by the rope made speaking difficult.

Ellingworth rested his elbows on the back of the chair, his entwined fingers making a platform on which to rest his closely shaved chin. Lafferty wasn't that clever, he deliberated. Having made it to New York, the Irishman should have kept going – changed his appearance, taken yet another identity and buried himself way out of sight another two thousand miles to the west – Montana, Utah, San Francisco. The trouble with these immigrants was that they had no conception of distance. Having crossed an ocean, they thought they were safe in the one place in America where it was most dangerous to stop.

In the shadow cast by the paraffin lamp, Ellingworth smiled, almost gently, at his prisoner. The fool had not even changed his appearance. Dyeing his flaming red hair a different colour and shaving off his moustache might have preserved his identity for a while longer. Ellingworth had merely instructed his men to maintain a low profile and wait – watching the bars and putting the word out among the Irishmen in the district.

New York was a big city, and because Lafferty, in a moment of sense, was using a name with the initials N.K., tracking down his quarry had taken a little longer than Ellingworth had anticipated. In the end Lafferty had turned up exactly where he had landed – on the Manhattan quayside. From that moment it had been a simple matter to choose an appropriate time and place, and arrange for two police officers to pick him up. That was another advantage of New York society, Ellingworth reflected. If you needed a genuine policeman for a job like this, it was merely a matter of paying.

'I'll tell you what it is we want, Martin,' he said softly, his voice edged with steel. 'We want to know, or to be correct our friends in England want to know, what happened just before Christmas. You recollect the matter, I'm sure. You were part of a team that committed a robbery in a small Midlands town. As we both know it went very wrong.'

Martin's head was pounding; the fumes from the lamp were making him feel sick. He should never have reneged on the Kelsford job. Desertion was the one thing that the Brotherhood did not allow to go unpunished. In the light cast by the smoking lamp he began to make out the features of the man facing him. White hair, worn long, well barbered and brushed back from his face. Clean shaven, and a long straight nose above thin lips and a strong jaw. Despite the heat he appeared to be expensively dressed in a dark frock coat over a white shirt, closed at the neck with a black bootlace tie.

'I shouldn't have run.' His voice was little more than a croak. 'The money was there in the tin. After I took it I decided to get out and make a new start.'

'Where is the money now, Martin?' The voice was soft, cajoling.

'Most of it's spent. It took a lot to get here, and then I had to live until I got set up.' Might as well be honest, he thought: it's bad enough as it is. The truth was he still had over half of George Camm's hundred pounds stashed under a loose board in his room. If he ever got out of this he was going to need that money.

The man's voice suddenly lost its avuncular note. 'Don't mess with me, Lafferty. You've got fifty-two gold sovereigns under a loose board in your apartment. Where are the other seven hundred and fifty?'

Lafferty's fear began to turn into panic. 'That's it! That's all I've got!'

Ellingworth's voice was flat and deadly. 'The money is secondary. The real question is what we're going to do about you killing Eddie Donnelly.'

Stunned, Martin Lafferty sat completely still on the chair to which he was tied. Staring into the shadows in front of him, like a rabbit mesmerised by a snake, he tried to take in what had just been said. 'Jesus, Mary Mother of God! I haven't killed anyone! I took the money from the cash tin – a hundred pounds – that's it!' The adrenalin pumping round his system lent a strength to his voice. 'Jesus, what's going on here?'

For the next hour Miles Ellingworth continued his interrogation of the red-haired Irishman. He was surprised at the tenacity with which his prisoner stuck to his story. Adamant that he knew nothing of Donnelly's death, Lafferty continued to maintain that all the money he had brought with him was from a theft committed before the main robbery.

The steam crane that Martin had heard working when he was brought into the warehouse began its deafening clatter again, forcing Ellingworth to pause for a moment. It was unloading a vessel in the harbour nearby. The time between the driver lowering his hook into the hold of the ship and screeching its way back up to deposit its load onto the wagons on the quay was about fifteen minutes. While the machine was lifting the cargo out the noise that it created made conversation inside the warehouse impossible.

Miles Ellingworth used the respite to marshal his thoughts. The man was being stupid. That he continued to deny the killing of his partner in crime was not surprising: to admit it was to invite certain death. That Lafferty was not seeking to make a deal that would enable him to hand back the money and escape from his present situation was less than sensible. Obviously, he mused, Lafferty was underestimating the gravity of his predicament. It was time to remedy the misunderstanding. The crane ceased its noise.

Ellingworth stood up and stretched his legs and arms to bring the circulation back. 'Untie him.' His demeanour was that of a man who has reached a decision.

Lafferty felt unseen hands releasing the ropes binding his ankles and then those round his wrists. The blood flowing back into his trapped limbs was agonising as the tight cords fell away. Two men appeared in his peripheral vision, one on either side of him. They hoisted him roughly to his feet. He was vaguely aware of a third man moving about somewhere in the background.

'You've chosen to be stupid, Mr Lafferty.' Ellingworth walked a few paces to stretch his legs before turning to speak again. 'My associates are very skilled, if somewhat unorthodox, in dealing with stupid people. I'll give you one last chance. The money is of a small amount: less than four thousand dollars. Definitely not worth the discomfort that you're going to be put to. But I'm determined to know what you've done with it before we deal with the matter of your killing Donnelly.'

'I don't know what you're talking about.' The fear emanating from every fibre of Lafferty's being was palpable, filling the warehouse like a drum roll in a cathedral.

During the last hour most of the questions that he had been asked did not even make sense to him. That something drastic had gone wrong after he and Devlin parted company was obvious. Somewhere along the line, apparently, Eddie had been killed and the proceeds of the robbery had vanished. His own disappearance could not have been more inappropriately timed. Without being able to give these men the answers, Martin knew his life was not worth much.

The silver-haired man shrugged in resignation and nodded to the men holding Lafferty. Keeping a tight grip on his arms, they pushed him across to a position between the wooden counter and the door that led into the body of the warehouse. Martin realised he was standing beneath a weighing device known as a steelyard, a simple piece of apparatus commonly used by butchers and fishmongers. Hanging by a small hook from a beam about six feet from the ground, it comprised a three foot length of steel, from which it derived its name, counterbalanced at one end by a heavy metal ball. Beneath it was a large hook for hanging carcasses, or big sea fish such as sharks and marlin, in order to weigh them. Swinging from the hook, the weight forced the steel bar upwards, whereupon the operator moved a counterbalance along the bar until it returned to the horizontal. The weight of the load was then read from the graduations cut into the bar.

Martin looked desperately at the two men holding him. One was a gaunt-looking man of about forty, dark curly hair tumbling out of a workman's cap pushed onto the back of his head. The other was younger, probably not much above twenty, with dark and shifty eyes and sallow cheeks; his straggly moustache did little to hide a livid white scar running from the side of his mouth across his cheek. The other man who had joined them was big, over six feet tall, with red hair, not a deep Titian colour like Lafferty's but a bright ginger. Martin judged him to be nearer fifty than forty. He was grossly overweight, the heavy leather belt supporting his baggy trousers lost in the folds of a vast, overhanging belly. Lafferty took in the purple-veined cheeks, the stubbled jaw that had not seen a razor for several days and the protruding pale blue eyes. It was the eyes that held him. Not their colour, nor the tiny red capillaries at the edges; it was their complete lack of expression that sent the first real chills through his body. Over his years with the Brotherhood Lafferty had from time to time come into contact with born killers, and he knew beyond doubt that he was looking at one now.

The big man opened his mouth as if he were about to speak, revealing twisted yellow, nicotine-stained teeth. Instead, without warning and with the force of a lashing mule, he buried his fist in Lafferty's stomach. As his victim doubled over the red-haired man brought his right knee up hard into Lafferty's face. As if it were happening to someone else, Martin heard a sharp crack and felt a spatter of blood as his front teeth snapped – before passing out on the warehouse floor.

When he came round, Lafferty was aware that one of his captors was holding him upright while another was doing something with his right hand. Consciousness returning, he realised his arm was being held aloft by the curly haired man, who with his free hand was positioning the hook of the steelyard in the middle of Martin's palm. He almost passed out again as he realised what the man was doing.

With a swift, powerful movement his captor dropped his full weight onto Lafferty's arm, forcing the hook up through his outstretched hand. The pain was excruciating. As if in a dream, he saw the bright metal hook, smeared with blood, protruding from the back of his hand. The pain was intense, but he was aware as warm blood began pulsing down his arm that he must keep a hold on consciousness for as long as possible. If he passed out now the weight of his entire body would be taken by the impaled hand.

The fat man was standing in front of him again. This time he was holding a long-barrelled heavy calibre pistol. With the care of a surgeon about to perform a delicate operation, he took hold of the forefinger of Martin's impaled right hand and extended it to its full length. Pressing the gun barrel against the second joint of the digit, he turned his face to Lafferty and grinned in anticipation; the breath he exhaled over his yellow teeth stank.

At an unseen signal he stepped back. Miles Ellingworth, once again hidden in the gloom, said, 'It's time to stop being silly, Lafferty. This is your last opportunity to tell me why you killed Donnelly and what you've done with the rest of the money.'

Martin did not reply. He knew now that his tormentors would never believe he had no answers.

Ellingworth continued. 'Spanner is quite an expert in this sort of interrogation. He's rarely been known to fail. Do you know why he's called Spanner?' The question was a rhetorical one, to which he neither received nor expected an answer. The prisoner was in such a state of terror that he was unable even to indicate he had heard the question. 'He's called Spanner because whenever he begins to work on a subject everyone's nuts tighten up.' Ellingworth realised it would not be long before Lafferty fainted from pure fear. Things needed to be moved along. 'I'm sure you know something about how firearms work, but let me explain this particular exercise to you.' He saw some form of response pass through Lafferty's eyes. 'A .44 calibre revolver fired at, say, an inch from the target will completely remove a man's finger. The advantage is that, apart from causing extreme pain, the muzzle flash at that range will cauterise the wound, reducing bleeding to a minimum. The process can therefore be repeated as many times as necessary – up to ten, that is.'

Seeing that his prisoner had passed out, Ellingworth gave a cursory nod to the fat man and, turning on his heel, purposefully walked away. A brilliant shaft of sunlight illuminated the shed as he opened the side door to step out into the warm Sunday morning.

In the half-light of the interior the youth with the scarred mouth poured a pannikin of cold water over Lafferty to revive him. Meanwhile the man named Spanner patiently waited for the noise of the crane to resume.

Chapter Sixteen

In the three months that had elapsed since his promotion Tom Norton had settled very comfortably into his new role as head of Kelsford Detective Department. Each week now, on a Monday morning, along with Fred Judd, he met the head constable in his office to report on the events of the previous week and discuss any criminal work in which his department was involved. Initially Tom had been surprised by the relaxed atmosphere of these meetings. At first he thought it was because he had been admitted to the upper ranks of the force, but had come to realise that this was not so. The three uniformed inspectors who were the other senior officers were not included in these discussions, making it apparent that he and Judd were regarded differently by Archer Robson.

At these regular parleys Tom learnt a lot, and quickly came to respect the other two men's abilities. He already knew Fred to be a capable administrator, but had never previously appreciated the complexity of his job, balancing the accounts, arranging duties and attending to the hundred and one other details that kept the wheels turning smoothly. He found Archer Robson to be perceptive in his analysis of problems and open to suggestions. This aspect of his character was something of a revelation to Tom, although on reflection he had been given a glimpse of it at Harriman's yard when Archer Robson headed off the editor of the *Kelsford Gazette*.

When Tom outlined his suspicions regarding the Irish Republican Brotherhood's involvement in the Shires robbery and the deaths of Donnelly and Harriman, the head constable listened intently. Sitting back in his chair, Archer Robson dropped his chin onto his chest while he evaluated what the detective had told him. Smoothing back the ends of his heavy drooping moustache, he made a face that was a mixture of concern and resignation. Things were going too well, he thought. With Langley out of the way he had been given the opportunity to make overdue changes, and his two senior inspectors were an essential part of his plans. Fred had long been his confidant, and deputy in all but name, and now he had Norton, who was proving to be everything he had hoped for. Inevitably there had to be a problem somewhere, and it looked as if it were about to present itself.

'All right, Thomas.' The soft Edinburgh accent delivered the words with heavy deliberation. 'Make the investigation of any Fenian activities a priority. Keep me informed of any developments – and don't discuss the matter outside this office.' His sideways glance included Judd, who gave a quick nod of agreement.

One of the reasons Archer Robson had decided to make these two men his senior assistants was that he had reservations about the other inspectors, all of whom he had inherited from his predecessor. Caleb Newcombe was a contemporary of Joseph Langley and, as such, his loyalty to the head constable was decidedly suspect; Lemuel Watkins was a shifty, colourless man whom Archer Robson did not trust on principle; and Cecil Bayliss had the appearance and intellect of a carthorse. Consequently Archer Robson did not want this latest information to become common knowledge.

'There's one other thing I should like to resolve, sir.' It was, Tom thought, an appropriate moment to deal with the matter. 'We have a small armoury, which I've never even seen. My understanding is that it's kept by you in case there's civil disorder, such as may arise from a serious Fenian or industrial disturbance. Do you think it might be appropriate to decide how it should be used?'

Archer Robson pushed his chair back and stood up. 'If you've never seen it, Thomas, then you'd better have a look,' he said good-humouredly, and, indicating for them to follow him, led the way through a door into a small ante-room. Measuring about eight foot by six, it appeared to be used as a store. Along one wall a series of shelves held piles of neatly stacked files, and on a wooden hanger next to the window was his dress uniform and sword, while the plume of a cocked hat poked out of a large cardboard box on the top shelf. Taking a key-ring from his pocket, the head constable undid a small padlock, which secured a built-in cupboard let into the end wall, at some time in the past used as a wardrobe. Inside, standing along one wall in a weapons rack, were half a dozen shotguns. On the shelf opposite, in a cardboard box along with some ammunition, were a similar number of revolvers. A cursory examination showed them to be of varying makes, calibre and age, which was no surprise to either Tom or Fred. It was common practice for every police force to retain any such items that came into police possession from whatever source to form the basis of an armoury. Immediately obvious to Tom was that the superintendent had ensured the guns were kept clean and properly maintained; probably a local gunsmith came in at regular intervals to service them.

'What's your suggestion, Thomas?' the Scotsman asked.

'We should make a list of all those officers who have military experience, and then decide which of them can be trusted with a gun when the occasion arises. After that, at regular intervals we should set up a firing range – possibly in the yard with sandbags – and let them familiarise themselves with the weapons. That way we'll know we have a secure system in place.'

The superintendent turned the idea over in his mind. 'Agreed. You can be responsible for arranging this, and for the storage of the guns.' Removing the padlock key from his key-ring he handed it to Tom. 'Arrange for the carpenter to build a secure gun cupboard in your office.'

Back in the detective office, Tom called a meeting of his staff. One of the first changes he had agreed with Archer Robson was an increase in manpower. That crime in the town could not be effectively investigated by four men was fairly obvious, and that the detectives needed to be sergeants was debatable. On this basis, Archer Robson had decided that rather than appoint another sergeant to fill the vacancy created by Tom's promotion he would bring in three constables to team up with the remaining detective sergeants. Looking at the group, Tom tried to assess what progress was being made.

His first choice for a new recruit had been Harry North, whom he had placed with Squires. The two were, he knew, making good progress. Young North, with his elegant style of dress and smooth manners, had the potential to become a very useful asset. Tom knew that Henry Farmer had taken a dislike to Harry, but he thought this was probably to be expected – they were far too alike. With Henry he had put Joel Dexter, a quiet and intelligent man in his mid-thirties. The problem with Henry was that he was a loner, so anyone working with him could be in for a difficult time. The third pair was Sam Braithwaite and Reuben Simmonds. Tom had mixed feelings about bringing Reuben into the department. Recently the relationship between Reuben and Tom's sister had progressed and they were now officially 'walking out'. While he did not want to be accused of favouritism, Tom felt that Reuben was the best available man to work with Sam. Of all of the group, Braithwaite was the one who concerned him. Since Tom's promotion he had studiously refused to acknowledge that there was any difference in their relationship: on more than one occasion he had failed to carry out an instruction properly, and when taken to task had become almost belligerent. That Braithwaite would never have questioned Langley's authority Tom knew perfectly well, and he decided that if things did not change he would have to address the matter.

For the next half-hour Tom went over what little information they had on Fenian activities and the possibility that they would establish a base in Kelsford. Although various suggestions were put forward, at the end of the meeting the consensus of opinion was that until something more happened all they could do was watch and wait.

'Need to make a few more contacts, eh, Tom?' Braithwaite winked, as he made his way out to the police court. 'I'm back on this evening. Reuben and I will visit a few pubs round and about – see what's happening.'

'No, Sam.' Tom was annoyed. Braithwaite knew the rules: he should no longer – in public at least – refer to him as 'Tom'. 'Tonight I want you and Reuben to go over to the warehousing project and keep your eyes open. Over the last two weeks there have been several thefts of materials from the site. Whoever's doing it must be bringing in a cart. The pair of you can find somewhere secure and do some watching.' A look of irritation passed over Braithwaite's pudgy features; he had been planning to introduce Reuben to one or two of his favourite drinking holes. Almost as if he could read the detective's mind, Tom said coldly, 'And stay out of the pubs. I'll be here when you finish at eleven o'clock.'

Even for Sam the implication was clear: come in smelling of ale and there will be trouble. Shrugging his shoulders, he made his way off to court. Promotion was going to Tom Norton's head, he reflected: under Joe Langley it was normal to go out watching and have a drink at the same time.

Unexpectedly for Tom it was not from Sam Braithwaite that his troubles derived that evening.

Because the military depot in Kelsford – Sevastopol Barracks – was primarily used as a holding and transit base for troops being moved around the district, many of the problems in the town emanated from the soldiery. Drunkenness and fighting were rife, and it was not uncommon for serious assaults to occur. During Joseph Langley's time in office it had been practice to lock up any arrested soldier, then hand him over to the military for the commanding officer at the barracks to mete out such punishment as he saw fit. To Tom this seemed wholly unsatisfactory. He knew very well that back at the depot the man would be confined to barracks for seven days and the matter would be swept under the carpet. At Tom's request the head constable had written a letter to Colonel Sinclair, the officer in charge at Sevastopol Barracks, informing him that in future any arrested military personnel of whatever rank would be charged and taken before the magistrates.

Just after half past ten, as Tom was tidying his desk ready to leave for home, a message arrived from the charge office. A military escort had arrived demanding that a soldier, arrested earlier in the evening for fighting in the Prince Albert, be released into their custody. Having quickly looked at the evidence, Tom made his way down to the charge office.

On his arrival it was obvious that battle lines had been drawn. A young blond army captain, his face suffused with anger, was involved in a heated discussion with Ambrose Quinn, the night sergeant. Breaking off in mid-sentence at the arrival of the detective inspector, the young officer turned his attentions to Tom.

'Are you in charge here?' he demanded in a peremptory tone.

Tom eyed him coldly, taking an instant dislike to the man. He could not have been much more than twenty-five, of medium height with a look of inbred arrogance. His demeanour took Tom straight back to the days when, as a serving soldier, he had been regarded by men such as this as less than the dirt under their polished boots. There were, he knew, few officers in the British Army who had earned their commissions through merit. The vast majority came from reasonably affluent backgrounds and had bought a commission, serving long enough either to satisfy their ego or to be promoted beyond their capabilities.

'My name is Norton, Detective Inspector Norton. In answer to your question, I'm the officer in charge of this police station. And who, sir, are you?'

Had the captain been less enraged, or more perceptive, he would have noticed the icy depths that had filled the other man's pale blue eyes. Ambrose Quinn recognised them, as did the sergeant in charge of the escort. They silently awaited the outcome of this clash of personalities, Quinn behind his charge desk, the army sergeant standing rigidly at ease on the opposite side of the room, flanked by two young soldiers.

'I, sir, am Captain Palmer-Daley, adjutant to Colonel Sinclair, the officer commanding Sevastopol Barracks, and I have come to collect one of my men – Private Albert Took – from your custody. You will, sir, kindly surrender him forthwith to my jurisdiction.'

Tom fixed Captain Palmer-Daley with a steady gaze. He silently continued his appraisal of the man, who was wearing the dark blue patrol jacket and flat forage cap of the Derbyshire Regiment, known locally as the Sherwood Foresters. Tom guessed he was not from a particularly wealthy family; his father couldn't afford the price of a guards regiment, which probably accounted for his attitude: the squire's son always had more edge than the duke's.

'Your man's been involved in a brawl and caused damage in the Prince Albert public house. He's been charged with criminal offences and will be taken before the police court at ten o'clock tomorrow morning.' Tom's voice was pitched at such a level that his words could just be heard by the accompanying soldiery. He had the measure of his opponent and was in perfect control of both the situation and himself. 'You may of course, if you so wish, present yourself before the court and speak on his behalf. After he has served any sentence that the magistrates see fit to impose he will of course be released to the military.'

'This is preposterous!' Not accustomed to his authority being challenged, and suddenly realising he might not prevail, the young officer decided to place his reliance on bluster. 'You have no right to keep this man. He is a soldier of the Queen, and as such is my responsibility.'

Ambrose Quinn relaxed and began to enjoy himself. He liked Tom and knew he had the better of this little upstart.

Transferring his gaze, Tom stared over the young officer's shoulder at the escort. As expected from a transit depot it was a mixed bunch. The sergeant, wearing the uniform of the Royal Field Artillery, was a man of about forty. Lightly built and like the officer of medium height, he stared stone-faced at a point somewhere between Tom's head and the wall behind him. The two soldiers standing either side of the sergeant in the 'at ease' position both carried the Staffordshire knot and Prince of Wales feathers of the 64th Foot.

Returning his attention to the matter in hand, Tom once more addressed the captain. 'Your commanding officer has been notified of the change in procedures. If, as it appears, the army does not concur with them, then I suggest you write to the Home Office. In the meantime, your man is not going anywhere until tomorrow morning.' That the matter was no longer open to further discussion was obvious to everyone in the room.

As if acting upon a prearranged cue, Ambrose Quinn, poker-faced behind his heavy whiskers, held open the door leading out into the yard. Captain Palmer-Daley, a mixture of rage and embarrassment on his face, issued a curt order to the escort and, without glancing to left or right, strode out into the night.

Bringing the escort to attention, equally poker-faced, the artillery sergeant marched his men out behind the officer. Inwardly he was elated, looking forward to regaling his fellow NCOs in the sergeants' mess with the tale of the adjutant's fall from grace at the hands of the local police.

Letting himself in through the front door of Sidwell Place, Tom noticed a piece of folded white paper that had been pushed through the letterbox lying on the tiled floor of the darkened hallway. Picking it up, he took it with him into the sitting room, where he struck a match and lit the gas mantle on the wall over the fireplace. Opening the paper, Tom saw that it was a note: TO INSPECTOR NORTON, I NEED TO SPEAK WITH YOU SIR, PLEASE BE IN THE RIFLEMAN TOMORROW AT LUNCHTIME. It was unsigned, and the shaky bold script indicated it had been written by an uneducated hand. Removing his necktie and collar, Tom sat down at the table to eat the cold beef and pickles that Ann had left out for him.

The evening's events were still fresh in his mind, and this latest missive intrigued him. While it was not unusual for detectives to receive messages from informants requesting discreet meetings, he was a little bothered that this one had been delivered to his home. Setting the note aside, he determined to visit the Rifleman as instructed, in the hope that his questions would be answered.

Tom settled back in his armchair for a bottle of beer and a quiet smoke before turning in for bed. Apart from thinking about his work, he was considering the likelihood that Ann would soon be remarrying and moving out. She was, he knew, very fond of Reuben. Tom wondered what he ought to give them as a wedding present; because he and his sister were so close he wanted to give her something worthwhile. He was certain she would want to stop working behind the bar of their father's pub once married, so it had occurred to him that he should try to set her up in a small business, to supplement Reuben's wage of twenty-seven and sixpence a week. Premises occupied by a small grocer's shop in Oxford Road, round the corner from Sidwell Place, had recently become vacant: the old lady who had run the shop for years had died a month ago and Tom knew the premises had not been rented again. From a cursory enquiry that he had made he knew the owner was asking seven and sixpence a week in rent for the shop and living accommodation.

With his promotion Tom's wages had leapt from thirty-two shillings a week to forty-two and six, which was, he knew, more than adequate for his needs. He also had some money put aside, and saw no reason why he should not use some of it. If he paid the first year's rent and bought the existing stock it would cost about £120. He would, he decided, speak to Ann and Reuben over the next couple of days.

As Tom began to relax his mind drifted idly away to happier days. He closed his eyes, remembering a holiday that he and Kate had taken in Blackpool. Strolling along the front, holding hands – he in shirtsleeves, she in a long cream skirt with a striped parasol which he had bought for her, carried over her shoulder . . . As he began to doze the image was replaced unbidden by one of Ruth Samuels, pushed up close to him in the gig, laughing light-heartedly at some comment he had made.

The following lunchtime, just before midday, Tom strolled into the almost empty taproom of the Rifleman – arriving before the place became busy with its lunchtime trade so he could watch who came in. To his surprise he had only just exchanged greetings with his father when the sergeant of the previous night's military escort followed him in and took up a place at the far end of the bar. For a fleeting moment Tom wondered if he could be the writer of the note, but quickly dismissed the possibility. Whoever delivered the message had put it through the door after Ann and Jamie went to bed and before Tom arrived home. At that time the soldier would have been engaged with Captain Palmer-Daley at the police station.

Ordering a pint of stout, the sergeant busied himself packing and lighting his clay pipe. He had seen Tom talking to the landlord, of that there was no doubt, but after the unpleasantness in the charge office Tom guessed he would be unwilling to speak to him. Tom idly studied the soldier in the long mirror behind the bar. Framed by a set of heavy mutton-chop whiskers, the otherwise clean-shaven face interested him. Carrying the same swarthy tan that Tom had taken so long to lose when he came back from India, it was the lived-in face of a man who has experienced life to the full. It was his eyes that told the story, Tom thought. They were a pale amber colour, as if lightened by years of squinting into the sun at distant horizons, and had a hardness that it was difficult to define.

Across one shoulder and tucked elegantly into his broad leather belt the sergeant wore a long scarlet sash, signalling that he was the depot recruiting sergeant. Last night it must have been his turn to be officer of the guard, hence his presence at Long Street. What interested Tom most were the three medal ribbons that he was wearing on his immaculately pressed tunic. They were the crimson and blue of the Distinguished Conduct Medal, awarded for gallantry, the Indian General Service Medal and the broad green and crimson of the Afghan Medal. Tom knew he was going to have to speak to the man. The Indian General Service ribbon, which he himself held, combined with the medal for the second Afghan War meant that as gunners they had served in the same regiment and probably in some of the same places.

Excusing himself from his conversation with his father, Tom left him serving a customer in the adjacent snug and moved along the bar. '*Teek Sarjant ji, kia aap kayser hey?*' he asked politely, enquiring after the sergeant's health.

'I am well, thank you, Inspector Sahib, and yourself?' replied the soldier in the same language.

Tom acknowledged the courtesy, and said, 'I'm sorry about the difficulties last night. Nothing personal. Your officer should have known better than to take the attitude he did. I couldn't let him win.'

'Captain Inigo Palmer-Daley, known to one and all as I Pee Daily, is a young upstart who will never be a soldier as long as he has a hole in his rifle barrel,' replied the sergeant bitterly. His voice betrayed West Country origins. 'And where, sir, did you learn to speak Hindi?'

The ice broken, for the next half-hour the two men chatted amicably. Inevitably the conversation centred on their mutual experiences on the North-West Frontier. The sergeant, whose name was Walter Mardlin, had been in the artillery for almost twenty years, although he had not gone out to India until 1876, the year after Tom returned to join the police force. In the conversation he mentioned that he had been part of the garrison besieged at Kandahar while on a temporary attachment to the 66th Foot. Tom wondered if it was there that the sergeant had won his DCM.

After a while the bar started to fill up with customers, and Tom began to cast around for the likely writer of his note. Taking his leave, Mardlin explained that he was in the process of looking for lodgings. He had only recently returned to England and had been living in barracks; now his wife had joined him with their young son.

'I might be able to help you,' Tom said. 'Go to this address and tell the woman I sent you.' Scribbling on a piece of paper, he wrote down Jane Holloway's address in Wordsworth Lane. Arthur's mother wanted to let her spare room, and was desperately in need of the money. As an afterthought he added, 'If your wife's looking for work tell her to come in here and see Ernie Norton, the landlord – he's my father. His barmaid may be leaving soon.'

Thanking him profusely, Walter Mardlin left to find his wife and to impart the news of their good fortune.

No sooner was Tom alone again than his sister came over to him. 'There's a strange little man in the kitchen who wants to speak to you.'

Going through into the pub's living quarters, behind the bar, Tom saw, perched on a high-backed chair and sipping at a pint pot, the untidy figure of Weasel Meakin. While Tom and Mardlin had been chatting in the bar he had slipped unobtrusively through the stable yard and tapped on the kitchen window to attract Ann's attention. Explaining he had an appointment with Mr Norton, he had been admitted to wait in the back room.

Tom placed him immediately as the little man who was serving food and drink at the Flixton canal site. He also remembered seeing him in Edie Knapp's beerhouse on his visit there with Langley before Christmas. The detective hoped that whatever this old gaolbird had to tell him was going to be worthwhile; he had already spent longer away from his office than he had intended. Extracting a Goodman's Special from his leather cigar case, Tom eyed the diminutive figure disdainfully. 'This had better be good,' he said.

Saul Meakin's story most certainly proved to be worth Tom's time. For some while now, the little man told him, he had been keeping a close watch on Clancy Taft. With the instincts of a homing pigeon looking for its roost, the Weasel had identified him as a key player in whatever was going on under cover of the Kelsford project.

For the last two weeks Meakin, presently employed as an odd job man by the Shires Canal Company, had been working at the canal basin diggings. It was an ideal opportunity to poke round the temporary offices and store sheds on the site, and he had lost no opportunity to fill his pockets with small and highly saleable items such as drawing instruments and surveyors' tools, along with a couple of half-sovereigns left in desk drawers.

The previous morning he had spotted a new face on the site, a tall, dark-haired man wearing a reefer jacket and workman's cap. Immediately interested, the Weasel watched as he went into Clancy Taft's wooden lean-to hut, which acted as his site office. Slipping round the side of the shack, Meakin was able to secrete himself behind some barrels that were stacked beneath the office window, left open against the summer heat. His acutely tuned ears picked up the newcomer's voice, which had a soft Irish accent. 'It's still not resolved. The bastard showed up in New York, would you believe. The Brothers picked him up and from what I can make out gave him a serious going-over. Nothing. Apparently his story was that he had robbed the pub takings without a word to us, then legged it to catch a boat to America. Liam's had a letter and some newspaper cuttings. Apparently the American police are still trying to identify the body that ended up in the East river – whatever that might be. Somehow or other all the fingers on his right hand had been blown off.'

Taft's voice came through the window. 'So who the fuck was it, Connor? Do you think it might have been Ike Harriman?'

'If it was, he hid the money well. I turned the house over before those coppers showed up. Not a penny piece, no sign of the bag, nothing. It's a pity he had to go so soon. I'd have liked to have kept an eye on him for a while, but he was the only one who could have identified me and we couldn't risk it. Anyway, I honestly don't think it was him.'

The voices died away for a few moments as the two men moved to the other end of the shed. Shortly afterwards the conversation floated through the window again; the subject had changed. Again it was the stranger who was speaking. 'We'll move the guns down here as soon as the warehouses are ready. It's only a day on the barge. They'll come in with a load of other crates. Don't worry, you'll get plenty of warning.'

'Do Howkins and Langran know about this?'

'No.' The reply was emphatic. 'They're so tied up in their own little swindle that they've no idea what's going on around them.' Again the voices moved away. Meakin heard the stranger, apparently near the doorway, say, 'The Yank's good. He's hinted at a side deal later, something to do with some jewellery that's coming his way . . .'

Weasel Meakin decided he had been underneath the window for too long, and silently slipped away behind the next shed and round to the front of Taft's office. He was just in time to see the stranger leaving. Checking that he was not being observed, Meakin trotted off at a discreet distance behind him. At this point his story petered out, despite his best attempts to bolster his efforts. Having followed the man into the town, the Weasel had lost him when he turned into an alley.

Tom eyed Meakin speculatively. At last the breakthrough that he had been waiting for had come. It was ironic, he thought, that after all their efforts the key to the enquiry was this strange little figure. Feeling in his waistcoat pocket, Tom pulled out a gold half-sovereign and handed it to his new informant. Meakin's eyes gleamed, both at the handsome payment for his work and with the knowledge that he had chosen his man correctly.

'When you give me the information that puts this man into my hands it's worth five pounds,' Tom said. 'Next time you want to speak to me come into the bar here and leave a message with the landlord. He'll know where to get hold of me.'

With a curt nod the little man slid off his chair and, after a cursory glance through the kitchen door into the yard to ensure he was not being observed, scuttled off.

Alone in the kitchen, Tom sat in his father's armchair next to the fireplace. Hands together and fingers steepled, he stared at the ceiling, lost in thought.

Chapter Seventeen

As Tom had expected, it was only a matter of a few weeks before Ann and Reuben announced their intention to be married before Christmas, and he lost no time in discussing with them his thoughts about their present. They were hugely grateful, as this solved the problem of where they should live as well as how they could increase their income. Reuben, at forty-one, was still a bachelor living in lodgings on the other side of town. The couple decided that as soon as the tenancy of the shop in Oxford Road had been secured he would move into the living accommodation above and make a start on preparing it for his new wife and stepson.

The legal matters regarding the tenancy of the shop were being dealt with on behalf of the landlord by the Kelsford Bank of Commerce. Tom, Ann and Reuben were waiting in the banking hall at Cumberland Place when Ruth spotted them as she came down the main staircase from the directors' suite.

It had been an extremely trying morning for Ruth and she was now on her way out to keep an appointment with Mannie Issitt, which she hoped would help her to cool down a little. The source of her annoyance lay in the usual Monday meeting with her fellow directors, Jakob Peters and Solomon Meyer. Both of them were first-generation Russians from neighbouring villages in the Ukraine, who, along with Isaac Samuels, had made their fortunes by hard work and clever financial dealing. Although Ruth had become a partner in the bank on her husband's death and therefore a member of the board of directors, she felt she had never been completely accepted by the two old men. While neither could fault her abilities, they were never able to come to terms with the fact that a woman should be treated on equal terms in the business world. Thus, while Ruth was included in much of the day-to-day running of the bank, she had grown accustomed to the fact that on certain issues Meyer and Peters came to mutual agreements before consulting her.

That she was about to be presented with another *fait accompli* was obvious when, upon taking their seats at the long boardroom table, they were joined by

Max Peters. Ruth's dislike for Max had not abated in the weeks since she had discovered that he was soon to be appointed to the board. Having taken over the warehousing project, the younger Peters had, she was aware, been spending a great deal of time in the company of Joshua Howkins – more than Ruth felt was good for the bank. She would have preferred to see Max distance himself and conduct their meetings in his office, where it would have been possible to maintain some advantage.

Solomon Meyer spoke first, brushing his hand through his iron-grey beard. 'We've invited Max here today, Ruth, to bring us up to date with our involvement in the warehousing scheme.' The fact that the explanation was solely for her benefit told Ruth that she was the only one present who was not already party to the situation.

Folding her hands in front of her on the table, Ruth looked around speculatively. Solomon returned to stroking his beard. Max Peters, immaculately attired in dark morning coat and grey trousers, a smug look on his pudgy face, waited for the signal to begin. His father, the oldest of the men, thin and frail, played absently with his watch-chain.

'The project is going extremely well,' began Max. Unlike Meyer, his well-modulated tones were the unmistakable product of an expensive English university education. 'By the end of next month all the canal work will have been completed, thus allowing barges instead of horse-drawn carts to bring in the remainder of the stone and brick to finish building the warehouses. They – the warehouses – are well under way, and will be ready for occupancy by Christmas. We have, I feel, been rather fortunate in managing to secure an increase in our holding in the project . . .'

'What holding?' Ruth's interruption stopped the young man in mid-flow. 'Howkins didn't want the bank to have a holding. He turned down a very good offer.'

A self-deprecating smile spread across Max Peters' soft features. 'That's changed, Ruth. Joshua and I discussed it and he came to see our point of view. We've now bought into the project as investors, which is why I'm here this morning. Late last Friday afternoon I signed the papers with Joshua on behalf of the bank and the project group.'

Ruth had a sense of foreboding. If Howkins and his associates had suddenly decided to 'allow' the bank to buy into their investment, it could only mean there were problems with cash flow. 'How much of an investment have you made?' she asked flatly.

'We now have a £100,000 share, which will generate at least thirty per cent return within two years.' Max's voice took on a degree of arrogance. Neither his father nor Meyer had approved of his actions when he told them what he had done. The overcautious old men were, Max fulminated, completely out of touch with the way in which modern business had to be conducted. Now this awkward bitch was going to ask him about things she didn't understand. God, he thought, how old men's follies remain to haunt us.

If Isaac Samuels hadn't been so eager to get between a young wench's thighs, Aaron Kosminski's daughter would still be selling cheap jewellery behind her father's shop counter. To compound the matter, since her teens she had been privy to the innermost workings of the Pipeline, putting her in possession of information about all of them that made her position virtually unassailable. To his chagrin, while Max was certain she had involved herself in liaisons over the years, the woman's discretion was such that he could uncover nothing that would give him an advantage over her.

'I don't like it!' Turning angrily away from Max Peters, Ruth addressed her co-directors. 'I hope you both knew about this before the agreement was signed, but it's fraught with danger. We originally agreed to a loan of £20,000, which was increased to a maximum of £30,000. That these people have been allowed to more than treble that figure is ridiculous! That we've allowed the situation to be altered from a straightforward loan to one in which we're dependent upon their projections is madness!' She shot a cold glare at the smug young man. 'They are Howkins' projections – not yours – are they not?' Receiving no answer, Ruth continued. 'What I also find worrying is that this deal was brokered late on a Friday afternoon near the close of banking. I'll wager that while we were all paying our respects at the synagogue, by Saturday lunchtime Howkins' lawyers had their end of the matter signed and sealed with the ink nicely dried . . .'

'I think you've made your point, Ruth,' interjected Jakob Peters in his thin reedy voice. 'That you don't approve will be noted. I don't think there's any profit in wild speculation. The bank's committed to what will without doubt prove to be a profitable enterprise.' He could not voice the fact that he fully shared her apprehension. Had his son spoken to him before completing the agreement he would have intervened. Now it was too late, and he could not allow Ruth's criticism to be upheld.

The meeting concluded, Ruth made her way down the thickly carpeted staircase to the main banking hall, preoccupied and in a less than good humour. She decided that she would have to decide whether to continue with the bank once Max Peters became a member of the board of directors, or sell her shares and move to a warmer climate.

The patiently waiting trio caught her eye, and Ruth recognised the smart straw boater that Tom Norton had been wearing on the day he had given her a lift back from Flixton. As a matter of courtesy she went over to greet him. Having been introduced to the prospective bride and groom, Ruth enquired the nature of their business at the bank and immediately showed an interest. 'Have you enquired about purchasing the lease as opposed to renting the premises?' she asked.

Ann and Reuben exchanged embarrassed glances. How could they tell this lady to whom they had only just been introduced that the shop was going to be a present? Tom, a little disconcerted, replied slowly. 'We don't know if the lease is for sale. If it is we'll need to discuss it with your legal clerk who's handling the matter. We have an appointment to see him.'

'Please come with me and we'll find somewhere more conducive to talk,' Ruth said, and without waiting for a reply she ushered them into a small side room. Leaving her new clients seated comfortably, she went off to relieve the legal clerk of the documents for 2 Oxford Road and to inform him that his services would not be required.

Returning a few minutes later, Ruth sat down and excused herself while she read through the papers. When she was satisfied that there were no likely complications she sat back and smiled. 'I think I may be able to persuade the owner of the shop to sell the lease to you. It may cost a little more initially, but the benefits would be very much to your advantage, Mrs Turner.'

Ann looked at Tom, a question in her eyes, worried that his kind gesture was going to be a financial burden. Picking up where the money was coming from, Ruth looked across at Tom.

'It would be a much sounder proposition,' she said tentatively.

'I'm not sure,' said Ann. 'It's awfully expensive, Tom.'

Tom shook his head. 'It isn't a problem. Kate came into a bit of money when her aunt died. It's just sitting in the bank, and I'd far sooner use it for this.' Giving his sister a reassuring smile, he turned to Ruth. 'Please, negotiate the best deal available and we'll be most grateful.'

'Leave it to me,' Ruth replied, and, shaking hands with her three visitors, she escorted them back into the main concourse.

Out in the street Reuben and Ann, still embarrassed that the cost of Tom's wedding present had increased considerably, said their goodbyes and set off to complete what Ann considered to be necessary shopping for the wedding.

Acting on an impulse, Tom turned round and went back into the bank. He didn't even know if Ruth would still be there, and couldn't believe his luck when he saw her at the main counter engaged in conversation with an elderly bank official. Seeing Tom, she broke off her discussion and, smiling pleasantly, joined him.

Suddenly unsure, the memory of her firm handclasp fresh in his mind, he said, 'Thank you for your help. The lease is a wedding present for Reuben and Ann. If it's more expensive please don't worry. Just contact me direct and I'll be happy to discuss it.'

'There's no problem, Mr Norton. So long as I have the papers in my possession no other client can rent the premises, and in the meantime I'll speak with the owners of the property.'

Taking a breath, and feeling like a raw youth, Tom continued. 'I really do appreciate your help. Could I take you to lunch, perhaps, to show my gratitude?'

Pausing for a second, Ruth quickly evaluated the situation. That the offer was more than a token of his gratitude was obvious, and she found it flattering that the tall policeman was interested in her – but her involvement with Henry Farmer could complicate matters. Making a swift decision, she gave her most charming smile and replied, 'Thank you, I'd like that.

Today's not possible and during the day tomorrow I have engagements, but I'm free in the evening for dinner.'

In her carriage on the way to Mannie Issitt's Ruth wondered if she was acting wisely. Her relationship with Henry was both discreet and convenient, but she would not attempt to deny that she found Thomas Norton attractive. He had an air about him that she found intriguing, and his slightly clumsy approach was rather charming. Anyway, she resolved, it was only an invitation to dinner; perhaps she was misreading the signs.

Entering the library of the house in Leaminster Gardens, Ruth found Mannie sitting in a deep leather armchair next to the fireplace. After they had exchanged greetings he invited her to take the seat opposite him. Going to the array of bottles on the sideboard, Mannie ignored the decanters of Spanish Jerez sherry and fine whiskies and selected a bottle of clear spirit, from which he poured two generous measures into cut-glass tumblers.

Issitt handed Ruth a glass of the vodka, sat down in his chair and took a sip of the drink. '*Za zdorovye*, Rushka.'

'Your health, Manfred,' Ruth replied, holding the glass appreciatively to the light.

'Almost a hundred per cent spirit from Finland,' he said, adding rather wistfully, 'Polish is difficult to come by at the moment.'

'I can take a hint,' she laughed. 'I'll send David round with a couple of bottles of Wyborowa.'

After their long association conversation between the two came easily. Ruth wondered whether to discuss the problems she was having at the bank but decided to keep her counsel for the time being. They had not seen each other since Ruth's return from Unghvar, and Manfred had, she thought, aged somewhat in the interval. His hair was becoming flecked along the sides with grey, the silver wings adding to his distinguished, urbane appearance. Doubting that he had any problems over money, she wondered if perhaps he and Rachel were going through a difficult period: Mannie had been known to wander occasionally over the years.

'A little job's come up that I'd appreciate your help with, Rushka,' he began.

The 'little job', it quickly transpired, was by no means little, and if it went wrong the political ramifications would be extensive. News had come via the Pipeline that a major jewel robbery had taken place at one of Tsar Alexander's country homes. The Romanovs owned a small country palace half a day's journey south of St Petersburg. It was there that the Tsarina Maria Fyodorovna was in the habit of spending the hot summer months with her son Prince Nikolay and his wife Princess Alexandra, away from the humid bustle of the city. In the middle of June the Tsarina had taken her entourage on a hunting trip to a forest lodge on the edge of the estate. During their absence a daring raid by a group of anarchists had taken place, and several items of jewellery belonging to the houseguests had been stolen from the palace.

Among the jewellery was a diamond necklace belonging to the princess, which was valued at several million roubles. Despite an extensive investigation by the state police, conducted in their usual incompetent manner, nothing was found. Arresting large numbers of the local inhabitants at random, they blundered round the countryside for several weeks while the real culprits were a hundred miles away within hours.

The anarchist group responsible for the theft, which called itself the Sons of Latvia, had enlisted the help of the Pipeline in order to dispose of the jewellery. Now, three months after the event, it was deemed safe to bring the haul out of Russia to be sold. Many of the items were being divided among wealthy collectors in Europe, but it was felt that the princess's necklace could not be dealt with in this manner: it was too identifiable to be allowed to remain in Europe, and in any case would be impossible to sell – as it was valued at over a million pounds sterling.

It had been decided that the Romanov necklace, as it was now known, should go across the Atlantic Ocean to the United States. A deal with a wealthy American buyer named Miles Ellingworth in New York had been arranged in Vienna, by Joachim Schallmeier. Ellingworth, Mannie assured Ruth, had the necessary contacts to ensure that once in his possession the item would disappear without trace. 'We'll use the same route as we do for emigrants,' he explained. 'The courier will come here, to Kelsford, by train from France. We'll take possession of the necklace and hold it temporarily in the vaults at Cumberland Place; I'll need to discuss that with Solly and Jakob nearer the time. Ellingworth has a business associate in Kelsford who's shortly returning to the States, so the necklace will be handed over to him on payment of the agreed sum, and the proceeds, less our commission, will be paid into a numbered bank account in Zurich.'

'What's my part in this?' asked Ruth. She was under no illusion that the story had been recounted to her for interest's sake. This sort of operation had been undertaken many times before by the Pipeline, which would make a handsome profit from its involvement.

'It'll take a few weeks to set up, so we're looking, I think, probably at the first or second week in October.' Mannie picked up his glass from the side table and gazed speculatively at the light reflecting from its crystal facets. 'I want you to go down to London for an all-expenses-paid day's shopping and then catch a train back home. On the return journey you'll make contact with the courier who will hand over the necklace. Bring it back here and place it in the bank vault, ready for the handover to our colonial cousins.' He made the operation sound simple – and, thinking it through, Ruth concluded it really was relatively straightforward. As far as she could see the most difficult part would be making contact with the courier.

'Don't worry about that,' Mannie told her, 'an identification system will be set up. If the courier doesn't approach you it'll mean something has gone wrong – in which case you just come home.'

Pouring them both another vodka, he sat in silence, watching patiently, while Ruth, lost in thought, reviewed his proposals. One thing about dealing with her was her thoroughness. Always calm and quick-witted, in Unghvar she had, he knew, saved the network from a potential disaster. If there were any flaws in the present plan she would spot them. He would have been most surprised had he known exactly what Ruth Samuels was thinking. The journey to meet the courier was, she felt, routine and could be left to Mannie to plan. As she sat sipping at her vodka she realised that, unwittingly, Manfred had shown her the perfect way in which to deal with Max Peters.

Looking out of the bay window at a thin drizzle of rain falling across the perfectly manicured lawn of the manor house at Great Olston, Lucas Sangster felt a headache coming on. He had spent the morning checking documents, writing letters and, like a circus performer, working out how he was going to keep all the balls he was juggling in the air. Just a few more months, he thought, and he would be able to leave this depressing climate and return to the warm Californian sunshine.

Because of his commitments in the Midlands, the American had left his Kensington home and taken up the lease on Olston Grange just before the previous Christmas. Five miles from Kelsford, it was a pleasant Georgian house, set in two acres of land and far enough from the road to ensure absolute privacy, while not being too large to make security difficult. Despite the luxurious surroundings Sangster still yearned for the open spaces of the great American West, where he could ride for days without setting eyes on another living person.

When he had told Arthur Cufflin that he had been a gold miner, Sangster was telling the truth. One of eight children, at the age of nineteen he had, almost unnoticed, slipped away from his parents' dirt farm on the outskirts of El Paso to make his fortune in the California goldfields. Unfortunately the gold rush was effectively over by the time he arrived. After a short period spent ineffectively panning in the California hills, Sangster, a big strong lad who had been brought up on heavy manual work, gravitated to working in the saloons that proliferated throughout the Western townships. Getting into trouble in this sort of environment was unavoidable. At the age of twenty, brawling with a drunken teamster in a San Francisco bar, he hit his opponent over the head with a wooden stool, killing him. Fleeing the California law enforcement officers, he arrived back in Texas just as his home state was declaring for the South in the spreading War of the States. A good horseman and an excellent shot, he managed, as a soldier of the Confederate Army, to survive the vicissitudes of battle until at the battle of Gettysburg a 'Minnie ball' in the chest ended the war for him. The big Texan was fortunate in that the bullet, glancing off a rib and damaging a lung, exited through his right side, avoiding the deadly process of field surgery but keeping him safely in hospital until the war was lost.

After the collapse of the Southern armies Sangster moved north to New York, where he was soon working as an enforcer for Miles Ellingworth. Before long he returned to San Francisco, this time as Ellingworth's trusted lieutenant in the far West. When the arms shipments to Europe became big business it was he whom Ellingworth chose to send to England to manage his affairs.

Bringing his mind back to the present, Sangster rubbed his aching temples and attempted to concentrate. The deal with the Irishmen was going smoothly. On occasions unpredictable, but with a flair for handling firearms and an ability to resolve problems swiftly, they were the closest thing to Americans that he had yet encountered. Less encouragingly, it had been necessary for him to visit London a couple of times to negotiate deals with a group of East European activists. He agreed wholeheartedly with Connor Devlin's assessment that they were dangerous people. Their lack of coordinated activity, combined with a predilection for gratuitous violence, made them loose cannons whose actions would sooner or later spell disaster for anyone involved with them.

Turning from the window, he moved back to his leather-topped writing desk to recheck the figures he had been working on. He had, he mused, just about got Joshua Howkins and his partners tied up nicely. Howkins was greedy, and had jumped at Sangster's scheme to buy out the quarry company in Derbyshire.

Of the £100,000 that had been acquired from the Bank of Kelsford, only £10,000 had been needed to purchase the ailing Batsford Stone through the untraceable bogus company that Sangster had set up in London. In his rush to complete the deal Max Peters had failed to appreciate a fundamental loophole in the contract to which he was committing the bank. He had not specified in what proportions the bank's investment should be assigned, leaving it to Howkins and his partners to obtain the best return possible. Consequently, on paper at least, the Kelsford Bank of Commerce now owned a £100,000 investment solely in Batsford Stone, which was about to collapse – leaving the money to disappear without trace.

As planned, the Shires Canal Company had, on Howkins' advice, paid £10,000 in advance for building stone from the quarry – thus covering Howkins' investment. When Batsford Stone was shortly declared bankrupt there would be much wringing of hands and the Shires would be forced to repurchase stone at an inflated price from a Midlands quarry, which Messrs Howkins and Sangster also owned. This time, however, the second quarry was a legitimate enterprise, which could deliver as many barges of cut and faced stone as were needed. Batsford Stone had already been sold to a firm of developers who wished to build houses on the site, leaving a very comfortable profit for all involved.

At Sangster's suggestion, Max Peters had been persuaded to make a personal investment of £10,000. It might be useful, when the investment crashed, to have some hold over the young banker. A second nice touch, which at the time eluded Howkins, was that the second quarry, Pennine Excavations, bought with the bank's money, had been registered solely in Sangster's name.

Over the years Sangster had learned the benefit of ensuring that every opportunity should be maximised. With this in mind he decided to offset any financial liabilities on his employers' behalf, and to ensure Howkins' future compliance by, as they said in America, burying him.

Summoning the parlourmaid from the next room, where she was diligently applying beeswax to the long Georgian dining table, he instructed her to tell the coachman to be ready to take him into Kelsford in thirty minutes.

As it happened, unbeknown to Sangster, circumstances and Howkins' personal greed were about to combine, making it easier for the American to achieve his aim than he could ever have hoped for.

Joshua Howkins had acquired his personal fortune by many devious and often dishonest means. When the Kelsford Warehousing Project first presented itself in need of financial backing he approached Lucas Sangster, whom he had met through a business acquaintance, and Brewitt Gotheridge and Oswald Langran, both of whom he had been involved with previously. Having secured the necessary £100,000 from the bank, Howkins decided it was an opportune time to dispense with Langran and Gotheridge's involvement in the enterprise. Engaging originally with Howkins and Sangster in what they knew to be a shady deal to acquire property in the area of the canal basin before building work commenced, Gotheridge and Langran had already made a considerable amount of money. From the outset Howkins had carefully avoided revealing to them the full extent of his intentions, and while they knew that some form of swindle might be on the cards in respect of the stone supply, neither knew that Howkins had bought the quarry as part of his overall design. Therefore, when he warned them in confidence of the imminent bankruptcy of Batsford Stone, which would, as he pointed out, jeopardise the entire deal, the two men were only too eager to take their profits and withdraw from any future involvement in the warehousing project. That he had used their names on the agreement to secure the bank's latest involvement Howkins neglected to tell them.

Divesting himself of Langran and Gotheridge had been easy. Joshua Howkins was not so sure about Lucas Sangster. The American had an air about him that indicated he was more than an enterprising entrepreneur. For the time being, Howkins decided, he would go along with Sangster as a partner and, should the opportunity to be rid of him present itself later, he would review the situation.

When his accounts clerk nervously announced that a Mr Sangster wished to speak to him, Howkins wondered if the American were psychic. Asking his assistant to show his visitor up, he pushed aside his suppliers' accounts and sat back in his chair. With luck this interruption would be more profitable than checking how many bags of sugar had been delivered to his Latimer Street shop.

'I have a proposition to put to you, Josh.' Sangster waved his unlit cigar in Howkins' direction. Howkins nodded curtly; he hated being called Josh.

Sangster slumped in an old armchair that formed part of the tiny office's furniture. The office, above Howkins' shop in Clumber Row, was little more than a dingy storeroom. It was, as he constantly told his long-suffering wife, parsimony, not philanthropy, that had made him the owner of Kelsford's only chain of grocery shops.

'If you're prepared to take a small risk I can put you in the way of earning a great deal of money.' The deep Texan accent was barely audible.

'Go on. I'm listening.' The little slit eyes in Howkins' goblin face were alight with the fire of avaricious anticipation.

Knowing that his fish was hooked, Sangster began to feed out the line. His proposal, outlined in a low voice over the next half-hour, was one that filled Howkins with both excitement and trepidation.

The truth was that Lucas Sangster was in a slight dilemma. When the consignment of rifles had been sent from Liverpool by barge to be stored in O'Dowd's barn there had been a mix-up at the docks, and ten crates had been left on the dockside. Now, labelled as machine parts, the cases were due to arrive at Kelsford by rail the following night. Sangster had to arrange for their safe storage. Naturally, this was not how matters were explained to Howkins. As far as he was concerned, Sangster had bought a small cargo of rifles from an American contact, and needed temporarily to store them before selling them on. Should Howkins wish to provide the urgently needed warehousing he could turn a nice profit for himself, with the prospect of another cargo at a later date.

The little grocer pushed his forefinger down the inside of his high celluloid collar and eased it from his scraggy neck. A trickle of sweat ran down into his shirt. This was something outside his experience, but it sounded too good to pass up. 'We would need transport.' His voice was hoarse with nerves.

The Texan felt the muscles in his neck and back relaxing; it had been even easier than he had anticipated. Oh, I can provide transport, you greedy, stupid little bastard, he thought. 'That's no problem. Meet me tomorrow night at the Midland station and we'll accept delivery of our little windfall.' Pushing the still unlit cigar into the corner of his mouth, Sangster held out his huge right fist and the two men shook on the deal.

At half past eight the following evening, while Lucas Sangster and Joshua Howkins, wrapped in heavy overcoats against the chilly September evening, stamped their feet on the station's goods platform, Ruth Samuels and Tom Norton were being served their main course in the dining room of the Stag and Pheasant Hotel.

Tom had been apprehensive all day about his forthcoming dinner engagement. One of the reasons he had decided to take Ruth to the Stag was that, although it was one of the best hotels in Kelsford, gentlemen did not have to dress for dinner. Tom did not possess an evening suit, and to have obtained one at short notice would have proved difficult. Collecting his partner in a hansom, he wondered if he had made an error of judgement. She was, he knew, accustomed to moving in the best society, and he had a sudden pang as he handed her up into the cab that dinner might be an embarrassing disaster: the ankle-length cape with fur collar that she was wearing must have cost as much as he earned in a year.

Ruth had made careful preparations, and was looking forward to the evening. A few discreet enquiries by her coachman had soon revealed that she and Tom would be eating at the Stag and Pheasant. This was, she thought, an ideal choice. It had a reputation for good food without being overly ostentatious, and she often lunched there with clients. Taking a gamble that her escort would not put on evening dress, Ruth selected a smart skirt that she had bought in Vienna, and had not yet worn, along with a high-necked white blouse and a simple pearl choker. Mirka, fussing round, was convinced that her mistress was too understated for a first meeting with a new man, and spent over an hour repeatedly piling up and letting down Ruth's hair, until at last in frustration, taking the pins and brushes from her, Ruth sent the maid to find a suitable dress ring for the occasion.

To Tom's surprise and Ruth's relief, the evening was going remarkably smoothly. Both were well travelled and lived busy lives, so without undue effort they were able to find mutually interesting topics of conversation. Slicing into a perfectly cooked rack of lamb, redolent with a tangy rosemary sauce, Tom explained that he had developed a taste for lamb in India, where, because of the dietary constraints imposed on the Indian Sepoys by their religions, neither pork nor beef were in ample supply. Delicately lifting a forkful of roast duck, Ruth nodded in polite interest and avoided pointing out to him that for identical reasons she herself was prohibited from eating pork. As he continued to talk it suddenly occurred to Ruth that either he had not realised she was Jewish, which she doubted, or it was irrelevant to him. Already thoroughly enjoying her meal and his company, she decided there were depths to Tom Norton that she was beginning to find attractive.

Looking at her across the table, Tom hoped that things were going as well as they appeared to be. He had eaten here before on birthdays and special occasions, the last time being his parents' fortieth wedding anniversary earlier that year. Before that it must have been Kate's last birthday. The recollection aroused pangs of guilt. The woman opposite was lovely: not pretty but, with her carefully stacked midnight black hair and slightly slanting deep brown eyes, one of the most attractive women he had ever seen.

She was speaking again. 'I've been reading in the papers about these dreadful murders in London, Tom.' Formalities dispensed with, they had been on first-name terms by the time the soup was served. 'Do you think they're really the work of a single man?'

Tom paused. The recent murders of Mary Ann Nichols and Annie

Chapman in Whitechapel had been a frequent talking point in the detective office. 'Two separate women killed in a period of nine days, within walking distance of each other – it's difficult to surmise that there is more than one killer at large. I'm also told that each suffered mutilations of a similar nature.' Tom was not certain that the Whitechapel murders were a suitable subject for polite chat over the dinner table with a beautiful woman; in addition, rumour had it that feelings were running high in the East End against foreigners and Jews, and the conversation could easily take a wrong turn.

Ruth was not to be deflected. 'That they are prostitutes is interesting. There were similar murders in Paris several years ago. I understand that the mutilations to these women in London indicate the killer could be a doctor.'

Tom was beginning to feel a little out of his depth. He knew absolutely nothing about any murders in France – this was something he would have to find out from Jesse Squires – and the fact that this engaging woman was calmly working her way through half a duck in orange sauce while discussing two of the most horrendous murders in recent years was unsettling.

'Like you, Ruth, I only know what's published in the newspapers. Unless there's some specific enquiry for us to make here in Kelsford, the London police won't tell us anything that's not public knowledge.' In different circumstances Tom would have been only too happy to have discussed something that had engaged his attention since the first murder in August.

'It is interesting, though,' said Ruth, taking a deep swallow of the chilled Chablis that Tom had poured for her.

The loading of the rifles was almost completed. Standing next to the wagon drawn up on the platform alongside the goods van, Sangster hunched deeper into his overcoat and the little man next to him dug into an inside pocket and pulled out a gold fob watch. 'Quarter to ten, and that's the last but one.' Despite the early autumn chill Joshua Howkins was inordinately pleased with the evening's work. Never averse to making a quick profit, he had come to the conclusion that, although in the eyes of the law it was definitely criminal, handling the odd shipment of guns was a sound business undertaking. Sangster had arranged for a local haulier to be at the goods yard of the Midland station to offload the 'machine parts' and take them to one of Howkins' empty warehouses, from where they would be collected in a couple of weeks by the purchaser he had in mind.

Howkins would have been less happy with the arrangements had he been party to a short meeting earlier that day between Lucas Sangster, Clancy Taft and Brindley Stokes in the back room of Crooked Edie's beerhouse in Lothair Street.

The final case hefted between them to shoulder height, Taft and Brindley made to drop it over the wagon's tailboard. To Howkins' dismay the case slid from their grip and crashed onto the timbered platform, bursting open. From a split panel at one side of the box protruded the unmistakable shape of a rifle butt.

Brindley bent over the damaged case and pulled the rifle clear. Straightening up, he carefully examined the gun in the dim light cast by the platform gas lamp. Moving round the wagon to get a better view, Taft joined him.

'Well now, gentlemen, what have we here?' Taft's voice was soft and accusing. 'These are unusual machine parts, are they not, Brindley?'

Swiftly glancing round to make certain that they were not observed, Sangster put his hands up, palms forward. 'This is bad,' he muttered to Howkins, whose pallor was sufficient to indicate that the staged incident was having the desired effect. 'We've got to do something here. Leave it to me.' Sangster moved a few paces forward and said in a voice loud enough for his stunned accomplice to hear, 'Come on, boys, five pounds each and you haven't seen a thing.'

Taft and Brindley exchanged looks, as if trying to make up their minds. 'Ten,' grunted the Scotsman, pushing his cap back on his head.

Sangster shrugged his shoulders and nodded in resignation, 'All right, ten – and you get to unload the next lot that comes in for another ten. Call round and see Mr Howkins first thing tomorrow morning at his office for your money.' It was all that Sangster could do not to burst out laughing. Howkins was so terrified at the prospect of being discovered that he had not been able to utter a word. He would have been even more terrified if he had known that once the guns were in his warehouse they were not going anywhere: they were Sangster's assurance that from now on Howkins would do exactly as he was told.

At a quarter past ten a hansom cab pulled up outside the house on Victoria Road, and Tom climbed out with Ruth to see her into the house. On the doorstep, her hand on the bell pull, Ruth paused before ringing it. Turning to face Tom, she said, 'Thank you for the meal and for your company. I can't remember when I last spent such an enjoyable evening.'

Standing close to her, Tom caught the whiff of her light and expensive perfume: it created an unexpectedly erotic effect as it blended subtly with the night air. He was not sure whether to kiss her hand or shake it. Instead he held it lightly in his own and said, 'May I see you again?'

Chapter Eighteen

That the woman was a police informer, Eugene Leschenko was now certain. Sitting in the bar of the Britannia, he sipped at his mug of tepid ale and watched her across the table chatting animatedly with Vassily Brovnic. She was probably, he thought, about forty, but the life she led had aged her prematurely. Lizzie Gustafsdotter, or Long Liz as everyone in the Britannia knew her, had at one time no doubt been a good-looking woman. The dark curly hair under the little bonnet surprisingly was showing no signs of grey, and her full lips, parted in a wide sensuous smile, revealed, despite several gaps, strong white teeth.

Both she and Vassily were drunk, and becoming noisy. When Lizzie's money ran out in a while she would make her way to her nearby lodgings to sleep it off. After dark, when the dim shadows cast by the gaslight were kinder to her ageing features, she would go out into Commercial Road and ply her trade – fourpence a trick with as many clients as she could pick up. The first fourpence was for her night's lodging; anything after that was beer money. Vassily was a fool. He was becoming more and more involved with the woman. At first it had merely been a casual acquaintance over drinks in the bar, but very quickly he had become one of her clients – and now he was talking about moving her into their lodgings.

Leschenko did not like England, and he particularly did not like London. After parting company with Ruth Samuels he had made his way, as planned, to Whitechapel. Here he quickly made contact with others of a similar disposition to himself: men and women who had either escaped from the political oppression of Eastern Europe or were wanted by the police of a host of other countries for crimes committed in the name of patriotism and politics.

In truth, Eugene Leschenko was by no means certain that his choice had been a good one. The living conditions in the square mile of slums between Bishopsgate and Cable Street were as bad as any he had encountered. The dingy unclean streets and the courtyards of squalid and overcrowded houses, linked together by a maze of filthy alleys, were a breeding ground for vice and disease. On every corner was a public house or drinking den that provided a refuge for the miserable flotsam that spent their waking hours in an alcoholic haze. Common lodging houses abounded in each of the mean streets, crowded with prostitutes and thieves. But these conditions guaranteed the one essential that those such as Leschenko required: anonymity.

After a very short time Eugene moved into a run-down two-bedroomed house in Varden Street with six other so-called anarchists. One of these was Vassily Brovnic, the man on the other side of the table. From the town of Nikolsburg in Moravia, Brovnic was the oldest of the group. He was, thought Leschenko, also the most stupid. Dedicated to the rule of the proletariat through rhetoric, the fat and ageing Moravian had spent the last ten years doing little more than spread anarchist doctrine in beerhouses. Now approaching forty, like Long Liz, his most useful purpose as far as Eugene could see was providing a roof over their heads.

As he pondered how to deal with Brovnic's companion, Leschenko wondered how the rest of the group would react if they knew about Lizzie's treachery. His fellow Latvian, Miroslav Draskovic, would, he knew, follow his lead. It was through Miroslav's good offices that he had been admitted into the anarchist cell in Varden Street. He was not sure about Hans Schneider and Oleg Cherkashin: both were friends of Brovnic, and subscribed to the outdated political rubbish that he preached. Nina and Klara, the two women in the group, were unknown quantities. Klara, so willing in bed, would as Eugene's mistress accept any decision he made. That left small and unattractive Nina Volputin. How she would vote he was not certain. Probably against the whore. Nina had a capacity for hate that rendered her at the best of times unbalanced, Leschenko felt. If he could sow the seeds of doubt in her twisted mind it would not be difficult to ally her with him.

Vassily was standing up, putting his hand out to steady himself against the window-ledge at the back of his seat. 'If you've got no more money I might as well go home, Lizzie.' His slurred tones boomed across the wide taproom, catching the attention of the licensee's wife who was engaged in conversation with a commercial traveller at the bar.

'That's right, you fat bastard: no more money to buy you ale!' Now also on her feet, the woman's good humour had been replaced by a drunken aggressiveness. 'Piss off and play with yourself, you useless bugger. You'll be back tonight, though, won't you, when I've got a couple of shillings in my bag.' Swaying dangerously while trying to maintain her balance, she knocked over Leschenko's pint pot, spilling ale onto the sawdust-covered floor. Replacing the glass that she was idly polishing on the shelf behind her, the landlady wrapped the bar towel round her right hand and, closing it into a fist, moved casually round the counter and across to the troublesome pair. Women like Lizzie Stride, or Gustafsdotter as she was known to the foreigners she was with, were a daily nuisance.

As she crossed the room Mrs Ringer made a small gesture to a big man with battered features sitting on a stool at the opposite end of the room. There was no point in Joe the doorkeeper getting involved at this stage. 'Time to go home, Lizzie.' Her voice was flat and expressionless, an instruction not a suggestion.

Lizzie Stride glared balefully at the landlady, ready for trouble, then thought better of it. Mrs Ringer was not someone to mess with. Only last week she had taken out two of Big Mary Connolly's teeth in a fight that had spilled out across the pub step into Dorset Street. Carefully maintaining her balance, Lizzie nodded her acquiescence and, pulling her tattered shawl closer to her thin shoulders, marched unsteadily towards the large swing doors. The stocky landlady walked with her, keeping in close; it was not too late for Lizzie to sweep up a glass and put it through a window.

A movement at one of the tables near the door caught Lizzie's eye. A short, dark-haired girl in her mid-twenties wearing a black crepe bonnet had broken off the soft and intimate conversation she was having with a thin market porter in order to watch the diversion with mild interest. Liz made to move towards the table. 'What's your problem then, Mary Kelly?' she demanded angrily. 'Stop laughing at me, you bitch – I'll have your fucking head off.' A beefy fist took hold of the loose material at the back of her dress and, almost lifting her from her feet, propelled her head first into the street.

On the way back to their lodgings, steering the unsteady Brovnic down Commercial Street past the myriad of parked market wagons and passing traffic, Leschenko wondered what to do about Vassily's woman. Lizzie Gustafsdotter had recently paid two or three visits to 95 Varden Street, and it was on the second of these that Eugene's suspicions had been aroused. It was the middle of the morning, earlier in the month. She and Vassily had been out to take some small items of jewellery to a local pawnbroker whom Vassily knew was not overly particular about the provenance of the items he handled.

Despite her dark hair and London accent, Long Liz claimed to be Swedish. Certainly on one occasion in the Ten Bells in Church Street she had spent over an hour in unintelligible conversation with a Swedish sailor. But it was her interest in a conversation between Klara Brandes and Hans Schneider that alerted Leschenko. Although all the occupants of Varden Street spoke some English, conversations were conducted in a variety of languages, primarily Russian or German. Klara had been born in Prague and Hans in Vienna; they shared their Jewish lineage.

With Vassily out in the tiny kitchen preparing tea, Eugene had been sitting on Brovnic's truckle bed behind the door, talking to Lizzie in broken English about life in the Baltic States, which she seemed to be relatively well informed about. He noticed she was only half-listening to his words, and was instead trying to overhear a conversation between Nina and Hans on the other side of the room. Mildly interested that Gustafsdotter appeared to understand

Yiddish, he later asked what they had been discussing. Hans told him that he and Miroslav were proposing to break into a grocer's shop in nearby Great Garden Street; Nina was to be their lookout. The Latvian might not have thought any more about the matter, except that on the evening the raid was to take place it had to be called off. On an early reconnaissance Klara spotted two policemen going into a house in Old Montague Street, opposite where the burglary was to take place.

Last night Lizzie had stayed over at the house, sleeping in the front room with Brovnic. Upstairs, in the bedroom that was occupied by Nina, Miroslav and Hans, a lengthy discussion had taken place about their planned robbery of a nearby dairy in Whitechapel Road. It was very simple. The coming Friday afternoon, when the wages for the milkmen were ready for each to collect when he finished his round, Eugene, accompanied by Oleg Cherkashin and Miroslav Draskovic, armed with the revolvers that Vassily kept in his loft, would walk into the pay office, snatch the money and make a dash into the adjoining back street. From there they would split up, mingle with the Friday afternoon crowds and make their way back to Varden Street. Eugene spent a long time convincing the others that the key to the success of his plan lay in its simplicity.

Leaving to use the outside privy, Eugene had detected a movement in the hallway as he descended the stairs and heard the door of Vassily's room quietly closing. At the foot of the stairs he paused to listen. At first he could only make out Vassily's soft snores, but, remaining motionless for a while, he eventually detected a light breathing on the other side of the door, then the sound of someone moving away across the room.

Leschenko was out the following morning before anyone else was stirring. Going to a derelict house at the end of the road, from where he could watch the front door of number 95, he had settled down to wait. Soon after nine o'clock the tall figure of Lizzie Gustafsdotter had come out. Closing the door behind her, she had made her way to Commercial Road, where she turned right and headed towards Lambeth Street, before taking a side road towards the railway yard. Leschenko now had little doubt where she was headed. Having passed the goods yard, he had watched from a safe distance as she went into Leman Street police station. Satisfied that his suspicions were correct, the Latvian had made his way to a coffee stall to consider his next move.

Still meditating upon the morning's events, Leschenko reached Varden Street, where his insistent knocking brought Nina to the door. Initially opening it just enough to identify him, she helped Eugene manoeuvre the befuddled Brovnic into the narrow passageway. Pushing him into the front room between them, they laid him on the stained mattress and, having pulled his boots off, left him snoring noisily.

'Drunken bastard,' Nina said matter of factly as they closed the door on the sleeping figure. Leschenko paused in his deliberations to look at her. Standing less than five feet tall, Nina Volputin was one of the least attractive women he could ever recollect seeing. Naturally small, a childhood spent ill-clothed and undernourished in the ghettos of her home town of Kremnitz in northern Hungary had left her stunted and ugly, with a disposition that matched her looks. Her only saving grace, thought the Latvian, was her hair. At present pinned up in an unstylish bun, the thick Titian tresses reached beyond her narrow waist when loosed. How Nina came to be in England or how she came to be living in Brovnic's house he did not know. That she had at some point been Brovnic's mistress was in little doubt, but then she and Klara had both, even in Leschenko's short association with them, slept with all the men in turn. In the closed society in which they moved such behaviour was accepted as normal. Although Klara was at present primarily involved with him, Eugene would not have been surprised – nor offended, for that matter – to find her curled up in bed with one of his fellow conspirators.

Having made his way up the greasy flight of stairs to the room off the top landing, he lay back on the rickety double bed underneath the window. The bulky form of Oleg Cherkashin was visible in the late afternoon light that filtered through the dirty, uncurtained window, dozing fitfully on a straw-filled palliasse in the opposite corner. Eyes wide open, gazing at the cracked plaster on the ceiling, Eugene continued to consider his dilemma. After a while he reached a decision. That Lizzie was an informer was in his mind sufficient for her to be dealt with, but the fact that she knew his identity was also crucial. When his grand design to initiate the Great Latvian Revolution was eventually put into action, it was imperative that his anonymity be protected until he was ready to reveal himself.

Leschenko resolved that it would be simpler not to discuss the matter with any other members of the household. Tomorrow was Saturday, which meant that the streets of Whitechapel would be busy. For many of the inhabitants, the week's work ended, they would be spending the best part of the day in the local alehouses. Later in the evening Lizzie Gustafsdotter and her sisters of the streets would be out relieving the men of what little money the landlords had allowed them to retain. A small flame of anticipation began to kindle in his brain as he decided how to deal with the woman.

The squeak of a noisy hinge on the bedroom door broke into his train of thought as Klara entered the room. Stooping silently over the recumbent shape of Cherkashin to ensure that he was asleep, she slipped off her plain black dress and dropped it over the end of the bed. Snuggling under the single blanket, she pulled it up to cover them both and busied herself undoing his trouser fly buttons.

Unlike Nina, Klara Brandes, the younger of the two women, was not unprepossessing. Her pale features, prevented from being good looking by an overly large and slightly pointed nose, were otherwise pleasant and well proportioned. At twenty-five, her slim body under the light chemise was firm and compliant.

Absently, his mind still occupied with other things, Eugene parted the unlaced bodice and caressed her small hard nipples. As her ministrations began to take effect he felt the fire in his brain slowly transfer to his belly and the girl's growing excitement at the erection that filled her hands. With a swift motion Klara pushed back the covering blanket and mounted him. Thrusting urgently at each other they climaxed quickly, she in a blaze of blinding passion, he in a darker world, far from the creaking bed and the tiny room that confined them.

Saturday morning dawned dull and miserable. Rain pattered on the cracked bedroom windowpane as Klara stirred and climbed out of the bed to use the chamber-pot. Oleg's mattress, she saw, was empty. He had obviously not returned from his previous night's activities. Back in bed she was pleasantly surprised to find that her partner was also awake and ready to make love again. Usually content with once or twice in the week, since yesterday afternoon he had been particularly demanding, and they had enjoyed each other's pleasures during the early evening and again twice in the night. It was sex as she had not previously experienced it with Eugene. Normally a considerate and easily pleased lover, these recent bouts had been hard and quick sessions of pure rutting. Yesterday evening he had even insisted on doing it while Oleg had been in the room with them, preparing to go out.

Leaving Klara to doze off again, Eugene got out of bed and, swilling his face in the cold water on the night stand, dressed quickly before slipping out of the room. It was half past seven and the overnight rain had slackened to a cold autumn drizzle. Turning up his jacket collar, Leschenko set off down Cannon Street in the direction of Dutfield's Yard in nearby Berners Street, and the tiny printing shop at the back of the International Working Men's Educational Club that housed the Yiddisher magazine *The Worker's Friend*.

The International Club, as it was known, was a centre for all manner of political activists and intriguers, drawing like a magnet every anarchist and revolutionary newly arrived in London. Nina Volputin, with the help of an elderly Jewish typesetter known only as Joachim, laboured in the tiny workshop at the end of the courtyard two or three days a week to produce the cheap anarchist publication that she and her friends hawked on the streets of East London for a halfpenny a copy. Leschenko had taken the keys from her the previous evening on the pretence that he would spend Saturday stripping down and cleaning the hand-operated printing press that churned out the broadsheet.

As he expected at this time in the morning the club's dilapidated and peeling front door was closed and locked tight. Leschenko turned down the side of the building into Dutfield's Yard. The heavy wooden yard gates were permanently held back in the open position because of the broken hinge that caused the far one to hang drunkenly.

Letting himself into the dismal print shop, Leschenko felt the damp air and sour odour of printing inks wrap round him. He heard an urgent scuffling sound as an unseen rodent scurried to the safety of its hole. It was still not fully light, and the Latvian applied a match to the stump of a candle to see what he was doing.

Hanging up his damp jacket and workman's cap, Eugene placed the carpetbag he was carrying on the rickety table that Nina pretentiously referred to as her editing desk and began to empty out its contents. First was his one and only spare jacket. Threadbare and worn, it was a nondescript dark green colour, which later nobody would be able to recollect whether they had seen or not. Next was a large double-peaked deerstalker hat along with a dark Raglan overcoat, both of which belonged to Vassily Brovnic; while the length of the coat was all right, when it was buttoned up he could have got Klara inside with him. Although both had seen better days, he knew that Brovnic would never have loaned them to him had he asked. Finally, from the bottom of the bag he withdrew a small oilstone and a large heavy lock knife.

Going to a shelf on which there were several bottles of printing ink, Leschenko rummaged about until he found what he was looking for: a small tin of machine oil. Returning to the table he cleared a space, and having poured a small amount of the oil onto the stone he carefully spread it with his fingers over the entire surface. Opening the lock knife, Eugene tested the edge with his thumb before placing the five-inch blade on the oiled stone and massaging the edge against it in small circular movements, testing the razor-like steel every few strokes. The knife was an old one that his father had given to him when he was a youth of fifteen in Daugavpils. Many years ago he had broken the final inch from the tip while opening the window of a pawnshop in Riga, before ransacking the contents of the back room. Afterwards it had taken him hours of patient grinding to reshape the broken end into a smooth round. The loss of its tip did nothing to detract from the knife's effectiveness. It had been his primary weapon for more years than he cared to remember, and he guarded its fine edge with the loving care that another might lavish on a child or a favourite pet. After about an hour the aroma of freshly baked bread caught his attention. Wiping the oil from its blade, he folded the knife and slipped it into his trouser pocket.

In the kitchen of the club Freda, the young fair-haired cook, was lifting a tray of dinner plate-sized loaves of bread from the oven onto the kitchen range. The tantalising smell served to remind Leschenko that he had not eaten since the previous day. Cheerfully the girl asked him in Yiddish if he wanted one.

Not understanding the question, Leschenko pointed to the bread and said in Russian, 'Breakfast. Yes.' This time it was the girl who looked nonplussed. Eugene tried again, this time in German.

'Ja,' smiled the girl, 'for breakfast, one loaf with a cup of tea, one penny.' Leschenko gave her the penny and took his food through into the deserted club room. It was, he thought, hardly worthy of the title. In reality it was a large front parlour with some old tables and chairs set round, at which the clients played interminable games of chess and hatched plots that were never going to mature. At the back of the room was a trestle table, behind which stood an old-fashioned walnut cabinet laden with bottles. Although the premises were not officially licensed, the few among the clients who had any money could purchase drinks if they wished. Upstairs were rooms – so he was told, he had never been up there – that could be hired for meetings, and a couple of others that were let out from time to time as nightly accommodation.

The girl brought his tea in an enamel mug. As she set it down on the table Leschenko asked, 'Where is Louis?'

'Herr Diemschutz has gone to the market today,' she replied politely. 'It is Saturday and he always goes to the market on a Saturday.'

The Latvian grunted. He had hoped to catch the club steward before he left for the market at Sydenham. Louis Diemschutz, in addition to managing the affairs of the club, also sold cheap jewellery, usually in the various street markets in the East End. 'And Frau Diemschutz?'

'I am sorry, mein Herr, she is also out at the moment.'

With a nod of dismissal, Leschenko returned his attention to tearing off a piece of the warm unleavened bread. Brovnic had given him a pair of cheap gold-plated earrings to dispose of through the club steward, and he was going to be annoyed that he had to wait another week for some extra beer money. Eugene replaced the trinkets in his pocket. Feeling a draught behind him, he turned to see who had just come in.

Two young men in shabby suits nodded to him and sat at the far side of the room. One, with a huge waxed moustache and high starched collar, ordered some bread and tea from the girl when she appeared from the kitchen. Paying scant attention to the Latvian, they buried their heads in quiet conversation. Leschenko was relieved that the two were strangers: it would not suit his purposes at the moment to be seen by someone who knew him. Finishing his food, he made his way back out through the kitchen into the yard before Hans or Oleg came in for a warm and some tea.

Back again in the cold workshop he decided against lighting the pot-bellied stove, which was the only source of heat. Wrapping himself in an old blanket, he settled down to while away the remainder of the day.

It was not until after eight o'clock in the evening that Leschenko left his hiding place. Dressed in the shabby green jacket, he quietly locked up the print shop and made his way to the yard gates, round the side of the building and into the club through the front door. It was busy now; the smoky room was packed with men from almost every country between Calais and St Petersburg. Most of the shabby tables were occupied by earnest young men engaged in concocting devious schemes. As usual, those with a few coppers were buying occasional drinks for their less fortunate fellows. There were very few women, and Eugene was pleased to note that no one from the Varden Street lodgings was in evidence. Sitting down on the edge of a group of men whom he knew vaguely to be from somewhere near Warsaw, he engaged in a debate about the merits of achieving an independent Poland through armed revolt.

At about half past nine Eugene slid unnoticed away from the table and into the passageway. He waited patiently for a few minutes until the rotund figure of the steward's wife pushed past him on her way from the kitchen into the main room. Quickly he slipped out through the kitchen door and into the pitch-black yard. Letting himself into the workshop, without lighting a candle he went to the table where he had laid out his change of clothing. Pulling on the large overcoat, he buttoned it up in the dark. It made him look considerably heavier than he was. With the peak of the deerstalker pulled down over his face, he locked the door behind him and, leaving the yard, turned right past the beerhouse on the corner.

It took Leschenko almost an hour to locate the woman. Drifting into crowded taprooms, he took a cursory look round the Saturday night customers before leaving without buying a drink. The rain, which had cleared up during the afternoon, was now falling lightly again, with the promise of becoming heavier as the night wore on. Eventually, peering in through the lighted windows of the Bricklayers in Settles Street, he found what he was looking for. Lizzie Gustafsdotter was leaning against the bar talking to a short and tubby young man in his mid-twenties.

Moving back out of the light, Leschenko concealed himself in a darkened entry opposite the pub and waited. It was about half an hour later when Lizzie emerged from the bar arm in arm with the young man, who by now was wearing a short dark overcoat and a cap usually favoured by sailors. To Eugene's surprise the couple ambled back along Commercial Road and into Berners Street, heading towards the International Club.

It was not to the club that Lizzie was heading with her client. She had been in on several occasions but was never particularly comfortable there. No one objected to her profession, but she was Scandinavian and did not fit in with the habitual East European clientele – while her fluent knowledge of Yiddish, acquired as a child in her native Gothenburg, served more to attract suspicion than acceptance. However, she had made some useful contacts there, including the fat Russian Vassily, who seemed to think that he was in love with her. As a precaution Lizzie always ensured she was known in the club by her maiden name of Gustafsdotter rather than her married name of Stride. It was a small detail, but worthwhile. The club was often the subject of police interest and in her calling the less that was known about her true identity the better.

Lizzie led the young warehouse clerk, whose name she had found out was Percy, to Dutfield's Yard next to the club. All the girls had their favourite places for servicing clients, depending on where they picked them up. The whole of Whitechapel was a haven of narrow alleys and secluded back yards, ideal for turning a quick trick. Since the murders of Mary Ann Nichols in August and Annie Chapman a week or two ago, places such as Bucks Row and the yards round Hanbury Street were studiously avoided. Lizzie had known both of the dead women, and the thought of some maniac murdering them and then slashing them about with a knife sickened and frightened her badly. At present she was living at Mrs Cooper's lodging house in Flower and Dean Street with four other women who plied the same trade as herself. They had discussed the possibility of working in pairs, so as to keep a watch on each other, but the nature of their calling made that almost impossible and they continued to drift along as before. The recent killings meant that the streets were flooded with extra policemen. As far as Lizzie was concerned they appeared not to have the remotest idea what they were about, and merely made it more difficult for her to work.

Dutfield's Yard was one of Lizzie's favourite places to work a client. It was a secluded court, but within sight of the street lamp and near the Bricklayers. Strolling at a leisurely pace down Berners Street, she only half-listened to the young man's inconsequential chatter. It was obvious to her that he was embarking on his first experience of this kind, and was both nervous and excited. She was more interested in ensuring that no patrolling policeman was watching them, or that anyone more sinister might be following in their tracks. As they reached the entrance to the yard Lizzie's keen ears caught the sound of a scuffling and grunting in the darkness just beyond the gate. Damnation! One of the other girls was using her spot.

Pausing near the gates, she said to the young clerk, in a voice loud enough for the other woman to hear, 'Do you want a quick drink, love? Come back in ten minutes.' By now Percy Thomson was not at all certain that he wanted to do anything other than go home. Out for an evening's drinking with two of his friends from work, he had somehow become entangled with this woman and accepted her offer of the ultimate enjoyment for the price of a few drinks and some coin of the realm. His mates had quietly melted away, and he was now in a dark back street feeling rather unwell and decidedly unsafe.

'No, I don't think so, thank you,' he stammered.

The woman looked at him appraisingly. 'Feeling a bit dodgy, darling?' she asked solicitously. The last thing she wanted was for him to be sick over her at the crucial moment. The lad nodded. As they passed the lighted window of a house with a fruit stall in the open window, he pulled a penny from his pocket and bought a bunch of grapes from the fruiterer who was packing away his produce for the night.

By now the persistent rain had become quite heavy, and they moved across the road to shelter in a doorway while Percy ate some of the grapes to settle his churning stomach. Lizzie wondered idly if it would be worth hitching her skirts and doing it here in the front door of the house. It was risky, but it would get the job done and she could be back in the pub in ten minutes. She dismissed the idea as she saw the figure of a man in an open door opposite, smoking his last pipe of the night and watching them suspiciously.

Ten minutes later two figures emerged from the entrance to the yard, and she gave a sigh of relief – immediately followed by a low exclamation of annoyance. Walking sedately down Fairclough Street directly across from where they were sheltering was the tall figure of a policeman. 'Sod it. Frigging copper!' she muttered.

To her annoyance the policeman disappeared into the beerhouse at the corner of the street, reappearing, wiping his moustache with the back of his hand, almost twenty-five minutes later. Secure in the knowledge that he would not return for at least half an hour, at last Lizzie moved across the road with her young client into the darkened yard.

Eugene Leschenko, whose presence behind them Lizzie had failed to detect, despite her backward glances, followed the proceedings from his viewpoint further down the street. He was irritated that it was all taking so long. As soon as Lizzie and her customer disappeared into the blackness, Eugene crossed the road after them and melted into a patch of shadow by the broken gate.

The sounds of the clumsy engagement a few feet away were short-lived. In under two minutes he heard the dull clink of change, and the young man hurriedly emerged into the street. In his rush to be away from the scene of his sordid adventure he bumped into the figure in the shadows and, with a small gasp of fright, almost ran back up Berners Street towards the inviting lamplight of Commercial Road.

Leschenko moved cautiously into the yard, momentarily blinded by the intensity of the blackness. 'Lizzie,' he hissed quietly. 'Lizzie, it's me, Eugene, I need to speak to you.' In the silence he heard a sharp intake of breath cracked with fear. 'It's me, Eugene,' he repeated. His eyes now accustomed to the gloom, he could see her thin shape, back to the wall, hands at her sides, palms pressed hard against the damp brickwork.

'Jesus Christ! You frightened me to bleeding death. I thought you was the Slasher!' He could see the terror shining in her eyes. 'What do you want?'

'I was coming out of the Club and saw you,' he said casually. The woman was calmer now. 'How much for business?'

Lizzie relaxed; this was familiar territory. 'For a friend threepence, and you can buy me a drink after.' The friendly smile was back, an expression of coquettish invitation. 'How do you like it?' she asked softly, moving closer to him.

Leschenko bent forward and whispered in her ear. Throwing her head back, she gave a soft laugh and, turning to face the wall, began to haul her skirts up. The lock knife, concealed by his side, was already open in his right hand. Grabbing the thick curly black hair at the back of the surprised woman's head with his left, he drew the knife across her throat in one smooth movement. She was dead almost before her killer had thrown her face forward onto the ground as a fountain of blood spurted from the severed artery in her neck. The whole thing had taken less than five seconds.

Being careful not to tread in any of the rapidly pooling blood, Eugene stepped to one side and watched as the twitching corpse lapsed into stillness. A sudden movement in the street caused him to freeze into immobility. A couple, who appeared to be extremely drunk, were standing arguing in the edge of the light cast by the street lamp. In the middle of the woman's harangue the man slapped her hard across the face, knocking her to the ground. With an imprecation he lurched off down the road, bellowing an unintelligible obscenity at some unseen passer-by on the other side of the street. Leschenko remained perfectly still, hardly breathing, while the woman gathered herself up and followed the man out of view.

Letting himself silently into the shadowy office of *The Worker's Friend*, Eugene stripped off the heavy overcoat and hat, and swilled his hands and the knife in a bowl of water at the sink. Carefully drying the knife, he hid it under a floorboard that he had loosened during the day.

Dressed once more in his green jacket, the Latvian secured the outer door of the workshop and was about to make his way to the kitchen door of the club when he heard the clatter of hooves as a pony pulling a small market cart swung into the yard from Berners Street. He would have been trapped in the middle of the courtyard had the pony not suddenly shied at the smell of the rapidly congealing blood, almost throwing the driver from his seat. Roundly cursing the horse for its obstinacy, Louis Diemschutz climbed down to poke with his whip at the inert bundle lying against the wall. Recoiling in horror at the sight of the bloodstained corpse, just visible in the dim illumination cast by the cart's single acetylene lamp, the steward dropped his whip and lurched out of the yard into the street, grabbing the wooden gatepost for support.

A few seconds later, peering in at the kitchen window, Leschenko saw Mrs Diemschutz hurry out into the club to see what the commotion was about. Slipping into the deserted kitchen he followed her unobtrusively into the clubroom, and seconds later joined the curious throng that spilled out into the street to view the latest victim of the Whitechapel murderer.

Chapter Nineteen

Tom's peaceful Sunday morning was disrupted by the clatter of hobnailed boots in the passage outside his office, followed immediately by Arthur Hollowday's spiky ginger head popping round his door.

'Telegram, sir! Boy's waiting at the front desk to see if there's a reply, sir!'

Tom put aside the sheet of paper on which he was working out a new duty roster, and gave the boy what he hoped was a stern look. Young Arthur was coming on in leaps and bounds since things had changed around the police station. Tom had never realised quite how frightened the lad had been of Joe Langley until a few nights ago when he had been talking to Walter Mardlin in the Rifleman. Mardlin's wife Julia now worked there as a barmaid, and he and Tom saw each other fairly regularly when Tom was not working. The Mardlins were now lodging with the Hollowday family, and Walter's son William had become firm friends with Arthur. The youngster had confided in his new friend that he had lived in dread of Tom's predecessor.

'You're supposed to knock on the door before entering, young Arthur,' Tom said, glaring theatrically across the wide desk.

Suitably abashed, Arthur replied, 'Yes, sir. Sorry, sir – and the boy is still waiting, sir.'

Tom opened the envelope and took out the single sheet of typed paper. It was timed at eight o'clock that morning, 30 September 1888, and addressed to HEAD OF DETECTIVES KELSFORD BOROUGH POLICE FORCE. The neatly typed text read:

> Holding in custody at Leman Street Police Station 'H' div metpol Russian alien Eugene Leschenko on sus involvement in murder Elizabeth Stride aka Elizabeth Gustafsdotter and other poss murders Whitechapel district stop bvd also involved

anarchist activities stop in possession papers indicating may have connections your force area stop if you wish to interview advise by return stop.

Signed
Abberline Detective Inspector

Tom Norton rubbed a hand across his jaw, then smoothed the ends of his moustache as he reread the telegram. He had never heard of anyone called Leschenko, and the telegram was not overly informative. Leaving Arthur waiting, he went down the corridor and let himself into Fred Judd's empty office, where the station telephone was located. After ten frustrating minutes he was finally assured by the Kelsford operator that the Leman Street police station was not on the telephone.

Returning to his own office, Tom scribbled out a reply to inform the officer in charge at Leman Street that he would take the next available train to London and would be in Whitechapel the following morning. Handing it to Arthur for the waiting telegram boy, he instructed him to go down to the railway station and enquire about the times of trains to London that afternoon.

Alone again, Tom reread the telegram. Even if Leman Street was not on the telephone, other stations must be. A telephone call would have given him the opportunity to find out what this was all about, instead of going off on what might prove to be a wild goose chase. Dropping the message onto his desk, he turned his mind to the problem it created for him.

It was five days since Tom had seen Ruth Samuels, and he could not get the woman out of his mind. When she had agreed to see him again he thought she was merely being polite. The following day, however, he received an invitation to dinner at Victoria Road on Sunday evening. For the first time in a long while Tom was having to examine his feelings and make certain decisions. He not only found Ruth physically attractive, but also felt a quality about her that he could not define. She had a personality and intelligence that bewitched him, but he knew that pursuing a relationship with her was going to be fraught with difficulties. An enormous social gap yawned between them. As a forty-five shillings a week police inspector he could hardly offer to take her out to the places she was accustomed to frequenting. There was a difference in their cultural backgrounds. She was Jewish, and he was very aware that the Jewish community in Kelsford was closed and separate: he doubted he would be accepted in her society any more than she would be in his. Then there was his job. Both his and Kate's circle of friends had, thanks to the nature of his work, been restricted: on many occasions they had cancelled social engagements at the last minute when he had to work unexpectedly. Tonight, Tom sighed, was no different. He was going to have to tell Ruth he could not attend the dinner party. That he would not be missed by the other guests he did not doubt; it was the fact that she might be insulted and might not give him another chance that bothered him.

A polite tap at the door announced young Arthur's return. The boy must have run all the way to the station and back, thought Tom. There was, Arthur informed him, one train only that afternoon, leaving Kelsford at half past three and arriving at St Pancras at a quarter to seven. Tom looked at the clock on the wall – it was half past nine – and nodded absently. Taking the cigar case from his inside pocket he ran his thumb across the polished leather: '... better than one of those hinged cases ...' The words echoed through his memory. 'What do I do, Kate?' he asked quietly as Arthur closed the door behind him. In truth, Tom knew there was only one thing he could do, and twenty minutes later he was admitted by Mirka Sloboda into the dining room at Victoria Road.

Ruth was both pleased and surprised to see him. That something was amiss she guessed straight away from the embarrassed expression on his face. She listened patiently while he hesitantly explained his dilemma. As he walked from Long Street to the house he had rehearsed what he intended to say, but could find no other way than to proffer a polite apology and make his escape.

'I really am sorry, Ruth. Please tender my apologies to your other guests for my rudeness. It is, I assure you, unavoidable that I go directly to London.' That he really wanted to say 'and would it be possible to see you another night?' was, of course, out of the question. He caught the look of mild surprise on Ruth's face. 'There's no problem, Tom, and there are no other guests. It was just you and me. We can arrange it for another evening when you get back.'

Now it was Tom's turn to be surprised. He could not believe what she was saying.

As far as Ruth was concerned the dinner engagement was unimportant. She paid close attention to what he was telling her: a Russian alien in custody in Whitechapel who had possible connections in Kelsford was of considerable importance. Ordering the parlourmaid to bring coffee, she said, 'If the man in custody is Russian, how are you going to interview him?'

'I hadn't really thought about it. Presumably the police at Leman Street will provide an interpreter.'

Ruth looked pensive. 'I speak fluent Russian, and I could easily be away from the bank for a couple of days.' She regarded him quizzically. 'It would be far better for you to take an interpreter with you, would it not?'

Tom was caught completely off guard. 'It's a brilliant idea,' he stammered, 'but it's totally impossible. I haven't booked any accommodation yet, and it wouldn't be proper ...'

Ruth cut him off in mid-sentence. 'It would be perfectly proper, I promise you.'

The proposition was too good for Tom to refuse. He had no idea what facilities there were at Leman Street police station, or whether this unknown Russian spoke any English or not. But the opportunity to spend a couple of days exclusively with Ruth Samuels was beyond anything he could have expected. Gratefully he accepted the offer.

For the next half-hour they discussed arrangements, and it was decided that Ruth should telegraph the hotel she normally used in London and book accommodation for them both, while Tom went back to Long Street and made the necessary arrangements for his absence. Once the matter was settled Ruth asked casually, 'Do you have a name for the man in custody? There are various dialects in Russia and his name may help me to know where he comes from.'

Tom pulled the cable from his pocket. 'Leschenko, Eugene Leschenko. It merely says he's a Russian.'

Half-expecting the answer, Ruth said, her face expressionless, 'No, it doesn't mean anything. Let's wait until we see him.'

As soon as Tom left, Ruth scribbled a note to Mannie telling him of the recent development, and that she would contact him when she returned from London. Sealing the letter in a heavy brown envelope, she sent David off with it to Leaminster Gardens. Next she wrote to Solomon Meyer, explaining that urgent Pipeline business was taking her away for a few days, and that she hoped to be back by the middle of the week. She knew very well that he would soon have all the details from Issitt.

Ruth was not sorry for the opportunity to be away from the bank for a while. She had recently discovered that Max Peters, apart from overcommitting the bank to the warehouse project, had also invested a large amount of his own personal capital in the scheme. The information came confidentially from Mannie – where he found out these things she did not know, but he was rarely wrong – and she could not lay it before the bank's board without compromising her source. At the moment it was better, she felt, if she avoided her partners and Max.

She was also very excited at the prospect of going to London with Tom, albeit on a business trip of sorts. Even though her feelings towards him were far from platonic, the dinner that she had planned was by no means intended as a seduction, purely a pleasant evening in his company in return for the meal at the Stag. Ruth was not even sure of his intentions, although she had to admit she was finding it more and more difficult to put him out of her mind. Biting her lip, she attempted to focus on the task in hand. Initially, she decided, she needed to find out what Leschenko had done, and more importantly what the link was that had been found with Kelsford.

Calling for Mirka, she asked her to send a telegram to the Viceroy Hotel in Tudor Square, just off Ludgate Circus, reserving her usual suite and an adjoining room for Tom. Then she went up to her bedroom to pack a small bag.

Tom and Ruth chatted easily on the train, as if they had known each other for years. He explained the difficulties of his new job and touched lightly on the fact that, with his sister's impending marriage, he would soon be living on his own at Sidwell Place. She talked about her business trips abroad and how she would like to visit America. The journey passed quickly. A few minutes after half past six the train pulled into St Pancras.

The hotel was a ten-minute ride in a hansom through Bloomsbury and across Holborn, and it was getting dark when the porter took their cases through the revolving doors of the hotel into the foyer. Looking round, Tom immediately began to have misgivings. The Viceroy Hotel was a modern four-storey building that accommodated over 200 guests in a style that, if not opulent, was certainly grand. From the hotel lobby, for those guests who did not want to avail themselves of the iron-gated lift, a magnificent staircase with a dark red Axminster carpet ran up to the first floor. To his right, residents in evening attire were making their way into the main dining room. Tom had come to London as a policeman on an enquiry, and would therefore be expected to stay overnight in one of the dozens of small commercial hotels that abounded in the city. He could imagine Superintendent Archer Robson's face when presented with the bill for an overnight stay in a place such as this.

Ruth was already in conversation with the desk clerk, who appeared to know her. 'Your usual suite, Mrs Samuels, and room thirty-two, which is adjacent,' he said respectfully, handing one set of keys to Ruth and the other to Tom.

'Thank you, Stanley,' she replied, smiling graciously at the bespectacled clerk, while remembering another such receptionist in a hotel at the foot of the Carpathian Mountains. 'Would you be good enough to have dinner for two served in my room in half an hour, please?' She looked quickly at Tom for confirmation.

'Don't worry,' she said quietly as they followed the porter to the lift gate. 'I haven't brought any evening clothes either. We'll have dinner in the room. I presume you'll be too busy for socialising.'

Tom smiled back. 'I hadn't expected anything quite so grand,' he murmured.

To set his mind at rest, Ruth replied, 'Please don't worry. The Bank of Commerce is paying for this. I can do a bit of bank business while we're down here.' She placed a restraining hand on his arm as she realised he was about to protest. 'I promise you – the bank will pay. Think nothing of it. Now just relax, have a meal and get an early night ready for tomorrow.'

Over an excellent dinner of grilled sirloin steak, washed down with a particularly good claret, in the sitting room of Ruth's second-floor suite, Tom outlined to her what little he knew of the Whitechapel murders. He had decided that if she was to be of any practical use as his interpreter it would be as well if she knew as much about the matter as he did. In truth, as he had told her earlier in the week, his knowledge was limited to little more than what was available in the newspapers.

During the early hours of Friday 31 August the body of a prostitute named Mary Ann Nichols had been found by two men in Bucks Row, a side street off Whitechapel Road. The woman's throat had been cut, and when the body was examined at the mortuary it was found that her abdomen had been slashed with a knife. A week later a second prostitute, Annie Chapman, had been found murdered in the yard of 29 Hanbury Street, a slum dwelling only a few minutes' walk from where the first murder had taken place. Again, the woman's stomach had been mutilated in such a way as to indicate that both victims had been killed by the same man. From police documents Tom knew that the mutilations were of a particularly horrific nature, which it was not necessary for Ruth to know.

The circumstances of the murder for which the man Leschenko was currently being held were not known to him; neither were any details of the victim. His purpose, Tom explained, was to find out what the link to any anarchist activities in Kelsford might be.

'Are there no other suspects?' Ruth asked.

'As far as I'm aware, no. There have been the usual rumours. A man nicknamed "Leather Apron" was arrested and later released, but otherwise I don't think they have any real ideas.'

Throughout Tom's discourse Ruth, listening intently, continued to munch her way through the succulent beefsteak. He noticed she appeared unmoved by the gruesome topic under discussion. Pouring more wine for them both, she asked, 'How do you propose to approach this man Leschenko?' She knew she faced a difficult task tomorrow. That Eugene could be implicated in the murders she did not doubt – but she also knew that it was unlikely he would compromise the Pipeline unnecessarily by disclosing that it was they who had brought him to England, thanks to the secretive nature of his life. Like Tom, though, she needed to have the address in Kelsford that had been found in his possession.

Tom, spearing a forkful of sirloin steak, paused contemplatively. Ruth's question was the very one that he had been asking himself ever since they left Kelsford. 'First we see if the address means anything to me. If it does then I'll have a definite line of approach. If it doesn't then I'll see what he says about it and go from there. I'm sorry if that's a bit vague, but sometimes that's how it has to be done.' Inwardly he was cursing the fact that he had been unable to contact Leman Street police by telephone to ascertain the address. If he had been in possession of it earlier he would have been able to set a watch on the house before he left Kelsford, and would now have been in a much stronger position.

Making an early start, Tom and Ruth presented themselves the next morning soon after seven o'clock in the spacious dining room. While Tom ordered kippers, toast and coffee for them both, Ruth studied the recently delivered early editions of the daily papers.

'You'd better take a look at this,' she said, handing him a copy of the *Daily News*. Under a banner headline was what the editor of the paper proudly proclaimed to be a copy of a letter written to the police and the Central News Agency.

Tom glanced through the piece quickly, then sat back in his chair to read it properly. Dated 25 September, the paragraph read:

Dear Boss, I keep on hearing the police have caught me but they won't fix me just yet. I have laughed when they look so clever and talk about being on the right track. That joke about Leather Apron gave me real fits. I am down on whores and I shan't quit ripping them till I do get buckled. Grand work the last job was. I gave the lady no time to squeal. How can they catch me now? I love my work and want to start again. You will soon hear of me with my little games. I saved some of the proper red stuff in a ginger beer bottle over the last job to write with but it went thick like glue and I can't use it. Red ink is fit enough I hope, ha, ha. The next job I do I shall clip the lady's ears off and send to the police officers just for jolly, wouldn't you. Keep this letter back till I do a bit more work then give it out straight. My knife's so nice and sharp I want to get to work right away if I get a chance.

Good luck,
Yours truly,
Jack the Ripper

Putting the paper down, Tom nodded absently to the waiter as he placed the dish of freshly smoked kippers in front of him. As the man made his way through the intervening tables towards the kitchens he separated a portion of the fish from its bone and said thoughtfully, 'So now the press have a name.'

Just after half past eight Tom and Ruth presented themselves at the front desk of Leman Street police station. A few minutes later a young uniformed constable showed them up the stairs and into the first-floor office of Detective Inspector Frederick Abberline. Although studiously polite, Abberline, a tall slim man with pointed features accentuated by a high forehead and thinning hair, was visibly displeased with the world. His large dark moustache sweeping out to join a set of bushy muttonchop whiskers was almost bristling. Tom had little doubt about the cause of his annoyance: lying on the desk in front of him was a copy of the *Daily News*, the offending article plainly visible.

'On your way out ask Sergeant Thick to join us will you, Pitchman,' Abberline said to the departing constable brusquely. 'I shall have to leave almost immediately, Mr Norton. This newspaper article is going to cause a great deal of trouble. I'm going across to Scotland Yard to see Mr Swanson, who is head of detectives. We'll have to try to limit the panic that this foolishness will generate.'

The conversation was interrupted by a gentle knock at the door, which heralded the arrival of a broadly built man in his early forties wearing a dark checked suit.

'Come in, Will.' Abberline waved the new arrival into the office.

'May I present Detective Inspector Norton of the Kelsford Borough Police, and Mrs . . .'

'Samuels,' said Tom smoothly. It was obvious that Abberline had failed to register Ruth's name when he had introduced her. Ruth inclined her head slightly and smiled demurely.

Sweeping his hand from one to another, Abberline continued, 'This is

Detective Sergeant Thick, with whom I shall have to leave you. Will is as well informed as any man on my staff in relation to the present enquiries, and indeed it was he who arrested Leschenko.'

Sergeant Thick's heavy moustache lifted in a cheery smile. 'Your man is downstairs in the cells, sir. Perhaps if we have a chat before you speak to him ...'

Further along the corridor, ensconced in the roomy office which Thick shared with the other detective officers of H Division, Tom and Ruth took stock of their surroundings while their host made a pot of tea in a tiny room off the main office. It was, Tom reflected, not unlike the Kelsford office or any other of the hundreds of police stations dotted round the country. Rows of shelves, containing folders, and pictures of known miscreants wanted for a host of minor offences adorned the limewashed walls. Large windows gazed down upon the carts and pedestrians passing along the busy street below. Between the rooftops opposite the railway yard in Lambeth Street and the warehouses behind in Gowers Walk could just be made out.

Returning with a tray containing three mugs of steaming tea, Will Thick placed it on his neatly arranged desk and invited his guests to help themselves.

Despite his unfortunate surname, Thick was far from being a dullard. Since joining the Metropolitan Police twenty years before, he had spent the majority of his service prowling the murky streets of Whitechapel. Along with his immediate superior, Fred Abberline, he was probably the most experienced officer engaged in investigating the murders by the man whom the press had today dubbed Jack the Ripper. Known by the local criminal fraternity as Johnny Upright, because of his reputation for honesty in a world where values were renowned for their flexibility, Thick was without doubt one of the most feared detectives on the division.

Detective Sergeant Thick had to tread very carefully. The letter published in the *Daily News* was going to create considerable difficulties for the police. Abberline, already besieged by an angry public, was infuriated that the killer had been allowed to take the initiative. His summons to Scotland Yard to see Detective Chief Inspector Donald Swanson and the Commissioner, Sir Charles Warren, was a bad omen. Unfortunately Sergeant Thick did not envisage the day becoming brighter. Earlier in the morning he and Abberline had discussed the Stride murder in the light of the provincial detective's ensuing visit, and had been in agreement that Norton should neither be told that Stride might have known Leschenko through her connections at 95 Varden Street, nor that she was one of Abberline's best informants.

Summoned from his bed to Dutfield's Yard during the early hours of Sunday morning, Will Thick had been perturbed to spot Eugene Leschenko in the crowd gathered by the yard gates. Although he did not know the man's name, he recognised him as a resident of the anarchist house in Varden Street, which meant he must have known and been on speaking terms with Long Liz. Shepherding the local residents back into their houses, Thick instructed one of the officers to arrest three of the men who had come out of the club whose stories warranted further enquiries, including Leschenko. By the middle of Sunday morning only the Latvian remained in Leman Street cells. A search of the room that Leschenko shared in Varden Street had revealed little other than some anarchist literature, a recent copy of *The Worker's Friend* and a slip of paper bearing the address 22 St Andrew's Street, Kelsford.

Aware that there were certain things he could not divulge, Sergeant Thick was equally aware that not to be in possession of some of the facts would make Norton's task of interviewing the man almost impossible.

Sipping at his tea, Will Thick gave Tom the edited account of how it was that Leschenko came to be arrested and in custody. 'We have a bigger problem with these murders than you might realise,' he said, with an air of resignation. Who was the woman? he wondered. It was a strange thing to do, to bring an interpreter with you, especially a woman. Obviously foreign herself, probably Jewish. Anyway, it made little difference. It was doubtful they were going to learn much from the man in the cells, and they were an inconvenience he could do without. If he told them what was soon going to be general knowledge, then with any luck he could make a start on his day's work.

'The feeling is that, in addition to Mary Ann Nichols and Annie Chapman, there may have been two earlier murders committed by this man. In April a prostitute named Emma Smith was robbed and murdered in Osborne Street near to the junction of Brick Lane and Wentworth Street, and then in August, on the night of Bank Holiday Monday, Martha Tabram was found murdered on a landing at George Yard Building. Both had,' he searched delicately for an appropriate description in deference to the woman's presence, 'suffered certain abdominal wounds similar to those inflicted in the later cases.'

'Is there anything in common between the victims?' asked Tom.

Thick considered for a moment. 'All were prostitutes living in poor surroundings. All were in or around their forties: the youngest was thirty-nine, the oldest forty-seven. Lizzie Stride was forty-five.'

'Will you be charging this man with anything, or are you just waiting for my interview?'

'To be honest, it's not him.' Thick sounded disappointed. 'We're releasing him once you've spoken to him. No one can verify his movements during the day, but he says that he was out and about all morning and afternoon in the markets. He spent the evening in the International Club. There are witnesses who say he was there all evening, for what that's worth: these foreigners will lie like troopers to protect each other.'

Ruth winced, but the detective, either oblivious or indifferent, continued. 'Lizzie left the pub in Settles Street soon after eleven o'clock, with a client. He is described as being young, dressed like a clerk and with an English accent. At a quarter to twelve or so she was seen in Berners Street with the same man: he bought some grapes from a fruiterer at 44 Berners Street. She was then seen in a doorway in Berners Street at half past twelve by the beat man, Constable Smith, as he turned the corner from Fairclough Street. She was with another client whom he couldn't see properly because it was dark. A man named William Marshall who lives nearby also saw her with this second man. Presumably she took the first client to Berners Street and "did him" in the doorway, then picked up a second client and took him into the doorway as well. The interesting bit is that a quarter of an hour later a little Jewish bloke named Israel Schwartz on his way home saw Lizzie arguing with a man outside the gates to Dutfield's Yard. The man hit her and knocked her to the ground. Then he shouted something foreign at Schwartz and another man across the road. Schwartz, thinking that it was a robbery, ran off towards the railway arches. I think the man who knocked her down was this "Ripper", who then dragged her into Dutfield's Yard and killed her. Shortly afterwards the club steward, Louis Diemschutz, found the body when he came home with his pony and trap.

'In answer to your original question, I don't think that this Leschenko person is our man. We're certain that the killer has a high degree of medical knowledge – is most likely a doctor. Now this letter to the Press Agency. Whoever wrote that has a strong command of the English language, and our man downstairs is just an ignorant Yid who can't string a sentence together.' Once again Ruth winced slightly, but kept her face impassive. 'There's a clincher,' Thick added, with an air of despondency. 'Half an hour after Leschenko was taken into custody another prostitute, Catherine Eddowes, was found murdered in Mitre Square – and believe me, that was this Ripper fellow.'

Tom thought about what he had been told as the sergeant went out to pour some more tea. He understood the difficulties caused by a series of unsolved crimes in a relatively small area, combined with a high level of public alarm. He had faced similar problems during the months since the Shires robbery and the killing of Eddie Donnelly. It bothered him, though, that this whole affair was being rushed. Assumptions were being made – that the killer was a doctor, that he was English and that this recent victim had entertained several unidentified clients before being killed by one of them. Instinctively Tom knew that the man he was going to interview was not going to tell him anything. The London police had detained him on the flimsiest of evidence, and were using a possible anarchist connection in Kelsford as a reason for keeping him in custody. That was why they had not supplied him with the address earlier. Armed with that, an enquiry made in Kelsford might have eliminated the need for his trip to London, thus precipitating the prisoner's earlier release.

From experience Tom judged that Sergeant Thick, while probably an able detective, had a brief to feed him selected information until, their own enquiries completed, they allowed him to interview the prisoner. No doubt a headline in the London papers later in the day would appear to the effect that a man had been in custody for some time and had been allowed to leave after extensive enquiries and interviews, pending further enquiries. A deliberately careless piece of wording would identify the man and the address at Varden Street and send the public howling after a red herring, while the police bought a little more time to search for the real killer.

As Tom expected, the interview with Eugene Leschenko was a complete waste of time. Seated at a small deal table in an interview room off the cellblock corridor, in the bowels of the building, with Ruth at his side on a chair that had been crammed in for her, he waited for the prisoner to be led in. The room was at most six feet by eight, and Ruth was very uncomfortable in the oppressive surroundings. The only light that filtered in was through a steel meshed grill some six feet up on one of the dark green painted brick walls. The door was made of heavy steel-lined timber with a huge double lock. In the centre at about shoulder height was an observation hatch twelve inches square and hinged at the bottom, permitting it to drop outwards and allow a meal plate to be passed through from the corridor. Ruth realised that she was sitting in a converted cell that could easily be restored to its former status. Wrapping her overcoat around her more tightly, she was pleased to feel the reassuring bulk of Tom beside her.

The door opened and Eugene Leschenko entered, wearing a pair of scruffy corduroy trousers and a disreputable green jacket that looked as if it had been slept in, followed by Detective Sergeant Thick. For the briefest moment a look of surprise passed through Leschenko's eyes as he saw Ruth sitting with the police officer. Taking the seat that Thick held out for him, the Latvian settled down and, leaning back in the chair, crossed his legs before giving Norton an arrogant stare. His mind was in turmoil. What on earth was the woman doing here? Had the Pipeline sent her to bail him out? He discounted the idea immediately. He would have to sit tight and take his lead from her. It was obvious she didn't want anyone to know they were acquainted.

Looking at him across the table, Ruth decided that Leschenko had definitely not prospered in London. The old coat had a verdigris tinge, and he had the sour odour of someone who has not seen a bath or clean clothes for some time. His dark wavy hair was long and unkempt, the length serving to accentuate the wave in his parting. He had, she noted, affected the huge waxed moustache that was becoming a badge for men of his persuasion; in his case it served merely to accentuate the pallor of his pockmarked cheeks. The only things that remained unchanged were the cold hazel eyes, now turned disdainfully on his interviewer.

As Tom had expected, speaking to the man was exceptionally difficult thanks to the meagre evidence in his possession. Taking his cigar case out, he offered Leschenko one and, when it was refused, took his time selecting and lighting his own. Tom used the interlude to assess the prisoner. Arrogant was his first impression. More importantly, that he had been in this situation before was obvious. Tom cursed Thick and Abberline for not giving him more information. Will Thick had given him the slip of paper that had been found among clothing in Leschenko's chest of drawers only half an hour before. The address in St Andrew's Street was a lodging house in the Downe Street district run by an Irish woman called Susan Burke – and the possibility that the man had Irish connections interested Tom immensely.

The interview proved almost impossible. It was never easy to talk through an interpreter, as the pauses for translation broke up any rhythm or pressure that an interviewer had to establish in order to throw the subject off-balance. Patently aware of this, Leschenko waited for Ruth to interpret each of Tom's questions, even though he understood much of what was said. Then, taking as long as he dared, he replied directly to the woman in Russian, studiously ignoring his interrogator.

After nearly an hour Tom decided to give up, in total frustration. Venturing one last shot, he looked directly into Leschenko's eyes and said, 'How well do you know Connor?' As Ruth began to speak in Russian, Tom made a sharp gesture with his right hand to silence her. Leschenko stared blankly at him. Tom repeated the question, and Leschenko deliberately looked away from him at Ruth. 'Look at me when I'm talking to you!' The edge in Tom's voice pulled the man's gaze back. With a small jolt Ruth realised what many others had found to their cost: this was not a man to play games with. Sitting perfectly still, Tom said coldly, 'When did you last contact O'Dowd?' This time he was sure a slight flicker went through the Latvian's cold eyes.

Deliberately turning from Tom to Ruth, Leschenko said in Russian, 'I do not understand the question.'

Tom knew that to continue with the interview was a waste of time and, nodding to Will Thick who was standing against the closed door, said, 'Take him back to his cell. We'll met again, Mr Leschenko: please don't think that we won't.'

Alone again in the interview room with Ruth, he let out a long deep sigh. 'Not quite a waste of time,' he said, smiling at her solemn face. 'Almost, but not quite.'

Ruth wanted to escape. She found it frightening, and could imagine for the first time what it might be like to be shut away in a cell, only to be let out when it suited someone else. Sensing her disquiet, Tom said, 'Don't worry. We'll be going in a minute. Thanks for your help.'

'I'm just sorry you didn't get more information,' she replied, wondering vaguely what part of the interview had not been a waste of time for him, and at the same time immensely relieved that the address in Downe Street was not connected with the Pipeline.

Returning to the charge office, they were joined a few minutes later by Will Thick. Tom decided he had been treated like a country cousin for long enough. 'One last thing, Sergeant, I'd like to go to the house at Varden Street to have a look round.'

Sergeant Thick looked a little disconcerted, although he had known all along it was possible that the Kelsford officer might make such a request, if he knew his job. 'We can by all means, sir, but you'll find nothing of interest there, I can assure you. We searched the house thoroughly.'

'I'd like to have a look,' Tom insisted. 'It never hurts to rattle a few cages.' He grinned disarmingly – apparently at Detective Sergeant Thick, but in reality at the image over his shoulder of Joseph Langley, nodding in dark approval.

202

Chapter Twenty

The house in Varden Street was a narrow and mean affair squeezed in, along with two similar dwellings, between a candle factory and a tripe dresser's shop. The malodorous steam from the latter, which carried the flaking legend EZRA ADKIN, PURVEYOR OF TRIPE AND TROTTERS, was carried on the breeze from its back yard boiler down the cobbled road. Thick had tried to discourage Tom from allowing Ruth to accompany them to the house. Until this point she had remained in the background, but now she felt justified in speaking for herself.

'Thank you for your consideration, Sergeant,' she had said politely, 'but there's a good reason for me to accompany you. In a household of foreigners my knowledge of what they're saying to each other could be extremely important. I know their habits, and I most certainly will not be affronted by the living conditions there.'

Tom was unsure. Ruth was a well-bred lady who, despite what she was saying, probably had little notion of the way such people lived.

On turning out of New Road they encountered the local policeman on his beat, the collar of his voluminous cape fixed tightly under his chin against the drizzle that had begun to fall. The constable, an elderly man with a large spade beard shot with grey, stopped to pay his respects to Sergeant Thick, on whose instruction he took up position at the corner of Varden Street and New Road.

Leading the small party, Thick hammered brusquely on the flimsy front door of Brovnic's house. The door was answered almost immediately, revealing the squat figure of Nina Volputin. Common sense told her that to attempt to refuse entry would be foolish: her initial glance, which identified the large figure of Sergeant Johnny Upright in his checked suit and bowler hat, was sufficient to tell her that if she prevaricated the door would be kicked out of her hands.

Entering the gloomy hallway, which stank of vegetables purchased earlier that morning from an adjacent costermonger's stall and stale cooking from the night before, they were confronted by the overweight Vassily Brovnic. The fat

Moravian had been drinking since early that morning, attempting to console himself at the loss of his 'beautiful Lizska'. Unlike the little Hungarian woman, he did not recognise Thick and immediately began to bluster. 'What are you wanting this time? You cannot come in. I will not allow it . . .' Vassily's voice rose to a strangled squeal as Detective Sergeant Thick ground a heavily booted foot onto the top of his soft slipper, and pushed the man's back against the peeling wallpaper.

'Be quiet, or I'll arrest you as a suspicious alien and have you down at Leman Street ready for a boat back to Russia.' Even with Vassily's limited knowledge of the English language it was obvious that he clearly understood the threat.

While Thick dealt with Brovnic, Tom indicated to Ruth to follow him up the uncarpeted staircase. As he climbed higher, Tom recognised the familiar feeling of his feet sticking to the filthy treads, and hoped that Ruth would know to hitch her dress up and not let it drag on the boards. At the top of the stairs he pushed open the door of the first room on the landing with his foot. Two single bed frames and a mattress laid out on the floor, along with an open cupboard that obviously passed for a wardrobe, were the only items in the room. Moving along the landing, he went into the front bedroom where Eugene Leschenko slept with Klara and Oleg. The dirty blanket on the bed was stained and smelly; the palliasse in the far corner was devoid of any covers.

Tom was going carefully through the drawers of the dilapidated night table when they were joined by Thick. 'You'll find nothing there, Mr Norton. As I said earlier we've turned this place over. Anything of interest has been taken to Leman Street.'

Nina and Vassily were on the landing outside. Brovnic had sobered up sufficiently not to further antagonise Sergeant Thick. It was obvious to the police officers that there was no one else in the house.

'The rest have flown the coop, Sergeant,' Tom said. 'I make it four, these two here and our man in the cells. About seven, would you say?'

Thick nodded his agreement. 'Yes, I'd agree with that, sir.'

Ruth touched Tom on the arm and put a finger to her lips. Out on the landing Brovnic was speaking in Russian to Nina.

'Have you warned the others that the police are here?' Vassily's voice was hushed.

'Da. I've put the plant pot in the window. None of them will come in as long as it's there.' Volputin was matter of fact. She was becoming tired of this latter-day revolutionary who conducted his conspiracies through an alcoholic haze.

Ruth leaned forward and whispered softly.

Tom looked meaningfully at Thick and said, 'Let's just take a look round the yard before we go.'

Once downstairs, Tom, followed by Ruth and the others, pushed through the shambles that was a kitchen and out into the minuscule back yard. Sergeant

Thick, bringing up the rear, detached himself long enough to remove the large potted aspidistra that Nina had placed in the window of the front room that looked out onto the street.

Out in the yard Tom noticed a short single-run ladder about eight feet long hanging from the wall on two pegs. He was puzzled. It was too short to reach the guttering running along the overhanging tiles, or even the first-floor bedroom window. Tom caught Thick's eye. The sergeant had searched the house the previous day and failed to spot the ladder. Now, with it in front of him, he still hadn't worked things out.

'Go to the corner and fetch the constable,' Tom ordered Ruth, without taking his eyes off Thick. He knew he was not going to be popular with the Metropolitan Police. They had arrested Leschenko on suspicion of being a political activist, among other things. Yesterday their search of the house had been fruitless; now he as an outsider had spotted what they had missed. He just hoped that Leschenko had not already been released.

It was less than a minute before the constable, his cape folded back over his shoulders to leave his arms free, let himself in through the entry gate followed by Ruth.

'Take these two into the front room. Don't allow them to talk to each other and keep her away from the window,' Tom ordered the officer. To Ruth he said, 'Please tell her in whatever language they're using exactly what I've just said.'

The look on Nina's face when she realised Ruth spoke Russian was one of pure poison. The constable glanced quickly at Thick for confirmation before shepherding Brovnic and the woman into the house. At a sign from Tom, Ruth followed them. In the yard Detective Sergeant Thick's ponderous features were suffused with barely contained rage. 'The loft! How could I have missed it? The sodding loft!'

'It's easily done,' Tom said kindly. 'Point is, we've seen it now. Come on, let's go.'

Stopping to find the paraffin lamp that they knew would be in the kitchen cupboard, they carried the ladder easily between them up the staircase to the landing. Pushing open the trap door into the roof space with the end of the ladder, Thick lit the lantern with a match and handed it up to Tom, who pushed his head and shoulders through into the loft. Shining the lamp round the cold dark space it took him a matter of seconds to find three brand new long-barrelled Colt 'Peace Maker' revolvers laid out in an old shoebox. In a separate box under some newspapers were half a dozen boxes of .45 ammunition.

When the detectives walked back into the sitting room Brovnic, standing by the bed that he and Lizzie Stride had so recently occupied, became visibly pale when he saw the boxes Thick was carrying. Tom, dusting the bits of dirt and cobweb from his suit, stood to one side. This was Thick's responsibility now.

With a grim smile of satisfaction the detective sergeant drew one of the large pistols from the shoebox and showed it to Brovnic. 'I've just recovered these items from a concealed space in the roof of your house, *Mister* Brovnic, and you are now well and truly under arrest.'

Vassily Brovnic looked helplessly at the officers. It was as if his whole future was opening up before him: trial, conviction, prison and deportation to Moravia. He suddenly threw his arms up, knocking the elderly constable backwards against the window, and made a lunge forward. Thick was experienced enough to have anticipated the move and, despite being hampered by the boxes of weapons he held, kicked the Moravian hard in the crotch, doubling him over and allowing Tom, who was moving forward fast, to straighten him up with a well-delivered upper cut.

Nina made a dive towards the sitting room door and the safety of the passageway. Thick and Tom both swung to grab at her, but they were off-balance and too far away to catch her. All that stood between Nina and freedom was Ruth Samuels who, unnoticed, had placed herself by the door into the hallway as Thick showed the guns to Vassily. Lips drawn back over her gums in a banshee screech, hands stretched out like claws, Nina threw herself at the woman in the doorway.

Tom froze, first in horror and then in fascination as Ruth straightened to her full height, transferred her weight onto her right foot and swung her bunched fist into Nina Volputin's face in one smooth movement. The blow, delivered from the shoulder, took Nina squarely in the mouth. Her head snapped back and she dropped to the floor as if she had been pole-axed, bleeding heavily from the nose and mouth.

Tom and Will stood in silent admiration as Ruth, nursing her right hand, said in a strained voice, 'Buggery, that hurt!'

Back at Leman Street the morning's activities ended on a mixed note. Vassily Brovnic and Nina Volputin, both looking considerably the worse for wear, were booked in and left in the cells to await interview by officers from Scotland Yard. In accordance with Detective Inspector Abberline's instructions, Eugene Leschenko was released from custody some ten minutes before Tom and Thick had walked with their prisoners into the police station.

Although Tom arranged matters so that Will Thick took all the credit for finding the arms cache in the loft, he knew the Metropolitan officers would be pleased to see him leave. However it was dressed up, those who mattered knew he had made them look slightly foolish.

Shaking hands on the front step of the police station, Will Thick said a polite goodbye to Tom and Ruth before turning back into the station, and the enquiring looks of his colleagues in the detective office. As they walked down the road towards Fenchurch Street station Tom mused on the extraordinary woman by his side.

'What are you looking for, Tom?' she asked, breaking into his reverie. Tom, caught unawares, did not immediately understand the question. His instinct was to blurt out, 'You. It's you I'm looking for,' but he doubted that was what she was asking.

'I'm sorry I brought you here,' he replied. 'Had I realised things were going to get out of hand I wouldn't have involved you. I'm taking you back to the hotel right now and we can catch an afternoon train back to Kelsford.'

#Slipping her arm companionably through his, she said, 'Stop overreacting. I'm not some shrinking violet who'll be blown away by the first summer breeze. I came here to help you and that's exactly what I want to do. You've not answered the question. What do you want from this place?'

Tom did not have to consider his answer this time. 'Leschenko is an anarchist. In his possession was the address of an Irish lodging house near Downe Street. There's a connection between the Irish in Kelsford and the Irish Republican Brotherhood, which we think was responsible for the Shires robbery. The Brotherhood has connections with these anarchist groups. The Brotherhood man who was killed in the Shires robbery was carrying an American handgun. We've just recovered some American pistols from Brovnic. If I can show that the Irish brotherhood and the anarchists are linked then I'm getting somewhere.'

Her next question took him by surprise. 'Do you know anybody – other than the Leman Street police – here in Whitechapel?'

'No. No, I don't.'

'I do,' she replied brightly, tucking her arm tighter under his.

Situated in Brick Lane near to Booth Street, Moses Grodzinski's workshop was a fifteen-minute walk. On the way Ruth explained that she had been a frequent visitor to Whitechapel in earlier years, thanks to her father's jewellery business and also when her mother suffered a prolonged illness. Aged ten, Ruth had lived with relatives for several months, at the shop to which she was now taking him.

The poverty and degradation on every street corner were depressing, and Ruth was glad that she had Tom with her. She felt safe. For as long as she could remember she had had to be strong and to compete with men as equals – but with him she did not feel this need. Even now, in broad daylight, their dress and relative affluence was attracting attention. Surly looking men and women stared speculatively from the doorways in which they were chatting or huddling against the chill autumn breeze that had replaced the light drizzle. A small, thin, shabbily dressed man with a neatly trimmed black beard and a club foot was demonstrating patent cough medicines from a suitcase in the middle of the pavement to a stoutly built housewife smoking a stubby clay pipe.

Tom's size and bleak face, along with the sturdy Malacca stick that swung casually in his hand, deterred any who might have been contemplating a swiftly executed street robbery. Few who saw the couple failed to identify the fair-haired man as a policeman.

As they passed along Thrawl Street, Ruth stared curiously at a gang of prostitutes assembled in the doorway of one of the seedy lodging houses.

Locked out of their rooms during the day, the women were either lounging in the doorway of the house, or sitting on one of the surrounding doorsteps, despite the chilly weather. Their dress was, Ruth noted, almost a uniform: without exception they wore a dirty old dark blue or black dress, a thin crocheted shawl of the same colour and a battered wide-brimmed hat or tiny crêpe bonnet. A couple of the older women wore aprons, once white but now a grimy indeterminate grey. Their buzz of conversation ceased as Ruth and Tom approached, walking down the middle of the road to avoid having to pick their way through the throng. Baleful stares followed their progress, and Ruth could feel six pairs of eyes boring into her back as she neared the corner of Brick Lane.

The man whom they were going to see, Moses Grodzinski, was Ruth's uncle – the brother of her mother Rachel. He was, Ruth explained, a goldsmith by trade and well informed about the comings and goings in Whitechapel. Exactly why he was so well informed she did not say, not least because Moses was an integral link in the London end of the Pipeline.

Tom was pleasantly surprised at how roomy and tidy the goldsmith's shop was. A broad counter separated three young men from the customers. Gaslights along the walls were already illuminated although it was only lunchtime, ensuring that the interior was well lit and welcoming. Awaiting the arrival from upstairs of Ruth's uncle, Tom quickly made a second, professional, assessment. The shop was large because the original premises had been knocked through into the house next door to double the floor space. The counter was extra wide in order to prevent anyone snatching an item from the assistant's grasp, and the lights were turned up high to ensure that no wily thief could palm an item undetected. Tom guessed that one of the three 'assistants', probably the burly young man who had just left to summon his employer, was not in fact a jeweller but a minder.

Tom's brief appraisal was interrupted by the arrival of a large, jolly man in his late sixties who kissed Ruth on the cheek and introduced himself as Moses Grodzinski. He was mildly surprised at the appearance of the rotund figure, attired in a morning suit and with a tiny embroidered skull-cap perched incongruously on the back of his shiny bald pate; Tom had irrationally expected a sinister Semitic figure resembling Dickens' Fagin to appear. His second surprise, on being shown up to the first floor, was that they were expected. Ruth whispered that the previous evening she had sent word to her uncle that it was possible they would be paying him a visit.

The goldsmith's living quarters were very comfortably appointed. Soft armchairs and expensive drapes were spread round the ample sitting room, which, like the shop downstairs, had been extended. A deep Persian carpet covered the floor, muffling the sounds of any comings and goings below. Hot sweet tea and a selection of tasty snacks, the like of which Tom had never encountered, served to remind him it was now well past lunchtime, and he was extremely hungry.

Family news exchanged, Moses politely turned his attention to Tom. 'Ruth tells me you're engaged in investigating the anarchists, Mr Norton. How may I help you?'

'I'm not sure, Mr Grodzinski. But tell me – I'm intrigued to find such a beautiful home in the middle of Whitechapel. Are you not afraid of being robbed?' The question was not an idle one. Grodzinski had to be more than a simple goldsmith.

Moses smiled and, shrugging his shoulders, eloquently held his hands out, palms upwards. Mannie Issitt had also sent word to expect the policeman's visit, along with the rider that, tactful as she was, he suspected Ruth had more than a passing interest in the man. 'To possess nice things is to invite disaster wherever you live. You're right, though. In this district the risks are higher than usual, but I've been here for many years. My wife, God rest her, died only last year, and now I live alone. Over the years I've made a living through business transactions. With those who can afford my products, I deal in gold. This trade, you understand, is with the many jewellers in the city, and I keep very little of any great value on the premises. With the local people – both the good and the bad – I have over the years been involved in small transactions, which have earned me their respect. So I am left in relative peace and security to enjoy my old age.' Grodzinski gave a Buddha-like beam, and proffered a plate of pastries with a creamy smoked fish filling.

Tom understood perfectly what he was being told. Moses was an influential moneylender. Over the years he had become established and prospered. By now, probably every villain in the district relied upon him for funds from time to time, so his continued safety was essential to their own well-being.

Pausing to ensure that his visitor had fully understood, Grodzinski continued. 'I do not, I assure you, engage in any illegal activities. I have always been, as my niece will tell you, a thoroughly honest citizen.'

Ruth smiled at Tom in agreement. What her uncle was saying was to all intents true. Without ever handling stolen property or being involving in other criminal practices, which would have reversed the balance of power between himself and the local criminal fraternity, the old man had established a unique power base. There were inevitably some matters that did not bear close scrutiny. Occasionally, for example, consignments of highly traceable gold had been discreetly smelted in the well-equipped workshop at the rear of the building, serving to enhance Moses' reputation as a man of considerable standing; while, as an important member of the London Pipeline, he regularly processed items of value on behalf of emigrants who were passing through on their way to a new life. The former he saw as an occupational opportunity indulged in by most men in his position, the latter as part of his responsibilities to the Jewish community. When the time came Ruth knew he would play an integral part in the onward transmission of the Romanov necklace.

'I need to know who this man Leschenko is, and what connections he may have with a group called the Irish Brotherhood,' Tom said tentatively. He had spent months on the puzzle, and expecting to be handed the answer on a plate was naïve, but any information would be useful.

Grodzinski inclined his head and, looking at the detective with an amused smile, said, 'You have not asked if he is also this man they are calling "Jack the Ripper"?'

It was Tom's turn to smile. 'Do you know?'

'Not definitely,' the goldsmith replied, 'but I would be surprised if he were. I'm fairly sure he killed Elizabeth Gustafsdotter, though.' Tom gave the man his full attention and remained silent while Moses sipped his tea. 'The police are chasing their tails over this murderer. One minute he is a Jew, the next a foreigner, yesterday he was a sadistic woman-hater, today he is a doctor selling body parts. They have no idea.' Turning to his niece, and speaking in English in deference to Tom, he continued. 'Feeling against us is running high at the moment. Everywhere there is panic. Several of our people have been attacked in the streets for no reason other than that they are Jews. A Polish boot finisher was arrested because he wears a leather apron similar to one that is supposed to be worn by the killer. You should not be on the streets after dark, Rushka.' There was real concern in his voice. 'I don't think this last killing was done by the same man. For a start, there were no mutilations to the body, which does not fit in with the other murders. Secondly, the doctor who examined the body says that the knife used to kill her had a rounded end, unlike the pointed weapon used before.' Tom wondered where Grodzinski got his detailed information from. 'On the other hand, Leschenko had good reason to kill the woman. I don't suppose the police at Leman Street told you that, Mr Norton?'

The question was a rhetorical one, and Tom merely shook his head slightly, not wishing to interrupt the older man's flow.

'Lizzie Gustafsdotter or more correctly Stride, was a regular visitor to that fat idiot Brovnic's house in Varden Street. She was passing information to Inspector Abberline concerning the movements of the anarchist cell that Leschenko seems to think he heads. He was seen following her on the morning before she was killed, and doubtless watched her go into Leman Street police station. Her husband – John Stride – is dead, by the way, but his nephew is a Metropolitan policeman. I'll bet they didn't tell you that either.' The Buddha-like figure chuckled at the frustration on Tom's face. 'I doubt anyone will ever prove it, but if I were a gambling man I would put money on the Latvian having killed the woman to silence her.'

Ruth offered Tom the plate of titbits. With a small gesture he politely refused them, his appetite suddenly gone. How much more information had Thick and Abberline withheld from him?

'With regard to the activities at Varden Street, they are dreamers – dangerous, but still dreamers. Fifteen years ago Brovnic was a forceful revolutionary; now he is a drunken orator who makes a living from disposing of stolen property and letting out the rooms in that fleapit to fools like

Leschenko. They have dispersed to different addresses across London, where they will lie low – regathering at a later date to listen to the Latvian's crazy plans to dominate half of Europe.' The contempt in his voice was cuttingly dismissive. 'The part that I think is of concern to you,' Grodzinski took a delicate bite from a small herring pastry, 'relates to the arms they're acquiring. You're quite correct in assuming that they are dealing with the Irish Brotherhood.' Tom was not surprised that Moses knew about the Brotherhood: he had realised almost immediately that he was speaking to a very powerful man in the murky world of the East End. Had it not been for the woman beside him he would never have known of his existence, let alone been privy to this information. 'For some months now the Brotherhood has been supplying weapons, through an American source, to some of the Russian and Balkan groups living here in London. These weapons, primarily Winchester rifles and Colt revolvers along with their ammunition, are shipped in from a supplier in the New York area. I would suggest that weapons are being smuggled into other parts of the country by the Brotherhood and stored in safe hideaways, either for their own use or for sale to other groups, in order to raise funds. Having effected an exchange with one of these European groups, the Brotherhood can – for a price – arrange onward transmission of the goods through an English port to the continent through their contacts.'

'Do you know who this American contact is?'

Moses shrugged. 'That he used to live in Kensington and called himself Lucas Sangster is all I can tell you. He left some months ago and we lost track of him.'

The recollection of Sangster at Flixton was clear in Tom's mind. 'Do the names O'Dowd or Connor mean anything to you?' he asked.

'Liam O'Dowd is the mainland commander of the Brotherhood and sometimes visits London. The name Connor means nothing to me, I'm afraid.'

Tom nodded. He guessed that in an hour he had learned more from this man than was known by the entire London police force. Bringing Ruth to London with him had been a stroke of genius.

'There is one thing that the Metropolitan Police seem to have overlooked,' Moses said thoughtfully. 'The woman – Nina Volputin – is involved in producing an anarchist broadsheet called *Der Arbeiterfreund – The Worker's Friend*. Although the title is German, the paper is published in Yiddish. It's complete *schmutter* – rubbish. Its print shop is in Dutfield's Yard. On Saturday Leschenko spent the day locked away in the workshop. The police, of course, don't know that.' He smiled benignly at the detective, and chuckled. 'I'm sure I need not tell you that the people at the International Club aren't going to tell the police if it's raining, never mind that one of their own people was hanging around the murder location all day.'

Tom winced, and wondered if Thick and Abberline stood the remotest chance of solving their murders in this closed community. He doubted it.

The main purpose of their visit achieved, Ruth chatted with her uncle about family matters for another hour before, with a deal of handshaking between the men and hugging of Ruth by Moses, they took their leave.

Back out in the street the light was beginning to fade as an early evening dusk replaced the dull October day. Tom was deep in thought as they strolled down Brick Lane.

'What are you thinking about?' Ruth asked, taking his arm.

'There's something I want to do,' he replied carefully. 'Once we get back to Whitechapel Road I'm going to put you in a hansom. You go back to the hotel while I pay a little visit to the premises of *The Worker's Friend*. It shouldn't take long, and I'll join you at the hotel in about an hour.' Ruth had half-expected some such suggestion, and without breaking her pace looked up at him and said, 'Good idea – and a bad one. A good idea to have a look at *Der Arbeiterfreund* before the local police make a connection; a bad idea to go alone.' Silencing Tom's protest, she continued. 'It's getting dark and you'll never find the yard on your own; I know where it is. On your own here after dark you'll attract attention. People could even mistake you for this Jack the Ripper. If I come with you we won't be so conspicuous. People might even think I'm a high-class hooker.'

'What on earth is a hooker?' Tom demanded.

Ruth stared at him in mock-amazement. 'During the American Civil War there was a Union general – Joseph Hooker – who had an enormous appetite for whores. Ever since then the American slang for a prostitute has been "hooker".' She almost burst out laughing at the outraged expression on the detective's face. 'Do you know nothing?' she asked mischievously, bustling past an umbrella seller who was attempting to draw their attention to the cheap wares on his handcart.

Although not yet five o'clock, daylight was already failing when they arrived at the entrance to Dutfield's Yard. Ruth had brought them to the broken gates via Back Church Lane and Fairclough Street, in order not to be seen passing the entrance to the International Club. The broken gates hung forlornly beneath an old cartwheel that was fixed at first-floor level to the wall of the adjacent club. Even at this early hour Ruth felt an eerie chill. She was, she knew, standing just feet from where a woman's throat had been slashed open less than forty-eight hours before. It did little for her confidence. Tom felt Ruth's uneasiness. Indicating the lighted house window a few yards away, he said quietly, 'Go to that fruit store and wait for me. I'll only be a few minutes.' He sensed that she was now, with good reason, becoming frightened. This was not a place for a woman to be wandering alone, and it was impossible to take her with him. He deeply regretted allowing her to accompany him.

Ruth squeezed his hand, then walked away to engage a doleful old man in conversation at the window of his fruit stall.

Checking to ensure he was not being observed, Tom slipped down the yard to the dilapidated stable block. Gently trying the door handle, he was surprised to find that it turned freely; the door swung open easily under the pressure of his shoulder. Someone had been in recently and neglected to lock the door on the way out, he thought. With Volputin arrested, presumably someone had been in to clear the place of any incriminating material. Closing the door behind him, Tom waited to allow his eyes to adjust to the dim light. The atmosphere was dank and airless, and it had the unmistakeable stale tang that is left behind when a room has been used by a vagrant. Not a sound broke the stillness. His eyes accustomed to the gloom, Tom saw the shadowy bulk of a printing press on his right and an old wooden desk a few feet in front of him.

Moving over to the desk, he struck a match, and in its flickering light he saw the butt end of a candle in a small iron holder among the papers. The match began to burn his fingers and, hurriedly extinguishing it, he lit another, applying it to the blackened tallow wick. In the flare of the candlelight he saw the desk was littered with papers, all in some form of incomprehensible script that he assumed to be Yiddish. He knew that he should not remain here too long: something was not right, but exactly what eluded him.

As he moved round the desk, Tom's foot suddenly caught something, making him stumble and grab the edge of the table to keep his balance. Dropping to his knees, he felt the rough boards of the uneven floor and quickly found what he was seeking. The thin rug beside the desk was folded back and a piece of loose floorboard had been pulled away to reveal a small cavity beneath.

Too late he realised what was wrong: why the door was unlatched and what the rank odour was. Desperately trying to scramble to his feet, Tom felt a heavy blow across the middle of his back as his assailant dropped his full weight onto him. A voluminous sack was pulled down over his head and shoulders, preventing him from struggling. The weight lifted momentarily before the man threw himself down again as hard as he could, both knees smashing into Tom's kidneys, knocking the breath from his body and causing him temporarily to pass out. The man thrust his hand into the floor cavity inches from Tom's head, withdrew the lock knife, and then, without paying any further attention to the policeman's inert form, leapt to his feet and ran to the unlocked door.

Ruth and the old man at the stall turned towards Dutfield's Yard at the clatter of boots. They were just in time to see a man in an old green jacket and corduroy trousers run from the yard and head full tilt up Berners Street towards Commercial Road. The fruiterer was still staring in bewilderment when the dark-haired woman, who seconds before had been chatting to him about the recent murder, gathered her skirts together and took off as fast as she could into the yard.

Tom was staggering out through the print shop door as Ruth sprinted towards him, hampered by her ankle-length dress. 'Leschenko!' he gasped. 'The bastard was in there.'

'I know,' she said urgently. 'I saw him. Are you all right? We need to get away from here quickly, before the police arrive.'

Tom, now fully recovered, nodded and grabbed her by the hand as they dashed out into Berners Street in the same direction as their quarry.

Chapter Twenty-One

Back at the Viceroy Hotel, while Ruth engaged the reception clerk in a fruitless search for some fictitious correspondence, Tom, hatless and dishevelled, made his way unnoticed up the stairs to the privacy of his room. He was furious that he had allowed himself to walk into an open trap. Cursing profusely, he soaked away the day's events in the hot bath that had been filled for him by the chambermaid.

As before, they had agreed to have dinner in Ruth's suite. On this occasion it was not simply to avoid the formalities of eating in the hotel dining room; they needed to discuss the events of the day. A few minutes before seven o'clock Tom gave a gentle tap on the door, and admitted himself to the suite with the spare key that Ruth had given him.

Sitting down on the commodious settee and looking at the elegant furnishings while Ruth was getting them drinks in the next room, Tom idly considered the social differences between himself and Mrs Samuels. The elegantly furnished room was one of a series that made up the hotel suite: in addition there were a bathroom, a bedroom, a dressing room and a small cubby-hole for a servant to sleep in. How much it was costing he had no idea. That he would have to allow her to make good her promise for the bank to pay was unavoidable. It was beyond his means, and the Kelsford police force would not entertain paying for such accommodation.

The door from the outer room opened and Ruth appeared, carrying a tray with a bottle of clear vodka and two glasses. She was wearing a loose, high-necked, plum-coloured top, tied at the waist with a broad sash, over a pair of baggy trousers that were gathered together just above the ankles. To his astonishment he saw her feet were bare. Aware of his bewilderment, Ruth busied herself pouring a generous measure of the spirit into the glasses. 'Is something wrong?' she asked softly, handing one to Tom.

Standing in front of him in the flowing Cossack tunic, her black hair freed from its pins and now hanging loosely down her back, she was, thought

Tom, the most beautiful woman he had ever seen. How could anything be wrong?

Receiving no immediate answer, Ruth smiled. 'You're accustomed to being in the company of English women – ladies who follow strictly formal patterns of behaviour. I'm different. During the day I'm part of the English banking world, and all that entails. At home I relax, put on comfortable clothes and become what I have always been – a middle-class Russian Jew.'

'You look breathtaking,' Tom murmured, entranced.

Leaning forward, she took the untouched glass from his hand. 'Be comfortable,' she said, her normally throaty voice now a deep husky whisper. 'There's another tunic in the dressing room.' The scent of expensive soap filled Tom's senses: her face was only inches from his, her breath sweet and exciting. Reaching forward, he pulled at the loosely tied sash, and the tunic fell open to reveal her heavy breasts. Scarcely knowing what he was doing, Tom pulled her gently towards him and took a hard dark nipple between his lips.

Their lovemaking, first on the carpet of the main room and then again in the soft double bed, was a wonderful and sensuous thing. For Tom, who had not experienced a woman since Kate died, it seemed like a release from the past and the beginning of a new future. For Ruth, who had not known what to expect, Tom was a kind and gentle lover, as aware of her needs as his own. One thing she now knew: she was in love with Thomas Norton.

Relaxing quietly together under the rumpled bed covers, both were temporarily lost in their own thoughts. Ruth leaned over to the bedside table and, reaching into the drawer, withdrew a long dark cheroot. Applying a match to it, she passed it over to Tom, who, lying on his back, an arm behind his head, took it in his free hand.

Studying the ornately sculptured ceiling, he said in a quiet voice, 'Two things . . .'

Leaning on one elbow, Ruth pushed back the wayward strands of hair that were stuck to her damp forehead and gently kissed him on the mouth. 'Go on,' she murmured.

'First, I love you. I mean, I'm in love with you now and for all time.' Tom had never thought he would hear himself say those words. He should, he knew, feel guilty about what had happened, about his overwhelming feelings for Ruth, but strangely he didn't. It seemed as if from somewhere, lifetimes away, Kate approved and had given them her blessing. He had no idea why or how he knew this, but that it was so he was certain.

'That's very good,' she replied, gently kissing him again, her husky voice filled with emotion, 'because I love you – now and for all time.' Moving closer, the aroma of the cigar filling the room already scented with their lovemaking, she asked softly, '. . . and second?'

'How do you know Eugene Leschenko?' There was no accusation in the question. It was uttered in the flat, defeated tones of a man who knows the question must be asked but does not want to hear the answer. Tom felt that, having just found a happiness he had never dreamt of gaining, it was about to be snatched away by the woman's reply.

Ruth lay back and closed her eyes briefly. 'How did you know?'

Tom took a pull at the cigar, then studied the glowing end for a second. They were no longer touching. Ruth felt a cold black void in the pit of her stomach. Exhaling the smoke, he turned towards her. He needed to see her face, to look into her eyes. If she were lying he had to know. 'When I asked Leschenko about O'Dowd there was a flicker in his eyes. Just momentarily, but it was there – recognition: he knew what I was talking about. I'd seen that look earlier, when he first came into the room, but I thought I must have been mistaken.' Tom paused to gather his thoughts. 'Years ago, when I was a child, there was a basketmaker's shop at the bottom of our square. Mr Brunski was a nice old boy: he and his wife had come over from Poland years before. They had no children, and my sister and I used to play in their back yard. Mr Brunski's name was Eugene, and the old lady's was Danuta. I can see them now. He always called her "Dani", and she called him "Ganek". Twice in the interview room you called Leschenko "Ganek". That's when I knew I wasn't wrong. When Leschenko walked into that room he recognised you.'

Ruth lay perfectly still, knowing better than to try to touch him. She believed Tom when he said he loved her, but he was also hurt and baffled. To make a mistake could cost her that love. Her mind made up, Ruth decided to tell him.

For half an hour Ruth talked quietly in the darkened room. She told Tom about the Pipeline and her involvement over the years, how she had come to be a trusted courier and a link with escapees. She told him about the trip to Unghvar and the botched mission that had resulted in Leschenko's flight to England. She told him about von Rasche's murder on the Vienna train.

When she had finished, Ruth Samuels climbed out of bed, emotionally drained, and picked up the discarded tunic from the floor. Putting it on, she pulled the sash tight round her waist and turned to face the man who so recently had been her lover. 'Telling you this could put my life in jeopardy. The Pipeline is not a benevolent organisation. People who have threatened its security in the past have been known to mysteriously disappear – just as Eugene Leschenko would have in Russia should it have proved necessary. You're not the first man with whom I have made love. You are, however, the first man I've ever loved. It's now up to you.'

Tom watched the straight back and swinging hips as she strode purposefully through into the living room. A few seconds later a respectful tap on the outer door signalled the arrival of a waiter with the dinner trolley. Going across to the hanger on the wardrobe door, Tom took down the spare cotton tunic and baggy trousers.

In the main room of the suite a meal had been laid out. Ruth was sitting apprehensively at the table, her hands folded in front of her, watching him. Tom looked at her long and hard for several seconds. 'We used to wear these outfits in Afghanistan when we were up in the hills. In polite society, though, the ladies wore more than just the tunic.'

The meal over, they sat curled up together on the large settee. Tom sprawled, while Ruth lay full length, her head in his lap. Idly running his fingers through her hair, he said, 'Do you have to be back tomorrow?'

Lazily, Ruth murmured, 'What have you in mind?'

'I thought that tomorrow we could have a holiday, take the day out and see the sights, then go back on Wednesday.'

'And that gives us an extra night, does it not?' she ventured, with a wicked grin.

Much later that night, while Tom slept cradled in her arms, Ruth lay awake in the dark, pondering her good fortune. All the men whom she had known in her life had wanted something from her. Isaac Samuels was looking for a business assistant in exchange for a secure lifestyle. Her partners at the bank tolerated her because she was Samuels' widow. Mannie Issitt needed her skills and resourcefulness to further his ambitions for the Pipeline. The men whom she had taken for lovers over the years had wanted her ample body. Now, for the first time, in Tom Norton she had found a man who loved her for herself, and she loved him.

During interludes in their lovemaking they had decided to keep things a secret for the time being. This was, Tom had said, more for the benefit of her reputation as a respectable widow and member of the Jewish community than for himself, but it would give him time to prepare his parents and his sister for the new development. Ruth also wondered if Tom had suspected her relationship with Henry Farmer and was giving her time to disentangle herself.

As she lay there, not wanting to move in case she disturbed him, Ruth's mind kept returning to the one thing she had not told Tom. During the interview she had told Leschenko in dialect Russian that, once he had been released by the police, he and a couple of his anarchist colleagues were to take a train to Kelsford and make contact with her: it was then that she had used the diminutive Ganek, to signal she had something unusual to communicate to him.

Even though the reason she needed Leschenko to be in Kelsford was a personal matter, of which Tom should never become aware, Ruth was deeply worried. Eventually, tired out, she drifted off to sleep, telling herself she could tell Tom later if all went well.

Tuesday morning dawned bright and sunny, with the merest hint of a light breeze to keep away any rain showers. Straight after breakfast Tom and Ruth set off to make a tour of the town. Strolling hand in hand, Ruth with a light parasol and Tom swinging his silver-headed cane, they looked like a young married couple out to see the sights. Arriving in Ludgate Circus, less than two hundred yards from their hotel, they boarded an open-topped omnibus in front of Thomas Cook's impressive offices and set off on their excursion.

Although over the years Tom had made several visits to London, his knowledge of the capital was not as extensive as Ruth's and he allowed her to plan their itinerary. By early evening, when an identical omnibus brought them back to Ludgate Circus, they had seen Buckingham Palace – which, she pointed out, thanks to an error by the architect had been built without any bathrooms – the column erected to Admiral Lord Nelson in Trafalgar Square, and had spent most of the afternoon in the British Museum.

It was almost seven o'clock before they collected their keys at the reception desk and took the lift up to the first floor, pleasantly tired and ready for a hot meal. Half an hour later they were soaking together in the huge steaming porcelain bath in Ruth's apartment. Passing her the cigar that they were sharing, Tom continued to wonder at this strange woman who had somehow come into his life and captivated him. On the surface she was a sophisticated businesswoman living her life in the musty atmosphere of the Kelsford Bank of Commerce, but beneath that veneer was a sensuous, exciting woman as much at home in the cold snows of Russia or the back streets of Whitechapel as she was in this luxuriously appointed suite.

Climbing out of the bath to dry herself, Ruth playfully slapped away a wandering hand. 'Stop it. The waiter will be here with dinner in a minute,' she admonished him.

'That's another thing.' He pointed the cigar accusingly at her. 'Why did they not serve dinner until after nine o'clock last night?'

Pausing, she made a face at him. 'What a stupid question!' she said, taking the cigar from his outstretched fingers and clamping it firmly between her teeth.

Tom was laughing heartily to himself as he buried his shoulders beneath the hot water, a trail of cigar smoke filtering in from the dressing room. Finding this woman was the best thing that had happened to him for years; he felt twenty again. Taking today as a holiday had been a wonderful idea, and the day was not over yet.

Remaining in London was a decision he was soon to regret.

While Tom and Ruth, wrapped in their bathrobes, ate a succulent roasted chicken and washed it down with a chilled Rhine wine, Henry Farmer was tidying up his desk before making his way home. Henry was slightly depressed and not a little unhappy that Ruth was in London with Tom Norton. Henry knew this was somewhat unfair of him. His relationship with Ruth was, by mutual if unspoken agreement, a purely physical one. Knowing Tom, he doubted if his friend would be interested in the woman anyway. Since Kate died, Tom had shown absolutely no inclination towards female companionship, and anyway his taste in women was for the fair-haired petite type, which Ruth definitely was not. Even so, Henry was forced to examine his own situation. He was fifty-five years old and not getting any younger. For over twenty years he had lived a bachelor life, going from day to day and taking his pleasures where he found them. Now, in late middle age, he was aware that this affair with Ruth was going to be his last, unless he elected to settle for an arrangement with a dumpy and unexciting widow of his own age.

Going through into Tom's office, Henry picked up the copy of the telegram on the Inspector's desk:

for attention Head Constable Kelsford Pol Long Street stop enqs will be complete by Wednesday stop returning Kelsford same evening stop request urgent meeting Thursday morning stop.
signed
Norton

Perhaps at last there was going to be a break in the stalemate. With any luck, he thought, Tom will bring back something useful. It would have been helpful if those tight-mouthed bastards in the Met had supplied details of the address they had found. Still, no use wishing. He would stop off for a pint at the Rifleman and let Ann Turner know that her brother would be home the next evening.

The familiar sound of Arthur Hollowday's clumsy hobnailed boots sounded along the passage, and the familiar freckled face and spiky hair poked round the door. 'Oh, there you are, Mr Farmer, sir. I was looking for you in the other office.'

'What is it, Arthur? I'm just going home.'

The boy paused to catch his breath. 'There's a man at the back gate in the yard, sir, wants to see Mr Norton. Says it's most urgent, sir.'

'What sort of a man?' asked Farmer, frowning. In Tom's absence, as senior detective sergeant, he was deputising for the inspector.

'Very strange, sir.' Arthur's voice dropped to a confidential whisper. 'Got a screwed-up face. I think he might be an informant – refuses to come in beyond the yard, sir.' The Weasel's unprepossessing appearance and secretive manner had considerably frightened the lad when, on his way out through the back gate of the station, he had been grabbed by the arm and dispatched to find the detective inspector.

Sending the boy off home through the police station's front entrance, Farmer made his way to the back yard. Lurking in the shadows near the stable doors was Saul Meakin. The little man was not pleased to find that Mr Norton was away. Making up his mind, he decided to take a risk and tell Farmer the reason for his visit. 'Has Mr Norton told you about the Irishman he's looking for? The one who's involved in the Shires fiddle?' he whispered urgently.

Farmer nodded. 'Yes, I know about him. The one you saw at the site.'

Meakin relaxed a little. 'This is urgent. I've just seen him in the Black Boy with some of the Irish lads from the dig. He won't be there long. If you come with me I'll show him to you.'

Telling Meakin to wait, Henry hurried back up to the detective inspector's office. Glancing into the sergeants' room, to his annoyance he found it was empty. His newly appointed partner, Joel Dexter, was searching the lodgings of a petty thief who was in the cells. Scribbling a note for Joel, to the effect that if he returned within the next half-hour they were to meet in Welbeck Street outside the public house, he pulled on his coat and went out into the passage. Pausing for a moment, he turned and retraced his steps. Five minutes later he was back in the stable yard, the reassuring weight of the heavy revolver pulling his overcoat pocket out of shape.

With Meakin trotting along in front, the pair arrived in Welbeck Street just in time to see Connor Devlin, the collar of his reefer jacket raised and peaked cap pulled down over his face, leave the tavern in the direction of the canal basin works.

Leaving the informant in the alley to wait for Joel, Farmer followed the Irishman into the lighted street, maintaining a careful distance. Staying out of sight was not easy, as Devlin halted every so often either to use the reflected light of the gas lamps in the shop windows to check if anyone was behind him or to pause long enough to apply a match to his pipe and glance round.

An equally old hand at this game of hide and seek, after ducking quickly out of sight a couple of times Henry judged that the man made checks about every two minutes, and was thus able to anticipate the halts. It took ten minutes or so for the Irishman to arrive at the canal workings on the north edge of the town.

The diggings, which occupied an area several hundred yards square, were completely surrounded by a six foot fence of timber shuttering, erected to block out the view of the inquisitive and to prevent the theft of materials and equipment from the site. The timber gates at the front that gave onto the aptly named Canal Street were securely locked. Ignoring these, Devlin made his way along the fence and round the corner onto the wasteland that constituted the second side of the compound. Moving along, he ran his hand over the heavy fence boards, counting. When he reached number twenty-seven he halted and pushed a long-bladed pocket knife into the joint with the preceding board. A small panel of three slats pulled away easily, allowing him to slip into the compound before lodging the boards back into place.

Once inside, Connor waited a moment to orientate himself. He was, he knew, standing on a ledge that ran all the way round the workings. Five feet wide, it gave access into the pit that had been dug to create the basin in which barges would unload and turn round. Any unwary thief who gained entry to the site in the dark was liable to step off the ledge – and down a twenty-foot drop onto the solid hardcore base that was being laid. Very carefully, he began to descend a wooden ladder that was roped to the side of the drop. At the bottom a series of tunnels, three hundred yards long and high enough for a man to walk through, were being dug to allow an exchange of water between the basin and the main canal, which ran out of the town and northwards at the back of the complex. Entering one of the tunnels, Connor took a lantern and a box of Vesta matches from a ledge just inside the entrance, and lighting the lamp he made his way deeper inside. Almost at the other end, about two hundred and seventy yards in, a side compartment had been cut by some of the navvies who were Brotherhood members: eight feet square and the height of the tunnel, it was large enough to store materials or contraband. It was here that a consignment of rifles was temporarily stored, unbeknownst to anyone except Devlin, Taft and Sangster. The purpose for his visit was to ensure that no damp had leaked into the hiding place. Later, when the basin was ready to be opened, the guns would be removed before the tunnels were permanently flooded.

As he padded along the claustrophobic tunnel that was only dimly illuminated by his lamp, Connor was unaware that he was accompanied by more than the unseen rodents he could hear scampering away from his heavy footfalls. Behind him, working his way along the passage in pitchblackness and illuminated only by occasional glimpses of the Irishman's lamp, was Henry Farmer.

The first indication Connor had that something was amiss was the sound of a short scuffle behind him. Startled by the sudden noise, his heart pounding, he flattened himself against the wall and brought up the gun in his right hand.

'It's all right. You were followed.' The eerie voice echoing softly in the passage was barely recognisable as Sangster's. Warily, Connor made his way back to where the Texan was standing next to the prone figure of the detective, lying face down on the ground. 'He's been on your tail halfway across town,' the American said in a low voice. 'He picked you up near that pub in Welbeck Street.' Connor silently cursed himself for his carelessness. 'Looks like a cop to me,' Sangster continued, bending over Farmer's prone figure and removing the pistol clutched in his outstretched hand. Breaking it open, he saw it was loaded with five bullets, the chamber under the hammer empty for safety. Matter-of-factly he handed the gun to Devlin. 'I didn't think your cops were armed,' he grunted.

Connor took the pistol from him and, swapping hands, tucked his own gun into the waistband of his trousers. As he closed the chamber Sangster saw that the Irishman was examining the butt of the revolver. In the dim light the Texan watched curiously as Connor ran his thumb over a small vee cut into the wooden butt grip. It was the sort of mark that a man might make to enable him to identify his own weapon. Lost in thought and holding the pistol carefully in both hands, Connor gently rubbed the ball of his thumb backwards and forwards over the notch. After a few moments his attention returned to the man on the ground as he groaned and started to recover consciousness.

Sangster moved to one side as the Irishman stepped carefully over the detective, straddling him with one foot on either side of his body. With a cold deliberation Connor Devlin cocked the pistol and, leaning forward, pressed the barrel firmly into the back of Farmer's head, just above the base of his neck. In the tunnel the noise from the shot was deafening. Farmer's body gave a jerk, then lay perfectly still.

Sangster, aware at the last second what the Irishman was going to do, had braced himself, and now, dropping to one knee, with a short-barrelled revolver held double-handed, covered the entrance to the tunnel. Satisfied that no one had been attracted by the gunshot, he stood up and brushed some mud from his trousers.

'Bastard.' Devlin's flat tone was that of both judge and executioner. Pulling back the flap of his jacket, he tucked Eddie Donnelly's Colt revolver into his belt.

Chapter Twenty-Two

Henry Farmer's bloodstained corpse was discovered early the following morning by two young lads on their way to school, lying face down in a drainage ditch at the side of Whittaker's Lane, a narrow track that led to the village of Spilsby, four miles from Kelsford.

The frightened boys ran the half-mile back along the tree-lined lane as if the devil himself were on their heels, to find their father, a farm labourer, who was returning home after milking. Having listened to their excited and confused story, he took them up to Low Water Farm, where they were made to repeat the details of their discovery to Berriman Storey who owned the land butting onto Whittaker's Lane – and for whom their father worked. Mr Storey dispatched his cowman to fetch Constable Booth from the police house in the next village of Cummingley, and went with the lads to the scene of their grisly discovery.

It was soon after half past nine when Constable Donovan Booth drew up in his dogcart next to the ditch in Whittaker's Lane. Farmer Storey, having sent the boys back home with instructions to remain there until the constable had spoken to them, was sitting on the five-bar gate twenty yards up the road from where Henry Farmer lay. Puffing sedately on an old briar pipe, Storey looked for all the world as if he were simply enjoying a smoke while waiting for one of his men to turn up with a load of cattle feed.

During his sixty years on earth Berriman Storey had seen most of the things that life was likely to throw at him. As a lad he had watched with the macabre curiosity of the young at the crippled and ruined men returning from the war in Crimea. During his middle years he had stood helplessly by while disease had robbed him of his six-year-old daughter and ten-year-old son. More recently crop failures during the last two seasons had seriously threatened his livelihood and those of the men who looked to him for employment. This latest event was not pleasant, but in truth he realised it was just another part of life's grim tapestry.

'Where is he then, Berriman?' The stout constable climbed down from the back of the trap and looped the pony's broad leather reins over the top bar of the gate.

Storey slid his thin frame nimbly from the gate and pushed his smouldering pipe into a jacket pocket. 'In the ditch, Donovan – over here.' The wiry little man pushed through the tall grass, still wet from the overnight rain. Water dripped off his brown leather gaiters and splashed under his boots.

The constable joined him and dropped on one knee to examine the corpse. He grimaced at the sight of the mutilated head. Much of Farmer's face had been blown away by the exit wound made by the .44 bullet. 'Is this how you found him?' he asked.

'No.' The older man shook his head and looked away from the dead eyes staring up at him out of the ruined face. Pulling the pipe from his pocket he sucked on it momentarily. A cloud of fresh smoke billowed from the still burning embers. 'He was face down, head in the water. I pulled him out and turned him over on his back. Looks to me like the poor bugger's been shot.'

Donovan Booth went through the dead man's pockets. They were empty: Devlin had seen to that before helping Taft to load the body onto one of his wagons. The constable stood up and pulled his tunic straight. At six feet tall and weighing in at over nineteen stones, he was the epitome of the village policeman. A florid face, pink with his recent exertions, and strawberry nose gave way to a large double chin, into the folds of which his tunic completely disappeared. There was speculation in the villages for which Donovan was responsible that his tiny dogcart had specially strengthened springs and that his unfortunate pony should have been a shire horse. Nonetheless, Booth knew his business. It might have taken over twenty years of regular visits to every public house in the district to achieve his imposing stature, but this did not mean he was a bucolic fool. Little happened in the Cummingley and Spilsby area that Constable Booth was unaware of, a fact that many a poacher and petty thief had reason to rue when brought before the local justices.

'He's not from round here, and he's not been dead that long,' the stout constable reflected. The total absence of any form of identity bothered him: it meant this was not a simple robbery. Casting about the muddy lane for any clues, he was careful not to disturb anything.

'Doctor coming?' Storey enquired laconically. He had returned to his place on the gate and was reaming out the bowl of his pipe before refilling it from a worn leather pouch that he had balanced on the gatepost.

'Yes. I sent for him same time as I sent word for Sergeant Newman to come over,' the constable replied absently. He was down on his knees again, meticulously running his fingers through the wet grass surrounding the body. The absence of any spent bullet or cartridge case confirmed what he had already surmised: that the dead man had been killed elsewhere. Looking over his shoulder he said, 'Can you go back and get a hay cart or flat-backed wagon? Then I can get him moved soon as Dr Marsden has looked at him.' It was more an instruction than a request.

By the middle of the morning, after a flurry of messages between the county and borough police headquarters, combined with Henry Farmer's failure to arrive for duty at eight o'clock, alarm bells were ringing at Long Street.

Soon after midday Robert Archer Robson and Fred Judd were standing in a musty barn at Low Water Farm about to take their leave. Personal feelings were mixed inextricably with professional worries about the implications of Farmer's killing. Gathered with them in the makeshift mortuary were the local doctor, Simes Marsden, and Detective Inspector Theodore Thresh of the county detective department. The chief constable of the county force, Hubert Snelgrove, was still to arrive.

Archer Robson shook hands with the county detective. 'I'll leave this in your hands for the moment, Mr Thresh,' he said politely. 'No doubt we'll be speaking again very soon.'

Outside in the pony and trap he said quietly to Judd, 'Go back through the village and round the long way to pick up the road.'

Judd slapped the reins across the pony's withers and set off at a brisk trot. He well knew why they were going back through the village, and it had nothing to do with the scenery. Archer Robson wanted to be away from the barn before his counterpart from the county arrived, thus avoiding any early discussion about who had responsibility for investigating the crime. He needed to establish very quickly where the murder had taken place. It was fairly obvious to both Archer Robson and Judd that Henry had been killed in the town and taken to where he was found. With any luck, Judd thought, Tom would be back to assist them later in the day.

After a light breakfast in the spacious dining room of the Viceroy, Tom and Ruth spent the morning ambling round the busy streets near Ludgate Circus, enjoying the morning sunshine. Both knew that after they had collected their bags and boarded the train at St Pancras life would become more complicated. Tom was acutely aware that his association with this dark-haired woman would be frowned upon by his own family and never accepted in Ruth's community. Ruth was preoccupied with her first responsibility, to break off her affair with Henry Farmer as gently as possible, while she also had to send a message to Mannie, confirming that the address in Leschenko's possession had nothing to do with the Pipeline.

Their minds half-occupied with their feelings for each other, half-occupied with the practicalities of their situation, Tom and Ruth boarded the passenger train for Kelsford at twenty-five past three.

As the afternoon began to wane into early evening Joshua Howkins turned the key in the heavy padlock on the barn door and gave it a tug to ensure that it was securely fastened. The dark-haired, surly Irishman who had accompanied Lucas Sangster when he arrived at Howkins' office at eight o'clock that morning held out his hand for the key. Howkins glared at him, then turned questioningly to Sangster.

'Give him the key, Josh.' The American's tone brooked no argument. 'Then we can arrange for things to be removed later without having to bother you.'

Howkins was desperately unhappy and not a little worried. He already had the wagonload of rifles and ammunition from the railway station hidden away in his premises in Downe Street, and when Sangster and the Irishman, referred to as Connor, had shown up at his office he had been less than pleased, and at first had refused to have anything to do with the handling of a second consignment. When his answer was a peremptory 'no' he was taken aback by Sangster's reaction. 'It's not a courtesy call, Josh. You're in this as deep as we are. You've already got half the items stored, and the rest – outside in the wagon, in your yard – are at serious risk of being discovered if we don't move them. Make no mistake, my friend, if we get caught you get caught, and we all go to prison together.' With a malicious grin he added, 'Now you find somewhere nice and safe for us to take that wagon and we can all breathe again.'

The businessman knew nothing about the murder of Henry Farmer, and Sangster decided that this was for the best. Put too much pressure on their unwilling ally and he might just do something silly.

Late the previous night Sangster and Devlin had resolved that the rifles stored in the tunnel would have to be shifted to a safer place, because of the death. Farmer's body was removed by Taft on a spoil cart under a pile of sacking and taken to Whittaker's Lane. Before the grey light of dawn was touching the early morning sky Taft was back in Kelsford, and the guns, still labelled as machine parts, were safely stacked on the back of a four-wheeled wagon. After that it was simply a matter of waiting for Howkins to show up at Clumber Row.

By now the awful realisation had dawned on Joshua Howkins that he was involved in something far more sinister and dangerous than a shady business deal. Searching his mind desperately for a location as far away as possible from Kelsford, he remembered the place out at Monckton, twelve miles south of the town. At the back of an old village shop that he had bought was a large empty storage barn. The location, on the Erewash Canal, was ideal for their purposes: it would be a simple matter for the guns to be transferred onto a barge – as soon as possible, he hoped – and removed.

'I said, give him the key, Josh!' The strain of the last few hours was beginning to tell on the American. He was deeply aware that to kill a policeman, whether in America or England, was to invite all sorts of trouble. He had already proposed to Devlin that once the guns were safely relocated it would be sensible to call a halt to their operations for a while, but to his annoyance the Irishman had regarded this as unwarranted interference and had left him in no doubt that such decisions were made by more senior men in the Brotherhood than himself. Sangster was also perturbed that Devlin appeared to relish the dangers created by Farmer's murder – commenting that the ruffling of a few feathers was no bad thing.

In silence the Irishman took the key from Howkins' hand and slipped it into his pocket. For the whole day he had not uttered more than half a dozen words in the hearing of the little man. He and Sangster climbed up onto the seat beside the carter, leaving Howkins to scramble in an undignified manner onto the tailboard of the wagon.

Sitting behind the plodding horse as it made its way along the lane to rejoin the main road, Lucas Sangster surreptitiously glanced at the dour Irishman beside him – observing, not for the first time, that the solitary and secretive life that Devlin led did little to improve his naturally surly demeanour.

Although killing the detective was risky, Sangster understood and approved of Connor's reasoning. Henry Farmer, having finished work on the night of the Shires robbery, was just about to call at the Prince Albert for a late evening pint when he had seen the three Irishmen leaving the alleyway at the rear of the pub. Farmer must have gone after Eddie Donnelly as the easiest one to follow. Realising that Donnelly was carrying the proceeds of the robbery in his satchel, Farmer killed him at Bridge Sixty-Four, taking the money and stashing it for later recovery. Where he had made a mistake was in keeping Eddie's gun. When Connor had recognised this it had signed his death warrant. Sangster allowed himself a bleak smile, remembering that the man who had been killed in New York was telling the truth after all.

Not unsurprisingly, Connor Devlin was following a similar line of thought. Although he was unconcerned about Martin Lafferty, who as a traitor to the cause would have died anyway, he was reassured that Liam O'Dowd would now know beyond any shadow of doubt that he was not involved in Eddie's murder or the disappearance of the Shires money.

The American, Connor ruminated, was over-cautious: a good man and reliable in a bad situation, as he had proved the previous night, but with different priorities. Lucas Sangster was primarily interested in protecting and promoting his weapons trafficking, whereas the Irishman aimed to foment unrest – and what better way could there be than the assassination of a politician or the occasional killing of a policeman or military leader? Regarding their present situation, he saw few problems, especially as the new hiding place for the weapons was alongside the canal. In a few days the *Trojan* would be coming through, probably with O'Dowd on board, giving him the opportunity to brief the commander on the end result of the Shires affair. While he questioned the sense of involving the grocer, Connor had to concede that Howkins' access to premises was currently extremely useful. Later he would reconsider the little man's position. Of one thing Connor was certain. As soon as they arrived in Kelsford he would pack his single bag at Susan Burke's and be away before nightfall. He had already stayed in St Andrew's Street for too long; it was time to move on.

Tom Norton was surprised, then uneasy, when he saw Fred Judd waiting on the platform of the station as the train pulled in. Seeing his expression, Ruth gave him a questioning look. 'Something's happening, my love,' Tom muttered. 'Time to become Mr Norton and Mrs Samuels again, I'm afraid.'

Reaching over, she took his hand gently in hers. 'Come over to the house as soon as you can. Mirka will know to let you in.' Much as she wanted to, she did not dare kiss him before they parted.

Stony-faced, Judd reached up and relieved Tom of their bags as the couple descended from the carriage. Tom realised something serious had happened. Ushering them to a corner table in the deserted buffet, Judd quickly summed up the day's events. Mistaking Ruth's sudden pallor, the policeman apologised for his indelicacy. 'I'm sorry, Mrs Samuels. I shouldn't have discussed this matter in front of a lady.'

'No, no, it's all right.' She raised her hand in a delicate motion of dismissal. 'I'm afraid I'm not a good traveller. The motion of the train has left me a little unwell.' Ruth was genuinely frightened that she might pass out. She felt physically sick. For the last two days she had been searching for a way to break off her liaison with Henry, and now he was dead: shot through the head and his body thrown in a ditch. Ruth felt an enormous guilt that she had not been able to talk to him. With a sudden pang she wondered if Tom had any idea about her involvement with Henry. Glancing quickly at him, she saw that although he was listening to Inspector Judd he was looking intently at her with an expression of compassion and worry.

Judd continued. 'The superintendent wants to see us both as soon as you're available, Tom.'

His brain in a whirl, Tom nodded. Before he could make any plans he needed to know what had already been done, if anything. It was obvious that 'as soon as you're available' meant immediately, which suited him. Looking pointedly at Ruth, he said, 'Mrs Samuels, I'm going to be detained for some time. Could I impose upon you to leave my bag at my house on your way home? My sister should be there.' Ruth understood the implied message. She would possibly not see him for a while.

Judd pulled out his pocket watch; it was almost a quarter to seven. 'He said that if you were on this train he'd meet us in half an hour.'

Tom nodded again, and, having put Ruth into one of the hansom cabs on the station forecourt, the two men set off at a brisk pace on foot to Long Street. On the way Tom, despite being preoccupied, briefed Fred on the results of his trip to London. 'Irrespective of what we're doing about Henry's murder, we'll have to put a watch on Susan Burke's from tomorrow,' he told his colleague. Judd agreed. Almost the entire workload was going to fall on the men of the detective department, so tomorrow he would have to draft in some reliable uniform officers and put them under Tom's direction.

At the railway station Fred Judd had been aware there was something going on between Tom and Ruth Samuels. It was nothing he could put his finger on, but he knew that if he searched long enough he would identify it. Turning into the front doors of the police station, he suddenly realised what it was. Tom had not thanked Mrs Samuels for her help or said goodbye to her, which meant they were intending to see each other again. He had not given her his address, which meant she already knew where he lived. Fred Judd felt quite pleased, not for having made the deduction, as he would keep it strictly to himself, but because Tom might just have found someone with whom he could be happy.

Robert Archer Robson's day had been a long and tiring one. After he and Judd had identified Farmer's body they hurried back to Long Street to begin their own enquiries. Because the body had been found outside the borough, the murder investigation would for the time being be officially conducted by the county constabulary. Archer Robson wanted this to alter quickly, and for the enquiry to be placed in his own hands.

Leaving Fred Judd to trace any possible relatives that Farmer might have had, although he was having little success, Archer Robson spent the rest of the day setting up the preliminaries of his own investigation.

In common with most borough police headquarters of the time, the head constable's living quarters were part of the main building, situated on the first floor. Soon after six o'clock Archer Robson joined his wife and their two daughters for a hasty meal. Afterwards he changed his shirt, shaved for the second time that day and returned to his office to await the return of his detective inspector.

On the way down the back stairs he noticed that the tooth that had been plaguing him was once again sending out warning twinges. Before too long he would have to take his courage in both hands and submit to the attentions of one or another of the town's dentists.

At a quarter past seven the head constable was joined by his two senior officers. After enquiring briefly about Tom's trip to London, he invited them to seat themselves in the deep leather armchairs either side of the fireplace. Producing a bottle of single malt whisky from a small cupboard at the back of the room, he poured generous measures into three glasses and handed one each to Tom and Fred.

Standing with his back to the fireplace, Archer Robson raised his glass and said solemnly, 'To Henry Farmer – and a job to be done.' Adding the inevitable 'Slàinte', he settled into the third chair. Sipping the whisky, he swilled it cautiously round his aching tooth before swallowing. For a few welcome moments it anaesthetised the troublesome molar while he gathered his thoughts. 'You can tell me about London shortly, Thomas. First we have more urgent business to deal with.' The soft brogue had an edge to it. 'I presume Fred has briefed you, so can I have an opinion?'

Tom sat back in his chair, the whisky's relaxing fire burning its way pleasantly through his system. 'Henry was working yesterday until late evening.

We know from the boy that he had a meeting in the yard here soon after eight o'clock with a mysterious little man who was looking for me.' Tom paused. Had he been in Kelsford instead of eating dinner with Ruth, it would not have been Henry who went to his death the previous night. Pushing the thought from his mind, he continued. 'I doubt that the meeting was a trap. The informant's name is Saul Meakin. He's been passing me information for some time concerning the Irish Republican Brotherhood. In particular he's been trying to identify the local commander. I imagine he located the man and, coming here to look for me, found Henry instead. We know Henry left a message for Joel Dexter to meet him in Welbeck Street. According to Fred, Joel picked the message up, but by the time he arrived outside the Black Boy Henry had gone. I think it most likely that Henry picked our man up, although we can't check that until Meakin contacts us again, followed him, and was ambushed and killed.' The others remained silent. 'Anything now is conjecture.' Archer Robson indicated for him to continue. 'There had to be a really good reason to kill Henry. Either he found out where our man was living, or he stumbled across something else so important that he couldn't be allowed to walk away. Afterwards, whoever killed him needed some form of transport to remove the body. A wagon or a cart, not a pony and trap.' A thought occurred to him. 'Fred, has Ducky Mallard had a look at the body?'

Judd nodded. 'Yes. I got him to go straight over to Storey's barn as soon as I knew that was where the county were taking it for their doctor's examination. Ducky helped the local man, an old boy called Marsden, to do the examination. I spoke to him just before I came down to meet you at the railway station. It was one shot to the back of the head, at very close range, probably from a heavy calibre handgun.' Fred closed his eyes for a moment while he composed himself, trying to blot out the memory of the figure laid out in the barn. 'The exit wound took most of his face off.'

His companions studied their whiskies, giving him time to recover. Tom silently gave thanks for his colleague's efficiency. It was crucial that their own medical practitioner had examined the body: now they would not have to rely on information fed to them by the county police, while at any subsequent trial Mallard, as Kelsford borough's own police surgeon, would be a far more reliable witness.

For a fleeting moment Tom allowed his thoughts to return to Ruth Samuels. That she had been involved with Henry before they went to London was no longer in question, any more than the fact that she would have broken it off as soon as she was back in Kelsford. Seeing the effect of the news on her in the station buffet, Tom had wanted to reach out and touch her hand, to tell her that he understood, but that had been impossible. Later, he thought, he would talk to her, and they could put the matter to rest for good.

Robert Archer Robson was the first to speak. 'So far, Thomas, I haven't kicked any doors in. I don't want to interfere with anything you may already have in hand.'

Tom smiled ruefully. He wondered just where the Scotsman had learned his trade before coming to England. 'I suggest we make general enquiries in all of the pubs in town, to find out if anyone saw Henry or anything suspicious. Let the uniformed beat officers do that. Meanwhile, the detective officers are to make specific enquiries at the Black Boy and in the surrounding area. Weasel Meakin saw our unknown Irishman at the warehouse diggings a short while ago, along with a carter named Taft and an American whom we know as Lucas Sangster. Taft has access to wagons, so I think we need to look closely at him. I'll talk about Sangster later when we discuss my trip to London. Until we have something positive we need to tread very carefully.'

The other two agreed and, after further consideration of who would do what, the head constable turned to the other pressing matter. 'Now, Thomas, you'd better tell us what's been happening in London.'

Tom reluctantly decided not to go to Victoria Road on his way home. It was late and he wanted to give Ann and Jamie the small gifts that he had brought back from London for them. Ruth had helped him choose a silk evening shawl for Ann and a smart new cap with a button top for Jamie. He wondered if his sister would detect the other woman's hand in his choice of presents.

When he arrived home Tom found that Reuben had come to the house for dinner, to hear his future brother-in-law's news. Despite the late hour, young Jamie had been allowed to stay up until his uncle's return. Sitting in his shirtsleeves over a home-made meat pie that Ann had been keeping for him in the oven, and a cold bottle of beer from the marble slab in the larder, Tom recounted the details of his excursion to the metropolis, deliberately leaving out Eugene Leschenko and the events at Varden Street. Reuben and Ann knew better than to ask about such things, and Jamie was mostly interested in his new cap.

'The papers say there's been another murder in Whitechapel, Tom,' said Reuben, helping himself to a portion of Ann's pie. Tom flashed him a glance and gave an almost imperceptible shake of his head. A look of concern appeared briefly on his sister's face. Reuben gave the slightest of nods and occupied himself with his dinner. His interest aroused, he knew he would have to wait until Tom briefed his colleagues the following day.

With Jamie off to bed and Reuben taking his leave soon after eleven, Tom and Ann found themselves alone in the sitting room. She brought him another glass of beer and tidied away the pots into the kitchen sink before standing behind his chair and placing her hands on his shoulders.

'So . . .', she asked softly. 'How did your trip go?'

'It was all right. Tiring but all right,' he replied lamely.

Ann ran her fingers across his shoulders and gently stroked the thick blond hair at the base of his neck. It was something she had done ever since she was a little girl. When Tom came out of the army she had idly stroked his neck as he told her stories about life in India. Latterly, when they had reminisced about their times with John and Kate, he would smoke a cigar while his sister gently massaged away the tension in his shoulders and neck.

Very slowly, Ann worked her hands back and forth. 'Is this just a fling or do you love her?'

'How did you know?'

'She came here with your things and wasn't in a hurry to leave. We talked about all sorts of things. She didn't need to tell me.'

'Does she know you realised?'

'I think so. Now answer my question. Do you love her?'

'We love each other, Ann. We'll keep it quiet for a while, but we want to be together.'

The hands stopped moving, palms laying flat across his shoulders. 'I hope you know what you're doing, Tom,' Ann said earnestly. 'She's a Jewess, and out of our class.'

The censure in her voice raised a sharp flash of anger in Tom. Stiffening his body, he got up abruptly from the chair and turned to face her. 'Yes, I do know that Ruth is Jewish, and I do know what I'm doing.' It was difficult to be angry with Ann: he knew she was only saying to his face what others would say behind his back. 'I'm not telling anyone but you. Please don't say anything to Mother or Father – and if you do say anything to Reuben he's to keep his mouth shut tight or he'll have me to deal with. Let's leave it at that for the time being.' Tom refrained from saying anything he might regret later – that he had given Ann and Reuben his unqualified blessing and hoped for the same from her, and that, like her, he had no wish to spend the rest of his life alone.

Tom made his way into the hall and off to bed, tired and deeply troubled.

'I do hope you know what you're doing, my dear,' Ann said quietly to herself as his footsteps disappeared up the stairs.

After a troubled night's sleep Tom, smartly dressed in his light grey suit and bowler hat, set off with Archer Robson to a meeting with Hubert Snelgrove, chief constable of the county police, at his headquarters at Sheffield Road on the outskirts of town. Relationships between the county and borough police were at best uneasy; and an investigation by the county into the murder of a borough detective was an extremely sensitive matter for all parties.

Snelgrove's offices, on the first floor of his country house headquarters, were far more elaborate than those of Kelsford borough's head constable. They were approached by a wide staircase, which led up from an expansive lobby, and an elegantly carpeted passageway, which was adorned with the photographs of his predecessors and their senior officers.

Archer Robson and Tom Norton were admitted to the chief constable's rooms by a deferential inspector, who Tom presumed to be Snelgrove's secretary, probably also responsible for administration. Tom thought briefly of Fred Judd and the draughty office that, as administrator for the borough, he occupied in the ground-floor passage at Long Street.

Pleasantries exchanged with Archer Robson, Snelgrove shot an enquiring look at Tom. 'Thomas Norton, my head of detectives,' Archer Robson explained smoothly. 'I thought we might benefit from his advice, and he has some information garnered on a recent trip to London from which we could both benefit, Hubert.'

'Had I known you were bringing your man with you I would have arranged for Inspector Thresh to have joined us – but he's out and about, trying to discover who killed your fellow Farmer.' That Snelgrove did not welcome Tom's presence was patently obvious. A tall man in his middle sixties with sloping shoulders and a broad paunch, he had, Tom knew from previous experience, an overly high opinion of his position and social standing. Snelgrove's unfortunate physique, combined with thin pointed features and a long straight nose looming over a wispy moustache, led him to be known by friends and enemies alike as Harry the Rat.

Ignoring the implied discourtesy, Archer Robson bit his tongue and replied, 'We're convinced that Detective Sergeant Farmer was actually murdered somewhere on the north side of the town, with his body later being dumped out at Spilsby.'

Snelgrove made a little *moue* with his mouth, causing a twitching movement of his moustache that at any other time would have made Tom burst out laughing. On this occasion he remained silent, his dislike for the man mounting by the minute. 'That remains to be seen, Robert. For the moment Thresh is still making enquiries, and I have to say we think Sergeant Farmer was killed very near to where he was found. Time will tell, will it not?'

Robert Archer Robson felt his anger mounting. In truth, this was little more than he had expected. Time was in short supply, but until he could show that Farmer had been killed in the town he knew there was little he could do. His next suggestion, that in view of the circumstances of the murder a joint enquiry between the two police forces would be sensible, with Norton and Thresh working together, met with a polite but definite refusal.

'I think not,' Hubert Snelgrove said with a deprecating smile. 'Theodore Thresh is a most capable officer, and possibly has more experience in these matters than Mr Norton.' Now it was Tom's turn to bridle.

'In that case experience may just tell him what's looking my people in the face, that Farmer wasn't killed where he was found!' retorted Archer Robson shortly, struggling to keep a grip on his temper.

'You said that Mr Norton might have information that could be relevant to us both?' Tom wondered if Snelgrove was ever going to address him directly. The county man, inwardly gloating, wanted to move the conversation away from the subject under discussion. The dead Kelsford detective had a reputation as a ladies' man, and Theo Thresh had specific instructions from Snelgrove to leave no stone unturned until he had discovered what Farmer was doing out at Spilsby when he was supposed to be on duty in Kelsford. Archer Robson's insistence that the killing had taken place in the town, along with his determination to bring his own man into the enquiry, confirmed the matter in Snelgrove's mind. Something was going on that was potentially embarrassing, and he was going to get to the bottom of it.

To Archer Robson and Tom's further frustration, the county chief constable refused point blank to acknowledge the worth of Tom's information concerning the activities of the Irish Republican Brotherhood in the district, dismissing as fantasy the likelihood that a political organisation was committing major crimes and trafficking in arms. Tom thought back to Vincent Millward's parting words, that if the existence of such matters was denied then there was no need to investigate them.

Having spent a little over an hour at Sheffield Road, the two Kelsford officers collected Archer Robson's pony and trap from the stables and set off back to Long Street at a trot. Neither spoke for several minutes until eventually Archer Robson's fury bubbled over. 'Ach, the man canna piss straight!' he snarled. Anger made the Scotsman's accent so thick that Tom had difficulty understanding what he was saying. 'Ah know what his game is. He wants to put a borough officer in his area doing things he should na . . .' Not sure how to respond, Tom remained silent. Calmer now, the head constable, his face set, turned to look at him. 'I want this murder solved, Thomas. Too many things have happened lately without any results. The Shires robbery, Donnelly's murder, then Harriman's, now one of our own men. It's not a criticism of you, as what's going on isn't simple, but it can't continue. Solve one of these crimes and you'll find the answers to the others. From now on you do whatever you think is necessary – you understand what I'm saying?'

Tom knew exactly what Archer Robson was saying. If he needed to go beyond his official remit the head constable would not question his actions. By the same token, if things went wrong he would be on his own.

Chapter Twenty-Three

By half past eleven Tom was sitting in his office, fuming. The meeting with the chief constable had – to say the least – not been a resounding success. Glaring at the pile of papers on his desk, he wondered how long it would be before he had the break he needed. That there would be one he was certain: in his experience, if you worked carefully and meticulously on a case it would eventually happen. His mood was not improved when Arthur Hollowday announced that he had a visitor.

Charles Kerrigan Kemp pulled back the chair Tom offered him and sat down heavily. He was considerably older than Tom had realised before, well over sixty and probably nearer to seventy. A thick-set man of medium height, his ponderous jowls and baggy eyes made him look more like a policeman than a newspaper editor. Although etched with deep lines, his pale face bore few signs of the years of late nights and alcohol that Tom knew to be an important part of his life.

Returning to his place behind the desk, Tom picked up his flat leather cigar case and proffered it to his visitor. Kerrigan Kemp declined politely. 'I don't use them, thank you,' he said, to Tom's mild surprise.

Changing his mind, Tom replaced the cigar case on the blotter and sat back in his chair. 'What can I do for you, Mr Kerrigan Kemp?'

'I thought it might be time for us to have a chat.' Kerrigan Kemp's eyes held Tom's in a long speculative gaze, before releasing him with an engaging smile. 'You don't trust me, do you?' The question was put without animosity – a statement of fact.

Looking directly at his visitor, Tom replied, 'I haven't really had very much contact with you.' He paused before continuing guardedly, 'I know you were quite close to my predecessor, but how good a thing that was I don't know.'

Kerrigan Kemp nodded his head lugubriously, the resemblance to a bloodhound becoming more pronounced. 'Would you, as the new head of detectives, permit me to explain something to you?' Tom, intrigued, gestured for the editor to continue. 'You and I can, by the nature of things, have one of two relationships. The first is that we stand and throw bricks at each other across the street. The second is that, as the occasion demands, we discuss things like the professionals that we are and come to certain agreements.' He paused. 'For instance, you're in the middle of investigating the particularly unfortunate murder of one of your officers. I can report that as the death of a dedicated policeman in the pursuit of some as yet undetermined felons. Alternatively, as we both know Henry Farmer had a history of philandering, I can ask whether he was possibly the victim of some other form of misadventure . . .' Before Tom had the opportunity to react, Kerrigan Kemp put up his hands and said, 'Please, I don't intend to do that. I knew Henry quite well. I'm giving you an example of what I'm talking about. You, on the other hand, can exclude me when a crime is committed from information that would be of considerable use if I were in possession of it earlier rather than later.'

Tom weighed what was being said. An alliance with Kerrigan Kemp was more sensible than some sort of a stand-off. It was, as always, a matter of judgement. Did the newspaper editor genuinely wish to establish a working relationship or had he an agenda that Tom was not yet aware of?

'You know me through your predecessor.' Kerrigan Kemp was speaking again. 'Joe Langley and I were acquainted for years. We usually met, as you're aware, at the Pack Horse. I have a routine. If I want to collect information I have to be available in certain places at certain times. Consequently, rain or shine, I'm in the Pack Horse every lunchtime. Joe was a drinker, so that was the natural place for us to meet. What I'm saying to you is that we can make life easier for each other without compromising our responsibilities.' Kerrigan Kemp sat back. He had proffered the olive branch; it was now up to the policeman.

Tom nodded his agreement. 'I think that what you're suggesting is eminently sensible.' He had made his mind up that, until something happened to prove him wrong, he would take the editor at face value.

About to stand up and shake hands with his guest, Tom realised that Kerrigan Kemp had not finished. Reaching into his jacket, the older man withdrew a foolscap envelope, folded in half to fit into his pocket. Pulling his chair in nearer to the desk, he took two photographs from the envelope and placed them side by side, facing Tom. It appeared that both had been taken for the *Gazette* – probably by Alfred Saunt – as part of their coverage of the canal project. The detective leaned forward and examined the first, which he immediately recognised. It was the Flixton canal cut, taken on the day earlier in the summer when he had given Ruth a lift home. It showed Ruth and the party from the bank; in the centre were Max Peters, Joshua Howkins and Lucas Sangster. The second picture showed a large piece of machinery at Kelsford basin, presumably removing spoil. After a few seconds Tom spotted why he was being shown it. In the background, standing near to the door of a timber hut, were three men. Reaching into his desk drawer, he took out a large magnifying glass and held it to the group.

'The big man on the left is Lucas Sangster,' he said absently, aware that he was telling Kerrigan Kemp what he already knew. 'The one in the middle is the building contractor, Clancy Taft, and I don't know the one on the right.' He bent closer, bringing up the magnification of the third man who was dressed in a workman's reefer and an old cap pulled down over his face.

'The man on the end is Southern Irish. He's not employed anywhere on either site, and he's a frequent visitor to Taft's office – which is that hut. He's rumoured to be an Irish Republican Brotherhood Officer.'

Tom breathed a deep sigh. At last he had found the man named Connor. 'Thank you. I need to do some work on this, but I promise I'll talk to you when I know more.'

Kerrigan Kemp heaved himself to his feet; the morning had proved worthwhile. 'Is it time we stopped calling each other mister?' he asked affably, his doleful face breaking into a smile as he held out his hand.

Tom smiled back. 'Yes I think so, Charles,' he replied, ringing the small brass bell on his desk to summon young Holloway. As if by magic the small figure appeared in the doorway. 'Would you show Mr Kerrigan Kemp through to the front office, please, Arthur?'

'Yes, sir, Mr Norton, sir.' With the removal of the terrifying figure of Inspector Langley Arthur's daily life had altered immeasurably, and he now attributed to Inspector Norton the same God-like qualities as his hero Inspector Judd. To Tom's surprise, Kerrigan Kemp turned to the lad and said, 'Well now, young Arthur, and how are you?'

'Very well, sir, thank you, sir.' The boy bobbed up and down like a cork.

'Give my regards to your mother, lad,' said Kerrigan Kemp, turning the boy round and steering him back through the door. On the spur of the moment he lightly tapped Arthur on the shoulder so he would wait outside in the corridor, came back into the office and closed the door. He spoke very quietly. 'There's one other thing that may be of assistance to you. I live on the London Road, just on the edge of town. Early yesterday morning, about twenty past eight, as I was leaving home, the three in the photograph passed my house driving a sheeted-down wagon and heading for Monckton village. Joshua Howkins was with them, and he looked like an aristocrat being given a lift on a tumbrel.' Kerrigan Kemp grinned wickedly; he did not like Howkins. 'Wherever they were going to, Joshua was not a happy man.'

As the footsteps faded, Tom heard a small squeaky voice echoing back along the walls of the passage, 'She's very well, sir, thank you, sir. We've got a soldier and his family living with us now, sir.'

Perhaps, just perhaps, thought Tom, this was what he needed. For a while he sat quietly pondering what the newspaper editor had told him. A sheeted wagon meant that something bulky was being moved; possibly whatever had resulted in Henry Farmer's murder. Where was it being taken from and where to? What was Howkins' involvement?

After about a quarter of an hour he reached for a sheet of paper and, dipping his pen into the open bottle of ink on his desk, carefully scribed a note, sealing it in a large brown envelope that he addressed to Mrs Samuels, Kelsford Bank of Commerce. Within seconds of Tom's bellow down the passageway, Arthur presented himself in front of his desk. 'Put on your cap and take this to the Bank of Commerce in Cumberland Place. Tell the messenger there that it's important and that you'll wait for a reply.' Arthur bobbed up and down and scuttled off.

It was another forty minutes before the boy returned, his freckled face flushed with exertion. Tom waited until he was alone again before opening the envelope. The note confirmed what he had been hoping for. Joshua Howkins had bought an empty village shop and outbuildings in Main Street, Monckton, during June of that year. The Bank of Commerce had acted as agents for the vendor. The note was signed 'Ruth'.

Tom wondered whether to contact Theodore Thresh at County Headquarters, then dismissed the idea. He had met Thresh very briefly a few months ago and the man seemed to be a competent detective, but after this morning's meeting with Snelgrove it was obvious that it would not be possible for Thresh to cooperate even if he was so inclined. Snelgrove had made his position abundantly clear, and would have briefed his man accordingly. Recollecting the meeting soured Tom's mood again. He pushed his chair back and went through into the detective office. Jesse Squires was there with Harry North, and Sam and Reuben were just walking in, having been to arrange observation of the house in St Andrew's Street. Joel Dexter, Tom knew, was down at the Black Boy in Welbeck Street, interviewing the licensee.

'How did it go?' Tom enquired dourly.

By common agreement the others ignored his ill humour; they were aware of the pressure which he was under. Early that morning, during a lengthy meeting, Tom had briefed them fully. It was necessary, he had decided, to trust his men with the knowledge that they needed to conduct their enquiries effectively and safely. He spent nearly an hour outlining the background and suspected activities of the Irish Republican Brotherhood, going on to relate the events at Varden Street, studiously leaving out any reference to his illicit visit to the print shop in Dutfield's Yard.

It was while answering their questions that Tom had been summoned to the meeting with the head constable at Sheffield Road. All of those now present were aware that the meeting had gone badly.

Sam Braithwaite looked gloomy. He had spent the last two hours in the back of a borrowed bread van wearing a baker's smock and being driven round the Downe Street area by Reuben. 'We've found one place that might do. Five houses up from Burke's on the opposite side is an unoccupied house. We can get into it from the back yard in Gower Row, but it's not going to be easy and once you're in you're stuck.'

Reuben slumped down heavily behind his desk. 'It'll mean two twelve hour shifts, changing over after dark each day, sir.' Since coming into the department Simmonds had been careful to observe the niceties of rank between himself and Tom. Looking at Braithwaite for confirmation, he said, 'We've spoken to Inspector Judd and he'll detail two uniform men to work in plain clothes with us. I'll take one shift and Sam the other.'

'Better get on with it then,' Tom growled. Jesse Squires looked down at the list of stolen property that he had been reading. Come back Joe Langley, all is forgiven, he thought uncharitably.

Signifying to the sergeants that he wished to speak to them, Tom returned to his office. As soon as the door was closed he began without preamble. 'We have certain problems that are going to make things quite difficult for us.' Tom knew he was beginning to act and sound more and more like Langley; he was also beginning to understand the isolation that his position brought. 'First we need to find out who killed Henry. From conversations I've had today it's apparent we're going to have to achieve that in the face of certain odds. Basically the county police are pursuing a line of enquiry that I think is totally misleading and will be counterproductive to anything we're doing – so when we find the killers there must be indisputable evidence that will send them to the gallows.'

Squires, his face serious, watched Tom in silence. Sam Braithwaite nodded, his former brashness put aside. It was obvious even to him that the days of 'Good Old Tom' were a thing of the past.

'What I'm getting at,' Tom continued, 'is that everything that's happened since last Christmas is tied together. I'm convinced that once we find out who killed Henry – and why – we'll have the key to unlock everything else that has been happening.' He paused to look round for a moment. These men were his friends, and he knew that he was unfairly venting his frustration over the morning's meeting. 'The second problem is that Mr Archer Robson and I went to see the chief constable of the county this morning, and he refuses point blank to accept the possibility of Brotherhood activity in this area. More importantly, he's dedicated to sinking this enquiry if he possibly can.' Tom watched looks of consternation pass over the faces of the other two men. 'He has, for his own reasons, decided that Henry was killed where he was found. I know that's complete rubbish, but the man is out to make the facts fit his theories. This means we have to work in a slightly unorthodox manner for a while. When this meeting is finished I have to pursue a little enquiry of my own. I'll not be back here until this time tomorrow.'

Tom pulled out his silver pocket watch and was surprised to find that it was ten minutes past one. The day was already slipping away from him. 'When I get back things might start to move fairly quickly, if we're lucky. We'll have another meeting here this time tomorrow.'

The two sergeants exchanged worried glances, 'Do you not think that Sam and I should come with you?' asked Squires. He could not add 'Tom', and 'Sir' still did not come easily.

'No. Thank you, but this isn't something I want to involve either of you in.' For a moment he was the old Tom again, and they both knew he appreciated the gesture.

Once Sam and Jesse had returned to their own office, Tom pulled another sheet of paper from his drawer and scribbled a short message, shouting for Arthur as he appended his signature. 'Take this to the Bank of Commerce,' he instructed the boy. 'When you get there you're to speak personally with Mrs Samuels. Bring her reply to me at my house. If she's not there bring the note back unopened.' As an afterthought he fished in his trouser pocket and handed the boy a sixpence. 'You're a good lad, Arthur. Be as quick as you can.'

Tom picked up his father's pony and trap from the Rifleman just before three o'clock, threw his hastily packed bag into the luggage pannier and set off for Victoria Road. On the way he called at the shop in Oxford Road, where Ann was filling the shelves with newly delivered stock to supplement what was already there. With her wedding to Reuben Simmonds fixed for a week on Saturday, she was devoting all her time to the shop. Tom quickly explained that he would be away overnight on a job.

'On your own?' she asked pointedly.

'Yes, sis, on my own,' he replied equally pointedly. 'Unless I meet some beautiful woman who seduces me on the way, in which case I'll let you know.'

Tom was lying. Ruth's reply to his second note had been a simple 'Yes', delivered verbally by young Arthur to Sidwell Place while Tom was packing. The lad was quite bemused when Mr Norton gave him another sixpence, and with a beaming smile told him to get off back to Long Street.

Easing the pony to a halt, Tom was greeted by Ruth's slightly intimidating maid, whose name, he recollected, was Mirka. With an imperious gesture she took the pony's rein from him and walked it round to the tradesmen's entrance, at the same time indicating Tom to go into the house through the open kitchen door.

Inside, Tom followed her along the passageway into the main drawing room, where he found Ruth wearing a plain blue travelling dress and matching broad-brimmed hat. After speaking briefly to the maid, in what Tom presumed to be Russian, she crossed the room and kissed him softly on the lips. Tom pulled her closer, and returned the kiss with sudden urgency. Breaking gently away, Ruth said, 'I got your note. I need to be back by tomorrow afternoon.'

Tom shot a hesitant glance at the maidservant, who glared back at him implacably.

'Don't worry. Mirka will say nothing,' Ruth said quietly, adding to Mirka, in Yiddish, 'Come along, you miserable witch. I told you this was serious, didn't I? Now put the bags in the trap so we can be going.'

'If he hurts you I'll kill him. This is madness – what will people say when they find out, for God's sake?' Mirka was genuinely worried. She had never seen her mistress involved in this way before, and was appalled that he was not even of the Faith.

Ruth took Mirka's hands and smiled. 'It'll be all right, Mirschka. I promise. No one will find out until we're ready.'

Mirka shrugged her shoulders in resignation and picked up Ruth's bag. 'Da, Princess, da,' she muttered.

Pleased with the exercise and change of scenery, the pony set a brisk pace on the main London Road out of Kelsford. Perched on the bench seat, Ruth listened intently while Tom explained where they were going. 'Monckton is a little village about three-quarters of an hour from here. I need to have a quiet look at some premises there after dark when there's nobody about.'

'The shop that Joshua Howkins bought.'

Tom nodded. 'I thought that if we drove through the village we could have a look round, so I can find out exactly where the place is. I think it may be the outbuildings rather than the shop that are important. Then we'll go another couple of miles to the next village, Grimley: there's a pub there where we can stay overnight. The advantage is that the two villages are connected by the canal – and along the towpath it's only about a mile. After dark I can slip off, have a look and be back in about an hour.'

'And what do we do in the meantime?' Ruth asked mischievously.

'I'll be conserving my strength,' Tom said severely.

Monckton was a couple of miles off the London Road, along a narrow country byway that cut through the fields and followed the route of the meandering canal. A sleepy little cluster of cottages spread along a single street, the village was primarily an agricultural settlement, but there was also passing trade from the canal barges that plied the Erewash Canal.

Casually gazing round as the pony walked slowly along, Tom spotted what he was looking for on the right-hand side: the shuttered windows and closed door of an old-fashioned general store. A board over the narrow front bore the legend JETHRO COULSON, PROVISIONS AND TRADE, EST. 1853. At the side was a narrow alleyway, just wide enough to drive a wagon down, at the end of which he could make out a low stone barn. Acknowledging a courteous 'Good afternoon' from an old man sitting on a kitchen chair in the open doorway of one of the cottages next door, Tom reined the pony to a halt. 'I was hoping to buy some tobacco, sir, but the shop appears to be closed,' he said, leaning out of the cart.

'I'm afraid so, sir,' replied the old gentleman, with the inherent countryman's politeness. His toothless mouth was drawn up in an amiable smile, his face tanned a deep shade of mahogany from years of exposure to the weather – the same years of hard work that had resulted in the arthritic hands resting on the stout ash stick propped between his knees, their joints contorted into impossible angles and shapes. Tom speculated that he would probably have been a grown man in his prime when the bells of the church at the top of the hill had rung out the end of the war in Crimea. And in all those years, Tom thought, he has probably never been further away from this pretty little village than the few miles to Kelsford market. 'Jethro Coulson died a while ago,' the old man continued. 'His son Matthew has sold the place, although I think it may open again afore long.'

'These things happen,' Tom said easily. 'I'm sure the loss of the village shop must be quite an inconvenience. You say you think it may open again?'

The old fellow inclined his head sagely. 'Some men delivered a wagonload of stock only yesterday, so it looks as if the old place might be back in business soon.' The toothless grin reappeared, and he gave a thin cackle of amusement. 'Old Jethro was a deal of a robber, though: we shall probably fare better with this newcomer.'

Tom returned the grin and raised his hat politely. 'Thank you for your time, sir,' he declared, and clicking to the pony moved sedately on.

As the road climbed up a short hill over the canal bridge and out of the village, they looked to their right at the lock gates and small white keeper's house next to the towpath. Saying nothing to Ruth, Tom paid special attention to the layout of the locks, which he would have to negotiate later that night in total darkness. Immediately over the canal bridge, facing an elegant stone church with a tall steeple, stood a large inn whose board declared it to be the Black Horse. From the size of it and the spacious yard at the rear, Tom presumed it was used by bargees and carters for the offloading of some of their cargos and for overnight accommodation of the occasional passengers that the boats carried up and down the waterways. The landlord, a slim, red-haired man in his late forties, was sweeping the front doorstep.

'Is this where we're staying?' asked Ruth.

'No. It's too close to the village. We're going on to the next place. The inn there is smaller but it'll suffice.'

The lane – it hardly deserved to be called a road – swung to the right just past the church and deteriorated into an unmade track that wound on for another two miles. After crossing the canal at a narrow hump-backed bridge, which the pony negotiated with difficulty, it led them into a tiny hamlet composed of half a dozen cottages, a butcher's shop and, from somewhere nearby, judging by the tantalising smell of fresh bread, a bakery. Standing to one side of the track, the Bell was a picturesque, white-fronted tavern of indeterminate age. A brightly painted board propped up outside declared the availability of Thompson's India Pale Ale and Burton Ales, along with a choice of Dewar's Best Scotch and Dunville's Old Irish Whiskey.

Tom hoped that Ruth would not think to ask him how he came to know of this place. The truth was that, many years before, he and Kate along with John and Ann had spent a weekend here one summer. They had stayed at the Bell and spent the days strolling in the country lanes and along the towpaths. Tom thought wistfully of the warm afternoons they had spent lounging in the grass, watching the laden barges passing through the locks.

Tying the pony to the rail set outside the pub, Tom led Ruth through the narrow porch and along the short passage into the taproom. It was exactly as he remembered it. There was a low oak-beamed bar with a short counter made up of scrubbed deal boards laid along a series of empty barrels, while to the right there was a large fireplace, with some polished tables beneath the low tiny-paned window that looked out onto the lane.

Even the licensee had not changed: a portly middle-aged man with pale blue eyes and a heavy grey moustache, which accorded well with his white hair and substantial paunch. He regarded the couple with interest, watching as Tom loosely wrapped the rein over the hitching rail before carefully handing the well-dressed lady down from the trap. At this time of year business was slow and the arrival of newcomers an infrequent occurrence. The landlord appraised them with a professional eye. The tall, fair-haired man was smart and well dressed, while she was conservatively but much more expensively attired – which meant they were not a married couple. The pony outside was tired but not lathered, so they had come a reasonable distance but at a relatively sedate pace, which could only mean they were from Kelsford.

Putting down the mallet with which he was about to tap a new barrel, he gave a welcoming smile and said, 'Good afternoon, young sir and madam. What can I get for you?'

While he pulled a pint of bitter for Tom and a large glass of red wine for Ruth, his wife in the kitchen busied herself cutting some cheese and pickle sandwiches for the famished pair. Tom and Ruth had the bar to themselves and were able to consume the food at their leisure, sitting at a table near the window.

As he replaced his empty pint pot on the table, Tom looked enquiringly at Ruth, who shook her head. It was getting on for six o'clock and she wanted to go up to the room that Tom had booked while ordering their drinks. One or two of the locals were now beginning to drift into the tavern, and they did not want to become involved in conversation with anyone.

The double room that the landlord had, with a deadpan expression, rented to Tom for the night in the name of Mr and Mrs Thornton, was at the back of the inn overlooking the stables. It was ideally situated for Tom's plan. 'We've got to be careful here, love,' he said.

Behind the dressing curtain Ruth was changing from her travelling outfit into one in which she could go down later for an evening meal. Shirt unbuttoned, his stiff collar and necktie thrown over a chair, Tom was lying on the soft double bed gazing up at the freshly painted white ceiling. 'What do you think I'm going to do? Parade about in a Cossack tunic?' The voice from behind the curtain was muffled and unclear. Tom grinned to himself and felt a distinct stirring at the recollection.

'No, you goose, I don't mean that. After supper I need to slide away without being seen, while you stay up here and get rid of anyone who might knock at the door.'

'Ah, that's all right then. I'm quite good at that.' The voice sounded cheery, and was no longer muffled.

With a rustle of fabric the curtain parted and Ruth emerged into the bedroom. She was naked.

Supper, served in the little snug just off the passageway opposite the bar, was more than filling. Freshly caught trout, followed by a rabbit pie covered with the lightest crust that Tom could ever recollect tasting, was followed by fresh crusty bread and a huge wedge of cheddar cheese. Both of them, to the disappointment of the landlady, drank sparingly of the excellent red wine: Tom had a busy night ahead of him and needed to keep a clear head. A chance question during the meal about whether or not Ruth could eat rabbit drew the tart response, 'I don't eat pork and I don't talk to strange men – but I do like large portions.' The affronted look on Tom's face sent her into fits of giggles, in which he quickly joined. He knew he was irretrievably lost to this beautiful, earthy woman.

Their supper finished, Tom consulted his pocket watch. It was five minutes to nine. 'Time to get off to bed, my dear,' he said loudly, for the benefit of the serving girl who had come in to clear away their dishes.

Five minutes later, dressed in an old pair of trousers and a jacket that he had brought along for the purpose, Tom climbed out of the bedroom window onto the sloping outhouse roof below. From there it was a simple matter to edge along the guttering to the downpipe eight feet away. Sliding his leg carefully over the edge, he felt for the covered top of the rain barrel, onto which he lowered himself before dropping safely to the ground.

Out in the lane, avoiding the taproom window, Tom made his way to the canal bridge, giving thanks for the cold moonlight that enabled him to see ahead for a few yards. From memory he knew that a small wooden stile on the far side of the bridge gave access to the towpath.

A twenty-minute walk along the canal brought him to the lock gates in Monckton, which he had to cross in order to get to the other side of the cut and the opening in the hedge that led to the main street. Climbing onto the gate in the dark and then edging across the narrow beam was fraught with danger. In the empty blackness beneath him he could hear a constant rushing sound as water under tons of pressure from the next chamber gushed through a loose paddle. Even though the black timbers were dry, it would still be easy to slip into the murky depths thirty feet below. Eighteen months ago the keeper at Town Locks just above Bridge Sixty-Four had slipped off his lock gates while coming home the worse for wear from the Prince Albert; his body had not been found until the following morning, by the first bargee to take his boat up through the locks. Edging cautiously along, Tom came to the end of the bar with a wave of relief and felt the reassuring iron step down to the ground. He began to shiver in the cold night air, suddenly aware that his body was bathed in perspiration.

Aware of the need to keep moving, he made his way along the narrow village street to the deserted shop where, feeling his way along the side of the building, he found the entrance to the alley. The wide single door of the barn was old, and the little paint left on it was cracked and peeling, but it was made of stout timber – and was secured by a newly fitted padlock and hasp. As he worked his way round the barn Tom came to a window at shoulder height. Close examination showed that it was a casement fitting, and it quickly yielded to the blade of his clasp knife. Easing the window open, he climbed through and carefully closed it behind him. Standing with his back against the wall, Tom listened intently in the darkness. After a momentary scuffling of tiny feet, as a bevy of mice disturbed in their nightly scavenging scattered to safety, the only sound was his own ragged breathing. Satisfied that he was alone, Tom pulled a piece of candle from his jacket pocket. The flare from the match temporarily blinded him, and it took several seconds for his vision to return to normal.

The barn had been used by its previous occupant as a storeroom, and the musty smell of vegetables hung heavily in the still atmosphere. It was, Tom judged, about twenty feet long and fifteen wide. Moving carefully round the walls he discovered that the stale smell was coming from a six foot high stack of rotting potatoes in the far corner in hundredweight hessian sacks, which must have been there since well before the late Mr Coulson's demise.

As he moved to the centre of the store, Tom found what he was looking for. Piled five high, in four rows, were neatly stowed packing cases, each about four feet long and eighteen inches deep. There were he counted, twenty-two of them, each with the words SONDERHEIM MACHINE PARTS INC., CHICAGO, ILLINOIS stencilled in bold letters on the side. The wooden lids were securely nailed down, and it was obvious that he could not open one without causing damage that would be immediately noticed.

Tom began a methodical inspection of the cases, hoping to find one that was damaged. He was engrossed in this when the sudden sound of voices outside, followed by a key turning in the padlock, brought him up sharply. Blowing out his candle and wafting away the smoke with his hand, his mind raced. He was at the far end of the barn behind the boxes, so there was a good chance his light had not been detected; he had to hope that the acrid smell of his candle would dissipate quickly. Stealthily Tom moved into the corner behind the rotting potatoes and crouched down, wishing he had a more substantial weapon than the pocket knife that he held open, blade up, in his hand.

With a slight creak the wide barn door opened, revealing the figures of two men illuminated in the light of an oil lamp held by the bigger of the two. Whoever had fixed the new hasp to the door had taken the trouble to grease the hinges at the same time. A draught of cold night air gusted in, stirring up the rancid atmosphere.

'Close the door, will you?' Connor Devlin's voice was harsh in the quiet of the night. Although no expert on Irish accents, Tom thought that he was probably from the south of the country.

'I told you everything would be all right.' Tom recognised the deep Western drawl immediately.

'You can't be too careful.' The Irishman again. 'Tomorrow I'll pull a couple of the lads off the Flixton job and bring them over. During the day they can get this place cleaned out, and at night they can sleep in here. Radbone will be here with the *Trojan* on Saturday afternoon. We'll manhandle the boxes over the bridge and onto the barge. If Amos leaves at first light on Sunday morning he'll be the other side of Kelsford by nine o'clock.'

The lamp was placed on one of two boxes that had been laid crossways on top of the stacks. From his hiding place Tom could just make out the back of Lucas Sangster's head, and for the first time he got a clear view of Devlin, his dark unshaven features illuminated by the lamp's glow. Tom knew he had seen the man before but could not place where. His back and legs were aching intolerably, and he was starting to worry that cramp would set in, but he dared not move a muscle.

'What are we going to do about Howkins?' the American asked.

'That's your problem. At the moment he's useful to us, and he's in so deep that he'll drown at the first slip. For the time being he'll do anything you say.'

'Hmm . . .' The big Texan appeared to be turning the matter over. 'He's got one shipment in Downe Street for the time being. He thinks that when that's moved out he's in the clear and done with us. What the silly bastard doesn't know is that we're onto his little scheme.' Sangster gave his throaty chuckle. 'He's got rid of his partners and thinks that when the dice stop rolling he'll sell his bankrupt quarry to a firm called Universal Stone, adding the price of the land to what he's picked up from the original deal. What he doesn't know is that Universal Stone is owned by my principals in New York. We have sufficient documentation to prove he was the original owner of Batsford Stone, and therefore the perpetrator of a massive fraud on the Shires Canal Company. So when he opens his negotiations with Universal Stone it'll be my pleasure to tell him whom he's dealing with, and relieve him of the cash he's taken from the Shires along with the deeds to the quarry . . . or he draws the Ace of Spades – his choice!'

Connor grunted, busy checking the boxes. The fate of the Kelsford grocer was of small consequence to him. In his cramped hiding place Tom was glad that he had not tampered with any of the crates, or indeed left his visit until the next night, when there would have been a reception committee waiting for him.

Sangster moved to the other side of the stacks. 'Where are these going?' he asked, running his hand over one of the pine cases.

'I don't know. I think Liam's coming down on the *Trojan*, so he'll deal with them.'

Tom's left leg was completely dead, and he knew his position could not be held for much longer. It was with gratitude that he heard the two men preparing to leave.

'Everything's all right here,' the Irishman said. 'We'll walk back up to the Black Horse and have a pint before we turn in.'

Tom waited in the darkness while the padlock was secured, and the voices had faded before he crawled out from behind the potatoes. He massaged his dead limb for some time before he could stand up, with acute pins and needles running through his feet and legs. Stiffly he hobbled about until the circulation had returned, before climbing out and closing the window. He was glad to be out of the claustrophobic barn, and wanted to be well away from the alley as soon as possible in case the men changed their minds and returned.

Tom's walk along the towpath was pleasant in the moonlight, once he had negotiated the lock gates. The cool air quickly drove the smell of rotting potatoes from his clothing and the clear starlit sky, along with a distinct drop in temperature, promised a cold night. Standing once more on the track outside the Bell, Tom was pleased to see that the taproom was still busy, with half a dozen locals at the bar in animated conversation with the landlord. Entering the back yard, he first went to the stable to quieten Trooper, his father's pony, who had picked up Tom's scent and had become restive, whinnying for attention. Gently stroking the animal's nose, Tom talked quietly until he settled down again, then made his way silently across the cobbles to the rain butt and up onto the sloping roof. As he edged along the slates Tom caught the aromatic tang of cigar smoke from the room above him, indicating Ruth's presence behind the open curtains. He realised for the first time since setting out how badly he needed a smoke.

Dropping lightly through the open window, Tom saw she was sitting fully dressed in the dark on a high-backed chair. Getting up, she kissed him quickly. 'How did it go?' she asked.

'Fine. We've got everything we need.'

Now that Tom was back, Ruth drew the curtains and moved over to the small writing table. Striking a match, she applied it to the wick of the oil lamp before replacing the tall glass chimney. Despite her apparent calm Tom realised from the pile of cigar stubs in the ashtray how worried she had been: she must have been chain-smoking since he left.

'If there are any of those left I'd really appreciate one,' he said.

Happy to have him back safely, Ruth replied primly, 'Actually I packed some of my own.'

Within half an hour they were snuggled comfortably under a pile of blankets in the substantial double bed that took up a third of the small room. Tom told her exactly what he had seen and heard in the barn. In turn she explained Howkins' involvement with the Shires project and with Batsford Stone. Privately she was exultant at the hold this new information gave her over Max Peters.

Much later they talked in the darkness about their plans for the future. Tom told her about the life and love he had shared with Kate. Ruth spoke about her marriage to Isaac Samuels. When she asked if he knew of her previous relationship with Henry Farmer, it occurred to Tom to deny it, but he decided to tell the truth; this was not a time for lies. Eventually they drifted off to sleep, comfortably in each other's arms, safe in the knowledge of their love for each other.

Chapter Twenty-Four

Tom Norton gazed round the police officers assembled before him in the muster room at Long Street police station; the old-fashioned clock on the back wall showed it to be five minutes before ten. Most of those gathered were older middle service men whom he knew and could rely on, but there were also two or three who had only recently joined the force, detailed by Fred Judd solely because he needed to make up the numbers. Tom supposed he should have chosen one of the other inspectors, Caleb Newcombe or Lemuel Watkins, to be his deputy on this raiding party, but Fred Judd had readily agreed to the proposition and Tom needed someone he could rely on.

Including the detectives, and Inspector Judd standing behind the muster desk with him, there were twenty-five officers waiting patiently to find out why they had been ordered to the police station at this time of night. That it was going to be a special job was obvious, and the buzz of conversation was filled with anticipation. Two sergeants, Alf Vendyback and Ambrose Quinn, stood to one side quietly conversing. Tom spotted young Daniel Chote. He wondered if the lad had escaped Bartie Horspool's displeasure over the incident with Queenie Bartholemew – and realised, with a slight jolt, that almost a year had passed since the incident.

Harry North, equipped with rod and line, had spent the day at Grimley Bridge, fishing in the still waters of the canal and waiting for the *Trojan* to pass on its way to Monckton Locks. After the boat had gone by he gathered up his tackle and strolled casually along the bank into Monckton village. There, while downing a pint of best bitter at the Black Horse, he watched as Devlin's men, together with two newcomers from the barge, loaded the consignment of packing cases into the body of the *Trojan* before concealing them under a large tarpaulin. Apart from the bargee and his wife, Harry reported that a swarthy, thickset man was travelling on the boat.

That this must be the mainland Brotherhood Commander, Liam O'Dowd,

Tom was certain. If he could be arrested when the cache of weapons was seized it would be a tremendous step forward. Additionally, from what he had overheard in the barn Tom knew that somewhere in Downe Street Joshua Howkins and Lucas Sangster were storing a further consignment of weapons, which he needed to trace before they were spirited away.

Calling the men to order, Tom took a deep breath and began to explain what they were going to do the following morning. His plan was simple.

If what Devlin had said was correct, the *Trojan* would be coming into Kelsford along the Erewash Canal sometime before nine o'clock in the morning. As soon as the barge was within the town limits Tom was entitled to board it, seize the illicit cargo and arrest the occupants – which was exactly what he intended to do. His plan was to ambush the boat as it passed through Town Locks. That it was a Sunday meant that relatively few barges would be working, which should make the task easier. He knew the Irishmen would probably be armed, and it was more than likely that they would attempt to fight it out.

The warm early autumn sunshine, combined with the peaceful stillness of a Sunday morning, lent a deceptive atmosphere of tranquillity to the barge as it glided slowly along the quiet waters of the canal. Liam O'Dowd perched on the stern seat, his arm draped over the tiller, puffing meditatively at a stubby clay pipe gripped between his teeth. He had a lot on his mind. The trip along the canals from Manchester had been uneventful, and an opportunity to work on his strategy to establish a Midlands base in Kelsford. He might, he thought, move to Kelsford himself, but at the moment it was safer travelling the inland waterways on the *Trojan* than hiding in one place. O'Dowd's plans had received an unexpected setback on his arrival at Monckton the previous day. He could not believe that Connor Devlin had been so stupid as to kill a police officer – and leaving the body to be discovered was inexcusable folly. Their meeting in the barn behind the shop had been a stormy one. O'Dowd felt that, having identified the detective as responsible for Eddie Donnelly's death, Connor should have realised the valuable potential for blackmail. A collaborator within the local constabulary – no matter how unwilling – could have benefited the Brotherhood immeasurably. Devlin, on the other hand, forcefully maintained that, in line with Brotherhood policy, the execution was completely justified. The resulting impasse was not helped by the bargee Radbone having to shift part of his cargo of seal oil to accommodate the crates, in O'Dowd's opinion creating unnecessary delay and risk.

A sulking Devlin, still licking his wounds, had left the boat some twenty minutes before, declaring his intention to drop back and ensure they were not being followed. Like a predatory animal sunning itself, O'Dowd gazed about in a leisurely manner, checking for any signs of danger. Amos Radbone, up in the bows of the barge tightening the tarpaulin ropes, had been joined by his elder son, Terence. His wife Eliza, also sucking on a short clay pipe, was busy in the tiny galley preparing the breakfast that, after passing through Town Locks, they would eat on the canal bank. Smoke from the wood-burning stove percolated lazily up the chimney next to the open cabin skylight.

Satisfied that nothing was amiss, Liam returned to his deliberations. The association with Lucas Sangster was proving to be highly successful. A ready supply of weapons was now being slowly but surely transferred across the Irish Sea from Liverpool to Ireland, where they quickly disappeared among the farmland and cottages of the patriots. Apart from at Kelsford and London, O'Dowd was being careful not to hoard weapons on the mainland. The dangers were greater and the time was not yet right for such a move. Their present cargo would be transferred to another barge heading for the east coast, for onward transmission to Hull and from there to Copenhagen. It was a simple matter for the weapons to be sold on from there to dissident groups in Eastern Europe. The Lafferty affair had not been entirely without advantage, he mused: the Brotherhood's contact with Sven Olafson had provided a very useful route into the Swedish underworld.

Although he would not admit it, Liam agreed in one respect with Connor Devlin. The anarchist faction was totally unreliable and dealing with them was fraught with danger – which was why he was sending this latest shipment to Copenhagen. A prime example was the problem that the American Sangster was experiencing as he tried to cover his tracks over a few pistols he had sold to a group of foreigners in Whitechapel. A police raid had found the guns in a shoebox in their house, and God alone knew how much they were telling the Metropolitan Police.

Lying prone on the top of a haystack a hundred yards from the canal, Jesse Squires watched through his telescope as Amos Radbone's young son Michael ducked low to lead the lumbering carthorse under Bishop's Lane Bridge. He smiled to himself with grim satisfaction: another ten minutes and the Irishmen would be on borough police territory. As the barge passed out of sight round the first bend Jesse scrambled down. Hiding behind the hayrick were Harry North and five uniformed policemen, along with the rented horses that had brought them out from the town. Leaving one man, Seth Morton, to look after the horses, Jesse dispatched North and two of the constables to their positions on the opposite side of the bridge, while he and the other two moved down onto the nearest bank.

Unaware that the *Trojan*'s arrival was only minutes away, the hidden police officers further along waited in their allotted positions. Two hundred and fifty yards beyond the bottom lock, in an empty coal barge that was tied up to the left bank with its tiny stern doors shut tight, were Fred Judd and Alf Vendyback, crammed into the ten foot six inches of cabin space with four officers. As there was only sufficient room for two of them to sit down at any one time, the general feeling was that if Sergeant Vendyback were a slimmer man it would be of benefit to one and all. Keeping a sharp eye out through a small aperture in the cabin wall, Judd allowed the banter to continue. The men were in a high state of tension and needed some slight relief.

Tied up on the opposite bank, fifty yards closer to the locks, was the seventy-two foot *Florentine*. Because the *Florentine* usually carried timber it had been deemed sensible for Sergeant Quinn and his men to lie in the clean hold under loosely tied sheeting. Sitting at the back of the boat, smoking a home-rolled cigarette, was Daniel Chote in the muffler and cap of a bargee.

Ambrose Quinn eased his position slightly to relieve his aching back. Cautiously he moved the double-barrelled shotgun to a better position. Peering out from under the edge of the covers, he whispered hoarsely to Chote, 'Can you see anything yet, boy?'

Daniel stretched and stared along the canal bank. Standing up did not aid his view, as they were positioned below the bottom lock gate. 'No, Sergeant,' he whispered back urgently.

'Keep your eyes open and listen for the whistle,' Quinn growled back, ungraciously. He had spent long enough in this stinking hold. More importantly, the four men with him were becoming restive and cramped; the last thing he wanted was for none of them to be able to move fast enough when Tom Norton gave the signal. He fingered the cartridges in his left-hand tunic pocket.

Last night, when Fred Judd had issued the firearms from the locked cupboard in Detective Inspector Norton's office, Quinn had opted for one of the double-barrelled twelve-bore shotguns. Half a dozen revolvers had been handed out to the detectives and anyone such as young Chote who would be in full view, while the rest of the twenty-odd men in the ambush party were given a shotgun and a supply of cartridges. The men briefed and the firearms issued, no one was allowed to leave the police station. Truckle beds were brought out of the store room for the constables and detectives to sleep on, while the sergeants and two inspectors retired to their respective offices to snatch some sleep, before moving out to their positions just before dawn. Declining an offer to join in a card school, which Alf Vendyback had set up with Joel Dexter and Harry North, Quinn made his way to the sergeants' office.

Closing the door, he took a small can of gun oil from the drawer of his desk. He broke open the shotgun, checked the barrels, stripped the weapon down and oiled it. His task finished, he reassembled the gun and worked the action several times until he was satisfied by its reliability. Next he turned his attention to the twenty cartridges that Fred had given him. Turning one over in his thick fingers, Quinn grunted in satisfaction. It was loaded with a heavy gauge shot, the sort used to fetch down a deer or other such large game. Standing the cartridge on end, he pulled a candle from the same drawer as the oil and, having lit it, turned his attention to carefully working open the crimped end of the cartridge.

In the ten years that he had spent in the Irish Guards – before, as rumour correctly had it, earning his living as a prize-fighter – Quinn had learned many things, one of them being that a gun has only one purpose: to kill. A shotgun was a devastating close-quarters weapon. Fired at a range of a few yards its blast would take a man's arm clean off or cut his torso in half. It had a major drawback, however. The greater the range the wider the spread of the shot, and consequently the less effective it became. At a range of thirty or forty yards the gun would bring down an animal such as a buck, but you could not guarantee it would kill a man. Ambrose Quinn's intention was to remedy this defect. As a boy, before he joined the army at the age of fifteen, he had lived with his parents and siblings on a small farm in County Wicklow. Although not interested in the political ambitions of most of the local men and youths in the district, he had nevertheless been aware of many of the practices that these aspirations engendered – one of which was how to ensure that when you shot a man he did not get up again to return your fire.

With the cartridge open and the wadding removed, Quinn carefully picked up the lighted candle and tipped in the melted wax, gently tapping the base of the cartridge on the table top to ensure that as much as possible ran down to mix with the lead shot before it started to set. Then he repeated the process until the mixture reached the point where the wadding could be inserted again and the cartridge resealed. Filling five of the cartridges in this manner was time-consuming, but at the end of half an hour he sat back pleased with his work. He now had five cartridges loaded with a solid charge of lead and wax. Each, loaded into the choke barrel of the gun with a standard cartridge in the other, was lethal. The solid shot alone would pass straight through a man, making an entry hole big enough to insert one of Quinn's massive fists into, and an exit wound that no physician in the world could repair.

Tom Norton's men were comfortably ensconced in the parlour of the lock-keeper's house. The availability of this hideaway was particularly fortuitous, and one of the prime reasons why Tom had chosen to site his ambush here. Following the untimely drowning of the previous lockkeeper, the position had gone to a police pensioner. He had only just retired after serving for twenty years in the borough force when he took the job, and was considered by Tom to be completely trustworthy. A late night visit to the cottage had ensured that he and his men would be admitted soon after four in the morning and hidden until the *Trojan* passed through.

The keeper's cottage had another advantage. From the upstairs bedroom Tom had a clear view of the five hundred yard straight that ran down to the wide turning basin at the top lock chamber. As he gazed, the *Trojan*'s bow appeared round the bend as it began its final run down to Town Locks.

Amos Radbone, his wizened face screwed up against the light as he scrutinised the approach to the turning basin, nodded to O'Dowd who had joined him at the front of the boat. 'All quiet.' His thick Irish accent, despite half a lifetime in England, was as pronounced as ever. O'Dowd agreed, and began to edge back along the side of the barge towards the cabin at the rear.

The smell of frying bacon was tantalising in the fresh air. He was famished, and looking forward to a hearty breakfast.

The first chamber was already filled, and it was a simple matter for Michael Radbone to unhitch Sultan, the big carthorse, from the plaited tow rope and lead him down to the far side, where he waited patiently while the horse began to graze. Looking after the nag, he reflected smugly, was a good card to draw. While Terence and his father worked the balance beams of the massive gates, he could stand idly by minding the horse.

Meanwhile his brother, having moved the barge through the top lock into the middle chamber, was winding furiously at the rack and pinion gear to raise the paddles and allow the excess water to drain into the bottom lock.

Tom stared anxiously at *Trojan*, now halfway through its passage down the locks, as Terence, his clean Sunday morning shirt stained with sweat, turned the crank. To ensure success with a minimum of violence, they needed to trap the barge at its lowest level in the chamber. From his vantage point behind the curtains, Tom watched as the young man continued to draw the paddles between the middle and bottom lock, allowing the water to gush through. With a slow dignity the barge began to drop lower as the water level fell, until finally the heads of the men on the deck disappeared from sight below the blue brick walls of the chamber.

With the windlass from the winding gear swinging lightly in his right hand, the youth took a break and leaned idly on the great beam of timber beside him. Once the levels in the bottom and the middle chambers were equal he would be able to swing the mitre gates open and allow the *Trojan* to drift through into the bottom lock.

As soon as the barge disappeared from view Tom flew down the stairs two at a time and into the tiny hallway, where Joel Dexter, a pistol in his hand, was waiting with the officers ready to surround the barge. Shouting to them to follow him, Tom threw the front door of the cottage open and, pausing only to blow three long blasts on his whistle, the signal for everyone to move, took off at a run for the middle lock.

At the sound of the whistle the previously tranquil scene was transformed to one of frenetic activity. Michael Radbone, seeing armed policemen spilling from the barge in front of him and on the lock behind, grabbed at the leather halter round Sultan's head and in one swift movement swung himself up onto the horse's back. Kicking his heels hard into the startled animal's ribs, he set off at a gallop towards the constables running in his direction. In a blur of activity he saw two of the men drop to their knees and try to get a sight on him as he charged headlong through them. A well-built man with a bushy beard wearing the pillbox cap of an inspector grabbed at the horse's head before being knocked backwards off-balance; the flash from his pistol scorched Michael's leg as he fired at him.

Ten yards further on Sultan's forelegs hit the tripwire that had been stretched across the towpath, sending him crashing to the ground and his rider somersaulting over his head. The force with which he hit the ground stunned the boy, and before he could recover his senses a pair of handcuffs had been slapped securely onto his wrists.

Thrusting aside the tarpaulin, Ambrose Quinn scrambled onto the canal bank and ran headlong towards the lower lock gates and towards Terence Radbone, with Daniel Chote close on his heels. Quinn held his shotgun at the port across his chest, right hand on the stock, forefinger along the outside of the trigger guard, his left hand gripping the barrel and two reload cartridges poking from between his fingers. Chote pointed his revolver at the man who only seconds before had been preparing to swing open the lock gates and bring the *Trojan* down into the lower chamber.

Terence Radbone, unable to believe what he was seeing as Norton's men emerged from the house, spun round as he caught sight of the second group of armed men running towards him from the *Florentine*. Dropping the windlass, he turned to face them. The leader, an older man and much bigger than the rest, was carrying what looked like a twelve-bore shotgun. His bulk appeared to be slowing him down, and he was being overtaken by a younger, slimmer figure pointing a handgun in his direction.

Grabbing at his belt, Radbone pulled a long-barrelled single-action Navy Colt from his waistband and fired off two quick shots in the direction of the men. Daniel was half a head in front of Sergeant Quinn when he felt something whistle past his left ear, and saw the brief muzzle flash of a revolver in the man's hand. Everything seemed to go into slow motion. First came the awful realisation that he was about to be killed, then the conviction that he had to do something to prevent this from happening. Still running, he aimed and pulled the trigger of his revolver, but nothing happened. In that frozen millisecond he had time first to be puzzled and then to understand why the weapon had failed to fire: he had not cocked it. As if in a dream he saw another spurt of flame from the pistol that was pointed at him before the world erupted in a flash of light, accompanied by the sound of two ear-shattering bangs – so close together that they appeared to be one.

To Chote's amazement it was not he who began to fall backwards, mortally wounded, but the man pointing the gun at him. The entire front of his sweat-stained white shirt was suddenly sprayed a bright crimson, and as he toppled backwards over the lock gate Daniel stared in fascination at the great hole that had appeared in his assailant's chest.

'Cover me, you fucking idiot!' Quinn's snarl brought Chote back to his senses. Dropping on one knee, he threw the revolver up in front of him, this time remembering to cock it and holding it double-handed as he had been taught, and swung the barrel in a hundred and eighty degree arc. Sergeant Quinn was also crouching, the shotgun broken across his knee with smoke drifting from the open breech, as in one smooth movement he spilled out the expended cartridges and rammed home the reloads. Daniel had hardly gathered his wits before, snapping the gun closed again, Quinn was on his feet and running forward, his left hand pulling two more cartridges from his side pocket. The whole thing had taken less than five seconds. Racing the final few yards to the lock gate, Daniel Chote knew he owed his life to the irascible sergeant.

Taken completely by surprise and at the bottom of the lock chamber, O'Dowd and the older Radbone were completely blind to what was going on above them. As soon as the shrill blast of a police whistle sounded O'Dowd grabbed two loaded Winchester rifles from the cabin in front of him and threw one of them across the roof to Radbone. Working the lever action to pump a shell into the breech of the gun, the Irish commander waited, tensely peering up at the edge of the brickwork above him.

Within seconds the sound of pistol shots and the double crash of a shotgun from the beam overhead signalled that Terence was in trouble; then his blasted body hurtled down onto the boxes in the hold, and came to rest at his father's feet.

From that moment O'Dowd knew he was trapped. Initially he had hoped this was some sort of routine Customs and Excise foray that he could either talk or shoot his way out of. The killing of Radbone's son at the first sign of armed resistance dashed that hope, signalling that this was a serious raid by men who were well prepared. As armed police appeared on either side of the lock above his head, shotguns and pistols pointed menacingly down into the barge, he shook his head angrily at Amos Radbone. Spitting contemptuously into the water, on Tom Norton's peremptory command he laid his rifle on the roof of the cabin and raised his hands.

Tom felt a mixture of elation and relief as the adrenalin began to subside. Staring down, he watched as the mainland commander of the Irish Republican Brotherhood, followed by the bargee and his wife, climbed silently up the rungs of the narrow iron ladder let into the brick wall of the lock. Once they were safely handcuffed the boat would be searched and its cargo removed. He could not believe that the operation had gone so smoothly. Calling across to Fred Judd and Ambrose Quinn, he received confirmation that none of their men had been injured. As O'Dowd appeared at the top of the ladder Tom stared long and hard at him. Neither man spoke: that would come later. O'Dowd spat again in Tom's direction as Joel Dexter applied handcuffs to his wrists, before leading him across to the lock-keeper's minuscule front garden to await the prison van. It was a pity that Connor had not been on the barge, thought Tom, but apart from that it had been a successful morning.

Making their way towards him along the canal bank were Jesse Squires and the rearguard party, each man carrying his shotgun broken and secure in the crook of his arm. Tom tucked the bulky Webley service revolver into his waistband and signalled to Ambrose Quinn to join him, then turned to raise a hand in salutation to the figure in a shapeless brown suit standing in the doorway of the lock-keeper's cottage. Charles Kerrigan Kemp returned the acknowledgement.

'Yes, sir?' The deep Irish brogue beside him brought Tom's attention back. Strange, he mused, how different men from the same background could be – Quinn and O'Dowd, both Irishmen but with nothing more in common than the language that they spoke.

'Ambrose,' he said softly, glancing round to ensure that they were not overheard, 'I don't know what you did to those cartridges, but if you have any left get rid of them – now!'

The Irishman stared dispassionately down at the mutilated body spread-eagled on the deck below them. 'Will that be all, sir?'

Before Tom could reply, the sound of hoof beats hammering along the towpath caused both men to swing round. Thundering along the canal bank, scattering Squires and his men into the hedge and the canal, Connor Devlin was galloping towards the locks on a bay gelding, a second horse flying along behind him on a trailing rein.

After his dispute with O'Dowd, Connor had taken himself off for a few minutes to smoke a pipe and calm down a little. The disagreement with the commander had been a serious one, and he needed to regain his equilibrium before they talked again so he didn't say something he would later regret. So it was that, some ten minutes after the *Trojan* passed under Bishop's Lane Bridge, he came across Seth Morton and the saddle horses.

Even as he stood behind the hedge watching Morton and appraising the situation, the sound of gunfire made him realise that he was probably already too late. It was an easy matter to overpower the elderly constable and, having tightened the horses' saddle girths, he set off cautiously along the towpath. In a couple of minutes he was behind Jesse Squires and his men. From his position in the saddle Connor had a clear view over the hedgerow and could see what was happening further along the canal. The tall detective inspector was standing next to the top lock gates talking to a big uniformed sergeant. Several other men were moving about aimlessly now that the excitement of the moment was over. All carried weapons. To one side were Amos Radbone, his wife and Michael. There was no sign of Terence. Further away, apparently being kept in isolation, was Liam O'Dowd in handcuffs. He had only one policeman with him, not very old, slimly built and wearing a dark grey suit. From his bowler hat, Connor presumed that he was a detective.

Ducking down in the saddle to avoid being spotted, Devlin took a moment to decide his course of action. Whoever had handcuffed Liam had been overconfident: his hands should either have been behind his back instead of in front of him, or he should have been cuffed to one of the policemen. In addition, the officers on the locks and near the Radbones had broken their shotguns and put away their pistols. It was a slim chance, but if he hit them fast enough he might be able to get Liam away. Crouching low over his mount's neck, revolver clasped in his right hand, the Irishman set off at full gallop.

Hurtling through the unprepared men on the towpath, Devlin fired two shots in the direction of the biggest group of policemen, near the cottage, causing them to dive for cover in confusion. Veering off to the left, he headed for O'Dowd. Understanding immediately what was happening, Liam swung both of his manacled hands up, using the full weight of his body, and hit the detective full in the face – for a split second relishing the sound of snapping teeth. As the policeman went down, O'Dowd grabbed at the stirrup of the second horse as Connor skidded to a halt beside him, firing this time in the direction of Tom and the big sergeant who were running from the lock gates. Tom, arm extended, returned fire with the pistol that he had pulled from under his jacket.

It almost worked. Liam, his boot in the stirrup, was pulling himself up into the saddle when Joel Dexter, one eye almost closed, his mouth split and pouring blood, struggled onto his knees and shot O'Dowd in the back. Seeing the blank look of astonishment in Liam's eyes, Devlin knew that he had been hit even before the commander's hands relaxed their grip on the pommel, his foot dropped from the stirrup and he slid slowly backwards to the ground. With a curse, Connor swung his weapon and, this time taking deliberate aim, fired twice into Dexter's chest, killing him instantly. Both horses reared, adding to the confusion and making any accurate shooting almost impossible. O'Dowd's horse, pulling free from the trailing rein, broke away towards the water.

Knowing that the day was lost, Connor hauled his own animal round and, kicking it into action, took off along the bank in the direction from which he had come.

Chapter Twenty-Five

Grabbing at the reins of the skittering mare as she went past him, Tom Norton ran a couple of paces alongside, gripping at the halter. Then, pulling himself up into the saddle and finding the stirrups with his feet, he took off like the wind after the Irishman. Inwardly he was cursing. At least Joel had succeeded in bringing down O'Dowd before he was killed. For Joel's death, if nothing else, Tom was determined to see the man ahead of him hang.

As he galloped up to Bishop's Lane Bridge, Tom saw a flash of movement as Devlin cleared the hump of the bridge and disappeared out of sight again. Off to his right a shaky Seth Morton, blood trickling from the wound on his head where Devlin had hit him with his pistol butt, was trying to recapture his charges. Reining in, Tom yelled, 'Tell them he's making for Sangster's!'

Without waiting for a reply, he set off at a gallop after Devlin. Olston Grange was the only logical place that the man could be heading for. If he could get there undetected he would have access to a fresh horse and different clothes before making off to safety. Tom was hopeful that the Irishmen had not realised the police had made the connection between their activities and the American. It would be some minutes before Fred Judd or any of the others could get to the horses and come after him; meantime he must not allow his quarry to escape.

It took Tom twenty minutes of hard riding across the fields before he saw the rooftops of Great Olston ahead of him. The term 'Great' was a misnomer. The village consisted of a half a dozen cottages and an alehouse, past which Tom clattered at full pelt, to the obvious consternation of the one or two residents who were not in church. Olston Grange was at the far end of the village, a tall red-brick pile, built in the early years of George III's reign and set in two acres of ground. Sliding from his saddle in the lane outside the house, Tom left the mare to roam loose and gather her wind while, pistol in hand, he began to work his way cautiously through the bushes along the side of the driveway up to the house, avoiding treading on the gravel path.

One of the tall oak front doors was swinging open and the Irishman's lathered bay was cropping the closely mown grass of the front lawn. Crouching down behind a tall immaculately topiaried bush, Tom paused. The open door and absence of any signs of life indicated that the man he was chasing was alone in the house. It was probable that if Sangster was not at home the servants had gone to church in the village. Tom needed either to capture the Irishman or prevent him from leaving until reinforcements arrived.

Kneeling on the damp soil behind the bush, he pulled out his revolver and, pushing down the stirrup latch with his thumb, broke it in half to check the load. It was one of the new double-action Webley service revolvers that had recently been brought into use by the British Army. Archer Robson had bought two on trial only a month ago; Jesse Squires had the other. As Tom pulled the barrel down with his free hand the star-shaped ejector threw the six expended cartridges onto the ground in an untidy heap before dropping smoothly back into place. Hurriedly reloading, Tom grimaced: he should have done this before coming up to the house. If anyone had been lying in wait for him he was carrying an empty gun. Snapping the pistol closed, he sprinted the remaining five yards to the open doorway.

The silence inside was oppressive. Dark wooden panels gave the entrance hall an air of uninviting gloom, which contrasted curiously with an all-pervading smell of furniture polish and beeswax. Ignoring the wide stone staircase clad in a plain green carpet, Tom moved to the first door on his right.

The door swung open at his touch and he stepped inside warily, pistol close to his body. It was a library and writing room. The ceiling-high bookshelves, he thought almost subconsciously, were probably for show, the volumes purchased by weight rather than for their content. Beneath an elegant window that looked out over the front lawn stood an expensive writing desk, the contents of which under different circumstances would have borne close examination.

Closing the door softly, Tom returned to the hallway and paused again to listen. From a room further along he heard a muffled footfall. Edging along the panelled wall, the expensive carpet deadening any sound he might make, he crept towards the source of the sound. Slipping in through the half-open door, he found himself in a huge old-fashioned ballroom, at least eighty feet long and almost as wide. Across one end ran a wide seating area separated from the dance floor by a series of high-carved stone arches that supported the minstrels' gallery above. It was easy to imagine annual hunt balls being held in this room, elegant dancers in their evening attire crowding the floor and gliding back and forth to Strauss waltzes, while the remainder of the guests took their ease on the ample chaise-longues or flirted discreetly behind the arches.

Now the ballroom was deserted, the light dimmed by half-drawn curtains at the tall windows on the far side. Whoever had been here had moved on. Keeping in the shadows, Tom moved deeper into the room. At the far end he could make out a large arched doorway through which the man he was following must have passed. With infinite caution he worked his way towards it.

As he got nearer he saw he was looking into a room that was the same as the one he was in now: a second ballroom. Suddenly his heart missed a beat. Through the portal, hiding behind a pillar, was the man called Connor. He was standing perfectly still, the back of his unbuttoned reefer jacket pressed up against the stonework. His left hand, pressed flat against his thigh, held a Colt revolver, barrel pointing down at the ground. Intent upon hiding, the man had not seen him yet.

Dropping flat on the floor, Tom began to work his way very slowly forward, to get close enough for a clear shot to disable the man. Reaching the next pillar, he stood up and flattened himself against it while he caught his breath. Suddenly he remembered where he had seen the Irishman before: with Langley in Crooked Edie's nearly a year before. Tom was just about to congratulate himself when he realised something was wrong. Another kaleidoscope of images ran through his mind. Images of a much more recent event. Of the man he was now watching, on horseback and firing a pistol at him as he and Ambrose charged down from the locks. Of the same man pointing his pistol at Joel Dexter and firing it into Dexter's heart before wheeling his horse round and galloping away. That man had been right-handed. Why, then, was he now holding the pistol in his left hand?

Purposefully Connor began to bring his arm up, pointing the Colt at Tom and taking careful aim. The explanation exploded in Tom's brain a split second before the Irishman fired. 'Jesus Christ!' There was no next room. The archway was a huge ornamental mirror. All the time he had been stalking Connor's mirror image the man had been behind him – waiting for an easy target.

Throwing himself flat, Tom felt the bullet pluck at his sleeve before it hit the mirror, shattering it into a million shards of flying glass. Hitting the ground and firing two shots in the general direction of the Irishman he began to roll towards the nearby sofa. Throwing an arm over the back of it, Tom fired again without bringing his head up. The response was a further volley of shots from the Irishman, followed by the sound of running feet. Leaping over the chaise-longue, the detective took off towards the door, which was now swinging loosely on its hinges. As he ran he tried to remember how many shots he had fired. Three: that meant he had three left.

Cautiously, Tom stepped back into the hallway – where the face of a choleric country gentleman in a Georgian velvet coat with breeches to match gazed down disdainfully from the wall. Waiting patiently, he could detect no further movement. Connor was either lying in wait or had made good his escape through the back of the house. The silence was shattered by the pounding of hooves outside, followed by the sound of gravel chippings being scattered to the winds as hard-ridden horses slithered to a halt. The front door was thrown open, revealing the figures of Fred Judd and Jesse Squires, pistols in their hands.

'Get down!' Tom bellowed. The two men dived for cover, Jesse at the foot of the stairs, Fred in the entrance to the library. Tom took the opportunity to reload, then, satisfied that the Irishman was no longer in the house, signalled for them to join him. 'Am I glad to see you two,' he said gratefully, still crouching warily in the shelter of the ballroom doorway.

'Took a while to get to the horses,' Fred Judd murmured, peering intently up through the ornate staircase. 'Where do you think he is?'

'Out at the back somewhere. Find the stables in time and we'll have him.'

'What about upstairs?' Jesse Squires already knew the answer.

Tom shook his head. 'No. This one's good. He's a professional. Only a fool would go upstairs where he could be trapped. We need to get to the stables fast.'

'Joel's dead, Tom.' There was a question in Squire's voice and in his eyes that was plain for the others to read.

Tom looked quickly at Judd. He knew that whatever decision he gave would be between them and no one else, for ever. He looked down at the Webley in his hand, briefly turning over his answer, then shook his head slowly. 'No. I want him alive.' Without looking back, he stood up and made his way through the great kitchens and out of the back door.

Fanning out, it took the three men less than a minute to locate the long white-painted stable block at the rear of the premises. A five-bar gate led from the stable yard to an anonymous track, which doubtless gave onto the lane to the village. Tom had seen buildings like this many times before: it would probably accommodate about twenty horses. Unlike those where each animal was kept in an individual stall, with a split door that allowed the horse to poke its head out into the yard, this one was built on the French style – an enclosed building with a single entrance in the centre. A passage ran the length of the building, with open stalls off it.

How many horses were there at the moment was anyone's guess, but the outer door was propped open by a baulk of timber, indicating that someone was inside. Tom gestured to the others to remain by the five-bar gate and cover him before bending low and moving as quickly as he dared across the yard. Staying to the right of the doorway, he flattened himself against the side of the building and, hugging his pistol to his chest, listened intently. Through the wall he heard the sound of harness being quietly moved around and the stamp of a horse's hoof as it was saddled up.

Tom knew that no matter how fast the rider urged his horse along the aisle between the stalls he would have to slow down to make the right-angle turn through the doorway into the yard. He calculated that he would have one or two seconds at most. With O'Dowd dead it was imperative that he took Devlin prisoner, to stand trial. He knew that if his plan went wrong he would be too close to the Irishman for Jesse or Fred to risk opening fire without hitting him.

The seconds ticked by. Tom checked to ensure there was nothing to obscure his view or cause him to stumble. He had a clear field of action, and

Devlin's weapon, in his right hand, would be on the far side of his horse's neck. Almost two minutes elapsed before Tom heard the man whispering to the horse and the creak of leather as he swung into the saddle. Rivulets of perspiration began to run down his back as he prepared himself.

A startled whinny came from the unseen animal as booted heels were clapped sharply into its flanks, propelling it along the passage. Two seconds later a black shadow loomed momentarily in the doorway, accompanied by a clatter of hooves, as Connor, dragging cruelly on the brown stallion's mouth, forced it into a turn through the door and into the yard.

The second that the horse and rider appeared in the doorway, Tom moved forward and swung inwards, the pistol held two-handed in front of him at eye level. It was a perfect shot. The round-nosed .455 lead bullet hit the stallion an inch behind its left eye, shattering the animal's skull and travelling deep in its brain. Dead on its feet but propelled by its own momentum, the stallion took two more massive strides before plunging headlong onto the cobbles five yards beyond Tom, pinning its stunned rider by the leg beneath its twitching body.

Lucas Sangster had spent the morning in Kelsford discussing the purchase of a consignment of rifles with Eugene Leschenko. Sangster was not particularly happy about doing business with Leschenko, whom he had last seen in the Ten Bells in Whitechapel with Vassily Brovnic. The potential problems that the raid at 95 Varden Street presented made Sangster extremely wary when he received a message from Leschenko that he was in Kelsford and needed to see him. Having turned the matter over, the Texan decided to see what Leschenko wanted. In his profession, few if any of the people with whom he was destined to conduct business were totally reliable, and as long as he exercised due caution a deal was a deal.

Early that morning, while the *Trojan* was still several miles away from Town Locks and the only people about were good Catholics off to early mass, Sangster met Leschenko at the back of a deserted factory in Collett Lane.

Even the early morning sunshine could not dispel the despondent air that hung over the grey Georgian building. Built fifty years ago as a factory that manufactured boot-blacking, it had passed through a succession of owners until, derelict, it had been bought by Joshua Howkins. Content to allow the three-storey building to stand empty, Howkins was biding his time until a few years hence when the nearby hovels would be pulled down. Through lack of maintenance the factory had deteriorated to its present state of dilapidation – although the steel bars at the lower windows and stout locks on all the doors meant it was anonymous and secure. For this reason Sangster had agreed to use it as a store for the rifles unloaded by Taft and Brindley at the railway station.

Leading his horse through the broken-down gates at the rear of the premises, Sangster, followed by Eugene Leschenko, crossed the cobbled yard to the secure double doors that gave access to what had once been a large loading bay. The doors opened as if by a pre-arranged signal to reveal the stocky figure of Brindley Stokes, a double-barrelled shotgun held loosely in his fist.

While Brindley secured the doors behind them, Sangster ushered the Latvian up a set of rickety stairs to the first floor and into a huge open storage space, which ran the entire length of the building. In the middle, neatly stacked in cases, stood the consignment of guns. Under one of the boarded windows was a smaller pile of ammunition boxes. A short middle-aged man with a pockmarked face under his two days' growth of beard moved respectfully out of earshot, cradling his shotgun in the crook of his arm.

As Leschenko walked round, touching the crates like a child examining his presents on Christmas morning, the American prised open the lid of one of the boxes. Withdrawing a Winchester 1886 repeating rifle, he handed it to his companion. Putting the gun up to his shoulder, the Latvian peered along the barrel, working the lever action and pulling the trigger several times without taking his eye away from the sights.

Sangster, the consummate salesman, spent the next quarter of an hour demonstrating the weapon. Finally replacing it in its box, he looked up from resealing the lid and said, 'Are you interested?'

'How many have you got?'

'How many can you afford? I'm selling them at four English pounds each, minimum of one hundred – plus ammunition.'

'Very soon there will be a lot of money coming to my group. Then we will buy from you as many as you can let us have. I will need sufficient to equip an army,' Leschenko replied grandly.

Slowly the American turned his gaze on him. It was a look that would have struck fear into the hearts of most men. 'What do you mean, you'll soon have money?' he hissed, the menace in his voice causing the pockmarked guard to move to a position where he could cover the foreigner.

'I need to know the availability of your guns,' replied Eugene loftily. 'Within a few days – a week or two at the most – a large amount of money will be in my hands, at which time I'll be back to buy all the guns you can give me.'

Sangster's anger was barely contained. 'Listen to me, you son of a bitch, you're wasting my time. Either you've got the money to do a deal or you haven't!' The man with the shotgun moved behind the Latvian, where he could get a clear shot if called upon. 'And if you haven't got the money I'm going to have to think very carefully about what you've seen here.' The Texan's words hung in the quiet atmosphere. A shaft of bright sunshine coming in through a gap in the window boards laid a sliver of white light across the pile of cases. Behind him Leschenko heard a flat double click as the hammers on the shotgun were pulled back. As if to emphasise the point Sangster stepped to one side. 'So, Mr Revolutionary, where does that leave us now?'

Eugene Leschenko ran his tongue over suddenly dry lips. That he had misjudged the situation was obvious. Vassily had told him that buying guns from these people was 'as easy as laying a two kopek whore'. The fat Moravian was a fool, Eugene realised, and now he was a bigger fool for believing him.

He should have waited until the money Ruth Samuels had promised him was actually in his possession. 'There's no need for this,' he said hoarsely, his lofty arrogance gone. 'I assure you that within a few days the money will be available.'

'It had better be, Mr Revolutionary, it had better be . . .' Sangster's voice left no doubt about the consequences should it not be so.

Once Leschenko had been escorted into Collett Lane, Sangster climbed onto his horse and began the leisurely ride back to Great Olston. Enjoying the morning sunshine, he stopped at the cabmen's coffee stall just off the High Street. Ordering a coffee from the man behind the counter, Sangster leaned casually against the wooden shack and surveyed his surroundings.

A couple of hansoms were pulled up at the cab rank. The horses were munching steadily at feed bags attached to their noses. Their owners, one a slim thin-faced man, his companion stout and with the mottled cheeks and nose of an inveterate drinker, were standing a few paces away chatting, and nodded a cursory good morning. Sangster was a regular visitor. Late night excursions to meet Clancy Taft and Devlin often ended with coffee on the way home. Sangster had learned his trade in the back streets of San Francisco and half a dozen other Western towns along the way. Never be in too much of a hurry was, he found, an adage worth following. Stopping at a place like this gave him the time to ensure he was not being followed, while a cab rank, whether in San Francisco or Kelsford, was where some of the most informed gossip could be picked up.

The hansom drivers were listening intently to a small man with a straggly moustache, wearing the shirtsleeves and cloth cap of a market porter. Sangster noticed his two-wheeled barrow next to the kerb, its long shaft and T-shaped handle pointing out precariously into the road. Wiping away the coffee from his straggly moustache with the back of a grimy hand, the porter continued to address his audience. 'I tell you, there's at least four dead. Shooting all over the place. I never even knew the coppers had guns!'

Sangster edged closer to the conversation. Draining his pot mug, he replaced it on the counter. 'Think I'll have another please,' he said, loudly enough to be heard by the men. 'Would you gentlemen care to join me?'

The drivers were accustomed to the newcomer's deep Texas drawl, and handed up their mugs for refills. The American usually stopped by late at night or in the early hours of the morning and chatted with whoever was about. A personable man who could tell a good story – he had been in the American War of the States – most of the drivers knew him to speak to.

'Something's been happening, huh?' Sangster put on his best Western accent for the benefit of the porter.

'Ozzie says there's been a shooting up at the cut. Some blokes on a barge.' The thin-faced driver suddenly had Sangster's undivided attention.

Determined not to be deprived of his story, Ozzie, with an annoyed glare at the cabbie, interrupted. 'Boggy Simms come into the market ten minutes ago and he seen it. There was a barge going through Town Locks. All of a sudden hundreds of coppers with guns come running from all over the place and started shooting. Then they nicked everybody on the boat. There was bodies all over the place.'

'Go on.' Sangster had forgotten about the drawl.

'Well, Boggy says it was all over in a couple of minutes. He hid at the back of the bridge, 'cause he's a bit doolally – then all of a sudden it started up again. Some bloke come riding up on a horse and he started shooting and one of the blokes who'd been arrested made a break for it and the coppers killed him. Shot him in the back, Boggy says. Then this bloke on the horse shoots one of the coppers and rides off. Boggy says there was bodies all over the place.'

Sangster rubbed a hand over his close-shaven jaw and took a deep breath. For a Sunday it was developing into quite a busy day, he thought. First the Latvian, now this. He pushed a large cigar into the corner of his mouth and begged a Vesta from the red-nosed cabbie.

Staying another ten minutes while he finished his rapidly cooling coffee, Sangster bid the men farewell and set off towards the London Road and Great Olston. Once out of sight, he speeded up, chewing thoughtfully on the end of the cigar and considering his situation in light of the morning's events. Sangster was a professional, and was fully aware that for any venture to be successful you had to know when to pull out to guarantee survival. That something had gone dramatically wrong with the transfer of the consignment was apparent. If the police had sufficient knowledge to lay down an armed ambush, it indicated that the Brotherhood's operations were blown open. He badly needed to know who had been killed or taken prisoner, and sincerely hoped that the only two who could identify him, O'Dowd and Devlin, were dead.

It was time, Sangster decided, to wind up his operation in Kelsford. Racking his brain as the horse jogged along, he could not see how the police could link him with the Irishmen: he had been very careful not to leave a trail. Closing down the Brotherhood connection should be fairly easy. First thing tomorrow morning he would draft a coded cable to Ellingworth. A detail that was bothering him was that Leschenko was now aware of the location of the weapons cache. It had been a mistake not to take him in blindfolded. That he could not complete a deal through lack of funds incensed the American.

A decision about Leschenko could be delayed for a few days, Sangster resolved. If the Latvian double-crossed him he would use some of Clancy's boys to deal with the man on a permanent basis. It would simply be another loose end to clear up. In any case he could not leave Kelsford for the time being: he had recently received a telegram from Miles Ellingworth concerning an urgent deal that he needed to complete with Max Peters.

Chapter Twenty-Six

That he had not been at home when Devlin arrived, hotly pursued by the police, was, Lucas Sangster later considered, one of the greatest pieces of fortune to come his way for some time. As he trotted in through the gates of Olston Grange he realised that the police were at his house well before his butler came out to tell him, because of the horses and a pony and trap outside the front door.

Dismounting and handing over the reins, Sangster made his way calmly into the house and towards the ballroom where, he was told, the senior police officer was waiting to speak with him. As he walked into the entrance hall the American's mind was racing. The man who had escaped from the ambush on a horse must have been Devlin, because only he knew where the Grange was: O'Dowd had never been there. It would now be impossible to deny that he knew Devlin.

In the ballroom he found a tall, dishevelled man with fair hair who introduced himself as Detective Inspector Norton. With him was a smaller and neater man in his early thirties, who did not at first glance have the appearance of a policeman. He was introduced as Detective Sergeant Squires.

In the hour that had elapsed since Connor had been taken away, Tom had made a swift but thorough search of the downstairs rooms of Olston Grange. The fact that he and Jesse had been interrupted by the return of the servants made little difference. There was, he realised, nothing to link Lucas Sangster with Devlin.

The American was much as Tom remembered him from the day at the Flixton workings, bluff and hearty, his voice booming out in the quiet room. 'How the hell did this man get in here, Inspector?' Sangster demanded. 'You say that you chased him across country from Town Locks after he shot a police officer? This is terrible, just terrible!'

'More importantly, why did he come here at all?' Tom asked. He had to be careful, as he did not have a shred of evidence to suggest a connection between Sangster and the men on the *Trojan*. He had a photograph that showed Sangster in the company of Taft and Connor and Kerrigan Kemp had seen the American on a wagon with them, but either of these could be explained away by a capable defence lawyer.

'Sure as hell beats me, Inspector. I can only suppose that he saw the house and broke in to get away from you.'

'The man's name is Connor. He had connections with the Flixton canal diggings and the warehousing project in the Kelsford Basin. I think you knew him.'

Tom waited, but was disappointed at the reaction. He had hoped that the American would deny it. Instead, pulling a new cigar from his inside pocket, Sangster paused for a moment, apparently lost in thought, before replying, 'If he's the man I'm thinking of he did some work at the basin cutting. I think I met him with a contractor I know – a man named Clancy Taft.' In a stroke of inspiration, he added, 'You say his name is Connor. Is that his first or last name?'

Tom hesitated for a second too long before he replied. 'Just Connor. You say you know him.'

Lucas Sangster felt a surge of elation. They didn't even have the Irishman's full name. This was a fishing expedition, and it was one in which the detective inspector was going to be disappointed. With a regretful smile and an eloquent shrug of the shoulders he said, 'I'm sorry, Inspector, I don't know the man other than to say I've seen him at the basin. I seem to remember him coming over to speak to Clancy when we were talking one morning.'

Tom was annoyed that he had given away more than he had wanted to, but it had been unavoidable. One thing was certain: he was going to make absolutely no progress with the American this morning. Before they spoke again he would need to have sufficient evidence to arrest the man.

'May we look round before we leave?' he asked politely. 'The man – Connor – was in the house for some minutes before I arrived. It's possible he left something in one of the rooms.'

Smiling amiably, Sangster invited them to go anywhere in the house they wished.

On Monday morning, to Tom's frustration, Joshua Howkins left a short note for his wife to say he needed to go to London on business, and disappeared. The grocer's trip to London was, Tom suspected, in view of the conversation he had overheard between Devlin and Sangster, directly linked to the announcement in the *Kelsford Gazette* that morning of the unexpected bankruptcy of Batsford Stone. The Shires Canal Company had immediately suspended all its operations while it reviewed the implications of its major supplier's insolvency, while the Kelsford Bank of Commerce was not available for comment. Without being able to interview Howkins any attempts by the detectives to find the second cache of weapons were futile. Tom decided he would have to be patient and wait for the grocer to return from his trip in order to interview him.

The fact that Howkins was chairman of the watch committee had repercussions, necessitating a lengthy discussion between Archer Robson and his head of detectives. Archer Robson was worried that it was going to be difficult to prove Howkins' involvement without revealing Tom's illicit visit to the barn at Monckton. Now more than ever it was of the utmost importance to locate the second consignment of weapons. In the meantime it was decided that Sam and Reuben should go to Monckton and obtain statements from the landlord of the Black Horse, in whose yard the cases had been stacked during loading. With any luck they might also be able to find a couple of villagers who had seen the transfer of the boxes from Howkins' shop to the barge.

Had Tom been aware of the true situation in relation to Joshua Howkins he would have been even more perturbed. On Sunday evening, several hours after Tom and Jesse had departed from Olston Grange, Lucas Sangster had received a further visitor – his surviving partner in crime. When the little man was shown into the library, Sangster was disturbed to see how shaken he was. It was obvious that Howkins had spent the day in a state of near panic. His shirt was rumpled and his high winged collar was grubby with fingermarks. The fact that Devlin had been arrested and O'Dowd shot the day before it was planned to disclose the collapse of Batsford Stone had shaken Howkins to the core.

'Ignore the fact that Connor has been arrested: that's a coincidence. Calm down and tell me what you plan to do about the scam,' the American said, handing him a large glass of Kentucky bourbon.

'For Christ's sake, do you have to refer to this as a scam? It's a business operation.' Howkins' alarm was so near to the surface that Sangster began to doubt whether the man would hold together long enough to carry out the next part of his scheme. 'Please yourself,' he replied, holding his glass up and watching the light from the oil lamp bouncing across the amber liquid. 'There's nothing to implicate you with this thing at the locks. You're holding a consignment of weapons for me. Nothing has changed there. As and when I decide the time is right I'll arrange for them to be moved, and your involvement will be over. Meantime, this other thing is totally your own affair.' Sangster watched carefully, then added, 'This is your nest egg, Josh. Now get off down to the company that's buying the site. What's its name?'

'Universal Stone.' The voice was stronger now. Either the bourbon was taking effect or Howkins' confidence was returning.

'That's good. Universal Stone. You go and seal your deal with them, then stow the money somewhere safe. All you have to do after that is keep your head down until this blows over.'

It was another hour before Howkins, considerably the worse for wear, steered his pony and trap unsteadily towards Kelsford. Seated comfortably in his leather armchair in the library, a fresh glass of bourbon from the depleted bottle at his elbow, Sangster studied the timetable of trains from Kelsford to London.

On Tuesday morning, having spent a disturbed and anxious night at the Shelton Park Hotel, Joshua Howkins descended from his cab outside an elegant three-storey Georgian house in Bloomsbury. Paying the driver, he turned and climbed the steps to the dark green front door, where he was admitted by a liveried footman.

Howkins was mildly puzzled. He had been expecting to find Universal Stone in an office block, but the surroundings in which he found himself resembled a gentlemen's club. This impression was confirmed when, a minute or two later, the same attendant guided him into an expensively furnished salon in which a score of well-dressed men were spread either singly or in pairs, ensconced in the deep leather armchairs that, along with a number of ornate side tables, occupied most of the room. Deferentially leading him to the far end, where an enormous log fire was roaring in a wide stone fireplace, the servant indicated a pair of armchairs, one of which had its back to him, obscuring his view of the occupant.

Feeling decidedly ill at ease in the unfamiliar surroundings, Howkins made his way to the fireplace. As he moved round the dark polished table and the armchair, a beefy hand waved him into the free chair.

'Take a seat, Josh. What would you like to drink?'

For a moment Howkins could not believe his eyes; then he began to feel sick. Whatever was happening here, Lucas Sangster should not be part of it.

'Two large brandies, please,' Sangster said to the waiter who had appeared at the arm of his chair. He knew that, sophisticated as it was, the Lansbury Club would not stock bourbon. His one complaint against English society was that it refused to accommodate anything that it considered to be foreign.

'Why are you here?' Howkins' voice sounded distant.

'We're both here to do business, Josh.' The American gave his throaty chuckle – which sounded to the little grocer like a cackle from the grave. 'I represent Universal Stone. Now let's discuss our latest little venture.'

It was worse than Howkins could have imagined. Over the next half-hour Sangster, despite all the Kelsford businessman's protests and pleadings, stripped the quarry swindle to its bones and rebuilt it before Howkins' eyes, this time with Universal Stone taking all. On Arthur Cufflin's advice, the Shires Canal Company had, since the middle of the summer, been paying cash on delivery for quarry stone. This meant that Howkins' original plan to obtain money for goods that, with the collapse of the firm, would never be delivered was not going to happen. Although this was an inconvenience it was not critical, as the major part of the fraud depended upon the subsequent sale of the company's assets. The fact that Howkins had divested himself of his original partners was a calculated risk. A much-increased profit margin required that he had to shoulder the financial burden of maintaining the bogus company alone. In order to do this, having first convinced the gullible Max Peters to extend his credit, Howkins proceeded to commit himself well beyond his safe limits. As his cash flow became more difficult he allowed Peters to buy into the swindle. That Peters was aware that the transactions to which he and the bank were now committed were of a dubious nature was an advantage to Howkins, allowing him to extend his credit still further. Failure now would mean his total ruin.

That the man sitting opposite was involved in Universal Stone was something that Howkins could never have anticipated. It was obvious that the American was going to negotiate the sale of Batsford Stone very much to his own advantage. The problem was that he also knew of Howkins' financial weakness and his consequent vulnerability. The bank would lose most of the £100,000 that it had invested, which while being a severe blow would not be unsustainable: it would survive, albeit severely damaged. With the inherent acumen of a banker, Max Peters had not gone beyond his means. The real loser was going to be Joshua Howkins.

'Lucas, you've got to give me a fair price for the quarry and the land,' he said, desperately seeking some salvation. His gnome-like face ashen, Howkins was still stunned at the American's duplicity. His one thought was to broker a deal in which Universal Stone would pay him sufficient money to allow him to break even and pay off the bank.

'Have you brought all the paperwork for me to look over?' asked Sangster smoothly, knowing full well that Howkins would have everything necessary in his possession. The American needed the documents in his hand before he delivered the *coup de grâce*. 'My principals are reasonable people, Josh. I'm sure we can work out a fair price. How much do you need to clear?'

Howkins did not have to search for his answer; he knew almost to the penny. 'The bank's in for a hundred thousand. I need the same again to settle my commitments.'

Sangster gave a low whistle. He could not believe that this avaricious little man had allowed himself to stake what must be all of his assets on one throw of the dice.

For the next fifteen minutes he read and cross-checked the papers. Twice, when Howkins made to speak, he silenced him with a gesture. Eventually the American looked up and nodded in satisfaction. Reaching into his inside pocket, he pulled out a single foolscap sheet and handed it across. 'Everything seems to be in order, Josh,' he beamed. 'We both sign this deed of sale and you're relieved of the burden of the late lamented Batsford Stone.'

The little man stared in disbelief at the legal document. His hand was trembling visibly, and Sangster began to worry that he was going to faint, or even have a heart attack. 'What's this?' he croaked. 'You're offering me a hundred pounds for the lot! Are you mad?'

Sangster leaned back in the deep armchair and folded his hands across his ample stomach. 'Certainly not, Josh. In the circumstances it's a very fair offer.

Let's look at it. You staked a lot – too much, it now appears – on being able to swindle everyone in sight out of a large fortune: your partners, the bank, the Shires Company, probably me as well if you got the chance. Unfortunately you were out of your league, and now the wheel's stopped spinning the ball hasn't landed where you expected it to.'

'I'll go to the police. I know far too much for you to get away with this.' Desperation had turned to anger, and Howkins was fighting for his life.

'No, you won't do that,' Sangster replied confidently. 'You're involved with Irish terrorists who are responsible for a series of crimes, including more than one murder, most of which will attract the death penalty. Did you know, by the way, that when Devlin and O'Dowd were caught they had the guns from your store at Monckton on board?' The question was rhetorical, and without waiting for an answer he continued. 'Then, of course, you collected a consignment of guns from Kelsford station and paid two of the labourers to keep quiet. After that you stored the weapons – nice shiny Winchesters all the way from America – in another warehouse that you own in Collett Lane. In fact they're still there now, just waiting for the police to call and collect them. No, you'll take the money and run if you have any sense, Josh.'

Half-watching the grocer in case he collapsed or attempted to do something silly, Sangster signalled to one of the club waiters. Reaching again into his jacket, he handed the man an envelope that was heavily sealed with melted wax. Written on it were the words Detective Inspector T. Norton and the address of Long Street police station. 'What time do you go to the post office, Jonathon?' he asked casually.

'In another twenty minutes, sir,' came the respectful reply.

Sangster inclined his head in acknowledgement and handed over the envelope. 'If you could oblige, please,' he drawled. 'Twenty minutes, Joshua, then that letter with everything in it goes to Kelsford police. By tomorrow they'll have a warrant out for you, and that deed of sale in your hand will be worthless.'

'I'm ruined.' Howkins slumped down in the chair looking like a discarded puppet. He seemed to have shrunk to half his size. Head forward, his snowy beard splayed across his shirt front. 'Christ Almighty, what am I going to do?'

Sangster gave a dry smile. 'If you're frightened of wolves don't go into the forest, Josh,' he murmured, dipping a pen into the inkstand that had been placed on the table next to his elbow.

When Howkins had left Sangster finished his drink and strolled out into the marble-floored foyer where, as instructed, the club servant was waiting for him. Taking the letter from the waiter's salver, the American pressed a half-guinea into the man's hand and, tearing the envelope in half, dropped it into a nearby waste-paper basket. After the American had disappeared into the busy street the waiter retrieved the discarded envelope from the basket, and was puzzled to find it contained a sheet of blank paper.

At precisely twenty-five to ten on Wednesday morning the manager and reception clerk of the Shelton Park Hotel were busy checking the list of guests due to arrive that day when a series of piercing screams sent them dashing up the main stairway of the hotel to the first floor. As they reached the corridor from which the screams had emanated they were greeted by the sight of a chambermaid vomiting on the carpet. Without pausing, the two men pushed past the hysterical woman through the open door of Room 139. Laid in an untidy heap across the double bed, his shirt and surrounding bedclothes stained a dark crimson, was the body of Joshua Howkins. Still clasped in his right hand was the open razor with which he had cut his throat.

The next few days were a busy time for Tom Norton and his men, as they prepared files of evidence against those in custody – ranging from the Radbones' illegal possession of firearms to murder in the case of Devlin.

The news of Howkins' suicide dealt a serious blow to Tom's hopes of quickly locating the arms that were hidden somewhere in Downe Street. For the time being Archer Robson, aware of the political implications of a prominent businessman, and chairman of the watch committee, being found dead in an hotel room, decided to allow the suicide to remain a mystery, grateful that it had occurred in London and not in Kelsford. News of Howkins' death was received among his business associates and fellow members of the town council with a decided lack of sentiment: he had never been a well-loved man. Charles Kerrigan Kemp, after a private conversation, agreed with Tom not to ask too many questions, on the promise of first-hand information as soon as anything emerged.

By arrangement with the magistrates all the prisoners, with the exception of Liam O'Dowd, were lodged in Kelsford gaol. The risk of the Brotherhood attempting to rescue them was very real, and their removal to a more secure place than Long Street police station had been dealt with urgently.

O'Dowd was the prisoner who presented a real difficulty for the police. Joel Dexter's bullet had passed between O'Dowd's shoulder blades and lodged in his left lung. For the present, although the bullet had been removed at Kelsford Royal Infirmary, it was still not known if he would survive the wound and the subsequent operation. For the time being he was in a private room at the hospital under armed guard.

It was only with the arrival, simultaneously on Monday afternoon, of Vincent Millward from Manchester and Detective Sergeant Walter Hibbert of the Metropolitan Police secret department, that Devlin's full identity was established. Millward, to Devlin's consternation, was able to identify him from his activities in Manchester, although the detective appeared not to know about the safe house in Swinburne Court.

After a brief time with the two officers Tom handed them over to Squires and Braithwaite, to assist in interviewing Devlin and his accomplices. As expected, neither of the visitors elicited anything more from the prisoners, and they left on the late afternoon trains. The prisoners maintained a wall of silence. The Radbones, father, mother and son, knew better than to admit anything, and were in any case mourning for their son and brother, 'murdered by the forces of the English Queen'. Devlin refused to say a word to Tom, and eventually the detective gave up, deciding to concentrate on putting together the case for the murder of Joel Dexter.

Kerrigan Kemp, for his part, devoted as much space in the *Gazette* as he could to the events at Town Locks, doing what it was not possible for the police themselves to do in the circumstances – linking the consignment of weapons to terrorist activities elsewhere, and asking the public to examine the possibility that this latest affair was related to the murders of a well-respected detective officer and Isaac Harriman, along with the outrage of the Shires payroll robbery. He was probably one of the happiest men in the town as sales of his paper soared.

The week, which seemed to fly by for Tom, dragged interminably for Ruth. Knowing that she would be worried when news of the shooting at Town Locks leaked out, Tom sent a brief message letting her know he was all right, but since then there had been no opportunity to see her. Ruth, appreciating the demands on his time, spent her days anxiously at home trying to occupy herself with domestic chores, and getting in Mirka's way. It was therefore a welcome interruption when she received word from Manfred Issitt that delivery of the Romanov necklace was scheduled for later that week.

Sitting in a comfortable armchair in the familiar library at Leaminster Gardens, Ruth listened attentively to Mannie while he briefed her. 'Go up to London on Thursday and stay at the Viceroy overnight. On Friday afternoon, travelling first class, take the twenty to two train from St Pancras back to Kelsford. On the journey you will be contacted by the courier who will give you the necklace. All that you need to do then, Rushka, is to take it to the bank, where you hand it over to Max.'

'How do I make contact with the courier?'

'You don't. The courier has been given a full description of you and will seek you out. I suggest that to make things easy you wear your dark blue dress and the broad-brimmed hat you bought in Vienna.'

Ruth gave a small grimace. It seemed unusually casual for such an important assignment, but she knew better than to question Mannie's arrangements. 'When I hand the package over what's Max going to do with it?'

Issitt paused for a moment, gazing into the fire. There was really no reason for Ruth to know anything more about the operation, but if something went wrong extra information could be helpful. 'The package will be kept in the vault at the bank until Sunday, when the courier for the final leg of the transfer picks it up. Then we're finished with the matter. The necklace's next stop will be somewhere in America.' Ruth nodded gratefully. That was what she needed to know.

Thursday morning was wet and miserable, and well suited to Tom Norton's mood. The previous evening, on receiving a message from Ruth that she was going to London for a couple of days, he had taken an hour out from work and gone to see her at Victoria Road. The hour had spread into two as, relieved to see each other again, they had talked about what had happened since they last parted. When he left the house late in the evening Tom knew she was going to London for the Pipeline. Although he did not know anything more, it bothered him considerably, and he knew he would not be happy until she was safely back.

Paying the hansom's florid driver a shilling, Tom pushed open his umbrella and held it over his head against the driving rain. As the cab departed he turned and looked across the road at the bleak uninviting gates of the borough lunatic asylum.

It had been his intention for some time to visit Joseph Langley. Tom knew he had been putting it off because he did not want to do it – but the previous night, after he left Victoria Road, he had made his mind up. The case against Devlin was complete, and the magistrates had committed him on a charge of murder to the next assize. The quest for the second arms cache was, in the absence of any further information, like searching for a needle in a haystack. To his added chagrin, Sam and Reuben's observation of Susan Burke's house had been totally unproductive, and he had cancelled it the day after Devlin's arrest.

Tom had never been inside the asylum before. The tall grey stone four-storey building, surrounded by an eight-foot wall, was at the top of a hill on the southern outskirts of the town. Near enough to Kelsford to be easily accessible, it was to an extent shielded from view by the high trees of the municipal cemetery opposite.

A double gate, let into the wall for delivery vans to pass through, housed a small keep door to enable those on foot to gain entry. It was here that Tom presented himself, ringing the bell. For some strange reason, now that the decision was made and he was here, Tom was quite looking forward to seeing the old man again. There were things he wanted to talk to him about and advice he wanted to seek. Although they had never been friends – Langley had no friends, nor did he ever seek to make any – Tom had always felt a sincere respect for his abilities, and now understood a lot more about his previous position.

The narrow door was opened by a uniformed gatekeeper. 'Detective Inspector Norton. I telephoned earlier and spoke to a Mr Latham concerning a visit to a patient.' It seemed ironic to Tom that while there was no telephone connection between Long Street and the Metropolitan Police, it was an easy matter to telephone the lunatic asylum from Fred Judd's office and arrange an appointment.

Admitting him, the attendant left him alone while he went to find the asylum superintendent. Shaking the rain from his umbrella, Tom looked round with more than a casual interest. Inside the gates, the attendant on reception duty was housed in a tiny hut slightly larger than a sentry box. It was of sufficient size for him to be seated out of the weather next to an open coke brazier that was glowing brightly against the inclement morning. The heady fumes from the coke were overpowering, and Tom wondered how the man could sit by it without passing out.

A wide and neatly tended gravel driveway, flanked by green lawns, led past an ornamental fountain before reaching the entrance to the main building. From the doors of this entrance a portly figure in the dark navy tunic and flat-topped kepi of the borough asylum was beckoning the policeman to join him.

Fletcher Latham greeted Tom warmly: visitors to the asylum were few and far between. Once a patient was admitted to the care of the institution, relatives and friends rarely continued to check their progress. The superintendent, thought Tom as they shook hands, resembled a jolly Father Christmas in blue serge, with twinkling eyes and a nicotine-stained white beard. Setting a brisk pace, he trotted off, leading Tom through a maze of anonymous passages and keeping for the most part a few paces ahead. 'Joseph Langley's been with us for almost five months now, and if I'm perfectly honest he's made little progress. His problem, as you're aware, is drink related. It's a never-ending circle – when he's in drink outside he's subject to *delirium tremens*; in here, with no drink available, he continues in a similar vein owing to the lack of it. He is, I fear, a classic example of how the demon drink can bring heartache to the world of man. Had he signed the pledge in earlier days he would, I'm sure, not be in his present lamentable state.'

Anticipating a temperance lecture, Tom hurriedly changed the subject. 'How many inmates do you have, Mr Latham?'

'The Lord has consigned well over a hundred to our care,' the superintendent replied, as he went through a door into another of the interminable corridors.

Tom bit his tongue, and avoided asking how many souls the local authority in its infinite wisdom had added to that number.

Before long Tom had completely lost his sense of direction, but knew they were deep inside the main building. As they passed through what appeared to be the dining hall towards an open area a muted hubbub became apparent. Although the sound appeared to be human voices it had an eerie quality that Tom could not place. Superintendent Latham led him into a wide ill-lit corridor which, to Tom's horror, was the nearest thing to bedlam he could imagine. Men and women in various states of dress and undress were wandering aimlessly up and down the stone-flagged floor. Almost without exception each was in a world of his or her own. Gazing around, Tom estimated quickly that there were between twenty and thirty of them, the majority being men. The stale smell of unwashed bodies hung like an oppressive cloud. Nothing in his experience could have prepared him for the pitiable scene.

An elderly man with bare feet, wearing only a striped cotton nightshirt, crossed in front of them, counting his paces aloud. On reaching fifteen he turned abruptly and began retracing his steps, starting again at one.

Tom was sickened by the abject state of the humanity surrounding him. Like the old man in the nightshirt, most of the inmates were relatively quiet; those who were talking at all seemed to be communing solely with the voices in their heads. It was the sound of their individual muttering that combined to create the low babel. On his left a pale-faced man of about thirty with shoulder-length matted hair, squatting on his haunches, was engaged in an animated conversation with himself, breaking off after every few words to shake his head and laugh at an inaudible joke.

Lengthening his pace, Tom headed for the door at the far end. Dark cell doorways to left and right indicated the living spaces occupied by these unfortunates, who at the end of their allotted exercise period would, he presumed, be shut away again. A thin man and a woman standing close together just inside one of the doorways caught his attention. The woman, a squat figure with the doughy features of an imbecile, had her thin dress unbuttoned almost to her navel, exposing flabby sagging breasts. The man, dressed in a dirty grey shirt and trousers, half-turned at the sound of their footsteps on the stone floor. Tom saw that his trousers were undone and the woman was masturbating him.

'Cover yourself up, Lizzie, and stop that. You've been told before. That's a bad thing to do.' The superintendent's tone was severe but not unkindly.

The woman did not reply. Her mouth was parted in a vacant grin, revealing the gaps in her twisted and discoloured teeth. Her hand continuing to move rhythmically back and forth along the man's erection.

'Dear God . . . how do you work in a place like this?' Tom asked his guide.

'You become accustomed to it, sir. These are the ones that can be trusted out for a while. There is, I regret to say, debauchery: there's nothing you can do to stop it. Once your visit is over I'll come back in here to keep an eye on them. Your man doesn't come out now. He used not to be too bad, but lately with no drink and the DTs he has to stay in his cell.'

At the end of the exercise corridor Latham unlocked the door; as soon as they were through he secured it behind them. They were now in a narrow gas-lit passage, almost identical to a prison cell block. The only sound was a high shrieking from the first cell. Dropping the flap, the superintendent indicated to Tom a figure writhing on the floor. The tight webbing jacket, secured by thick leather straps, that encased the unfortunate from head to toe made it impossible to see whether it was a man or a woman. The animal screams made Tom's stomach turn as he recollected what the attendant had just said about Langley: 'with no drink and the DTs he has to stay in his cell'.

They stopped two doors further along and, selecting a master key, Fletcher Latham unlocked and opened it. Seated on the single bench seat, looking vacantly into space with his back to the brick wall, sat Joseph Langley. Like the man in the exercise corridor, he was wearing only a cotton shirt and a pair of stained trousers. Without the benefit of a belt or braces to support them, the trousers bagged loosely at his shrunken waist, and it was obvious that in order to walk without them falling down Langley would have to hold them up with his hands. It was his face that was most shocking. Aggressive strength had been replaced by a vacuous empty expression, while the piercing eyes were dead and sunk deep into their sockets. Tom reckoned the old man had lost between two and three stone in weight since he had last seen him, and had aged almost beyond recognition.

The room was ten feet by six, painted dull green and virtually the same as a police station cell that was used for drunks overnight. A shaft of light was admitted through a tiny barred window set high in the wall. Apart from a slop bucket in one corner there was no furniture, and there were no personal effects to identify the occupant.

'You've got a visitor, Joseph.' The superintendent spoke in a slow clear voice.

The figure on the bench made no reply. There was no indication he was even aware of their presence. A drool of spittle began to trickle slowly from the corner of his mouth into his long unkempt beard. The stench seeping from under the lid of the loosely covered bucket was nauseating.

Tom felt an immense pity welling up. The Joseph Langley he knew had been strong-willed, meticulously efficient and single-minded, his sole weakness a love of strong drink. A man who relished power and control over the lives of others – who had gone home one night and had a bad dream, as a result of which he had been locked away from the world for ever. Which, Tom wondered, was the more barbarous, the world in which the old man was now living or that from which he had been removed? The one thing that was plain for anyone to see was that Joseph was now completely mad.

'Hello, Joe.' Tom spoke quietly, hoping that the sound of his voice would evoke some response. Langley continued to stare blankly at a point somewhere between the dark reaches of his mind and infinity. Reaching into his pocket, Tom pulled out the two-ounce packet of Bondsman that he had brought. He shot a look of enquiry at Latham, who signified his assent.

'He can have it, my dear sir, by all means, but he won't be able to smoke it. They're not allowed matches or anything inflammable.'

Tom nodded in understanding. Bondsman was Langley's favourite: he used to smoke an ounce of it a day. To his surprise, the old man's gaze had dropped and the dead eyes were staring at the packet in Tom's hand. Tom held it out tentatively. A thin arm extended slowly towards him, the wrist no thicker than a child's. Tom saw that the dirty nails of the claw-like fingers were uncut and discoloured. Very gently he pushed the packet into the outstretched hand. Equally gently Langley's fingers closed round it and, without looking, pulled it close to the emaciated body. Then his blank eyes fixed on the cell floor again, the trail of spittle joined by a second.

Tom knew he had to leave, to escape from this house of horrors into the outside world. Turning abruptly, he nodded to Latham and walked out into the corridor where, totally defeated, he slumped against the wall while the superintendent double-locked the cell door. Gathering himself for the journey back through the throng of inmates in the next room, Tom strode off down the corridor. The animal screams from the end cell had, he realised, ceased. Suddenly, from the dark hole behind him, he heard a thin reedy voice raised in anguish. 'Thomas . . . ? Thomaaas . . . !' Tom felt his gorge rising.

Chapter Twenty-Seven

Standing on platform one at St Pancras station, Ruth experienced the feeling of isolation that often overcame her in such places. The rain that she had left the day before in Kelsford was now hammering down on the vaulted roof, adding to her mood. So far she had seen no one who looked remotely likely to be her contact. She could only assume that he or she had boarded the train before her arrival. A few feet further along the platform two army officers broke off their conversation to give her an appraising stare. One of them, in a dark green tunic and braided forage cap, gave a decidedly ungentlemanly leer. The look she returned would have deterred even the most ambitious admirer.

Mirka gave sixpence to the porter, who stowed their shopping and overnight bags in the otherwise empty first-class compartment. With a polite touch of his cap, he moved off to assist a well-dressed gentleman and his wife with their suitcases. Once aboard, Ruth continued to scrutinise the platform for any late arrivals. The two officers were once more in earnest conversation. Their presence served only to remind her of Colonel Franz von Rasche and the nightmare journey on the Vienna Express.

Settling into her seat as the train pulled gently out of the station and through the suburbs towards open countryside, she began to wonder if something had gone wrong and the handover was not going to take place at all. Wrapped in a voluminous brown overcoat, the figure sitting opposite mumbled something unintelligible in Russian. 'What did you say?' she asked.

'I said that I don't like London and I don't like trains; they're noisy, cold and dirty. And where is this kulak who's supposed to have met us?' Mirka slumped morosely in her seat, glaring out of the window at the passing fields.

'How do you know it's a kulak we're supposed to be meeting?' Mirka had been in a mood since they left Kelsford. Ruth imagined there had been further trouble between her and David over some infidelity, real or imagined.

'It's obvious that only a rich land-owning kulak would be able to make such a journey out of the old country.'

Ruth glared across the swaying carriage. It was time Mirka and David Capewell were married, she decided, so this bickering would end. 'If you can't talk sense then be quiet,' she said coldly. The other woman lapsed into a sulky silence that lasted for the next eighty miles, until the locomotive pulled into Market Harborough station.

At the last moment, as the guard began his walk along the coaches to check that all doors were secured, a man and woman wearing anonymous clothing suddenly appeared from the station buffet. Crossing the platform, they climbed swiftly up through an open carriage door and disappeared from view.

'I think this is it,' Ruth said softly.

It was some minutes after the train left Market Harborough and was gathering speed along the straight approaching East Langton that two shadowy figures appeared in the corridor, and the door of their compartment slid open. Ruth scrambled to her feet in astonishment and grabbed Lukeria Yavlinskiy in a tight embrace. Grinning like a small boy, Grigoriy followed her in. After the initial greetings and excited chatter the Yavlinskiys explained their presence in England as they settled comfortably into the plush seats.

For some considerable time they had been planning to escape from the shadow of the two mighty empires under which they lived. With the inevitability of a comet hurtling towards the sun, sooner or later the monolithic dynasty of Franz Josef would collide with the Imperialist Romanovs on the far side of the Carpathians. Before that happened the Yavlinskiys wanted to be living safely in a different part of the world. Two recent events had provided both the catalyst and the means for them to carry out their plan. The first was the theft by the Sons of Latvia of the Romanov necklace and the ensuing sale of it to the Pipeline. Ruth wondered wryly how much the Pipeline, in the form of Joachim Schallmeier, had paid these people, but she knew it would only be a fraction of its true value. The second was the fact that Lukeria was two months pregnant. Spurred on by a desperate desire for their child to be born either in England or the United States, they volunteered to make the hazardous journey with the necklace across Europe. In exchange for their undertaking, the Pipeline agreed to pay the couple's passage to America and, once there, to make sufficient funds available for Grigoriy to set up a small printing business in one of the rapidly expanding Midwest towns.

As things turned out they had encountered no difficulties. Taking a week's leave from his job at the Kaiserhof, Grigoriy and Lukeria packed only sufficient possessions as would fit into two suitcases and climbed aboard the Vienna Express. By the time anyone in Unghvar realised they had disappeared they were on the train from Paris to Boulogne.

Safely in London, they had spent three days at Moses Grodzinski's home in Brick Lane. Ruth did not doubt that her uncle's role was to examine and verify the authenticity of the jewels, and to report to the Pipeline that all was well before the couriers moved on. It was his suggestion, with security in mind, that they should catch an earlier train to Market Harborough.

Lukeria put a hand inside her coat and, unbuttoning the front of her loose-fitting dress, pulled out an oilskin package sown with a stout sailmaker's thread. Taking it from her, Ruth excused herself and went along the corridor to the ladies' lavatory.

The remainder of the journey seemed to fly by, and all too soon the driver began to slow as they came into Kelsford Midland station. Descending from the train to take their parting, Lukeria and Grigoriy hugged first Ruth then Mirka. 'I shall miss you,' confided Lukeria to Ruth. 'Do you think you'll ever be able to come and see us in America?'

Ruth nodded tearfully; the unexpected encounter combined with the swift parting was affecting her. 'Yes, Lushka,' she replied. 'Possibly soon.'

Watching the train pull away on the final leg of its journey to Sheffield, where the Yavlinskiys would change for Liverpool, Ruth wiped her eyes and, putting her arm round Mirka's shoulder, set off towards the steps to the main concourse, where David would be waiting for them with the brougham. It was not merely the parting that was upsetting her. For some reason she did not understand, Ruth felt a deep envy of her friend for the unborn child she was carrying.

It was five minutes past five when David pulled up outside Kelsford Bank of Commerce. Although the main banking hall was closed there was still plenty of activity, with cashiers balancing the tills and the clerks finishing up the day's business. Leaving Mirka to wait outside, Ruth made her way through the double doors and up the central staircase to the management suite. Turning left, she headed for Max Peters' office. The panelled door was ajar and she entered without knocking. Max was looking out of the window into Cumberland Place, and had obviously seen her arrive. Turning to face her, he gave Ruth a nervous smile.

'Have you got it?' he asked urgently.

Ruth studied the pudgy young man standing before her. His habitual immaculate uniform of dark morning coat and grey trousers did little to conceal the signs of strain on his face or the dark circles under his eyes. If she had not known better she might have assumed that the stress was the result of his concern about the present undertaking, and the responsibility of looking after almost a million pounds-worth of diamonds. Cynically she chose to believe it had more to do with the recent death of Joshua Howkins, and the loss of a large amount of money. Enjoying herself immensely, Ruth wondered how much he had actually lost. It was, she knew, well in excess of £20,000. Possibly forty, even fifty.

'Yes, Maxwell, I've got it.' Turning away from him, she opened her overcoat and, from a concealed pocket inside, withdrew the parcel. The hand that took it from her was clammy, and she saw that Peters was beginning to perspire. 'I don't know why you're sweating,' she said coldly. 'I'm the one who's taken all the risks.' She knew that this was the first time Max had ever been involved in operational work; he usually just arranged funding.

'Have you checked it?' he demanded nervously.

'I've brought you the package as it was dispatched and given to me,' Ruth replied deliberately. 'It was sealed then and it's sealed now. If you choose to open it that's your responsibility, but I'll need a witness.'

Max studied the parcel in his hands indecisively. He knew that through his inexperience he was making a fool of himself – to this woman whom he so heartily detested. 'No, you're right. We'll put it in the vault as arranged.'

'You put it in the vault: my part is ended. I've completed my handover to you, and now I'm going home.' Ruth knew she was being unnecessarily awkward, but her dislike of Peters was getting the better of her.

'You think you're very clever, don't you, Mrs Samuels?' The bitterness and frustration of the last few days gave Max Peters' voice an edge that bordered on hysteria. With the death of Joshua Howkins he had lost the greater part of his personal fortune, and unless something dramatic happened very quickly he would have to go to his father for help. That, he knew, would be an extremely delicate matter. His action in extending Howkins' credit was already the subject of the partners' severe censure, and when it was discovered how deeply he had committed the bank it was highly unlikely he would be given the directorship that he so coveted. 'Let me tell you this, you cocky bitch. In a month's time, when I'm a member of the board of this bank, you'll not have such an easy ride. I'll have you out before the end of next year – that I promise you!' Without another word, the parcel firmly in his hand, he brushed past her and out of the room. Alone in the walnut-panelled office, Ruth smiled to herself.

It was late that night when Tom arrived at Victoria Road. Although he had not sent word Ruth was pleased to see him, but perturbed at how worn out he looked. Instructing Mirka to prepare some food, she took Tom through into the drawing room.

'You look tired.' Her voice was full of concern. She knew the stresses that he had been under during the past week.

'I've had a bad day,' he said, not wanting to discuss his visit to the asylum, 'and I've been worried out of my mind about you. I want you to stop this Pipeline business.' Blurting this out before he could stop himself, Tom knew he had made a mistake from the sudden hardening in her expression. He had been allowed to see into her hidden life and now he was interfering. He realised that he should have known better, as Ruth was not a woman to be told what she could or could not do; but his anxiety for her safety overrode his better judgement.

Ruth felt the anger rising in her chest, then unexpectedly it started to diminish. There was something in Tom's eyes, a haunted look that later she would have to know about. Relaxing, she leaned forward, kissed him softly, then pulled away. 'I've already made my mind up about that. I'll not be doing any more work for them.' Tom's relief was tangible. He put his arms round her and held her for a long time. She could feel the tension draining away, but she knew there was something more; it was what she had seen in his eyes. 'Can you stay tonight?' she asked.

He nodded. 'With the wedding tomorrow Ann and Jamie have moved to the shop, and Kelsford police can do without me.' He did not add that he had only been home to sleep once that week, otherwise catnapping in his office.

'Good,' she smiled. 'I'm famished, and I've got a lot to tell you.'

As had become their habit, they lay side by side under the bedclothes and talked once the lovemaking was over. Tonight was different. Instead of clearing away the ghosts of the past, they quietly made plans for the future.

Tom told her of his trip to see Joseph Langley. Ruth quickly realised this was the source of his earlier unease and listened without interrupting. Even though he disliked discussing the horrors of the asylum, and dwelt upon Langley and his deterioration, it was impossible to conceal his overall revulsion for the place. The memory of the avuncular superintendent, trotting round and chattering about temperance and the Lord committing souls to his care, kept intruding into his mind. Tom wondered if spending his life within the walls of the asylum had not unbalanced him a little.

Lying on his side, Tom contemplated Ruth's profile as she regarded the corniced ceiling. Her nose was slightly too long and straight to be classic, he thought, and her chin just a touch too aggressive . . .

'What are you thinking?' she asked, turning to face him.

Silent for a moment, wondering how best to phrase it, Tom ran his fingers over her shoulder and gently down to her well-rounded flank. 'I want to stop this hiding. I want us to get married.'

Ruth did not answer for a while. She had no problem with the proposal; it was a matter of timing. Sitting up, she pulled the covers around her and, reaching into the drawer, took out a cigar; nowadays she always kept Goodman's in the bedside table. Following what had become almost a ritual, she lit it and then, after inhaling deeply on the pungent tobacco, passed it to Tom. Leaning on an elbow, she said thoughtfully, 'Yes, I'd like to marry you too, and you're right: it's time to come out into the open.' The encounter with Max Peters had affected her as profoundly as had Tom's with Joseph Langley. It was time to stop complying with the wishes of other people and become her own woman again. There would, she knew, be problems over marriage, if only because of their religious differences, but this was not insoluble. As regards to making their relationship public knowledge the opportunity was immediately to hand. 'Tomorrow. We'll do it tomorrow.'

Having come to terms with her brother's involvement with Ruth Samuels, Ann had given them her blessing. His mother and father knew nothing, but Tom would have been surprised if Reuben was still ignorant. Without being prompted, Ann had included Ruth among her wedding guests, and she was included in the party at the top table because of her social standing. It would be a simple matter for Tom to ensure he sat next to her at the reception, and make it plain that they were there as a couple.

They talked for a long while afterwards about the prospect of their own marriage, and Ruth told Tom about the Romanov necklace.

In deference to the tradition that the sun always shines on a wedding, Saturday morning was bright and cheerful, despite a chill wind that was blowing in from the east. The weather held and at two o'clock the happy couple, with Sam Braithwaite as best man and Jamie as page, were duly married at St Mary Magdalene's Church in Old Friars.

David Capewell picked Tom up in the brougham from Sidwell Place and then returned to Victoria Road to collect his mistress. Ruth, who loved weddings, both Jewish and Christian, had been careful not to dress in such a way as to upstage the bride. Mirka tutted and fumed as the morning ticked by and her mistress refused to accept any of the choices of dress that she laid out for her. Eventually they settled upon a smart cream skirt and cut-away three-button jacket in the same colour, over a high-necked white blouse and ivory waistcoat and topped off with a small, narrow-brimmed hat trimmed with cream ribbons. The effect, Tom thought, was stunning. Taking her seat next to him in the carriage, Ruth reached over and removed the pin from his dark silk cravat, replacing it with a small antique stickpin that she took from her sleeve. 'An early wedding present,' she said, kissing him on the cheek.

After the ceremony the wedding party repaired to the first-floor room of the Rifleman. Seated together, and chatting like an old married couple, Tom and Ruth were given several enquiring glances by other guests. Short of an official declaration, they could not have made their situation more apparent.

During the unavoidable speeches Tom gazed contentedly round the room. The party was a relatively small one; Jesse and Susan Squires were next to Sam Braithwaite and Harry North, and Walter and Julia Mardlin were at the next table. Since Julia had taken Ann's job at the Rifleman they had become good friends, while Tom often dropped in for a pint with Walter when they were off duty. As the guests mingled before taking their leave, Walter touched Tom on the arm and said quietly, 'Are congratulations in order for you as well?'

Barely audibly, Tom replied, 'We think so, when things have settled down a bit.' Mardlin beamed and nodded his approval, before confidentially passing the news onto his wife.

After the bride and groom had departed for their new home in Oxford Road and the majority of the guests had left, Tom indicated to his parents that he wished to speak to them. In the kitchen, where it seemed like only a week or two before that he had secretly met Saul Meakin, Tom told his parents of his plan to marry Ruth. To his surprise they accepted the tidings well, better than he expected, which led him to suspect that his sister had already primed them, so they had time to become accustomed to the idea. His mother gave Ruth a kiss and a hug, while Ernie shook hands with his son and wished them both well. It occurred to Tom that, with Ann now married, they were probably concerned about him living on his own at Sidwell Place.

Ruby Norton suggested they should spend the evening together and that they and Ruth could get to know each other better over a quiet drink and supper. Ruth agreed, tremendously relieved at how easy they were making it. She doubted that the Jewish elders would be so accommodating when they found out.

The evening of good food and pleasant conversation came to an end soon after eleven o'clock when Ernest went downstairs to close the bar. Ruth, although she had been careful to drink only wine throughout the festivities, was by now beginning to feel the effects and was relieved to make what she hoped was a dignified exit on Tom's arm. Had she but known it, the Nortons, initially extremely nervous of this wealthy society lady, had taken a firm liking to her. Far from being a snob or socialite as they feared she might be, Ruth had impressed them with her down-to-earth nature, and an ability to hold drink that would have warmed the heart of any licensed victualler.

In the hansom cab on the way back to Victoria Road, Ruth snuggled up close to Tom. 'You can stay tonight provided all that you want to do is sleep,' she mumbled.

'I'm sorry, but I didn't understand a word of that,' he replied, laughing heartily at the fact that this was the first time he had ever seen her drunk.

Max Peters spent the following day in a state of nervous anxiety. As the afternoon ticked away towards evening he checked the clock incessantly. It was five to six now. The American should be here in the next few minutes, he thought, glad that his ordeal was almost over. Whatever he might think of Ruth Samuels, the woman had, he knew, the one quality he lacked – nerves of steel.

He looked at the clock for the hundredth time: three minutes to six. The package, which he had collected personally from the bank's vault at a quarter to six still sealed in its oiled silk wrapping, lay on the rosewood desk in front of him.

A discreet tap on the office door by the elderly watchman who was responsible for security at weekends heralded the arrival of the man for whom he was waiting. Seconds later Max was face to face with the big American whom he had last seen at the Flixton canal site earlier in the year.

'I wondered if it might be you,' he said nervously, 'what with your involvement with Joshua Howkins and all.'

Sangster gave the banker an expressionless stare. 'What involvement would that be, Mr Peters?'

Max shuffled his feet and dropped his gaze. 'Sorry, my mistake,' he said in a low voice.

'You have the item I've come to collect?' Unlike Peters, the American was in perfect control. Realising that the banker was an amateur, which was potentially dangerous, Sangster wanted to take possession of the goods and leave as quickly as possible. He was booked onto the eighteen minutes to seven train to London, and by nightfall he could ensure that the necklace was hidden away securely, ready for onward transmission.

Peters handed over the bulky package hastily, like a child playing pass the parcel. Taking from his pocket a tiny penknife that he used for cutting the ends of cigars, the Texan carefully parted the stitches and opened out the oilskin. A glittering array of diamonds, linked together by some unknown craftsman to form a three-tiered necklace of shimmering light, slid out onto the desktop. Max Peters let out a gasp. He could imagine it adorning the throat of a Russian princess at an imperial ball.

The American was more sanguine. 'They all seem to be there, Maxie,' he said in a satisfied tone. The necklace appeared to have a life of its own as he allowed it to flow through his fingers back into its wrapping, before he placed it in the large leather Gladstone bag that he had brought with him.

'Is that all there is to it?' Max could hardly believe that after all his waiting and worrying everything had been handled so quickly.

Moving towards the door, Sangster halted, turned and smiled thinly, 'You had better hope so, Maxie, because if there's anything wrong I'll definitely be back.'

Downstairs in the empty foyer of the bank the watchman and Sangster's two escorts, provided by Clancy Taft, were waiting patiently. At a nod from Peters the watchman unfastened the side door and Taft's men stepped out into the street. Having checked that all was in order, they signalled to Sangster, and the three men climbed into a waiting hansom. As they left Cumberland Square a second hansom, parked further along, moved off at a discreet distance behind them.

Eugene Leschenko had waited all his adult life for this day. His dream of leading the Great Latvian Revolution and taking his place alongside such men as Józef Piłsudski in Poland and Giuseppe Garibaldi in Italy was now within his grasp.

Checking his cheap pocket watch against the kitchen clock propped on the mantel shelf, he saw that they agreed: twenty-nine minutes past six. Miroslav and Hans, along with Klara and Oleg, were already at the station waiting for the courier.

Their plan was simple. The men were to spread out and mingle with passengers on the station forecourt where the cab would drop off its fare. Klara would remain at the main entrance and keep a lookout for any police. Each was in possession of a detailed description of the American, whom Eugene had been assured was the courier. As soon as he climbed out of the cab they would overpower him and take the diamonds, then split up to confuse any pursuit and disappear into the surrounding streets. Because Sangster knew him, Eugene could not go to the station with the others.

Sitting at the bare kitchen table, Leschenko pushed aside the empty glasses with which they had toasted the mission before everyone left and drummed his fingers nervously. He was becoming bored with spending his life in hiding.

Having left London, he had come to Kelsford as instructed by Ruth Samuels, finding accommodation in an empty house in Century Courtyard near St Andrew's Street. The Latvian did not know that he was within a five-minute walk of Connor Devlin's hideaway at Susan Burke's. His house, which had two bedrooms upstairs and a kitchen and tiny parlour below, belonged to an old Jewish cobbler who lived in the shop next door. It was, even by Leschenko's diminished standards, a hovel. The only amenities were cold running water, a gas cooker and a mantle in the parlour. A communal privy was shared with the four other houses in the courtyard. With nowhere else to go now that Brovnic and Nina Volputin were in custody, the rest of the group joined him to await details of the work that Ruth had for them.

Eugene could still feel the icy thrill that shot through his body when the woman told him he was to steal back the Romanov necklace. The sensation was almost sexual; he could not believe what was being offered. Ruth Samuels would give them the time and day along with details of the handover. All that they had to do was intercept the American at the railway station before he could board the train, and rob him. Ruth would then give Eugene £100,000 when he handed the necklace over.

The Latvian scratched his armpit, into which a flea had found its way from the straw mattress where he and Klara slept. A slow smile of satisfaction spread across his unshaven jaw as he stroked the ends of his waxed moustache. Privately he had decided to amend Mrs Samuels' master plan to accommodate his own ambitions. Why should he take £100,000 for an item worth a million, he asked himself? Once his people were in possession of the necklace they would quietly disappear to Paris. Eugene was certain that his anarchist contacts there would be able to dispose of the necklace for much more money than the Samuels woman was offering. After that he would have sufficient resources to set up a movement in Latvia that within six months would take him to the pinnacle of his political ambitions: the establishment of an independent government with himself at its head. For this reason, he did not want Sangster to know he was part of the group involved in the forthcoming robbery; later he was going to need the guns stored in the American's warehouse.

Drawing the cork from the small stone jar in front of him, Leschenko poured a generous measure of dark rum into one of the dirty glasses. He grimaced in satisfaction as the potent liquor hit the back of his throat. Soon he would be back home again, drinking hundred per cent proof grain vodka; meanwhile all he could do was wait until the others returned.

Lucas Sangster took a long careful look out of the hansom cab window before opening the door. Padraig Brady checked the other one, then nodded. 'It seems all right, sir.' Ever cautious, the American was in no hurry to descend. Brady and his partner McAteer were, Clancy had assured him, totally reliable, but he would still wait until he was personally satisfied that the coast was clear. There were very few people about in the gathering gloom of the station forecourt. A middle-aged man and his wife carrying heavy suitcases emerged from the entrance to the booking hall, and the man started to come over to see if the cab was available. The driver, another of Taft's men, made a short negative gesture with his whip, and the couple went off towards another hansom.

Standing in the booking hall entrance were two foreign-looking men in their early thirties smoking cigars. From the way they were comparing times on their watches it looked as if they were waiting to meet someone on a later train. At the tall vaulted arch leading out into the main road a thickset man in his twenties with a Van Dyck beard was chatting to a pale-faced young woman. Neither had any luggage to indicate they were about to make a journey. Nice figure under the shabby overcoat, thought Sangster idly, but her nose was too big for her to be attractive.

Out in the street he could see that the second hansom with Taft and two more of his men had just pulled up; they were to remain outside as back-up in case something should go wrong. Sangster was well aware that this was the most dangerous part of the operation: it was always possible that they had been followed from the bank. Once he was aboard the train to London, though, he would be reasonably safe. Making up his mind, Sangster pushed open the door.

Watching from the booking hall entrance, Miroslav Draskovic and Hans Schneider dropped their cigars and began to run the ten yards to where the man, now out of the cab, was turning to close the door. At the same moment Oleg Cherkashin, breaking away from Klara, came in from the opposite side.

As they began to run both Miroslav and Hans realised that the American was not in fact closing the door but speaking to someone else inside the cab. In the seconds it took them to cross the forecourt two men, short batons in their hands, bundled out of the cab to face them. Oleg saw what was happening just before his companions began to grapple with the two bodyguards and Sangster, putting himself behind his men, shouted to the driver. Grabbing at the back of Sangster's overcoat, Oleg attempted to drag him off the hansom step. Holding the door frame with his left hand, Sangster brought the butt of the pistol in his right hand back and down in a savage blow, catching Oleg across the forehead and opening up a gash three inches long. Momentarily stunned, Cherkashin released his grip and stumbled back. The cab was already moving towards the street as Sangster slammed the door behind him. Realising their quarry had escaped, Miroslav and Hans, aided by Oleg, broke away from McAteer and Brady and began to run – this time for their lives. The hansom, ploughing through the station gateway, blocked off Taft and his men just long enough for the three would-be robbers to escape through the goods entrance to the station and out into Coal Lane at the back of the loading dock. Despite giving chase, Taft and his companions did not find them again.

Some considerable time later, mud-spattered and its horse blown, Sangster's cab pulled up outside Derby's railway station. Its single passenger boarded the first train travelling north, away from London and any other reception party that might be waiting for him. Sitting alone in his firstclass compartment with the blinds drawn, Lucas Sangster put his mind to the evening's events. After some consideration he decided that once he had handed over the package to the ship's captain in Liverpool, for the final leg of its journey, he would return to London and make a few enquiries. Additionally, he deliberated, when he went back to America in January he would invite Max Peters along with him for a short holiday. It would, he felt, be most productive to introduce the devious little banker to one or two influential gentlemen in New York. A certain 'Mr Spanner' would be most interested to make his acquaintance.

The incident was reported to the police at Long Street station by a worried stationmaster, perturbed at the violence that had erupted on his forecourt. It took a further half-hour for news to filter through from the front enquiry desk to Jesse Squires in the detective office, who in turn passed it on to Tom Norton.

The only occupants of the office at half past seven on a Sunday evening were Sam Braithwaite and Jesse Squires. Coming through, Tom pulled up a chair and sat down. He lit a Goodman's Special and passed his cigar case to the others. 'Presuming that this is not just a fight between rival factions over a matter we know nothing of – what do you think, gentlemen?'

Sam inhaled deeply on his cigar and, picking a piece of loose tobacco from his lower lip, considered his reply. 'Claude Inskip – the stationmaster – isn't given to panicking. I've known him since I was a kid. My dad was a porter at the station until he died. So if Claude says there was a serious fight I think we should listen to him. From what he says the men in the hansom spoke with Irish accents, while the others appeared to be foreigners. The Irish we know about. What about the foreigners?'

'I think there are two questions we need to think about.' Jesse took up the debate. 'We know who the Paddies are, but we don't know about the others – although it's fairly safe to presume they're one of the anarchist groups. Secondly, we don't know why they were fighting. The inference is that the foreigners attacked the Irish. If it was a gang fight of some sort, then why did the foreigners initiate it when they were patently outnumbered?'

Sam looked pensive. 'I agree with Jesse. The only foreign groups that we know of are the East European anarchists. Up to now there's been no indication of any such cells operating in Kelsford, but with the way things have been going in the last few months anything's possible. It seems likely that the Paddies had something the others wanted – witness one of them jumping back in the hansom and it taking off like the Charge of the Light Brigade – and that it all went wrong. And from the description of the man in the cab it's got to be our American, Sangster – not an Irishman at all.'

Tom took a pull at his cigar and peered at the other two through the haze of tobacco smoke. He knew exactly what the American was carrying. What he did not know was who had tried to relieve him of it. Pensively he said, 'Yes, I agree it was probably Sangster. The fact he made off confirms that something highly illegal was taking place. Jesse, give the description of these foreigners to the men who are on night-shift, and we'll see what happens. Meanwhile, let's get off home for an early night.'

Tom suddenly had an eerie feeling that Joseph Langley was sitting in the corner of the room, mocking him.

Chapter Twenty-Eight

Saul Meakin was in a bad mood. Three months had elapsed since he had moved into the room at 54 Dakin Street with Queenie Bartholemew. It was certainly not a love match; the fact they both frequented Crooked Edie's initially put them on speaking terms, which gradually gravitated towards a business arrangement. In exchange for a free lodging the Weasel kept watch for Queenie while she was soliciting, and ensured that the approach of a policeman on his beat did not interfere with her working. The disadvantage for the little man was that on the occasions when she brought a client back to the room he had to go out or hide in the clothes cupboard. This evening she had arrived back with a drunken soldier from the barracks, and made it plain to Weasel that she wanted him out for the next half-hour.

Turning his coat collar up against the cold night air, Meakin trudged off along Dakin Street towards Hanover Row and the Green Parrot. Hope she gets rid of him before he sobers up, he thought maliciously, otherwise he'll want his money back when he sees her with the light on. It was half past ten; he would go back no later than eleven. Like the inquisitive little rodent after whom he was named, Weasel could not resist the opportunity to slip into the darkened Century Courtyard. There might be something left out worth stealing, he thought, or he might get a view through an uncurtained window of some woman – perhaps more attractive than Queenie Bartholemew – getting undressed for bed.

A light in the downstairs room of the house at the far end drew him like a moth. Sidling up to the glass, he peered in cautiously. There were four men and a woman in the front room, and from their raised voices it was apparent that they were arguing. They were speaking in a foreign language, and one of them had a gun.

Earlier that evening, on his first visit of the night to the Green Parrot, there was talk in the bar about a fight at the railway station that evening.

Meakin, always interested in any information however apparently irrelevant, listened closely. The cause of the disturbance was not clear, but it had been caused by a bunch of foreigners, 'bleedin' Russian Yids' the burly coal heaver with the twisted back was telling his companion who, from the smell of him, Meakin decided, was enjoying a few pints before going to his night's employment removing night soil on the dilly wagon. Whatever the situation, Weasel was reasonably sure that Mr Norton down at Long Street would be interested in locating these foreigners, and he set off at a trot towards the town centre.

In the house Leschenko, who when he was told of the failed robbery had gone into an uncontrollable rage, was still furious with his companions. His dreams of a triumphal return to Latvia had suddenly turned to ashes; he was in a dangerous mood. A pistol lay on the table in front of him, and he threatened to kill anyone who tried to leave the house. They had all experienced his temper before. Waving the Mauser at Miroslav, he hissed, 'And you, you yellow-gutted sister shagger – you're not fit to call yourself a Latvian, even less a patriot! We had it in our hands! The means to carry through the revolution, and you ran away!'

Draskovic knew he needed to be careful. All evening Eugene had, between bouts of rage and depression, been steadily emptying the stone flask of rum. Although the worst of his tongue-lashing seemed to have subsided, he was still extremely unpredictable. There was little doubt in Draskovic's mind that, despite what the police thought, Leschenko was responsible for cutting the woman's throat in Dutfield's Yard. 'Listen to me. We were outnumbered. There were two hansom cabs of bodyguards with the man. No one told us that. He was supposed to be alone.' It was, he thought, the twentieth time that he had made this statement, and it made no difference to their leader.

Leschenko pointed the gun unsteadily at him. 'I should kill you, you miserable coward.'

Weasel had not gone more than three streets away from Century Courtyard when, turning into Appleton Road East, he encountered Sergeant Ambrose Quinn and two constables. Downe Street was not in a district where policemen patrolled singly. This evening, as night duty sergeant, Quinn had decided to walk the two officers detailed to cover this part of Downe Street from the police station to their beat. The sight of Weasel Meakin scuttling along, obviously on some nefarious errand, was not to be ignored.

'Just what's your hurry, then?' Quinn demanded, placing himself in the little man's path.

Weasel, making a swift appraisal of the situation, decided to impart his information directly to the police officers and collect his information money from Inspector Norton later. Quickly, and in low tones, he spoke. The sergeant listened and, looking up at the night sky for a moment, as if seeking confirmation of the decision he was about to make, said, 'You'd better show us this house.'

The sharp rapping on the front door brought a sudden halt to the dispute. Schneider held his hand up for silence, and the clamour of argument ceased abruptly. Klara doused the oil lamp, plunging them into darkness. Everyone remained still.

Outside a voice with a distinctly Irish accent, and the unmistakeable tone of someone not used to being ignored, commanded, 'Police! Open the door immediately!'

Leschenko picked up the Mauser and cocked it. Putting a hand to his lips, he moved silently into the hall and knelt on one knee at the side of the stairwell, the gun trained on the front door. Klara and Miroslav ran quickly past him and up the stairs to the top of the landing. There was another pistol in the bedroom, but Draskovic did not know if he would have time to get it before the police came in. Schneider and Cherkashin pushed their backs against the wall of the parlour and waited.

The insistent voice came again through the thin door panels. 'We know you're in there. We saw you put out the light. Open the door now or we'll break it down.'

They all remained immobile, hardly daring to breathe. A brief silence was followed by a splintering sound as Quinn's boot hit the door just below the lock. His second kick smashed the keep from the frame and the door burst open, letting a draught of cold air into the hall and silhouetting the huge figure of the sergeant in the moonlight.

The crash of the shot and simultaneous blinding muzzle flash of Leschenko's revolver were numbing in the confined space of the hallway. The first bullet took Ambrose Quinn in the throat; the second hit him in the chest. Because of his bulk the impact did not succeed in knocking him backwards, and momentum carried him forward into the hallway where he collapsed, dying, at the foot of the stairs.

Following immediately on Quinn's heels, Constable Noah Rodwell had no chance to avoid the same fate as his sergeant. Two more shots in quick succession hit him in the chest barely an inch apart, killing him instantly. Walter Swain, the third officer, spinning round and attempting to run for cover, was shot by Leschenko in the back, falling to the ground on the hard cobbles just a yard away.

Eugene Leschenko stood up straight, the smoking pistol still pointing at the doorway. The first of the others to move was Hans Schneider. 'Come on, we've got to go!' His voice was charged with panic. 'We have to leave, *sofort, du verdammtes Arschloch!*'

With the calmness of a man who is in total control, Leschenko replied coldly, 'Yes, we have to leave now. Drag those two inside and shut the door. No packing, just your coats. Miroslav, bring the other gun. Move. We've got no time.'

In under five minutes they were assembled in the hallway. A small group of neighbours had gathered in the courtyard, trying to see what was going on behind the splintered front door. It was an area where the arrival of three policemen at a house after dark was a matter for little curiosity, but the sound of shots was a different matter. On Leschenko's order the anarchists burst out into the courtyard at a run when the broken door was thrown open. Leschenko and Draskovic fired a couple of shots each over the heads of their neighbours, sending them scattering for cover and deterring any pursuit. Within seconds they were out of the courtyard and running for their lives.

Stopping after a few minutes, several streets away, Leschenko signalled for them to gather in the gateway to a small gas mantle factory. Listening intently, they heard the sound of police whistles as officers from the next beat, attracted by the gunfire, arrived in Century Courtyard. So far there were no sounds of pursuit. Catching his breath, Leschenko explained very quickly where they were going, and the five of them moved on, more cautiously now.

Weasel had almost been caught out when Leschenko stopped, but it was not difficult for one man to come to a halt undetected while following a group. Having guided the police to the house in Century Courtyard, Meakin had slid away and waited out of sight behind a rain barrel at the courtyard entrance as Sergeant Quinn began to bang on the door. What followed left him speechless and terrified. As he watched two of the men drag the bodies into the house, he had remained frozen in his hiding place. As people began to emerge from the adjoining houses and the foreigners made their frantic getaway, Meakin had decided to risk following them. It was pure avarice that motivated him. He knew that the killers' hiding place would be worth at least fifty pounds from Inspector Norton, and there might even be an official reward as well.

From the deep doorway of a hardware store he watched as the four men and the woman moved off again, turning right at the end of the road. Another ten minutes brought them to Collett Lane. At a signal from the one with the big moustache, who appeared to be their leader, they moved to where the back of the premises gave onto an area of waste ground, keeping close to the old factory wall, and disappeared from Meakin's view.

Whispering to the others to keep quiet, Eugene positioned Hans on one side of the gate at the back of the factory and Oleg on the other, then rapped gently on the panelling – two short, two spaced, two short, exactly as Sangster had done the previous Sunday.

The sound of footsteps on the other side of the gate, followed by the bolt being drawn, told Leschenko what he wanted to know: as on his previous visit one man was on the gate while the other remained inside the building. A quiet voice asked, 'What is it?'

Muffling his tones, Eugene replied, 'I've got an urgent message from Mr Sangster. He gave me an envelope and told me to bring it here.'

A second bolt slid back and the gate swung open a few inches to reveal the pockmarked man, shotgun at the ready. 'Give it to me then,' he grunted.

'Not so loud, you fool. Do you want to let everyone know where we are?' The censure in Leschenko's voice was sufficient to put the man off his guard slightly, and, as an automatic reaction to the words, he shifted his gaze momentarily to check up and down the alley. It was precisely what the Latvian wanted. Stepping in close to the man, he thrust the barrel of the Mauser under his jaw and pulled the trigger. The sound of the shot, muffled by the scarf wrapped round the gun, still sounded loud enough to be heard inside the building. Stepping over the body, Leschenko moved stealthily towards the doors of the loading bay while Oleg and Hans hauled the inert figure inside the yard and secured the gates. From inside he could hear stertorous breathing.

'Brough? Is everything all right out there? What the hell was that bang?' Brindley Stokes sounded nervous.

Eugene remained silent. The sound of the heavy lock turning as Stokes decided to investigate set a fresh charge of adrenalin pumping through his system. Cautiously, he pushed the revolver back into his belt and opened his lock knife. Stokes stepped into the light as the door swung back, shotgun trailing loosely at his side. The Latvian, pressed against the wall, seemed to melt into the brickwork.

He need not have worried. Stokes' attention focused on the figures at the opposite side of the yard and the man lying prone in the gateway. Dropping to one knee, he threw the shotgun up to his shoulder. Stepping in behind him, before he could even sight the weapon, Leschenko pulled the man's head back and drew the blade of the knife across his throat.

Now that they had secured access to the building, the anarchists were able to work at a less frantic pace. Dragging the two bodies out of sight into the loading bay, they secured the outer gates and the doors before making their way across the ground floor and up the stairs into the storage area. Once they were on the first floor, where the guns were hidden, everyone began to relax a little. The light from the oil lamp that Stokes had left burning gave adequate illumination for Eugene to show his companions the arsenal of weapons and ammunition.

'What are we proposing to do now?' asked Klara matter-of-factly. Although there had been no opportunity for discussion, she and the others seemed to appreciate the position they were in. There was not a country in the world where you could gun down three unarmed policemen and not expect the pursuit and retribution to be unrelenting.

Leschenko, hands clasped behind his back, began to pace up and down. 'We're safe here for a while. No one other than the American Sangster and his men know of this place. With the police crawling all over Downe Street and Sangster occupied disposing of that necklace, his men will stay away for a day or two at least.' He paused to pull a Winchester from one of the boxes. 'Tomorrow morning, as soon as there are people about, we'll slip away from here, quietly make our way to the station and catch a train out of here.'

'It may not be as simple as that, Eugene.' Klara, as ever, was the objective member of the group. 'The other people in that shit heap where we were living will have given our descriptions to the police. They'll be checking everyone at the station, and anywhere else.'

'These English are fools,' Leschenko replied loftily, resuming his pacing. 'Remember, I have been arrested by them once and hoodwinked them with ridiculous ease. Tomorrow we'll leave here and meet again in London.'

The others exchanged surreptitious glances. Not for the first time they were beginning to suspect that their self-styled leader was slightly unbalanced. He had completely underestimated the security surrounding the Romanov necklace when it left the Kelsford Bank of Commerce, and his shooting of the policemen was an act of absolute folly.

'Any of you who don't trust my judgement should say so now,' he said, a dangerous edge to his voice. He gave a hollow laugh. 'And if it doesn't work out we have enough weapons here to hold off an army.'

Saul Meakin hurried through the silent byways back to Century Courtyard, where a great throng of people was gathering round the narrow entrance from Porter Street. Pushing his way to the front, he was confronted by two constables who had blocked off the entrance to the courtyard. 'I must speak to Inspector Norton,' he whispered.

'He's busy. Get on your way, you nosey little bugger!' Constable Ewart Buck was still visibly shaken by what he had seen in the hallway of the house behind him. Had Ambrose Quinn chosen to walk him and Seth Drew out to their beat instead of Noah and Walter, it would have been him lying dead in the hallway now.

Meakin saw there was only one way to get past the officer – and of speaking to Norton without the growing crowd of onlookers suspecting what was happening, always a prime consideration when one earned a living as an informant. 'Fuck you!' he shouted, in a voice loud enough to attract the attention of the tall bowler-hatted figure on the other side of the yard – and gave the startled officer a sharp push in the chest.

Caught off-balance, Buck reeled backwards, grabbing at the little man's coat and holding on tight. Keeping his footing, the policeman swung Meakin off his feet and sent him crashing to the ground.

'What the bloody hell is going on?' Tom bellowed as he dashed across to the struggling pair.

'Need to talk to you, sir,' Weasel gasped, in a voice just loud enough for the detective to hear. With the grip that Ewart Buck had on his neck and throat, it would have been impossible to do more than croak.

'Nick him, and bring him into the yard where we can deal with him.'

Tom was shaken to his foundations by what had happened, as was everyone else at the scene of the murders. He had been about to leave Long Street with Sam and Jesse just before eleven o'clock when word of a shooting in Century Courtyard came in. Arriving at the scene of the crime twenty minutes later, he could not believe the carnage that greeted him. Walter Swain and Noah Rodwell were spread-eagled in the hallway, blocking the front door, while Ambrose was dead at the foot of the staircase. Jesse and Sam were trying to piece together what had happened from the neighbours while Tom awaited the arrival of the head constable and Dr Mallard.

Forcing himself to appear casual, he said, 'All right, Ewart, go back to the entrance. This one isn't going anywhere.' Releasing his hold, Buck glared venomously at Meakin and strode back to his position with PC Drew.

'What do you know about this?' Tom asked quietly.

Meakin had just finished relating his story when Archer Robson and Mallard arrived, closely followed by Kerrigan Kemp. Leaving the doctor to examine the bodies, Tom took the head constable into the tiny kitchen, where he told him as much as he knew, including the information about the killers' hideaway. 'It's a disused blacking factory. I know the location quite well. The front's on Collett Lane and there's a walled delivery yard at the back that gives out onto waste ground and the railway lines. If it's what I think it may be we could have major problems.' Tom kept his voice low.

'You think it's the weapon store we've been looking for?' Archer Robson's mind was working along the same lines as Tom's.

'It's likely. They obviously have knowledge of Sangster and his activities. Maybe they've traced his movements to the old factory and worked out what it is. If we're right we can surround the place while it's still dark and deal with them tomorrow morning in daylight.'

Archer Robson took a long minute to reply. 'We need to do the job properly. Do you want me to stay here while you work out what to do with the factory, or do you want me to sort out that end of things?'

Tom did not need to consider his decision, although he respected Archer Robson for allowing him the choice. 'I'll take the factory – but I'm going to need more men than I have at present. If I go back and turn out as many officers as I've got firearms for, would you be prepared to bring in the army to help us?'

Archer Robson nodded. 'Cover the place first. It's midnight now. I'll get word to the commanding officer at Sevastopol Barracks to turn out a company of armed troops to work with you. It won't be light for another four or five hours, so you should have time to get everything in place. Good luck, Thomas.'

Briefly shaking hands before parting, the two men went back into the hallway: Archer Robson to deal with the grisly business of clearing up the murder scene, Tom to catch the killers.

By half past two Tom Norton had a total of fifteen officers, including Inspector Caleb Newcombe and Sergeant Alf Vendyback, at strategic positions around the blacking factory in Collett Lane, armed with shotguns and revolvers. Fred Judd, who had been summoned from his bed, was at Long Street liaising with the army.

Tom, Jesse Squires and Harry North were crouching behind the darkened first-floor windows of Weissman's clothing factory, opposite the anarchists' hiding place. Harry pressed the release mechanism on his pistol and checked the action by spinning the chamber, for the third time in as many minutes.

'Will you put that sodding gun down and concentrate on what's going on across the road?' snarled Squires.

'Be quiet, both of you. Harry, close the gun and leave it alone before you shoot one of us,' growled Tom sourly.

In the resulting silence he checked that everything was in place. From where they were they could see directly over the road, fifty feet away, the boarded windows of the old blacking factory, the feeble light of a single oil lamp filtering through several gaps. That, at least, was confirmation that Meakin had brought them to the right place.

To the left, a hundred yards down the road, Sam Braithwaite, Reuben Simmonds and three uniformed men were crouching behind a barricade of hastily stacked beer barrels, brought from the yard of the nearby Fleur-de-Lis. At the opposite end of Collett Lane Caleb Newcombe and his men had quietly manhandled a four-wheeled carter's wagon, its wheels muffled with sacking, to a position across the junction with Raglan Street. Alf Vendyback was in position on the waste ground at the rear, covering the double gates. Charles Kerrigan Kemp was in the background, discussing something with a figure in an ankle-length overcoat who was busily setting up a tripod and camera.

Tom badly needed the soldiers to arrive. Archer Robson had, he knew, sent word to the barracks for the commanding officer to be woken and given his message. Their firepower was essential: if the anarchists, as he suspected, were sitting on an arsenal of weapons, then the shotguns and pistols with which his men were armed would be ineffective. He needed heavy calibre military rifles.

Another hour elapsed, and a thin grey light began to break through the night sky behind the derelict factory. Tom spotted two files of red-coated soldiers, one on each side of the road and hugging the fronts of the houses, making their way cautiously up Collett Lane to Braithwaite's men behind the barrels. An officer in a dark blue tunic spoke briefly to Sam, then, signalling to the Senior NCO beside him and keeping in the cover of the buildings, he darted across to the doorway of Weissman's and disappeared.

A minute later Tom was joined at the window by Captain Palmer-Daley. Walter Mardlin took up a position next to Jesse Squires below one of the windowsills, a Martini-Henry rifle in his hands. Although he could not speak to him while his officer was present, Tom was pleased to see him: Walter's experience might be invaluable as the night wore on. Tom moved further away, back into the workshop, to where the women's sewing benches were situated – near enough to be aware of any developments but far enough not to be overheard. 'I'm pleased to see you, Captain. Your assistance is much appreciated.'

'Let's clearly understand, Detective Inspector, that I'm in sole control of any soldiery here, and any police action that takes place is entirely your responsibility. My men will contain any situation and offer protection to your officers. However, any action you initiate against the people in the building opposite you alone must answer for.'

Tom wondered how long the officer had been rehearsing his little speech. It was obvious that the incident between them in the charge office had left the young captain with a grudge that he intended to continue. Whatever happened in the next few hours Tom was going to be on his own: no shared discussions or joint decisions.

Tom remained poker-faced. 'Of course, Captain. May we now discuss the deployment of your force?'

While Palmer-Daley remained with Tom, Sergeant Mardlin slipped off to ensure that his men took up the positions that they had been allocated. Because Sevastopol Barracks was a transit camp it had not been practicable for the Commanding Officer Colonel Sinclair to muster a complete company: the best that could be managed at such short notice was twenty men. Five were left under Palmer-Daley's direct control with Tom and his men, in the room overlooking Collett Lane. This was where they anticipated the major action would take place. Three more were left at each end of the street on the barricades, which the police were already manning, and the remainder were sent through a side alley to the wasteland at the back of the yard and loading bay.

It was twenty-five past four when Sergeant Mardlin reappeared in Weissman's workroom. Outside a clammy mist hung a few feet above the cobbled roadway. Taking a quick look to left and right from the window, Tom could just make out shadowy forms crouching in the cover of the building line, the soldiers distinguishable from the policemen by their trailing rifles, despite the darkness still enshrouding the street below.

'It's a good time to rush the building. We could be in before these people knew what was happening.' Palmer-Daley's tone indicated it was not a suggestion, which could later be construed as collaboration. The tone was a clear criticism at the lack of action on Tom's part.

'No. Time's on our side. As long as we stay under cover they'll have to make the first move. As far as we know they have no food or water in there. I'm prepared to sit here all day.'

Inigo Palmer-Daley snorted disparagingly. This was the sort of reaction he had expected from a civilian police officer who was allowed to command what should have been a military operation. On being awoken as duty officer during the night and told of the situation, he had been annoyed that Colonel Sinclair had briefed him to take his instructions from the senior police officer, in everything except matters relating to the safety of his men. It was patently obvious to anyone with a grasp of strategy that now was the time to attack, while the enemy was asleep.

His pistol still holstered, hands behind his back, he walked determinedly to the middle window and looked out. There was no sign of life opposite. From the corner of his eye he caught sight of Walter Mardlin at the next window, rifle barrel resting on the sill, looking across at him anxiously. Sergeant Mardlin DCM: because he had served in India and shot a few natives the man thought he knew everything. What a timid bastard to hide away under a window from a few untrained foreigners.

Mardlin, his profile hardly visible beneath the sill, began to put his hand up to warn the officer to get away from the window when the glass exploded inwards, and Palmer-Daley was knocked off his feet by the impact of a .44 Winchester rifle bullet.

Chapter Twenty-Nine

Having made his proposals for their escape the following morning, Leschenko set his companions to loosening the boards at the windows and creating gaps through which, if necessary, they could establish a field of fire. Breaking open the case on the top of the nearest stack, he handed a Winchester and a box of ammunition to each of them. As an extra precaution he propped a second loaded rifle against each of the windows, along with a small pile of ammunition boxes. He instructed two of the group, Oleg and Hans, to position themselves at the windows that ran along the back of the room and had a view over the rear yard and the wasteland beyond.

Preparations completed, he and Miroslav went to explore the remainder of the warehouse. The ground floor was damp and musty, and as they looked to see if there was anything that might be of use to them Miroslav almost fell into a large hole. A section of floorboards had been removed, presumably to effect repairs elsewhere in the factory. Next to the gap they discovered that Howkins had stored tins of paint. They had obviously been there for some time, as those at the bottom of the stack were corroded and had leaked, leaving a small lake of dried paint. Examining the labels in the flickering lamplight, they saw that all the tins bore War Office insignia. Either Howkins had purchased a bulk consignment or, in common with the rifles, they were illegal.

Leschenko and Draskovic returned to the first floor, then climbed the rickety staircase to the one above. Two unmade palliasses, the blankets untidily thrown back, indicated that this was used by the guards as living quarters. An ancient coke-burning stove had been set up next to the back wall, with a makeshift chimney poked out through the broken window next to it. The remains of a loaf of bread and a greasy shoulder of mutton stood next to unwashed plates on an upturned box. Behind the box there was a half-empty crate of Starbright Pale Ale.

Gathering up the bread and the meat, Eugene and Miroslav pushed half a dozen of the bottles of beer into their pockets and rejoined the others. No one had eaten since late afternoon on Sunday and the simple fare, washed down by the cold ale, was soon consumed. Worn out by the previous day's events, they all settled down to get some rest.

Thin shafts of grey light were filtering through the gaps in the window boards when Klara awoke. She and Eugene had lain down on his old green coat near the stairwell, and she had fallen into a deep sleep. Not sure why she had woken, Klara listened intently for a full minute, but could detect nothing out of the ordinary. Shifting her position to ease her cramped muscles, she pulled herself onto her hands and knees.

'What are you doing?' demanded Leschenko, immediately awake.

'I'm going for a pee,' she whispered, trying not to disturb the others, and without waiting for his reply she stood up and made her way cautiously down the narrow wooden stairs to find a private corner on the floor below.

As she returned, Klara crossed to the nearest gap in the boards and peered out of the window. What she saw in the rapidly growing daylight sent shivers of fear coursing through her body. Along the road a barricade of beer barrels had been erected, behind which blue-helmeted figures were crouching. Some wore the scarlet tunics of soldiers, others the dark uniforms of police. Looking to the left, she saw that the other end of the road was blocked off as well. 'Wake up! Everyone, wake up!' she hissed urgently.

Leschenko eased the board further to one side and checked up and down the road. Doubtless the factory opposite was teeming with Imperialist troops and police. Who, he wondered, was the Ochrana spy who had led them to this hideout. Looking over his shoulder at his four companions, he wondered. Hans, the German, brought up in the Austro-Hungarian Empire. Miroslav or Oleg, the cowards who had allowed Sangster to escape – if indeed they had not already betrayed him. Klara, the Bohemian Jewess. Was she really in league with the Pipeline? Had she betrayed them to the police? If it was one of them he would find out, and he would kill the traitor himself.

'We will fight,' Leschenko said in a flat, determined voice. 'We're in a strong position and have more ammunition than they can dream of. After nightfall those of us who are left will escape across the wasteland at the back.'

From their expressions it was obvious that the others did not share his confidence. The last few hours had led them, too late, to identify the flaws in his leadership.

A movement on the first floor of the clothing factory opposite caught Leschenko's attention. Kneeling down, he worked the lever of his rifle to push a shell into the breech. The figure of an army officer in a patrol jacket was silhouetted at one of the windows. Eugene could clearly see his blond side-whiskers and the silver badge on his forage cap. Taking careful aim, he pulled the trigger and watched the man fly backwards as if kicked in the chest by a mule.

Without taking his eyes from the building opposite, Walter Mardlin gave the order, 'Open fire, five rounds rapid!' Taking quick aim, he sent five rounds in quick succession at the boards covering the window. As soon as his men stopped firing he turned to see what was happening behind him.

Palmer-Daley, bleeding heavily from a wound in the right side of his chest, was being manhandled to a safe position by Squires and North. Tom and the sergeant crawled along the floor to where he was lying. The captain's face was ashen and he had already lost consciousness, whether from the severity of the wound or from shock it was impossible to judge. Mardlin pulled a field dressing from his pack and, ripping open the blue tunic, applied it to the wound.

'The Fire Brigade ambulance is standing by at the back of the building in Duke Street, sir,' gasped North; it was heavy work moving an unconscious man.

'Get him down to it, then come back here as fast as you can. For Christ's sake be careful.' Not for the first time Tom gave thanks for Fred Judd's organisational skills. He would bet a month's salary that Judd had also made sure Arthur Mallard would be with the ambulance.

Palmer-Daley was the first. Tom wondered how many more there would be before the day was out.

'I told you Palmer-Daley was a stupid bastard. Not even a raw recruit would stand in front of an open window.' Mardlin was down on one knee beside Tom, watching the darkened windows opposite. After the volley there had been no further signs of movement.

'Will your men take orders from me?' Tom asked.

Mardlin nodded. 'If I tell them to.'

'In that case we'll play a waiting game. During the day they'll get hungry and thirsty: as far as we know they haven't got any provisions. If it's still going on this evening we'll rush them after dark – but it should be over before then.'

Both men knew that unless the anarchists lost their nerve, or were killed by sniper fire, it would be difficult to shift them without incurring heavy casualties, even though they were outnumbered. That they intended to fight had been made obvious.

'Is there any chance of getting a field piece onto the waste ground and blowing out the yard gates?' Tom asked speculatively.

Mardlin shook his head. 'We need to stay out of rifle range. Their ranging shots could do damage to our own men on this side of the building. You'd do better to put charges against the gates and blow them in.'

This time it was Tom who shook his head. 'Too risky. The sappers would have to come in under their rifles. Forget it.'

Several shots from the far end of the blacking factory ricocheted noisily as a careless member of Braithwaite's team showed his helmet above the barricade.

As the morning progressed the bright sunshine of early autumn took the chill off the austere workshop where Tom and his men waited patiently, for something that would allow them to take the initiative. The slightest movements from the street or in Weissman's drew a hail of bullets from the defenders, who had stripped the boards from the windows to widen their field of fire. The deadly effectiveness of the Winchester repeating rifles was worryingly apparent. Tom had given orders that the police and soldiery were to fire on any target that presented itself.

Inside the warehouse the atmosphere was charged with tension. Leschenko paced back and forth, a rifle in one hand, the Mauser in the other. Holding out during the day and escaping after dark was, they all knew, their only hope of survival. Huddled by the wall at the far side of the room overlooking the waste ground, Oleg Cherkashin took a quick look over the windowsill to see what was happening. All appeared to be quiet. Since daylight had revealed their situation, any moves by the police on the wasteland to close in on the building had been prevented by Hans and Oleg, both good shots, who amply demonstrated the difficulty of approaching a defended position across open ground.

Dropping down again, Oleg stole a look at the next window, six feet away. Hans Schneider was sprawled next to it, back against the wall, his feet splayed out in front of him, his rifle across his knees. Worn out by the last few hours, the Austrian had slipped into an uneasy sleep. In contrast to Oleg's thin moustache and narrow Van Dyck beard between his lower lip and the cleft in his chin, Hans wore a thick neatly trimmed spade beard. Its normally manicured edges were, Oleg noted, blurred with two days' growth of untidy whiskers. Two days in which all of their lives had been irrevocably changed. Cherkashin wondered if, with his own dirty shirt and stubbled face, he looked as unkempt and grubby as Schneider. None of the others looked much better. Across the room Miroslav, his braces hanging loose and a pistol thrust into the back of his trousers, was manning the firing point at the far end, while Eugene and Klara stared intently from opposite sides of a middle window, which, now devoid of boarding and glass, was letting in a refreshing breeze. It must, Oleg thought, be about nine o'clock.

He stole another look at Hans, who was oblivious to what was going on around him. Everyone else had their backs to him. With infinite caution Oleg stood up and moved to the centre of the room where the ammunition boxes were stacked. To anyone watching he was going to collect a fresh box of cartridges. As his hand reached out to the top packing case a bullet from one of the barricades whistled through the opening by Leschenko. Immediately the three defenders began to shoot down into the street.

Cherkashin quickly picked up the oil lamp from the top of the box. In two strides he was on the wooden stairs leading down to the floor below, and began to tiptoe down the narrow flight. His disappearance had not been noticed. Afterwards it would be too late; Eugene would not be able to spare anyone from the gunfight to come and find him. Oleg had made his mind up that he had no intention of dying for a lunatic and doomed ideal, and intended to slip down to the ground floor and find a way out. That there had to be more than one door he was certain – a staff entrance or a small delivery bay. If he could find it he would hide away until dark, and then make an escape attempt.

In the closed-up ground floor it was still pitch black. Moving away from the stairwell, Oleg struck a match and lifted the chimney of the lamp. As the wick flickered into life he heard Leschenko's angry voice at the top of the stairs. 'Oleg! Are you down there? What the bloody hell are you doing? Get back up here now!'

Shielding the glow of the lamp from the view of anyone above, Cherkashin moved towards the middle of the room. Ten feet away he could see a stack of tins, and decided to investigate them before working his way round the walls. He could hear Leschenko's voice – angry now and accusing. Oleg decided to hide behind the stack of tins: if Eugene came downstairs he would shoot him. If that happened they might even stand a chance of surrendering.

A clatter of boots sounded on the stairs. 'You treacherous bastard, Cherkashin. Where are you?' It was Leschenko, and there was murder in his voice.

Oleg darted quickly towards the tins. If he were quick enough he could get a shot at the Latvian before his eyes became accustomed to the poor light. Without warning his right foot stepped out into empty space, where the floorboards had been removed. He felt a sudden chill of terror as, losing his balance, he began to fall. In a frantic effort to save himself he allowed the rifle to drop from his right hand into the darkness below. As he threw out his left in a vain hope of catching onto something substantial, he flung the lamp away from him.

Lying twenty feet down on the rubble-strewn floor of the disused cellar, the Moravian was aware of an incredible pain in his left leg below the knee. Easing himself onto an elbow, he realised that he had been temporarily knocked out by the fall, and that he was seriously injured. The pain in his leg was intense, and he knew it must be broken. Cracked ribs made breathing a separate agony.

What he was going to do Oleg did not know. As he lay there, something caught his befuddled attention: a bright light was shining through the split floorboards above him. His first thought was that the others were looking for him with the spare lamp, and he felt a tiny ray of hope. He could say he had come downstairs to search for an escape route for all of them. Then something else began to register: the bright light was accompanied by a crackling, roaring sound. Dear God, the building was on fire!

Gathering all his strength, Oleg attempted to reach the rifle, so he could use it as a crutch. The pain from his broken leg was beyond anything he had ever imagined. As he passed out the last thing he saw was a long splintered shard of bone poking from his trousers where his shin should have been. So deep was the unconsciousness into which his attempted movement put him that even the pieces of burning timber falling from the disintegrating floor overhead and setting his clothes alight did not wake him.

Leschenko staggered back up the stairs, coughing from the thick black smoke that was billowing up behind him.

'*Was passiert?*' yelled Hans. By now everyone was aware of Oleg's defection.

'Bastard's set fire to the place,' gasped Leschenko. 'He fell down a hole in the floor and his lamp smashed on that paint. It's going like a torch!'

On the other side of the road Tom Norton was becoming worried. Two more soldiers and one of the policemen manning the barricades in Collett Lane had been wounded by the sniper fire. He was beginning to wonder if his plan to sit the defenders out was practicable. From their vantage point on the first floor the anarchists had a clear field of fire. At the back of the premises most of the police and soldiers had withdrawn another fifty yards to take cover in some railway trucks. A runner from Fred Judd had brought a message, asking Tom if he wanted the head constable to come in and take command. Tom declined. This was his problem and he would solve it himself; besides, Archer Robson would have enough to do dealing with the shootings in Century Courtyard.

An exultant shout from Harry North brought him scrambling back to his viewpoint. 'Smoke, sir! Far end of the building at the bottom!'

Everyone's attention fixed on the ominous twists of black smoke pouring from the ground floor. The indistinct sound of an explosion was followed by a sheet of flame erupting from the end window.

'All of you, keep your heads down!' Tom felt a surge of elation. How it had happened he could only guess – but it didn't matter: it altered the entire situation. Now he could win. Amidst the clamour of excitement at first they did not hear the dull, thumping noise of something being dragged clumsily up the staircase. As the noise got closer they turned and watched in puzzled curiosity as a tiny figure, swathed in ammunition bandoliers and dragging several more behind him, poked his spiky ginger head above the stairs. Hardly able to stand under the weight of the cartridge belts, Arthur Hollowday dragged his load across the floor, his spindly legs buckling under his efforts.

'Ammunition, Mr Norton, sir!' he panted excitedly. 'Brought it from the wagon at the back. Thought you'd need it, sir.'

Tom and Walter were the first to react. In a flash Tom knew that Judd would never have permitted the boy to come here; he must have slipped away without anyone's knowledge.

'Jesus Christ! What are you doing here, boy? Get out!' Dropping his rifle, Mardlin threw himself across the room towards the lad.

'Rapid fire! Give cover!' Tom bellowed at the soldiers, who were gaping at the small figure. Already the sudden movements in the workroom had drawn fire from the blacking factory, and as Mardlin sprang up to grab the boy a hail of rifle bullets hit the plaster of the workroom and spattered round the walls.

The burst of shooting was over in a matter of seconds. Tom, crouching low, sprinted across to where the sergeant was lying prone, covering the boy with his body. 'Are you all right, Walter?' he gasped.

Mardlin gave an affirmative grunt and rolled to one side, keeping Arthur between them. 'You stupid boy, Arthur! How the hell did you get up here? Christ, you gave me a fright. Come on, let's get you off home . . . Oh Jesus . . .'

Arthur had a surprised expression on his freckled face. It was impossible to tell if it was because of the unexpected confusion that his arrival had caused, or whether it was because of the small round hole in his right temple, where a rifle bullet had hit him a split second before Walter Mardlin had taken him off his feet.

Rolling away, Tom ran to the window and, standing in full view, emptied his revolver at the figure of Klara Brandes kneeling in the window opposite, a smoking Winchester in her hands. He now knew exactly what he had to do. Deliberately he walked back to where the child's body lay, impervious to the renewed firing. Pausing for a second to look down, Tom picked up one of the ammunition packs and threw it across his shoulder. Next he went to the corner and picked up a spare Martini-Henry. Checking it was loaded, he continued to the stairs.

A quiet voice said, 'I'll come with you, Tom.'

Silently he nodded, drained of all emotion. Without looking back, he said, 'Take charge here, Sergeant Squires.'

Tom quickly outlined the basics of his plan to Mardlin as they sprinted round the back of the building into Raglan Street, where Caleb Newcombe's barricade was across the junction with Collett Lane. Earlier in the morning, from his elevated viewpoint, Tom had seen that one of the borough fire engines had been brought into Raglan Street. In the present situation, though, there was no way that the firemen could tackle the blaze in the blacking factory. Tom and Walter needed a piece of their equipment.

Out of breath and panting, Tom found the fire superintendent and explained what needed to happen. Two minutes later, with a ten-foot ladder between them, he and Mardlin were standing against a house wall just inside Collett Lane. On a command from Inspector Newcombe, the soldiers and policemen behind the carter's wagon poured a deluge of fire at the windows of the warehouse, while Tom and Walter made a dash to the alley that led along the side of the old factory, separated from the large yard with double gates by an eight-foot wall. They knew they had to hurry: Leschenko and his group were probably already trying to escape from the burning building, and Tom and Walter would have to move fast to cut them off. Throwing the ladder against the wall, Tom stripped off his jacket and dropped it on the ground; Mardlin did likewise with his tunic. Tom climbed up quickly and poked his head cautiously over the top. It was better than he could have hoped for. This part of the yard was cut back in an L shape to follow the wall of disused stables, creating a narrow walkway. Tom realised that if they went into this space they would be out of sight of everyone outside, and consequently could expect no backup. Reaching down, he took the ammunition bandoliers and then the rifles from Walter, slinging them over his shoulders before dropping down into the walkway. Seconds later he was joined by his companion.

They moved warily to where the walkway gave onto the open yard. It was perfect. A five-foot high stack of crates had been abandoned ahead of them, almost blocking off the confined area and making it virtually invisible to anyone coming into the yard. There was a clear view of the loading bay, so anyone crossing the forecourt would come into their line of fire.

Leschenko knew he had to make a decision quickly. The floor beneath their feet was becoming hot, thick smoke was beginning to fill the room and flames were licking up through the floorboards at the far end. It would only be a matter of minutes before the stairs were alight and they were trapped. Eugene hoped that Oleg Cherkashin did not die quickly.

'We've got to get out!' bellowed Miroslav in his ear, the roaring of the fire beneath them making it difficult to hear what anyone was saying.

Leschenko nodded. Waving to the others, he shouted, 'The yard! We'll make for the yard and hold out there.'

Taking Klara's hand, he began to descend the burning staircase. The four of them only just reached the bottom before the flames erupted up the stairwell into the room they had just left. The heat and smoke were unbearable, and Eugene knew they had to get out before they were overcome or lost their sense of direction. Dropping to his knees, with Klara holding onto his belt, he began to crawl towards the loading bay door. As he did so her grip slipped, and she gave an involuntary scream. Pausing, Leschenko took precious seconds to reach back and grab her wrist, guiding her hand back to his belt. Glancing back, he saw her face was smoke-blackened and sooty, and her eyes were closed. For a fleeting moment he caught sight of Hans and Miroslav holding onto her skirt.

The smoke was so dense that the Latvian had to crawl on his belly to drag oxygen into his lungs. He knew that if he opened the door and admitted new air into the enclosed space, the entire room could explode in a fireball. It was a chance they had to take. A few feet further on his outstretched hand reached the wall, which was already warm to the touch. Inching along, he found what he was looking for: the timber of the doorframe. Realising that he had stopped, the others crawled alongside. Unable to speak, the Latvian closed his fist and shook it in a gesture of triumph. Taking as deep a breath as he could in the scorching smoke, he grabbed the now unconscious Klara round the waist and stood up, feeling desperately for the door handle. It took him five endless seconds to find it, and he thanked his stars that, being brass, it was not yet too hot for him to grip. With the last of his strength he pulled. Fortunately the heat had not yet warped the door. Dragging it ajar, Leschenko forced himself and Klara out into clean air. Miroslav and Hans just had time to follow before a mighty roar indicated that the fire behind them was feeding on the new source of oxygen. Hans slammed the door tight and collapsed with the others in the confined passageway that led to the loading bay doors.

It was several minutes before, coughing and gasping, they were able to take stock. They all had singed hair and scorched clothing, while Klara's dress was badly torn and smouldering. Overcome by a fit of coughing, Leschenko eventually recovered his breath and spat up a globule of black phlegm. From the upper storey came first the repeated firecracker sounds of ammunition exploding, then a mighty crash as one of the floors collapsed.

'We have to keep moving. It's only a matter of time before this part goes up as well.' The others nodded dully. As if to emphasise Leschenko's words, the door through which they had just passed began to crackle, a dull, hungry glow showing round its edges.

'What weapons have we got?' asked Hans.

The result was not impressive. Leschenko had kept hold of his Winchester, which had five shots in the magazine. Klara and Hans had lost their weapons in the desperate crawl through the smoke. Miroslav, by some miracle, had kept hold of his rifle, and still had the old Russian army pistol stuffed into the back of his trousers; this he gave to Hans.

'Can we surrender?' asked Klara resignedly.

The expression on Leschenko's face sent a fresh chill of fear rushing through her. 'I'll kill any one of you who tries to surrender,' he snarled. 'We'll get out of this or die trying. Do you understand?' None of them had the strength to argue. 'The first thing we must do is get into the yard before they realise where we are, and establish defensive positions round the walls. I'll go out first with Miroslav. You and Klara will follow us, Hans – *versteht?*'

The young Austrian nodded, and smiled weakly at the woman, who seemed too far gone to care.

Standing up, Leschenko eased open one of the double doors.

Tom and Walter waited patiently behind the stacked crates. It had been almost ten minutes since they had found their vantage point. The Martini-Henry rifles, their long barrels resting on the crates in front of them, were pulled snugly into their shoulders; stacks of loose cartridges were by their right hands. Each had pulled the rifle sling tight into his elbow to ensure a steady aim. They knew there was only one way out of the burning building. Then a slight movement caught their attention: one of the double doors was being swung open. Tom flexed his fingers and minutely adjusted his grip on the rifle stock. A deep and fathomless quality had entered his pale blue eyes. Both men's faces held a remorseless expression, totally devoid of mercy.

Two figures carrying rifles slipped through the half-open door and dropped from the loading bay to the ground. If Tom was surprised to recognise one of them as Eugene Leschenko, it did not register on his implacable features. Leschenko turned and spoke quietly to someone behind the half-open door. Another man, of slight build, aged about thirty and with thin Semitic features, accompanied by the woman Tom had seen at the window with the Winchester, now appeared. The woman no longer had a rifle and the man was carrying a pistol.

'Hold your fire,' Tom murmured softly.

The group began to move guardedly across the yard, stopping and looking round after a few paces, as if assessing what their best course of action would be. Taking careful aim at the Latvian, Tom took up the first pressure on his trigger and said in a low voice, 'Take the right and fire when you're ready.'

Exhaling, he checked his aim and shot Eugene Leschenko in the chest. At the same moment there was the sharp crack of Mardlin's rifle, and Draskovic spun round like a broken doll before pitching on his back onto the greasy cobbles. Without pausing for thought, Tom and Walter worked the levers on their rifles and, having cleared the action, rammed fresh cartridges into the breech. Hans Schneider paused for a second in utter confusion before raising his pistol and swinging it round in front of him as he frantically attempted to locate his attackers. Mardlin shot him cleanly through the heart. Klara Brandes began to scream, throwing her hands up in surrender, '*Nicht schiessen, nicht schiessen!*' Tom watched as, hands thrown up in supplication, she dropped to her knees, weeping. The image of a small spiky-haired boy filled his vision for several seconds before he squeezed the trigger.

Reloading, the two men walked forward, pausing at each body in turn to confirm they were dead. Bending down, Mardlin picked up the Winchester that was a few yards from Draskovic and walked over to Klara Brandes, who lay gazing sightlessly at the sky, the bullet hole exactly above the bridge of her nose. Pausing, he looked down dispassionately before dropping the rifle across her body. Neither noticed the slight movement of Leschenko's head as he followed their progress. With the last of his strength, the Latvian freed the Mauser from under his jacket, pointed it at Tom and fired. A hammer blow hit Tom in his right thigh, knocking him three feet before he dropped to the ground. For a moment he did not know what had happened. Then the sharp crack of Walter's rifle sounded, and he knew that one of the anarchists had shot him.

Seconds later, Walter was kneeling beside him, pulling a field dressing from his shirt pocket and swearing. 'Bastard. How could I have been so careless? Sorry, Tom, I really thought he was dead.'

Strangely there was no pain in his leg; it just felt as if a lead weight had been attached to it. Tom's hand felt wet, and when he put it up before his face it was smeared a bright red. With the sound of a shell exploding, the loading bay doors blew out, and a section of the roof collapsed, showering the yard with sparks and blazing baulks of timber. Mardlin had discarded the field dressing and was pulling as tight as possible the leather belt he had taken from his waist and strapped round Tom's upper leg. Tom was still puzzled by why his hand was red when he lost consciousness.

Chapter Thirty

L ying in his hospital bed propped up among the white pillows, Liam O'Dowd looked exactly what he was, a sick and broken man. Flecks of white showed in the thick dark beard that now covered his pallid features. Constant pain from the bullet wound along with the collapse of his life's work combined to make the man look considerably older than his fifty-odd years.

Despite his discomfort and weakness, the Brotherhood commander shot Tom a glance laden with malice as, leaning heavily on his Malacca walking stick, the detective entered the room in the side ward on the top floor of Kelsford Royal Infirmary. The ward, normally reserved for private patients who could afford to pay for their treatment, had been selected carefully by Fred Judd for its position and ease of defence should the need arise, although he had not told the infirmary's board of governors this.

Looking down at the man in the hospital bed, Tom could in some way empathise with him as the pain of his own wound was still fresh. He had spent several weeks in hospital while the doctors, having removed the bullet from his thigh and repaired his shattered hip bone, attempted to deal with the damage. The healing process had left the injured leg shorter than the other, and it was doubtful if he would be able to walk again without the aid of a stick.

Two months had elapsed since the ambush, and O'Dowd was still seriously ill. With the ever-present possibility that the Brotherhood might decide to make one last effort to release their leader, Judd had arranged for the Irishman to be housed as securely as possible while Tom was in hospital. Two armed policemen in the corridor outside his room and two more on patrol in the hospital grounds twenty-four hours a day had proved an enormous strain on the force's manpower, and two days before it had been agreed that O'Dowd should be moved to the hospital wing of Kelsford gaol. Tom derived a small measure of satisfaction from the knowledge that if a rescue operation were mounted the Irishman would almost certainly die, because of his present condition.

Only recently released from hospital himself, this was the third time that Tom had been into the sick room in an attempt to interview the man. On each occasion, as in his efforts to talk to Devlin, he had met with a wall of silence. Regarding the man lying propped up beneath the crisp white sheets, he could not avoid making a comparison with the conditions in which Joseph Langley was being kept.

Pulling up a chair, Tom decided it was time to adopt a different approach. Ensuring that the constable out in the corridor could not overhear him, he bent forward slightly and said in a soft voice, 'Michael Radbone has cracked, Liam.' The Irishman gave no indication that he had heard him. 'We know all about the deal you and the Yankee set up. Sangster is in custody at Long Street. He's been telling us how everything got into the store at Monckton. We're arresting Howkins.'

Tom paused. That all of this was lies, based on the conversation that he had overheard in the barn, was irrelevant. He needed something to make O'Dowd think he was finished, and had to take a chance that news of Howkins' suicide had not reached him.

For the first time he saw a change in the Irishman's eyes. Defiance was now diluted by concern. 'Then you'll not be needing to talk to me, will you? You can go and shag yourself.' The retort was full of venom but lacking in confidence. Tom realised that a fundamental change had taken place. Age and failure had suddenly taken their toll. Liam O'Dowd was disillusioned after a lifetime in the shadows working for an unseen goal, and more importantly he was frightened.

'When we arrest Howkins he's going to crack open like a rotten log.' Tom's voice was relentless, and the Irishman closed his eyes. 'He's the biggest mistake you ever made, and you know it. He's the amateur. We know all about the consignment you've lost in Collett Lane. Sangster is busy telling us where the Winchesters on the barge came from, and how you and your boys moved them out of Howkins' barn onto the *Trojan*. Howkins will fill in the rest of it, and then, my friend, you and Devlin will hang together.'

Liam O'Dowd kept his eyes tightly closed. Devlin was responsible for all this. Killing the policeman in the canal tunnel had been a huge miscalculation. It had unleashed the forces of law and order in a way that nothing else could have done – and Devlin's bad luck had transferred itself to him.

'You're a sick man, Liam. Taking a bullet at your age isn't good. Even if you escape the gallows you won't survive a year in prison. You've only got one lung now, and the doctors say your only real hope of seeing old age is to take it nice and easy by the fireside. The first winter infection going round the chokey and you're a dead man.' The detective was enjoying himself. There was a time when the Brotherhood commander would have put a gun to his head for baiting him in this manner. His next words caught O'Dowd unawares. 'How would you like to go back to Ireland, Liam?'

Tuesday 11 December 1888 dawned cold and miserable. No snow had fallen yet, but by late afternoon the lowering sky through Connor Devlin's cell window promised that it was on its way. Connor smiled ruefully: the least he could have hoped for on his last full day on earth was for the sun to shine. He continued to pace, as he had done all day, up and down the eight foot length of the condemned cell. One of the few books that he had read, many years ago, was about a man who was condemned to die. The character had spent a great deal of time counting the number of paces he was taking and the number of bricks in the cell walls. Neither occupation interested Connor; he had other things on his mind.

Outside in the narrow tiled corridor sat two uniformed guards. Procedure demanded that after sentence Devlin should be watched twenty-four hours a day, in case he thwarted justice by taking his own life ahead of the hangman. Had he wished, one or both of the officers would have remained in the cell with him, playing cards or chatting, but company was the last thing the prisoner wanted.

Born a Catholic, Connor's religious beliefs had lapsed at an early age, after he had decided to enter the Brotherhood. It was, he felt, an irreconcilable contradiction to worship a God who had sole power over life and death when he and others like him were exercising that same sanction. For his entire adult life his energies had been channelled into the beliefs of the Irish Republican Brotherhood. While others attended Sunday mass, he presided over planning meetings. Along with Liam O'Dowd, he had been one of the Brotherhood's most powerful men. Now he had been secretly informed that Liam was dead.

Since the ambush at Town Locks, Liam's condition had remained serious. Unwilling to sentence him in his absence, the authorities had not set a date for his trial – which would not be necessary now. A bout of pneumonia brought on by the damp winter cold had been too much for his weakened condition. It was ironic, thought Devlin, that they had parted under such bad circumstances. He regretted that the last conversation between them had been acrimonious.

Watching the evening dusk gather through the bars of the tiny cell, Connor made up his mind. Liam was right: the execution of Henry Farmer had been a stupid mistake, and must not be allowed to compromise the plans for the Brotherhood's base in Kelsford.

A dark form blocked out the small amount of light coming in through the observation hatch as one of the prison officers, a sallow-faced individual with a neatly trimmed beard, unlocked the steel-lined door. 'Time for supper, Devlin.' Albert Granger placed a tin plate of beef stew and potatoes on the bench next to the condemned man. Prisoners under sentence of death were, by some quirk, allowed the best food available, and the meal had been brought in from the kitchen of a nearby pub.

Granger sat on the bench beside Devlin: condemned prisoners were not to be left alone with such instruments as a knife and fork. Checking through the half-open cell door, he saw that his shift mate was observing the proceedings attentively.

It was strange, thought Connor, that despite the circumstances he was still hungry; perhaps it was some form of nervous reaction. Handing the empty plate to Granger, he said, 'Ask the governor if he and the priest can come and speak to me.' Nodding, the warder closed and double-locked the cell door; it was a request often made by men in this situation.

It was half past six when the governor of Kelsford Gaol and Father Michael Lilley were let into the condemned cell. Cutting short the priest's platitudes, Devlin spoke directly to the governor.

'Have you pen and paper?'

The governor signalled to his officers at their table in the passage. Albert Granger brought in the writing materials.

'Tell him to bring the table in, then sit down and write.' Connor spoke in a quiet authoritative voice.

'That will not be necessary, my son,' intervened the priest. 'If it's your last will and testament it can be written down at the bench beside you.'

'It's nothing to do with any last will and testament, and I was speaking to the governor. I only want you here so that no one says later that what I say is a figment of the imagination of the authorities.' Devlin, picking up the man's slight Belfast accent, had taken an instant dislike to him.

Gilchrist was interested, and again signified to the warders to bring in the wooden table. It was not the first time in his long career that a man about to die had confessed to his crimes in this life in the hope of achieving salvation in the next.

For nearly an hour Connor Devlin spoke slowly in a low clear voice, stopping from time to time in order to ensure that the scribbling prison officer was getting down everything he said. First he explained how after the robbery of the agent at the Prince Albert he and Martin Lafferty went off in one direction on horseback while Eddie Donnelly made his way down to the canal bank to rendezvous with the barge that was due to collect him. Connor deliberately left out the identity of the barge or the Radbones' involvement. He told them how, as soon as he and Lafferty parted company, he had galloped back to the canal instead of setting off for Sheffield as planned, and had waited under Bridge Sixty-Four for Donnelly to arrive, to steal the proceeds of the robbery. He had cut it fine and had barely had time to reach the bridge before Eddie, wet and bedraggled, ducked under the brickwork. That Eddie had to be killed was inevitable. The risk of him identifying Connor was too great to allow him to live. Taking the stolen money, Devlin then continued with the original plan. He caught the train in Sheffield next morning, and threw the Gladstone bag out of the window as the locomotive chugged its way up a gradient somewhere in the Pennines.

That Martin Lafferty, for reasons best known to himself, then chose to abscond with the contents of George Camm's money box was a bonus that

Connor could never have dreamed of. The interview with Liam at the house in Swinburne Court was probably the most difficult part of the operation – when there was a real risk that his guilt would be dealt with on the basis of adequate suspicion. Once that had not happened, he knew Liam was satisfied that Martin Lafferty was the guilty party.

Ike Harriman's death was, Connor explained coldly, more of an administrative matter than anything else. He needed to return to Kelsford in complete safety, and because Harriman could identify him he had to be removed. The Irishman allowed himself a grim chuckle. Having searched the house to ensure there was nothing there to connect him to Harriman, he had just left the yard when he almost bumped into the detectives walking up to the stables. Two minutes earlier and they would have caught him coming out of the house.

So long as Martin remained at large and sought by the Brotherhood, Connor was safe. But when Lafferty was traced by Miles Ellingworth's men in New York, and refused to confess to the crime of which he knew nothing, it brought a host of suspicions back into the Brotherhood commander's fertile brain. Connor knew that, for his own safety, he needed to find some way to close the matter once and for all. The opportunity came when, quite by accident, he was almost caught in the tunnel at the canal basin workings by Henry Farmer. By pure luck it was Eddie's revolver that Connor was carrying when he was surprised by the detective. At this point the Irishman paused in his story. He could not tell the listening men that when Sangster handed him Henry's revolver, which he had taken from the armoury cupboard before setting out, he had slipped it into his belt and brought Eddie's back up. The version that Connor dictated to Albert Granger was that he alone surprised the detective and shot him. Subsequently, he continued, he had showed the revolver to O'Dowd and told him he had recovered it from Farmer before killing him – acting as judge and jury.

His story finished, Connor heaved a sigh. Now he could meet the hangman with equanimity. The confession had nothing to do with conscience or fear of his own mortality; he had just redressed the errors he had made. With the confession in his hands, Thomas Norton would finally be able to close the case. At a later date the next appointed commander would be able to pick up the plans to create a mainland base for the Irish Republican Brotherhood here in Kelsford. He hoped that when he met Liam in the next world he would be satisfied.

The next morning, almost a year to the day after Arthur Cufflin was robbed, a crowd began to gather in the early morning cold outside the gates of Kelsford Borough Gaol. It was a long while since there had been an execution in the town, and this one was going to be special: it was Connor Devlin, the Irishman who had shot the policeman at Town Locks in the big fight with the gun runners.

By a quarter to eight, with a fine sleet falling, the crowd numbered well in excess of two hundred. Inside the prison yard, immediately in front of the gallows that the prison carpenter had erected, a tarpaulin had been put up in order that the dignitaries present should not get wet. Solemn-faced, the prison governor and head constable stood at one side, quietly chatting. Detective Inspector Norton, leaning heavily on his malacca cane, was standing by the chair that had been provided for him and that he was steadfastly declining to use. With him were Dr Mallard who, after the execution, would be required to perform a post-mortem and give a certificate of death, and Charles Kerrigan Kemp, who the governor had agreed should be present so that the event was accurately reported.

At ten minutes to eight the governor excused himself and went down to the cell block. As the minutes ticked by Tom eased his weight onto his good leg and pulled out his pocket watch. It was three minutes to eight. He began to wonder if he would have to avail himself of the seat after all. His leg and hip were aching intolerably, and his doctor had instructed him not to stand or walk unnecessarily for another month. Leschenko's bullet had hit him in the right thigh, smashing the bone and narrowly missing a main artery. If it had not been for Walter Mardlin's prompt action in applying a tourniquet, Tom would probably have bled to death before help arrived.

From a doorway in the prison yard behind the gallows a party of men emerged. At its head was Connor Devlin, his hands secured behind his back, flanked by two warders on each side. Following them were the prison governor and a Catholic priest. As he climbed the short set of steps up to the scaffold, Devlin was unable to balance without the use of his hands. When he swayed slightly, looking as if he was about to topple backwards, two of the warders put their hands on his back and he completed the ascent.

Before fixing the rope round Devlin's neck, the hangman made to place a large black hood over his head. With a sharp movement Connor said something curtly to the executioner, who looked enquiringly at the prison governor – who nodded, and made a small sign with his hand to indicate that the hood could be dispensed with.

'His only request has been that he shall not be hooded – he wants to see what's happening,' Archer Robson said to Tom in a low voice. 'Governor's agreed to it, but it's most irregular. Jack Ketch doesn't seem very happy, though.' The hangman had gone over to the governor, as if seeking clarification of his instructions.

Connor Devlin stared arrogantly at the spectators while the rope was secured and carefully adjusted. His gaze fixed for several long seconds on Tom Norton, as if he were determined to remember his face throughout the eternity that was imminent. Stepping back, the hangman moved to the trapdoor handle, awaiting the signal. Devlin's gaze suddenly shifted to a point behind the audience, and for the first time since he had walked onto the scaffold his face became animated. Tom and Archer Robson swung round. At an open window on the first floor of the prison, wearing a nightshirt and supported by two hospital orderlies, stood Liam O'Dowd.

Connor opened his mouth as if searching for words, the hempen rope restricting movement. 'Liam,' he yelled. 'Liam, we've been fools! It was all for naught . . .'

The sound of the clock in the bell tower along with the clatter of the drop as the hangman threw his weight against the release lever drowned out his final words.

An eerie silence hung over the prison yard.

Chapter Thirty-One

Detective Superintendent Daniel Chote looked out of his office window at the busy street below. A motorised delivery van was steering a cautious path round 'Jammy' Hallam's bread van; Jammy's horse, restive and unpredictable, was stamping a hoof and snorting as the puffing monster slid past it in the narrow thoroughfare. It would not be long, mused Chote, before there were nearly as many motor cars as there were horses, and then they would have to widen Long Street and High Street and all the other roads leading through the town.

Pacing aimlessly, he stared down at his empty desktop. Usually it would be cluttered with crime files and messages that demanded his urgent attention, but not today. On his last day before retirement Daniel had cleared his desk by ten o'clock. Anything left undone could be attended to by his successor, whoever that might be.

He looked round the room for the hundredth time that morning, and reflected upon the five years that he had spent as head of Kelsford Borough's detective department. He was the first to be made superintendent; his predecessors had all been inspectors. Before him it had been old Jesse Squires, who had been detective inspector for twenty years after he took over from Thomas Norton in May 1889, when Tom retired after being injured in the Collett Lane siege.

Jesse Squires knew his job and was good to work for, Daniel thought. Innovative and clever, he had made all sorts of changes over the years – photographing prisoners, installing telephones, even suggesting that the force bought a motor car; but the head constable had turned that one down flat.

In Daniel's opinion, Thomas Norton was better, probably the best. Perhaps that was because he had helped him out when he was a probationer. What was the woman's name? Queenie Bartholemew, that was it. Funny how after nearly thirty years he could remember her raddled miserable face. Still, she had succeeded in hoodwinking him and, had it not been for

Tom he would have been in serious trouble with that miserable old sod Sergeant Horspool.

The reminiscence took him back. Poor old Ambrose Quinn, who had saved his life down at Town Locks when he shot Terence Radbone. At least Radbone had a gun in his hand when Quinn killed him, not like those Russian bastards who murdered Ambrose at the house in Century Courtyard. He remembered watching the courtyard being pulled down as condemned property about ten years ago, and thinking of the men who had been murdered there for nothing.

It was Tom and an army sergeant from the barracks who had exacted justice for that. The truth about what happened at that old blacking factory had never really been known. It was all over when the soldier opened the yard gates to let reinforcements in: the anarchists were dead and Tom was badly wounded – he had never walked properly again.

Unbidden, the memory of the little office boy who had been killed by the sniper came into his mind. Arthur Hollowday – he recollected him quite clearly. Nice lad, from a very poor background. He remembered how badly Inspector Judd had taken the death. Tom Norton, unable to work, had left soon after the siege and moved away with Ruth Samuels, the banker. The soldier and his wife still lived in Kelsford, though. What was their name? Mardlin, that was it: they worked for Reuben and Ann at the Rifleman.

The memories crowding into his mind, Chote went to the old gun cupboard, long ago replaced by a gun safe built into the back of the charge office and now only used for storing old files. Pushing through to the back, he dragged out a dust-covered box that had not seen the light of day for more years than he could recollect. It contained all the paperwork for Tom's other famous case: the trial of Connor Devlin for the murder of Detective Constable Joel Dexter.

Chote carried it back into his office and began to sift through its contents. One of the first items he found was a copy of the *Kelsford Gazette* dated Wednesday 12 December 1888. It was twenty-six years since he had last seen this. Daniel scrutinised it again with interest.

> *POLICE KILLER ADMITS TO OTHER MURDERS*
> Special Report by Chas Kerrigan Kemp
>
> Earlier this morning, Connor Devlin, an Irishman from the
> Manchester area, was hanged at Kelsford Gaol for his part in
> the battle between police and Irish Nationalists at Town Locks
> on Sunday 7th October this year, in the course of which he shot
> and killed Detective Joel Dexter of the Borough Police Force.
> It has been revealed that before going to the scaffold, Devlin
> in an act of remorse and doubtless seeking to meet his Eternal
> Maker with a clear conscience, confessed to the Prison Governor,

Mr. Jordan Gilchrist, and the Prison Padre, Father Michael Lilley, the commission of several other crimes. The first of these was the murder of one of his accomplices, a man named Edwin Donnelly, while effecting their escape from the scene of what has become known as the Shires Robbery. Later crimes for which the doomed man admitted responsibility were the killings of well-known local Horse Dealer, Mr. Isaac Harriman, and the cowardly murder of Detective Sergeant Henry Farmer. The full details of the confessions, which are at present in the hands of the local police, are not yet known. The prisoner, who declined to be hooded, met his fate with equanimity. At the moment sentence was carried out, he turned his face towards the heavens and declared, 'what fools we have been, it was all for naught'. The executioner then released the trap upon which he was standing and the unfortunate man was dispatched.

Putting the newspaper to one side, Daniel began to work his way through the papers in the box until he came across the faded confession dictated by Devlin in his cell. He was about to drop it back into the box when he spotted a small package tied with white string and closed with sealing wax, bearing the coat of arms of the borough gaol and in pale blue ink the name 'Devlin, Connor'. It was the domestic record of the prisoner's stay in prison, which the governor must have forwarded to the police sometime after the execution, so it could be stored with other relevant papers. Pulling the package towards him, the notation on the bottom confirmed his assumption. In the neat handwriting with which Daniel had become very familiar over the years was written, 'Delivered from HMP Kelsford, 25th May 1889, domestic documents in relation to Connor Devlin, executed Wednesday, 12th December 1888. For storage with the main file. J. Squires, Detective Inspector.'

Pausing a moment, Daniel did a quick calculation. The file must have come in a couple of weeks after Thomas Norton had retired. It was a purely administrative procedure, and Squires had never even opened it.

Curious to find out about Devlin's last hours, Daniel Chote broke the sealing wax and opened the package. Inside were some twenty sheets of paper covered in double-sided entries relating to the food given to the prisoner, records of visits to him and details of his appearances before the assize court. The last sheet of paper related to the day before Devlin's execution. Daniel sat for some time staring at one of the entries: '11th December, Tuesday, 2.35pm. Visit by Detective Inspector Norton, Kelsford Police. On authority of Detective Inspector, visit unsupervised. Visit ended 3.47pm. Signed: A. Granger (Warder).'

Daniel Chote removed all the papers from the box and began to go through them with meticulous care. At the end of an hour each of the documents had been examined and replaced. Nowhere was there any reference to Tom Norton visiting the condemned man on the afternoon before sentence was carried out.

Getting up from his chair, the detective superintendent pulled out the gold hunter that had been presented to him the night before, at his retirement dinner. Clicking it open, he checked the time and saw he was due to see the head constable in fifteen minutes for a farewell glass of sherry before leaving the building for the last time.

How he had done it, Daniel Chote had no way of knowing, and there was no way of finding out. Thomas Norton had retired in early May 1889 and now lived abroad. Had he remained as detective inspector a few weeks longer the prison papers would certainly not have survived. Somehow that afternoon Tom had found a way to convince Devlin to confess to his crimes before he died, and now he – Daniel – was the only other person privy to the secret.

He certainly knew now what it was that Connor Devlin was attempting to say before the hangman cut him short. The question was, what was he going to do about it? A gentle knock at the door interrupted his deliberations, and the head constable appeared in the doorway. 'Ah, glad to find you're still here, Daniel,' he said genially. 'I'll walk with you upstairs. There are a few members of the watch committee who would like to wish you well in your retirement.'

Smiling in polite acknowledgement, Daniel slipped the slim package of papers into his inside pocket and followed the head constable out through the door.

Thomas Norton put aside the letter and gazed out over the screen of pine trees that ran along the gravel drive towards tall wrought-iron gates.

Pulling out a large white handkerchief and removing his steel-framed spectacles, he wiped a runny eye. His sight was not as good as it used to be, but for sixty-three he was not, he thought, in bad shape. The blond hair and moustache were now the snowy white that seems only to be granted to fair-haired people. Age had thickened his slim figure, but he could still walk five miles a day with the aid of his stick, in search of a brace of rabbits or the occasional hare.

Replacing his glasses, Tom picked up the letter from Jamie and read it for a second time. Marcel, the *facteur*, had come trudging up the drive with it from the village a short while ago. As was his custom, having delivered the mail the postman had adjourned to the kitchens to partake of a well-earned aperitif and a plate of Mirka's delicious pastries. They would soon have to consider whether Mirka and David should retire, he thought idly. Although the warm climate of southern France had proved beneficial, Mirka's arthritis was making it more difficult for her to cook and run the château.

Easing back in the cane chair and relishing the hot summer sunshine on the balcony, he decided to let the matter take care of itself. The present arrangement was satisfactory to all concerned. Mirka ran the domestic side of things, ruling the servants with a rod of iron, while David managed the estate and dealt with the tenant farmers. Their son Stefan would be returning soon, having completed his university studies, and would perhaps take over the reins from his father.

Feeling in the pocket of his white linen jacket, Tom pulled out the old flat cigar case and, pulling the top open, removed one of the long thin cheroots. From habit, he ran his fingers over the polished leather as he did twenty times a day, and, as it did every time, a small clear voice from a different lifetime echoed clearly in his mind: '… better than those hinged cases …'. After almost thirty years Tom could still see her finely cut features and thick chestnut hair when he closed his eyes. He often wondered how different his life might have been had she lived. In the years since Kate died and he and Ruth had been together he had never ceased to wonder how he could love two women without any conflict.

Applying a match to his cigar, he brought his attention back to the family letter; he received one every month, from either his mother or Jamie. After Tom's father had given up the pub some ten years before, Reuben and Ann had sold their shop in Oxford Road and taken over the Rifleman. Jamie had decided to study law, and was currently a partner in a well-established practice in the town. The news of most interest this time was the retirement of Daniel Chote. It was curious, he thought, that all he could remember about young Chote was the incident when Queenie Bartholemew gave a false name and address. Who would have thought, he mused, that the young probationary constable would one day take his place as head of the detective department.

Tom closed his eyes and pulled at the cigar, turning his face to the morning sunshine, enjoying the warm rays on his face. It was a glorious day. This summer had been the hottest that he could remember in the twenty-five years that they had lived here in Saint Martin. They could not, he thought, have chosen a more perfect place to settle than in the Haute-Loire district of France's Massif Central. Below them, the river from which the region took its name began its winding seven hundred mile journey to join the Bay of Biscay beyond Nantes. Behind the château stood the impressive mass of Mont Mézenc. During the winter months Ruth and Stefan Capewell had spent most of their days skiing across the steep mountain slopes.

Jamie, Tom reflected, was about the same age he had been when all this had begun – the cold wet December night that he had killed Eddie Donnelly. Every day since he had told himself that he never intended it to happen.

Making his way home from a late shift on the evening of the Shires payroll robbery, it was Tom and not Henry Farmer who spotted the three Irishmen splitting up and going their separate ways. Deciding to follow Donnelly, Tom quickly realised that the man was heading for the canal. Taking a chance, he decided that rather than follow him down Beggar's Lane he would come in along the canal bank from the opposite direction. Running hard, Tom made it to the bridge at Scriven's Walk in a little under five minutes and was crouching low in the shelter of the brickwork out of the pouring rain well before Donnelly, ploughing along the muddy towpath, made it to the bridge. The barge hook that Tom had picked up from the deck of one of the moored boats as he passed was clenched tightly in his left hand; the slope of the brickwork would not allow him to swing it with his right.

Waiting patiently, Tom heard the squelch of boots approaching and knew his guess about the man's destination had been correct. Standing up as straight as the bridge would allow, he hefted the hook and tested its balance. Suddenly what little light there was at the opposite end of the bridge was blocked out by Donnelly. It was at this point that Tom made a miscalculation. Swinging the hook with all the force that he could muster, he aimed a blow at the middle of Donnelly's body; but did not allow for the Irishman being bent double under the slope of the wall. His head was up as he peered forward into the darkness, and Tom's blow, taking him full in the face, killed him instantly.

Standing in the claustrophobic space, Tom was close to panic with the realisation of what he had done. Gradually cold reasoning took over, prompted by an overwhelming instinct for self-preservation. Checking swiftly that he was alone and unobserved, he carefully removed the heavy Gladstone bag from the dead man's grip and then, almost as an afterthought, tugged the long pistol from his belt. That was his mistake, although at the time it was a sensible precaution. As the dead man was on his way to rendezvous with someone, it was logical to suppose that if he encountered that person before he could hide the money Tom would be in trouble, and might be glad of a weapon. Afterwards he was never able to explain to himself why, after hiding the moneybag at the back of his garden shed before going into the house in Sidwell Place, he had not also disposed of the gun. Like Vassily Brovnic, he had hidden it away in a box in the loft, where it remained until Robert Archer Robson directed that the police armoury should be relocated in the detective inspector's office in Long Street. The back of the gun cupboard in his office seemed the safest place for the Colt. After a while Tom had even wondered if it might not come in useful when they caught up with the leaders of the Brotherhood. Perhaps, he reasoned, an opportunity might arise to return it to Devlin or O'Dowd before triumphantly recovering it in suitable circumstances. The one good thing to come out of the whole business, he reflected, was that his appropriation of the money had enabled him to set Ann and Reuben up in the shop in Oxford Road.

That Tom's plan to use the gun never came to fruition, and the fact that it resulted in Henry Farmer's death, still haunted him. Before leaving the police station all those years ago to trail Devlin, Henry, in possession of the armoury keys during Tom's absence in London, had prudently decided to take a firearm with him. The fact that his hand came to rest on the box containing Donnelly's pistol was sheer bad luck. In his hurry the significance of there only being five rounds of ammunition – sufficient to load the weapon once – had not registered; he had simply loaded the gun and left to accompany Weasel Meakin to Welbeck Street. Connor Devlin's outrage when Lucas Sangster handed him what he immediately recognised as Eddie's gun was genuine, and his immediate assumption was that Henry had the weapon because he was Donnelly's killer. The resulting murder would, Tom knew, always be on his conscience.

Once Devlin and O'Dowd were both in custody, for the first time he had an opportunity to tidy matters up and to ensure that, whatever the rights and wrongs of the matter, Devlin confessed to Henry Farmer's murder. On the day that Tom visited O'Dowd in the infirmary he had the basis of a plan in his mind. It depended totally upon the Brotherhood commander's state of mind: that his long spell in hospital, hovering between life and death, would have depressed him sufficiently to make him receptive to a proposition. If O'Dowd could convince Devlin to make a statement to the effect that he had killed Eddie Donnelly, and at the same time admit to the murders of Isaac Harriman and Henry Farmer in addition to the one for which he was about to hang, justice would in Tom's eyes be well and truly served.

O'Dowd was in a worse state than Tom could have hoped. With the severity of his wound rendering him a permanent invalid, his abiding wish was to return home to Ireland and to spend his last few years in peace. The fires of political ambition were dwindling to will-o'-the-wisps flickering over a treacherous swamp.

By the time he left the hospital room Tom was in possession of a letter from O'Dowd to Devlin, instructing him, as his last act of sacrifice for the Irish Republican Brotherhood, to confess to the crimes. The reason given was that O'Dowd, near death, needed to secure the future of the Brotherhood. If Connor complied, and additionally took responsibility for the death of Eddie Donnelly, then all police enquiries would end with his execution and the Brotherhood would be free to resume its activities undisturbed. Tom was to give Devlin the letter, and tell him that the Brotherhood commander had died in hospital after writing it. Afterwards, in exchange for the confessions, O'Dowd's part in the arms deals was to be played down and he would be charged with minor offences. After discussions with the head constable, Tom was to arrange that the commander was returned to Ireland to serve out any prison sentence that he was given.

The plan had worked almost perfectly. Presented on the day before his execution with the letter, and the information that Liam had succumbed to an infection of the lungs resulting from the gunshot wound, Connor Devlin had nodded once and handed the paper back to Tom. The handwriting was indisputably Liam's and the order not beyond reason. It was an instruction that Connor himself would have issued had their roles had been reversed. The complication came when, standing on the gallows, Devlin caught sight of O'Dowd as he was transferred from the infirmary to the prison hospital block. It was not sentiment on O'Dowd's part, reflected Tom, that had almost proved the undoing of his plan. The commander had insisted on pausing at the window, not to bid a final farewell to his brother in arms but to ensure, after his own act of treachery, that Devlin was hanged at the appointed time.

Catching sight of O'Dowd in those last seconds, Connor Devlin, realising that in some way he had been duped, was attempting to pass a final message to the man in the window. He was not calling out 'It was all for naught' but was trying to say 'It was all for Norton'.

To Tom's everlasting gratitude, the hangman threw his weight against the lever of the drop, and cut short the accusing voice for all time.

Tom was involved in the killing of Eddie Donnelly and its consequences by accident, but the Romanov necklace was another matter entirely. He knew clearly when he had been released from so many constraints and allowed himself to join the woman whom he loved in the theft and disposal of the Romanov necklace. It was the day he visited Joseph Langley in Kelsford Borough Asylum. The horror of what he saw there would stay with him until he died. It was not merely Langley's physical deterioration, although that had sickened him, but what had been done to the old man. An appalling recognition had come to Tom that no matter how strong and resilient a man was, it counted for nothing if that man inadvertently stepped outside the accepted boundaries set by society.

For almost forty years Joseph Langley, despite the unorthodox nature of his methods, had served the community of Kelsford. That he was suffering from an illness was never in dispute – but that illness was not such that he deserved, without any redress or means of appeal, to be taken forcibly from his home in the middle of the night and thrown into a cell for the rest of his natural life, turning him into a drooling maniac in the process. Immeasurably affected, Tom had tried to explain his feelings to Ruth the night before Ann and Reuben's wedding as they lay in her bed – pouring out the horror of what he had seen. That it had affected his view of life he was in no doubt; but the fact that Ruth was in a position to help him change his circumstances had come as a considerable shock.

Knowing that fate had arranged matters with impeccable timing, Ruth explained what she had done. The simplicity of her plan was blindingly brilliant. Between Manfred Issitt alerting her to the theft of the Romanov necklace and her taking possession of the jewels from the Yavlinskiys, Ruth made a journey to London, about which even the faithful Mirka knew nothing. Travelling there and back in the day, Ruth, who, as Max Peters always averred, should have remained behind her father's shop counter selling jewellery, paid a visit to a small but extremely high-class establishment in Golders Green. Had Max ever known what she was doing that day, he would have regretted for the rest of his life the repeated allusions to her background that he was so fond of making. Although she had not been to Levin and Bernstein's since she was a young woman of twenty, Ruth took the precaution of wearing the dark weeds and veil of a newly bereaved widow. In the shop she spent nearly an hour examining and selecting a diamond necklace that was of high quality, and ostentatious enough to be worn by a member of the aristocracy. The one she finally settled upon matched as closely as possible the description she had in her possession of the Romanov necklace. Like its counterpart, it was made up of four interwoven loops of diamonds set off with an emerald clasp. The difference was that this one, while costing £500, was of very inferior stones and worth only a fraction of the price of the Russian necklace.

Bernhard Bernstein was a little surprised when the tall woman in black (which was, Ruth ensured, the best description he would ever be able to give of her), paid in cash. It was an enormous sum of money for a woman to be carrying around the streets of London in her handbag, but on the other hand it suited him better than a cheque. She was, he presumed, a young widow (without, it had to be said, a lot of taste), intent on spending some of her late husband's money. It was a pity, he thought, that she had not sought his advice: for the money she had spent he could have directed her towards a much better quality and far more tasteful item. Ruth, on the other hand, going back to the railway station in the cab that had been waiting outside for her, only regretted that she was not in a position to buy it wholesale – at a third of the price.

Back in Kelsford it had been a simple matter to stitch her purchase into an oilskin package of the sort that she knew the Pipeline used for such transfers.

After accepting the real necklace from Lukeria Yavlinskiy, she had merely gone to the ladies' lavatory on the pretext of hiding the package, and swapped it for the one from Levin and Bernstein's.

The one thing that made the plan infallible was, Ruth explained to Tom, pulling the sheets up under her chin, that after the real necklace had been examined by her uncle and declared genuine no-one would question whether it was genuine until it arrived in the United States. She was trusted implicitly by the Pipeline, while Peters was known to be devious and, following the Howkins affair, in deep financial trouble. Any suspicion would fall immediately on him. Meanwhile she would, after a reasonable time, sell her interest in the bank to her partners, so she could move away with Tom and dispose of the real necklace at her leisure.

Turning the proposition over in the quiet of the bedroom, it had not taken Tom long to reach a decision. No-one would get hurt other than the unlovable Max Peters, along with whoever the American connection turned out to be. In this respect he had little doubt that the necklace would be handled by Lucas Sangster, on behalf of whatever organisation it was that he worked for in the States.

Weighing up the subsequent events, Tom realised he could not have foreseen the tragedy that was to follow. No-one could have anticipated Eugene Leschenko's involvement and the mayhem that it caused. He had thought it through time after time. The only conceivable solution that he could reach was that the Latvian's presence in Kelsford was directly linked to an arms deal that he must have been transacting with Sangster, and that he had stumbled upon the transfer of the necklace by accident. Otherwise, how could he have known the location of the blacking factory in Collett Lane?

A voice from behind him brought Tom out of his reverie. The tall matronly figure standing in the open doorway leading from the first-floor lounge had lost none of her physical attraction with the years. Her black hair hardly touched with grey, Ruth Norton still looked barely a day over forty, although she had just turned fifty-nine.

'Do you want coffee or a Ricard?' she asked in the familiar husky voice.

'Dr Viard says that coffee is bad for my heart,' he replied amiably. 'Better make it a large Ricard, I think.'

Ruth nodded and, leaning against the door frame, paused for a few moments to enjoy the sunshine. She knew what her husband was thinking about – and had spent a lot of time herself putting things into perspective. Tom still spent hours going over what had happened all those years ago, and Ruth knew he blamed himself for Henry's death; whatever she said made little difference.

After the shootings at Collett Lane Tom had taken a long while to recover, not just from the effects of his disability but psychologically. Apart from Tom and Walter, she alone knew what had happened in the loading yard. The fact that Tom had taken justice into his own hands did not bother her as much as it did him: he had done what was necessary and she respected him for it. The men – and the woman, for she had taken an equal part – who committed the murders in Century Courtyard and the siege of Collett Lane deserved to die.

Ruth had sold her interest in the bank to Solomon Meyer and Jakob Peters, for a substantial amount of money: the interest that Isaac Samuels had left to her was worth in excess of £150,000. In the aftermath of the losses they had incurred in the collapse of Batsford Stone, Meyer and Peters asked her not to sell for six months, as it would take that time to recover from the financial losses they had incurred – and the early departure of a partner could badly affect public confidence.

Ruth agreed to the request, but immediately withdrew from taking any active part in the management of the bank. She spent much of her time nursing Tom, no longer particularly caring whether other people knew of their relationship or what they said behind their backs. Tom had been more than happy to bring out their affair into the open, and apart from one or two of her social acquaintances most people had accepted the situation.

When not with Tom, Ruth had travelled extensively in central France searching for the place where they should settle down, eventually finding the Château des Trois Reines near the tiny village of St Martin. All this time the Romanov necklace remained in the safe built into the wall of her bedroom. No-one other than herself and Tom knew of its existence.

During the early months of 1889 Max Peters, whose disgrace at the bank had been to a great extent covered up by his father, took a holiday in the United States. There was a general feeling that his absence was greatly welcomed by his father and Solomon Meyer, as it allowed them to repair the damage he had caused. Not long after his arrival he was killed after what was reported in the *New York Times* as 'an extended drinking session with some associates', when he took a fatal fall from a fifteenth-floor hotel room onto the busy street below. Neither Tom nor Ruth ever accepted this was an accident, rather that Max had been punished for what was perceived by the American organisation to be the theft of their property.

At the end of the agreed six months, in June 1889, her share of the bank settled and the house in Victoria Road sold, Ruth said goodbye to Mannie Issitt and moved to live in St Martin, where she was joined shortly afterwards by Tom. On 22 July they were married, and the following year their son Samuel was born. Eighteen months later, on a cold winter's morning in February 1892, Ruth gave birth to their second child, Irene.

With the money gained from liquidating Ruth's assets in England, the purchase of the thirty-room château with its rolling acres had presented no problem. The important thing was that they were in no rush to dispose of the Romanov necklace.

That the American purchasers of the necklace had been swindled was common knowledge among those in the clandestine jewellery industry. The consensus was that the real necklace had been disposed of by Max Peters to Eugene Leschenko and his associates for sufficient money to save Peters from bankruptcy, brought about by his disastrous involvement with Joshua Howkins. The theory was that the attempted robbery of Lucas Sangster at Kelsford railway station was a blind, orchestrated by Peters. Had it been successful, the Americans would never have known that Max had handed over a fake set of jewels. Consequently, the accepted conclusion among those who mattered was that either the real Romanov necklace had been lost in the fire during the siege at Collett Lane, or Max Peters had managed to dispose of it after Leschenko's death.

Ruth and Tom agreed that the longer they waited before disposing of the diamonds the better. To this end, soon after they had settled in at their new home Ruth suggested to her father that as she now lived in France they should expand the Kosminski jewellery business onto the continent. If he were prepared to go into partnership with her and open a shop in Paris, she would undertake, once the venture was established, to open more shops elsewhere in France. Thanks to Ruth's innate business acumen, within two years Kosminski's had outlets in Paris, Rouen, Marseille and half a dozen other cities across the country; and she was well on the way to becoming a millionaire in her own right.

After three years the couple decided it would be safe to deal with the Romanov necklace.

Each of the fifty-three diamonds, each one baguette-cut, in its own individual silver setting with a gold backing, was between one and a half and two carats; none was more than two and a half. Individually the stones were extremely valuable, but the necklace's unique quality and consequent value were dependent upon the setting. With her knowledge of the jewellery trade, Ruth could in complete safety dismantle the necklace, take the stones from their settings and dispose of them individually through her shops, while the emerald clasp could be broken down, re-cut and set: Ruth intended to keep it as a personal memento.

An integral part of the scheme was that for a period Ruth and Tom should make trips twice a year to South Africa. There, for two or three weeks at a time, they moved round the mining townships between Cape Town, Johannesburg and Kimberley so Ruth could buy small quantities of high-quality cut diamonds. Trading mainly with the agents for the de Beers Diamond Corporation, she made discreet and well-judged purchases of stones that were in the same category as those from the Romanov necklace. It was a prolonged and tortuous process. Several visits over almost four years were necessary because high-grade diamonds of the size and quality that Ruth was buying were not readily available, and competition from other major European jewellers was keen.

Bringing the newly acquired diamonds back to France, Ruth carefully placed them in her safe at the château, substituting those from the Romanov necklace that closest matched her bills of purchase. When the process was completed the Russian diamonds were sent to her craftsmen to be set into rings and other pieces, before being sold to the cream of French society. And, as Ruth pointed out to her admiring husband, hidden away in the château was a fortune in legitimate diamonds – for all of which she had duplicated bills of purchase.

Ruth looked out over the pine trees. Life had been kind to them, she reflected. Samuel, having gone to university in England, was now in London at the head office of Kosminski's learning about the business empire that he, along with his sister, would one day inherit. Irene, newly married, was living in Paris now and eagerly planning a family. Apart from a few aches and pains, Ruth and Tom still enjoyed good health, although his hip caused him more discomfort as he got older.

The one thing that Tom must never know was the mistake she had made in bringing Eugene Leschenko to Kelsford. Her intention had been for Leschenko to steal the Romanov necklace from Sangster once she had swapped it for the fake, thus preventing the substitution from ever being discovered: she had never had the slightest doubt that Leschenko would double-cross her and take the necklace for his own purposes. This would save her having to find the promised £100,000, and Leschenko would not know of his mistake until he tried to dispose of his spoils somewhere in Eastern Europe. That the robbery had gone wrong was unfortunate, but not in itself a disaster: she had realised that as soon as the exchange was discovered by Sangster all suspicion would fall on Max Peters, and indeed this had happened. The shootings of Ambrose Quinn and the other officers appalled her, and she knew the blame would always lie indirectly with her.

With Leschenko dead for more than a quarter of a century, she knew her secret would go to the grave with her.

Bringing two tall glasses of Ricard and iced water out onto the balcony, Ruth sat down in a cane chair next to her husband and, taking a sip, helped herself to a cheroot from his case.

'Is there much in the papers, Tom?' she asked dreamily.

'Usual political stuff,' he said, picking up that morning's copy of *Le Monde*. 'One of Franz Josef's nephews got himself shot yesterday in Sarajevo by a Serbian nationalist. No doubt it'll upset the old Emperor.'